THE PENGUIN CLASSICS

FOUNDER EDITOR (1944–64): E. V. RIEU

HONORÉ DE BALZAC was born at Tours in 1799, the son of a civil servant. He spent nearly six years as a boarder in a Vendôme school, then went to live in Paris, working as a lawyer's clerk then as a hack-writer. Between 1820 and 1824 he wrote a number of novels under various pseudonyms, many of them in collaboration, after which he unsuccessfully tried his luck at publishing, printing and type-founding. At the age of thirty, heavily in debt, he returned to litera-ture with a dedicated fury and wrote the first novel to appear under his own name, *The Chouans*. During the next twenty years he wrote about ninety novels and shorter stories, among them many master-pieces, to which he gave the comprehensive title, *The Human Comedy*. He died in 1850, a few months after his marriage to Evelina Hanska, the Polish countess with whom he had maintained amorous relations for eighteen years.

DONALD ADAMSON was born in 1939 and educated at Manchester Grammar School and Magdalen College, Oxford, where he read French and German. He then studied at the Sorbonne and spent a year in Paris and Chantilly researching into Balzac. He now teaches at Goldsmiths' College, London. His first book, *The Genesis of 'Le Cousin Pons'* (1966), was followed by a second Oxford thesis, on Balzac and the visual arts, which gained him a Doctorate of Philo-sophy. He is also joint author of a history of the Beauclerk family, and has edited the first biographical memoir on T. S. Eliot. He is currently writing a biography of Pascal. He has also translated *The Black Sheep* by Balzac for the Penguin Classics. He is married, with two sons, and lives in Kent.

Honoré de Balzac

URSULE MIROUËT

TRANSLATED AND
WITH AN INTRODUCTION BY
DONALD ADAMSON

PENGUIN BOOKS

Penguin Books Ltd, Harmondsworth, Middlesex, England
Penguin Books, 625 Madison Avenue, New York, New York 10022, U.S.A.
Penguin Books Australia Ltd, Ringwood, Victoria, Australia
Penguin Books Canada Ltd, 41 Steelcase Road West, Markham, Ontario, Canada
Penguin Books (N.Z.) Ltd, 182-190 Wairau Road, Auckland 10, New Zealand

—

This translation published 1976

—

—

Made and printed in Great Britain
by Richard Clay (The Chaucer Press) Ltd
Bungay, Suffolk
Set in Monotype Garamond

Introduction

IN the course of their disillusioning study of literature, Flaubert's heroes Bouvard and Pécuchet tackle the varied assortment of novels which make up *The Human Comedy*. They admire Balzac's range and intensity – a Babylonian macrocosm viewed as minutely as a speck of dust – and they praise him for his penetration in bringing to light aspects of the modern world to which they had never given a thought. Finally, however, reverting to the perennial theme of Flaubert's unfinished masterpiece, Pécuchet expresses his disillusionment: Balzac, he argues disdainfully, 'believes in the occult sciences, in monarchy and in aristocracy; he is fascinated by rogues; he handles millions as if they were centimes; and his middle-class folk are not middle-class folk at all, but colossi'. Flaubert does not tell us whether his heroes had been reading *Ursule Mirouët* (curiously, *Ursule Mirouët* has a minor character named Bouvard), but Pécuchet's viewpoint could well have been grounded, however one-sidedly, on a novel which Gide considered one of the most revealing in Balzac's work.

Balzac does indeed believe in the occult sciences to a much greater extent than any other novelist of comparable stature (of whom there are few); and of the ninety-four novels that comprise *The Human Comedy*, four – *Louis Lambert*, *Séraphîta*, *Ursule Mirouët* and *Cousin Pons* – best illustrate his theosophical bent. *Cousin Pons* even contains a 'Treatise on the Occult Sciences', while Chapter Six of *Ursule Mirouët* bears the title 'A Brief Digression on Magnetism'. In *Ursule Mirouët*, moreover, the doctor's conversion to Christianity is motivated by the supernatural; the postmaster's theft of the will and scrips is shown to be against the will of Heaven; and the ending could not have occurred but for Dr Minoret's appearance in a dream from the dead. To Balzac, who claimed that *Ursule Mirouët* was 'the work of a Catholic' but who was not a practising Catholic in the accepted sense, the world was a Manichaean contrast of good and evil, in which through meditation – not through the Church or its sacraments – man can attain an inner spiritual world. From this spiritual world God and His angels are actively concerned, though not always successfully, with the furtherance of good on earth.

Balzac is hypersensitively aware of both these worlds, and of the discordance between them; and so great, to his mind, is the contrast between the material and the spiritual that he tends to magnify the gulf. The good are often made to seem angelic, the wicked positively Mephistophelean. The sums of money which haunt the dreams of evil men eager to enrich themselves are so vast that great passions and temptations are in action. Throughout *The Human Comedy* Balzac does indeed handle millions as if they were centimes: witness the 17 million francs (or roughly £4¼ million*) belonging to Eugénie Grandet's father. Friends such as Zulma Carraud objected to the vastness of the sums Balzac conjures up, but to him that vastness was essential if the struggles for money were to achieve their maximum ferocity. His two and a half years' apprenticeship in lawyers' offices in Paris, before he decided to break with the prospect of a legal career and become a novelist, gave him that indispensable insight into the workings of finance and the law without which his later ambition of writing a systematic account of early nineteenth-century French society would have been impossible. As a businessman, after the failure of his first attempt to become a writer, he became familiar with the manipulation of investments and balance-sheets, whilst the fact that he failed in his business projects reveals the huge worldly successes of his evil men in an ironic light.

Balzac's experiences of the seamy side of life in two lawyers' offices led to a profound understanding of the psychology of rogues. As Pécuchet remarks, such men did indeed fascinate him – the more so as roguery takes an infinite variety of forms:

*For present purposes, the franc of the 1830s can be reckoned as equivalent to 25p. Thus, Dr Minoret's fortune is equivalent in modern exchange to about £350,000; his barouche, at 2,000 francs, cost the rough equivalent of £500 (second-hand); his house, auctioned for 50,000 francs, fetched £12,500 at present values. In relation to the general cost of living, house prices are much higher now than in 1835! *Livres* and *écus* (but not always *sous*) have been standardized in terms of the franc.

'virtue has only one form, evil has a thousand', the novelist himself remarks in his *Treatise on Fashionable Life*. With its total of 2,472 named characters, *The Human Comedy* contains many less than a thousand rogues; but each of them – whether the man of straw in *César Birotteau*, or the double-dealing barrister in *Cousin Pons*, or the dissolute, thieving son in *The Black Sheep* – is memorable as an individual in his own right. Of all the practitioners of roguery, however, none is more fascinating to Balzac than the one who gets away with huge crimes scot-free. Nucingen, so prominent in *Old Goriot*, is the wiliest of all the rogues in *The Human Comedy*: a banker who can engineer a liquidation of his own assets, or plan an investment portfolio on a client's behalf, simply and solely to further his own ends – enriching himself but bankrupting others by what is tantamount to legalized crime. Though utterly lacking in Nucingen's mental agility, and even endowed with a rudimentary sense of remorse, the burly postmaster Minoret-Levrault is cast in the same mould. The burning of Dr Minoret's will is not a *legalized* crime (Minoret-Levrault would have been too stupid to think up loopholes in the law) but a crime which, in the ordinary processes of life, would have escaped *undetected*: only the doctor's supernatural intervention reveals the crime against which Heaven had warned the postmaster; the only punishment meted out to the offender is again ordained by Heaven, in the shape of Désiré's fatal accident. The crime that is not a crime engaged Balzac's creative imagination, off and on, for a quarter of a century. 'There are many more crimes in high society than amongst the lower orders,' he jots in an early notebook. 'Uneducated people go to the scaffold for stealing a clock ... The fashionable man steals a will.' Goupil's occult persecution of Ursule is another instance of criminal behaviour just within the law. In other novels, such as *The Black Sheep*, it is the practice of duelling which is the legalized instrument of crime; but the undetectable crime of burning a will is absolutely central to Balzac's thought.

There is, therefore, a grain of truth in Pécuchet's criticism that Balzac's 'middle-class folk are not middle-class folk at all, but colossi'. Nucingen is certainly a colossus of intelligence and cunning, as is Vautrin with his seemingly limitless knowledge of the ways and inhabitants of the world. The rather obtuse Minoret-Levrault is a physical colossus, and on fourteen separate occasions in *Ursule Mirouët* is specifically referred to as such. Nevertheless, the middle-class people in this novel – which means practically everyone – are not, by and large, magnified beyond recognition as lifelike human beings. Indeed, *Ursule Mirouët* is remarkable for its truth to life, and Balzac even described it in 1842 as the masterpiece of all the studies of human society that he had written up to that date. The burning of wills and duelling with human obstacles to one's self-advancement constitute a colossal assault on innocence and justice, for which the only possible amends are on a cosmic scale; but the Massins, Levraults and Crémières are of the same prosaic earthiness, the same blinkered Philistine cunning, that Balzac must have seen satirized in Gavarni's and Monnier's lithographs, and rampant in bourgeois people everywhere – not excluding Nemours itself, which he visited with his friend Albéric Second to gain background information in May 1841. In a shady notary's clerk such as Goupil the only approach to a colossal dimension is the evil leer in the eyes, and twisted malevolence of the mind, which at one turning-point in the novel leads Balzac to equate him specifically with Mephistopheles.

As a self-appointed historian of French social life in the first half of the nineteenth century, Balzac was acutely conscious of the new, immense and steadily growing significance of money. Writing in the throes of the French industrial revolution, he chronicled the industrial, commercial and financial processes – property speculation, printing and publishing techniques, newspaper flotation, etc. – to which that revolution had given rise. Yet he was much less interested in man as a technological agent than as a moral being; was man to remain in control of the financial and technological processes he had unleashed? The fascination of the legalized and undetected crime lay precisely in the fact that it placed traditional morality in jeopardy. The industrial revolution seemed to Balzac to have brought about not only a revolution but a disintegration in traditional values. Hence the importance in *The Human Comedy* of the last

8

two features – aristocracy and monarchy – mentioned so scathingly by Flaubert's hero. Balzac sought and urged a social framework which would contain, mould and discipline man's natural instincts. Of the twin pillars of this political and moral edifice, the Monarchy and the Catholic Church, nothing is seen in *Ursule Mirouët* except for the benign goodness of Abbé Chaperon. 'Christianity,' Balzac writes in his Preface to *The Human Comedy*, 'and especially Catholicism ... [is] a complete system for the repression of man's depraved tendencies, and the greatest element of social order'; but it is not fearsome in its repressiveness, as the jovial mildness of Chaperon shows. In Balzac's Utopian social framework the principal agent of secular power would be the aristocracy, disciplining and edifying the untrammelled self-interest of a bourgeoisie whose idol was material gain. In this context, the scene between Savinien de Portenduère and his mother before the young man embarks on his brief naval career is of crucial significance. Madame de Portenduère is certainly not a person who would easily attract esteem and popularity nowadays; even her son would no doubt be regarded as too insipid and sentimental for modern liking. Balzac's point, however, as the young man solemnly swears in the room where his father died that the family honour is unscathed, is that here is a system of values at utter variance with the supine acquisitiveness of tradespeople: a system of leadership, discipline and self-sacrifice. To Balzac, as to Vigny, it was these ancient traditional values that had been called into question by the developments of the modern world. Leadership, discipline and self-sacrifice are the qualities most conspicuously lacking in Minoret-Levrault, Massin and Crémière; not even Désiré Minoret dies a hero's death (like Racine's Hippolyte), but only the travesty of one. Balzac was no starry-eyed idealist, however. Whilst hinting at a Utopian social solution in *Ursule Mirouët*, he knew only too well, and had already said so in *The Duchesse de Langeais*, that the aristocracy had failed to measure up to its social responsibilities in the years following the turbulence of the French Revolution and Napoleonic fiasco. Savinien's debts and imprisonment in Sainte-Pélagie are a minor indication of the same major weakness and irresponsibility, from which the young viscount is redeemed by Dr Minoret's exertions, but from which no power could redeem the French aristocracy on a national scale. As a parent, Madame de Portenduère is blinded by totally outdated notions of class distinction: under the system still prevailing in the 1830s she had the legal right to block her son's marriage completely until he had reached the age of twenty-six. Thus, both in the survival of an outdated snobbery from the age of 'morality' and 'honour' and in the heirs' legalistic concern over the inheritance, abstract notions of Family override natural affection.

The 'heirs', or Minoret nephews and cousins, have an unquestionable legal right to the doctor's fortune, regardless of his personal wishes and despite their manifest lack of affection towards him. This is a fact which Dr Minoret accepts, to the extent of making a distinction between 'settled estate' and 'savings' and also of refusing to become Ursule's husband in a marriage of convenience. The law permits Madame de Portenduère to delay her son's marriage. It allows the nephews' and cousins' claim to the inheritance. Its very procedures are a harassment to Ursule after her godfather's death. It is powerless to prevent Goupil's tricks, crueller than many 'crimes'. Yet, through the public prosecutor, it vigorously supports the orphaned heroine. It is rational, sympathetic and informal in the public prosecutor's dealings with Bongrand and Zélie. And, Désiré Minoret believes, 'though justice could not always punish everything, it would eventually find everything out and would bear the facts in mind'. It has a power of omniscience, a collective memory and a capacity for eventual action which far transcend the law's imperfect machinery. Indeed, justice also seems to have something of a regenerative quality in that it separates Désiré's outlook from that of his parents and even brings about Goupil's redemption once he has become a notary.

On all sides, Balzac believed, the obligations and privileges of family life were being dissolved by self-interest. 'I regard the family, and not the individual, as the true foundation of society,' he wrote in the general preface to his works. And he dreamed of winning the Montyon prize, specially intended to reward books that promoted the dignity and usefulness of the family. *Eugénie Grandet*, *The Black Sheep* and *Cousin Pons*, Balzac's other inheritance novels, show us the family at variance with itself, or definitely worsted, or left out of the will. *Ursule Mirouët* is unique in the fact that there is no struggle for a fortune. The members of the 'family' have an accepted status. Approximately half of Dr Minoret's fortune is destined for them. The theft of the other half is a crime which would not have occurred but for the law's rigid rules of inheritance. It is a crime against that higher family: the doctor's ward, goddaughter, spiritual charge, and niece, the daughter of a man who was Minoret's father-in-law's illegitimate offspring! Both in her unique relationship to the doctor and in the relationship of her own father to his natural father, Ursule outshines the legalistic 'heirs' through ties not of consanguinity but of the heart.

*

To Balzac, this novel was a 'remarkable *tour de force*, its only parallel being *César Birotteau*'. Both works were the outcome of prolonged thought, and both presented almost unparalleled difficulties. Both projects lay for six years in a state of suspended animation in the novelist's mind before he could finally write them up. The problem was how to create interest in a story in which no violent collision between the characters arose, where no critical moral dilemmas were experienced, and where the nephews' and cousins' bustle and animation confront the lethargy and passiveness of old age and inexperienced youth, and easily win in worldly terms. Balzac, who went specially to Nemours to verify the details of the novel he was about to write, also seems to have conceived of *Ursule Mirouët* as a statement of the dehumanizing consequences of the cash nexus in general. In one of the most revealing asides in the novel, he refers to Ursule's 'physical and mental collapse that would have brought pity to the hearts of the fiercest men – excepting heirs to fortunes'. The antics of expectant heirs in their dealings with rich uncles and cousins are not so much a Dance of Death as a Dance of Mammon in which each participant plays his allotted, predictable part. It is only to be expected that aspirants to a fortune will show no pity. Sometimes, in furtherance of their greed, they will *calculate*, or cruelly exploit the emotions of those who stand to benefit them. This is the lesson learned by Eugène de Rastignac in *Old Goriot*. No one exploits any emotion in *Ursule Mirouët*, however, if only because no deep human emotion exists except between Dr Minoret and Ursule, and between the Minoret-Levraults and their son. In deciding to leave between 45 and 48 per cent* of his fortune to the Minoret-Levraults, Massins and Crémières, the doctor has a cool, dispassionate awareness of the obligations of family ties – and of the commonsense expediency of protecting Ursule after his death by buying off the nephews' and cousins' hostility. Thus, no violent collision between the two sides arises, not even over the theft of the scrips, since that is a furtive gesture unsuspected by Massin and Crémière. Nor does the postmaster experience any moral crisis whatever prior to the burning and theft. At the outset of the novel it may even seem right, because it is both lawful and encouraged by the law, that the nephews and cousins should receive about half of Dr Minoret's money. There is much in Balzac's view of *Ursule Mirouët* to support George Eliot's belief that *The Human Comedy* lacks a coherent system of moral values. The cash nexus has presented man with unrivalled opportunities for criminal and sinful behaviour, and his moral stature appears to have diminished accordingly. What, if anything, does Balzac propose as a corrective?

Through the clear signs of the supernatural at work in this novel, Balzac is apparently trying to evoke some sense of eternal destiny. To George Eliot this would have been too facile and weak-minded a solution, a poor substitute for a positivist ethic, but for Balzac – who had learned theosophy at his mother's knee and who consulted trance mediums and fortune-tellers – life offered innumerable reminders of a transcendent reality. Whereas his father, an obvious prototype of Dr Minoret, was an eighteenth-century rationalist and deist-agnostic in the manner of Voltaire, his mother represented another aspect of that century, which besides Voltaire, Rousseau and Montesquieu also produced Saint-Germain and Cagliostro. The union of rationalism and occultism in his parents'

*Largely depending on the current quotation of the 3 per cents.

12

marriage is paralleled, in Balzac's outlook, by a unique blend of realism and spiritualism of which *Ursule Mirouët* is the clearest expression. To those who are prone to deride Madame Balzac's 'weak-mindedness' it must be emphasized that Swedenborg, with all his apparent 'irrationality', flourished in the Age of Reason. To those who poke fun at Balzac's belief in animal magnetism it should equally be stressed that Mesmer's theories produced a sensation towards the end of the eighteenth century and commanded the support of many intelligent men. Balzac merely echoes the opinion of many of his educated contemporaries when claiming in *Ursule Mirouët* that Mesmer's findings would revolutionize therapeutic medicine and that 'rationalist' methods of healing were ill-founded. He, like countless others, accepted Mesmer's teaching that the will-power and nervous system of human beings, as of all animals, could be influenced and indeed directed by the transmission of thought, viewed as an imponderable fluid inducing hypnotism. 'Genuine feelings have their own magnetic appeal,' he comments in the critical scene where Savinien is shown sitting by Ursule's piano, looking to all the world like Parmigianino's celebrated portrait, and diffusing a quality of spiritual radiance. But the feelings of Ursule and Savinien for one another, symbolized by the music through which they approach a celestial world, are not the only forms of genuine emotion in this novel; in their sordid lust for riches Minoret-Levrault, Massin and Crémière provide an alternative magnetic field. The whole of the action in *Ursule Mirouët* takes place against the background of an underlying spiritual reality – as when Dr Minoret is able to promise Ursule that she has only to call for him if she needs him and he will return from the dead.

This spiritual reality is only indirectly manifested in organized religion. Until his conversion Dr Minoret is not a Christian, yet even before the conversion the agnostic doctor and a Catholic priest are the closest of friends and stand together against the forces of materialism – even where that materialism assumes a pretence of religion. For all its sensational impact on Nemours, Dr Minoret's conversion (Balzac argues) is entirely consistent with reason and scientific law. It is only 'miraculous' in that miracles show the reality of a supernatural world, a world which of itself is not contrary to reason. Liguori's premonition of the death of Clement XIV, cited by Chaperon as evidence of the 'miraculous', is not miraculous in the sense of that word used by the Christian philosopher Malebranche, for whom a 'miracle' – a breaking of the physical regularity of the universe – would have proved God's non-existence. The experiences with the medium in Paris are based on a theory of telepathy which Balzac considered scientifically sound. To him, as a follower of Mesmer, thought and perception could be transmitted across vast distances by a process akin to the conduction of electricity. In the scene in which the agnostic's last remaining doubts are dispelled, Balzac stresses that there is even something electrical – and hence scientific and grounded in reason – about the doctor's ultimate conversion, caused not so much by the telepathic experiences themselves as by the energizing quality of Ursule's angelic purity and receptiveness to religious grace. As the interpreter of this spiritual world to those who have 'ears to hear', Balzac actually states that the sacrament of the eucharist somehow imbues Ursule with deeper qualities of the soul. Unlike his successor Flaubert, whose narrative position is never clear, he thus places himself firmly on the side of the angels. Though not a churchgoer, he writes as a religious man. Only once, in his hesitant reference to Spinoza, does he waver for an instant in his rebuttal of philosophic materialism.

*

As is implied by the title of the novel, its merit as a work of imaginative literature may depend largely on the character of the heroine. Is Ursule an acceptable portrait of a young woman in love and an affectionate goddaughter? Less than a year after writing *Ursule Mirouët*, Balzac admitted in his general preface to *The Human Comedy* that only Raphael had proved able to create many convincing portraits of virgins. And a virgin Ursule undoubtedly is, with all the energy and abundance of life which Balzac believed to be the attribute of chastity. It is perhaps not too fanciful to suggest that her Christian name is intended to evoke St Ursula, virgin and martyr: but a martyr different from Balzac's others in that, unlike for example the music master Schmucke who is her near counterpart in *Cousin Pons*, she finally regains human contentment. Ursule Mirouët, Balzac remarked, is Eugénie Grandet's happy sister. The preface to *The Human Comedy* emphasizes the difficulty of describing a woman's passion: even Scott, whom Balzac revered so deeply, usually failed in this. To the modern reader Ursule may well appear as the literary equivalent of a Greuze portrait, insipid and sentimental. A fact that he is in danger of overlooking is that for over half the story she is only fifteen. Even in the days of Women's Lib, too much sophistication must not be demanded of a young teenager! Indeed, for a girl of fifteen, Ursule is certainly not a child; she is just as happy as a child, at least in the earlier part of the book. Social and personal habits have changed, however, in the last 130 years and with our more astringent outlook we may tend to shrink from the scene in which she throws herself at her godfather's feet and kisses his hands; 'I nearly missed saying my prayers' is another of the things that may present her in a false light. When her fiancé tries to kiss her forehead, she almost faints and the eager young man has to be cautioned by the doctor; a sudden excess of emotion could cost her her life. Extremely emotional, demonstrative behaviour is out of fashion nowadays, at any rate within the purview of the modern novel; it belongs to a literary convention which in the 1840s was as powerful in *The Old Curiosity Shop* as it was in *Ursule Mirouët*. In the context of her own time Ursule was probably a perfectly attractive delightful girl, full of vivacity and sex appeal. We must beware of writing her off as a chocolate-box heroine.

What is true of her characterization may be applied with almost equal force to Savinien. He has, of course, the manly virtues of courage, tenacity and idealism, and he is older and more mature than Ursule. Balzac takes him extremely seriously as a character, never choosing to satirize him. And yet his conduct is definitely deserving of satire, and to this extent his is a more nuanced portrait than Ursule's. Just as the aristocratic virtues are now largely ignored in the money-grubbing world of the 1830s (as are the aristocratic families themselves –

Savinien actually complains to his mother that no one bothers any more whether you are a Portenduère), so in his outlook and personal qualities a young nobleman like Savinien is maladjusted to present conditions. Even after the humiliation of a month in Sainte-Pélagie he still intends to enter politics, for which he seems totally unsuited. Ironically, he hopes to become a politician for high-minded, edifying reasons – to give the sort of moral leadership to society which Balzac blames the aristocracy in general for failing to give. Henri de Marsay, Maxime de Trailles, Rastignac and Sixte du Châtelet – some of the successful politicians in other novels – enter politics, on the other hand, for purely selfish motives of self-aggrandizement and, being skilful in calculation, prove a success. Although Savinien's life as a dandy bears some resemblance to Rastignac's (running up debts whilst his mother skimps and saves), he is entirely lacking in the latter's determination, will-power and ability. He even asks Rastignac, Maxime de Trailles and others for the secret of their success – they having begun life with no greater advantages than he – but, not having found that secret for himself, he is unable to extract it from others. The talismanic presence of Ursule's love and wealth is of immense good fortune to him, for in his weakness and simplicity he might otherwise have foundered in the same difficulties that befell Lucien de Rubempré. As many of Balzac's characters move from one novel to another, appearing first in one in a major capacity and then perhaps in another as a supernumerary, we know from other works in *The Human Comedy* the future marked out for Ursule and himself. In marriage – as is clearly foreshadowed in the ending of *Ursule Mirouët* – they are destined to be blissfully happy; but in terms of worldly success Savinien is to rise no higher than to a position in local politics.

Balzac has been charged – by F. R. Leavis, amongst others – with glamorizing his characters, investing them with a sublimity or degradation unfound in the reality of daily life. Thus, Ursule tends to be seen as a paragon of virtue and beauty and Savinien as a model of courage and strength (though in reality his portrait is, as we have seen, more complex). Polarizing his characters into the hostile forces of vice and virtue, Balzac surrounds the kindness and gentleness of Ursule, Savinien, Dr Minoret, Chaperon and Bongrand with the malevolent, scheming cupidity of the Minoret-Levraults, Massins and Crémières – too ably assisted in their infernal purposes by the Mephistophelean Goupil. The conflict over half (or thereabouts) of Dr Minoret's inheritance, if conflict it is, unleashes a giant confrontation between light and darkness, in which even the supernatural world itself becomes actively involved. The assault of the principalities and powers on innocent goodness is viewed by Balzac in terms of property, but the cosmic onslaught could equally – as in, say, Balzac's own *Lily of the Valley* or Conrad's *Heart of Darkness* – have been viewed in other terms. The conflict in *Ursule Mirouët* is no doubt viewed in terms of property because money is one of the most powerful motivators of human evil. But the novel is by no means solely about a conflict over 760,000 francs,* nor is money presented exclusively as a loathsome bone of contention. Considered within the narrow ambit of an inheritance novel, *Ursule Mirouët* would suffer from a serious flaw in construction, for what is the relevance of Dr Minoret's conversion to the squabbling between his heirs over his inheritance? Even if he had remained an agnostic, he would still have bequeathed about half his fortune to his nephews and cousins and about half to his goddaughter; and Minoret-Levrault would presumably still have stolen the will and scrips. The cosmic duel of light and darkness is also to be seen in the dispelling of Dr Minoret's seemingly invincible ignorance, and the final turning of his eyes towards the light. This sudden enlightenment of his soul is of little or no account to the inheritance story, though it fills his nephews and cousins with amusing consternation as to the motives and consequences of his churchgoing. In the plot of *Ursule Mirouët*, little in fact is of account to the inheritance story since there is so little intelligent resistance of evil by either the doctor or the heroine. The only possible relevance of the conversion to the inheritance plot is in the ghostly apparition at the end, but Balzac's inner theosophical

*Owing to the rising trend in Government funds between 1830 and 1836, the sum actually increases from 540,000 francs to 960,000 francs during the course of the novel.

convictions are so divorced from his external support of Catholic forms that the link between proselytism and crime-detection remains tenuous.

If the characters often appear too glamorous or enhanced in *The Human Comedy*, money is usually too little so. It too easily appears as the filthy lucre which misers grudgingly hoard, and for which sordid people struggle relentlessly. Balzac in fact recognizes it as the motive force of a capitalist world and in such novels as *The Deputy for Arcis* emphasizes the fact. It is a force with its own mysterious magnetic properties, unevenly and inexplicably divided amongst mankind and only indirectly related to the magnetic fields of vice and virtue whose rivalry it promotes. Helping to sustain Ursule in her life and beauty, it is also the means by which Dr Minoret contributes – both literally and metaphorically – to the redemption of Savinien, and thus to the redemption of the French aristocracy in general.

Redemption and rebirth: these are the twin themes of *Ursule Mirouët*. Through music and love, Balzac tells us in the third scene of Ursule's piano-playing, she is 'spiritually reborn'. 'Will you give me life for a second time?' Savinien says to her, asking for a pledge of their engagement before he sets out on his naval career. Through his conversion Dr Minoret is also reborn into a new, deeper and fuller life. Love and sacramental religion are the instruments of spiritual rebirth in this novel, and as instruments they are closely interrelated: Minoret enters the fulness of sacramental religion through his love for Ursule; the love of Savinien and Ursule finds its deepest fulfilment in the sacrament of marriage. Through his acceptance of the Christian faith, the doctor is reborn – and redeemed – from the philosophic materialism of later eighteenth-century thinkers. Except for the one diffident reference to Spinoza, *Ursule Mirouët* is strong and consistent in its rejection of philosophic materialism; but its rejection of human materialism – the fierce, heartless, greedy ambition of Zélie Minoret-Levrault, the postmaster's terrible crassness, the diabolical machinations of Goupil – is firmer and more insistent still. In Ursule's dreamlike premonitions of Savinien's letters, in the doctor's reappearance both to Ursule and Minoret-Levrault after death, in his confidence *as a doctor* that such reappearances are possible, and in the status of music as the gateway to an eternal world, Balzac affirms the presence of a supernatural force aiding the still, small voice of holiness as heard, and overheard, in the private conclaves of Ursule, the doctor, Chaperon and Bongrand: how different these conclaves are from the heirs' consultation with Dionis where, rather as in a Beethoven symphony, loud noise – even cacophony – is followed by bursts of silence! Beethoven and Balzac are alike in emphasizing life's soaring aspirations of spirit, contrapuntal with darkness and despair.

D.A.

To Mademoiselle Sophie Surville

IT is a real pleasure, my dear niece, to dedicate to you a book whose subject and details have had the approval (so difficult to win) of a young girl to whom the world is as yet unknown, and who does not compromise any of the noble principles of a religious education. You girls are a formidable section of the reading public; you must only be allowed to read books that are as pure as your heart is pure, and you are forbidden certain kinds of reading-matter just as you are prevented from seeing Society as it really is. So does it not fill an author's heart with pride when he has pleased you? May God grant that love has not deceived you! Who can tell? Only the future, which I hope you will live to see, and which perhaps will be denied to

Your uncle,
BALZAC

PART ONE

1. The Heirs are Alarmed

ENTERING Nemours from the direction of Paris, you pass along the Canal du Loing whose banks form both countrified ramparts and picturesque walks in this pretty little town. Since 1830 several houses have unfortunately been built on this side of the bridge. If this kind of suburb grows, the appearance of the town will lose its graceful originality. But in 1829, at a time when the roadsides were unobstructed, the postmaster,* a tall, stout man aged about sixty, sitting at the highest point of the bridge, could on a fine morning perfectly take into his line of vision what (in the language of his own profession) is called a 'tail-ribbon'. The September weather was lavishing its riches, the atmosphere was blazing above the grass and pebbles, no clouds marred the blue of the heavens, whose purity – vivid everywhere, even on the horizon – indicated that the air was extremely rarefied. And so Minoret-Levrault (for such was the postmaster's name) had to cup one of his hands over his eyes so as not to be dazzled. Like a man impatient at having to wait, he sometimes looked towards the delightful meadows which spread out on the right-hand side of the road, with their second crops of hay, and sometimes to the wooded hillside stretching to the left from Nemours to Bouron. In the Loing valley, where noises from the road echoed as they were reflected back from the hill, he could hear his own horses galloping and his postilions cracking their whips. Do you not really have to be a postmaster to grow impatient at the sight of a meadow with cattle like those painted by Paul Potter, grazing beneath a sky like one in a Raphael painting, beside a canal shaded with trees in Hobbema's manner? Anyone familiar with Nemours knows that in that town nature is as beautiful as art, the function of which is to give nature a spiritual dimension: at Nemours, the country-side itself is imbued with ideas and leads to reflection. But faced with Minoret-Levrault, an artist would have left the

*Not the modern sense of postmaster, but a businessman owning and running a stagecoach office.

25

picturesque spot to go and sketch this bourgeois – a man so common as to be original. Combine all the characteristics of a brutish man, and you produce Caliban, who is certainly not without his own particular grandeur. Wherever Form is dominant, Feeling vanishes. The postmaster gave living proof of this axiom: his face was one of those in which it is hard for the thoughtful observer to see any trace of a soul beneath the florid tints of gross, coarsening flesh. His ribbed cap of blue cloth, with its little peak, fitted closely to a head which, in its large dimensions, proved that Gall's science of phrenology has not yet broached the subject of exceptions. The grey, apparently shiny hair protruding from beneath the cap would have demonstrated that hair goes white for other reasons than intellectual fatigue or personal grief. On each side of his head, his wide ears were almost scarred at the edges by the eroding activity of a blood stream so copious that it seemed ready to spurt forth at the slightest effort. The purplish-blue tints of his complexion showed through a surface skin brown from exposure to the sun. His grey eyes – alert, sunken and hidden beneath bushy black eyebrows – were like those of the Kalmucks who came in 1815; though they shone at times, it was only in the reflection of some covetous thought. His nose, which was flat from the bridge downwards, turned up suddenly like the leg of a cauldron. Thick lips were in harmony with an almost repulsive double chin, on which the beard (trimmed barely twice a week) kept a shabby, threadbare silk neckerchief in place; his neck, though very short, was lined with fat; full cheeks completed this picture of powerful stupidity, such as sculptors impress upon their caryatids. Minoret-Levrault was like these statues, except that they support a building whereas he was hard put to it to support himself. There are many such Atlases without a world on their shoulders. The man's torso was a block-like mass; he was like a bull rearing up on its hind legs. He had powerful arms and thick, broad, hard, strong hands, well capable of and well used to handling the whip, reins and fork, hands which no postilion ventured to defy. The huge belly of this gigantic man was supported by thighs as thick as the body of any normal adult, and by feet the size of an elephant's. Anger was obviously an emotion he

26

rarely experienced, but it must have been terrible, indeed apoplectic, when it did break out. Though he was violent and incapable of reflection, he had never done anything to justify the sinister portents written in the lines of his face. Whenever anyone trembled in his presence, his postilions would say: 'It's all right! He's not a bad fellow!'

The Nemours 'master' (such is the abbreviation of 'postmaster' common in many parts of France) was wearing a short shooting-jacket in bottle-green velvet, green drill trousers with green stripes, and a loose-fitting yellow goat's-hair waistcoat; in his waistcoat pocket was an outsize snuff-box, the black circular outline of which could be seen. Fat snuff-boxes belong to men with snub noses: this is an almost invariable rule.

As a son of the Revolution and a spectator of the Imperial saga, Minoret-Levrault had never concerned himself with politics; as for his religious views, he had only once set foot inside a church, and that was to get married; the principles he observed in his private life were those of the Civil Code: he believed he could do anything outside the law's reach or not forbidden by the law. He had only ever read the departmental newspaper of Seine-et-Oise, together with some information of a professional kind. He was considered a skilful farmer; but his knowledge of farming was purely practical. Thus, Minoret-Levrault's intellectual life in no way belied his physical appearance. It was for this reason that he hardly ever spoke; and that, before he did begin to speak, he always took a pinch of snuff to give himself time not to think up ideas but to find words. If he had been talkative, he would have seemed a failure. When you consider that this elephantine man, lacking both a trunk and a mind, is called *Minoret-Levrault*, must you not agree with Sterne that names have an occult significance, sometimes mocking and sometimes foretelling character? Despite his obvious inadequacies he had managed in thirty-six years, with the help of the Revolution, to accumulate 30,000 francs a year in investment income, invested in meadows, woods and arable fields. The fact that Minoret was still working, with financial interests both in the Nemours stage-coach company and in the Le Gâtinais carrying business in

Paris, was not so much due to force of habit as for the benefit of his only son, for whom he was planning a handsome future. This boy, who had become (in the peasants' phrase) a 'young gentleman', had just completed his legal studies and at the start of the next legal term was due to take his oath as a probationary barrister. Monsieur and Madame Minoret-Levrault (everybody must realize that behind this colossus of a man was a women without whom he would never have made such a fine fortune) gave their son freedom in the choice of his career: he could have become a Parisian notary, a public prosecutor somewhere or other, a divisional tax-collector anywhere, a bill-broker or a postmaster. What whim could a young man deny himself, what condition in life was he debarred from aspiring to, when his father was a man of whom it was said from Montargis to Essonne: 'Old Minoret doesn't know his own wealth!' Four years before the opening of this story, this remark had received fresh confirmation when Minoret built himself a superb house and stables after selling his coaching-inn and moving his business from the high street to the quay. These new buildings had cost 200,000 francs, but gossip for seventy-five miles around doubled that figure. The Nemours posting-house needs a great many horses: in the Paris direction it goes as far as Fontainebleau, and further afield serves the roads to Montargis and Montereau; whatever the direction, each stage is a long one, and the sandy road to Montargis calls for that mythical third horse, which is always charged for on the bill but is never seen. A man of Minoret's size and wealth, with such a business behind him, could therefore without any inaccuracy be called the 'master of Nemours'. Although he had never given a thought either to God or the Devil, and though he was a practical materialist in the same way that he was a practical farmer, a practical egoist and a practical miser, Minoret had enjoyed unalloyed happiness until now, if a purely material existence can be regarded as happiness. At the sight of the lump of hairless flesh enveloping this man's upmost vertebra and pressing in on his cerebellum, and (even more particularly) on hearing his thin, high-pitched voice that contrasted so ludicrously with his build, a physiologist would have fully realized why this tall, stout, thickset farmer worshipped his only son, and why perhaps he had waited for him so long – as in fact was indicated by the child's Christian name, Désiré. If love, as the expression of a strong bodily constitution, holds out a promise of the greatest things in a man, philosophers will understand the reasons for Minoret's inadequacy. Désiré's mother, whom the son very fortunately resembled, rivalled his father in indulging his whims. No child could have preserved his simple natural disposition in the face of such idolatry, and Désiré, aware of the extent of his power, knew how to milk his mother's money-box and delve into his father's purse, giving each of his parents the impression that he was only appealing to him or her for help. At Nemours Désiré played a part infinitely superior to that played by a prince of the blood royal in his father's capital; in Paris he had wanted to gratify all his whims just as he gratified them in his little home town; each year in Paris he had spent over twelve thousand francs. But through spending this sum he had acquired ideas that would never have occurred to him at Nemours: he had cast off the manners of a provincial, he had realized what power money has, and viewed a magistrate's career as a stepping-stone to higher things. During this last year he had spent ten thousand francs more, through his friendships with artists, journalists and their mistresses. A fairly disquieting confidential letter would, if necessary, have explained why the postmaster was anxiously on the look-out, a letter in which his son was asking for support for his marriage; but Madame Minoret-Levrault, busy preparing a sumptuous luncheon to celebrate the law graduate's triumphant return, had sent her husband out on to the road, telling him to get on horseback if he could not see the coach. The coach which was due to bring home their only son usually arrives at Nemours about five in the morning, and it was now striking nine o'clock! What could have caused such a delay? Had they overturned? Was Désiré alive? Or had he only a broken leg?

Three bursts of whip-cracks rang out, rending the air like rifle fire, the postilions' red waistcoats came into view, ten horses neighed, the postmaster took off his cap and waved it in the air, he was seen! The postilion with the best mount, who was bringing back two dapple-grey barouche horses, spurred his animal on, got ahead of five plump coach-horses (the Minorets of the stables!) and three Berlin horses, and rode up to the postmaster.

'Have you seen *La Ducler*?'

On the highways, fairly fantastic names are given to stage-coaches: people talk of *La Caillard*, *La Ducler* (the carriage running between Nemours and Paris) and *Le Grand-Bureau*. Every newly established business is known as *La Concurrence!** In the days when the Lecomtes were in business, their carriages were known as *La Comtesse*. '*Caillard* hasn't caught up with *La Comtesse*, but *Le Grand-Bureau* has nicely singed her dress all the same . . .!' '*La Caillard* and *Le Grand-Bureau* have massacred *Les Françaises.*'† Whenever you see a postilion riding hell for leather, even refusing a glass of wine, ask the coachman why: he'll tell you, with his nose high in the air, and his eyes peering into the distance: '*La Concurrence* is ahead of us!' 'And we can't see her!' the postilion will add. 'The scoundrel can't have allowed his passengers any time to eat!' 'Has he got any passengers?' the coachman will answer. 'Lay into Polignac, then!' All sluggish horses are known as Polignac. Such are the jokes and such is the gist of the conversation between postilions and coachmen riding on top of their carriages. There are as many forms of slang in France as there are professions.

'Is *La Ducler* . . .?'

'Bringing Monsieur Désiré?' the postilion replied, interrupting his master. 'You must have heard us, our whips were cracking loud enough; we thought you would be waiting in the road!'

'Well, why is the coach four hours late?'

'The hoop came loose from one of the rear wheels between Essonne and Ponthierry. But there wasn't any accident; luckily, Cabirolle noticed it as we were going up the hill.'

Just then a woman of about thirty-six came up to the postmaster. She was dressed in her Sunday best; the peals of the

* Competition!
† The Messageries Françaises, or French Stagecoach Company.

church bell in Nemours were calling the people to Sunday mass.

'Well, cousin,' she said, 'you wouldn't believe me! Uncle is in the high street, on his way to high mass with Ursule.'

Despite the modern poetic laws concerning local colour, it is impossible to push truth to the extent of repeating the horrible abuse, larded with oaths, which this news – seemingly so undramatic – brought forth from Minoret-Levrault's wide mouth. His high-pitched voice became a hiss. His face took on the look which lower-class people ingeniously call 'a touch of sunstroke', or sudden flush.

'Are you sure?' he asked, after his first outburst of anger.

The postilions passed by with their horses, saluting their master as they went, but he appeared neither to have seen nor heard them. Instead of waiting for his son, Minoret-Levrault walked back up the high street with his cousin.

'Didn't I always tell you?' she went on. 'When Dr Minoret loses his reason, that little hypocrite will turn him into a religious maniac; and as ruling the mind means ruling the purse, she will collar our inheritance.'

'But, Madame Massin ...' said the postmaster, dumb-stricken.

'Oh yes!' Madame Massin continued, cutting her cousin short, 'you'll take Massin's line: Can a little girl of fifteen think up and carry out such plans? Changing a man's opinions when he's eighty-three and has only ever set foot inside a church to get married, who has such a hatred of priests that he didn't even go to church with the child on the day of her first communion! Well then, if Dr Minoret does hate priests, why has he spent nearly every evening of the week for the last fifteen years with Abbé Chaperon? The old hypocrite has always given Ursule twenty francs towards the candle when she hands back the consecrated bread. And don't you remember the present Ursule gave the church to thank the priest for instructing her for her first communion? She spent all her money on it, and her godfather made it up for her – twice over. You men don't notice anything! When I heard these details, I said to myself: 'Well, that's the end of that!' An uncle with a fortune to bequeath doesn't behave like that, unless he has intentions towards that little brat picked up out of the gutter.'

'No, cousin,' the postmaster went on. 'Perhaps it's just an accident that the old fellow is taking Ursule to church. It's a fine day, and Uncle is out for a walk.'

'Uncle has a prayer-book in his hands – and such a sanctimonious look on his face! Anyway, you'll see him.'

'They've been playing a very close game,' the fat postmaster conceded. 'La Bougival told me that religion was never discussed between the doctor and Abbé Chaperon. Besides, our parish priest is the most honest man in the world. He would give a pauper the very last coin he had. He is incapable of an evil deed; and as for cheating us out of our inheritance . . .'

'But it's stealing,' Madame Massin burst out.

'It's worse than stealing!' cried Minoret-Levrault, driven to exasperation by his talkative cousin's remark.

'I know,' she went on, 'that Abbé Chaperon is an honest man, even though he's a priest; but he would be capable of anything if it helped the poor! He must have undermined, completely undermined, Uncle from below, till the doctor's become a religious humbug. We were feeling quite easy about it all, and now someone's gone and corrupted him. A man who's never believed in anything! a man of principle! Oh yes! we're done for, we are. My husband is all of a dither.'

Madame Massin's words were like so many arrows piercing the flesh of her stout cousin. Despite his corpulence, she forced him to walk at her pace – to the great surprise of people on their way to church. She wanted to catch up with Uncle Minoret and point him out to the postmaster.

From the direction of Le Gâtinais, Nemours is overlooked by a hill along which run the Montargis road and the river Loing. The church, over whose stones Time has thrown its rich black mantle (no doubt it was rebuilt in the fourteenth century by the Guise family, for whom Nemours was created a duchy), stands at one end of the little town, framed beneath a great arch. With monuments, as with men, position is everything. Shaded by a few trees, and thrown into relief by a neat little square, this solitary church produces a grandiose effect. As he came out into the square, the Nemours postmaster could see his uncle walking arm in arm with the young girl named Ursule, both of them holding their prayer-books as they entered the church. In the porch the old man doffed his hat, and his head – as completely white as a mountain peak crowned with snow – shone against the soft shadows of the church wall.

'Well, Minoret, what do you think about your uncle's conversion?' asked the Nemours tax-collector, a man named Crémière.

'What do you want me to think?' replied the postmaster, offering him a pinch of snuff.

'Well said, Levrault! You can't say what you think, if one of our illustrious authors was right in claiming that a man must think his words before speaking his thoughts,' a young man maliciously interjected as he came walking up; in Nemours he played the same part that Mephistopheles plays in Goethe's *Faust*.

Named Goupil, this rascal was the head clerk in the office of Monsieur Crémière-Dionis, the Nemours notary. Despite a previous record of almost dissolute behaviour, Goupil had been taken into Dionis's practice when, after squandering all his paternal inheritance in Paris (his father had been a well-to-do farmer who hoped he would become a notary), his complete penury made it impossible for him to continue there. At the sight of Goupil, one immediately realized that he had been in a hurry to enjoy life; to obtain satisfactions, he had to pay dearly for them. Despite his small stature, this twenty-seven-year-old clerk had a chest as well developed as that of a man aged forty. Short, thin legs, a large face with a complexion as blotchy as the sky before a storm, and a bald forehead threw his unusual build into even greater prominence. This was why his face seemed to belong to a hunchback whose hump was inside his body. One peculiar feature of this pale, sour face confirmed the existence of an invisible deformity. His nose was curved and twisted like the noses of many hunchbacks, and went from right to left instead of being exactly in the middle of his face. His mouth, drawn in at the corners like a Sardinian's, was always ready to break out into an ironical grimace. His hair, sparse and reddish in colour, hung lankly, occasionally revealing the skull. His hands, fat and badly joined to overlong arms, were claw-like and hardly ever clean. Goupil's shoes were fit to be thrown on to a rubbish heap, his floss-silk stockings were threadbare and almost greasy with filth; his waistcoats pitifully shabby, with even the moulds missing from a few of their buttons. An old silk handkerchief did service as a cravat. Everything about his dress indicated the cynical destitution to which he was condemned by his passions. This sinister general appearance was dominated by two goat-like eyes with yellow-ringed pupils, eyes that were both lewd and cowardly. No one in Nemours was more feared or respected than Goupil. Armed with the licence permitted by his ugliness, he had that detestable wit peculiar to those who are entirely without self-restraint, and he used his wit to avenge the disappointments of permanent jealousy. He would compose the satirical couplets that are sung at carnival-time, he organized abusive serenades, and produced the small local newspaper single-handed. Dionis was a shrewd but deceitful man, and even fairly timid as a result; fear prompted him to keep Goupil in his employment, as much as the latter's extreme intelligence and profound knowledge of the ins and outs of local affairs. But so deep was the employer's distrust of his clerk that he himself took charge of the petty cash, would not give him a room in his own house, kept him at arm's length, and did not entrust him with any confidential or delicate matter. And so, concealing the resentment he felt at the latter's behaviour, the clerk flattered his employer; planning revenge, he kept a careful eye on Madame Dionis. His keen intelligence made him a quick worker.

'Oh yes! you are already laughing at our misfortune,' the postmaster replied as the clerk stood rubbing his hands.

As Goupil basely flattered all Désiré's passions, having been his boon companion for the last five years, the postmaster treated him fairly cavalierly, not suspecting what a horrible fund of ill-will was building up in Goupil's heart at each new wound. Realizing that his need for money was greater than other men's, the clerk – well aware of his superiority to the whole of the bourgeoisie in Nemours – wanted to

34

make a fortune for himself, and relied on his friendship with Désiré to buy one of the three legal practices in town: the clerkship of the Civil Court of Conciliation, the office of one of the tipstaffs, or Dionis's notary's practice. Hence the patience with which he endured the postmaster's railing and Madame Minoret-Levrault's scorn, hence the infamous part he played in Désiré's life: for the last two years, Désiré had left him to console the unfortunate maidens deserted at the end of each university vacation. Thus Goupil devoured the crumbs of the irregular affairs he himself had arranged.

'If I had been the old man's nephew, he wouldn't have appointed God his joint heir along with me,' the clerk replied, baring his few black, threatening teeth in a hideously sneering laugh.

Just then Massin-Levrault junior, the clerk of the Police Court, caught up with his wife as he came walking along with Madame Crémière, the wife of the Nemours tax-collector. This man, one of the harshest members of the middle-class community in the little town, had a face like a Tartar's: small eyes as round as oak-apples beneath a low forehead, frizzy hair, an oily complexion, large rimless ears, a mouth that had practically no lips, and a sparse growth of beard. In his manner he had the pitiless gentleness of money-lenders, whose behaviour is based on fixed principles. He spoke like a man who has lost his voice. To sum him up: he used his wife and eldest daughter to make copies for him of the Court's sentences.

Madame Crémière was a stout woman with dubiously blond hair, a very freckled complexion, and dresses that were a little too tight for her. She was friendly with Madame Dionis, and was considered an educated woman – because she read novels. This wife of the lowliest type of financier, full of pretensions to elegance and wit, was awaiting her uncle's inheritance before she could *really begin to live in style*, decorate her drawing-room and be at home to the middle class of Nemours; her husband refused to buy her any of the Carcel lamps, lithographs and knick-knacks that the notary's wife had. She was terribly afraid of Goupil, who was always

35

on the look-out for her *vertical collapses* and gossiped about them around town (*vertical collapses* was her expression for 'verbal lapses'). One day Madame Dionis remarked to her that she had no idea what toothwash to use, and Madame Crémière replied: 'Use one containing opium.'

Almost all the collateral relations of old Dr Minoret were now gathered together in the market place, and so widespread was people's impression of the importance of the event that brought them together that groups of peasants and peasant women, carrying their red umbrellas and all dressed in those bright colours that make festival days so picturesque in the countryside, stood watching the Minoret relations. In little towns halfway in size between towns and large villages, people who do not go to mass stand in the market place discussing business. In Nemours divine service coincides with a weekly market frequently attended by householders within a radius of a mile and a half. This explains the united front presented by the peasantry against the middle classes on questions of food prices and wage rates.

'So what would you have done?' the Nemours postmaster asked Goupil.

'I would have made myself as necessary to him as the air he breathes. But, in the first place, you had no idea how to tackle him! An inheritance must be as carefully wooed as a beautiful woman; if you don't try hard enough, both will escape you. If my boss's wife was here, she'd tell you how apt the comparison is!'

'But Monsieur Bongrand has just told me we needn't worry,' replied the clerk of the Civil Court.

'Yes, but that could mean lots of things,' laughed Goupil. 'I'd have liked to hear your crafty conciliative magistrate saying that! If there *was* no hope, if I knew everything *was* lost – because, after all, he nearly lives with your uncle – then I'd say: "You needn't worry!"'

During this last sentence Goupil's face had such a comical smile, to which he gave such an obvious meaning, that the family suspected that the clerk of the Civil Court of Conciliation had become ensnared in the toils of his wily magistrate. The tax-collector, a stout little man as insignificant as any tax-collector should be, and as worthless as any woman of wit and humour could possibly hope for, struck terror into his co-heir Massin with the words: 'What did I tell you?'

Since deceitful people always attribute their deceitfulness to others, Massin looked askance at the conciliative magistrate who just then was standing near the church chatting with the Marquis du Rouvre, one of his former clients.

'If I knew that . . .' he said.

'You would counteract his support for the Marquis du Rouvre, who has several times been arrested for debt – he's playing up to him just now with his advice,' said Goupil, insinuating thoughts of revenge into the clerk of the Court's mind. 'But sing small with your boss: he's a cunning fellow, and must have some influence over your uncle; he can still prevent him from leaving everything to the Church.'

'Bah! Whatever happens, it won't kill us,' said Minoret-Levrault, opening his huge snuff-box.

'You won't live off it either,' Goupil answered, causing the two women to shudder. More rapidly than their husbands, they saw how much they would be deprived of by the loss of this inheritance, which in their imaginations had so often been laid out on worldly goods. 'Anyway, we'll drown this little anxiety in floods of champagne, shan't we, old man, by celebrating Désiré's return?' he added, striking the colossus in the belly, and inviting himself just in case he was overlooked.

2. The Uncle Worth a Fortune

BEFORE proceeding further with the story, precise people will perhaps appreciate a kind of advance inventory summary at this point – a summary which is in fact fairly necessary if we are to know the varying degrees of kinship that united these three family men and their wives to the old man who had so suddenly been converted to religion. Such criss-crossing of family ties in the provinces may give rise to many an instructive thought.

In Nemours there are no more than three or four families of the lower, obscure aristocracy, amongst whom the Portenduères were foremost at that time. These exclusive families are on visiting terms with the landed nobility of the neighbourhood, the chief of which were the d'Aiglemonts, owners of the fine estate at Saint-Lange, and the Marquis du Rouvre, whose heavily mortgaged properties were watched by the middle classes with a jealous eye. The town-dwelling nobility have no fortunes. Madame de Portenduère's only possessions were her town house and a farm producing a rental of 4,700 francs a year. In opposition to this minuscule Faubourg Saint-Germain are a group of ten or a dozen rich men, retired millers and tradespeople, a miniature bourgeoisie beneath whom the small retailers, proletariat and peasantry carry on their lives. As in the Swiss cantons and several other small areas, the middle classes present the unusual feature of being permeated by a few indigenous families: families which were perhaps Gaulish in origin, reigning over an area, invading it, and making almost all its inhabitants cousins. In the reign of Louis XI, a period in which the Third Estate eventually transformed their nicknames into proper surnames and when a few of the latter even mingled with the names of the feudal nobility, the middle classes of Nemours consisted of the Minorets, the Massins, the Levraults and the Crémières. By the time of Louis XIII's reign, these four families had already produced Massin-Crémières, Levrault-Massins, Massin-Minorets, Minoret-Minorets, Crémière-Levraults, Levrault-Minoret-Massins, Massin-Levraults, Minoret-Massins, Massin-Massins and Crémière-Massins, the whole thing further complicated with junior, eldest son, Crémière-François, Levrault-Jacques, Jean-Minoret, etc., etc., etc., enough to have driven any Père Anselme of ordinary families mad, if ordinary families ever had any need for a genealogist. The permutations of this fourfold domestic kaleidoscope were made so complicated by births and marriages that the family trees of the bourgeois of Nemours would have confused even the painstaking authors of the Almanach de Gotha themselves, despite the atomistic science with which they trace the zigzag lines of German matrimonial alliances. Over a long period of time the Minorets ran the tanneries and the Crémières the mills, whilst the Massins were in trade, and the Levraults remained farmers. Fortunately for the area, these four families sent out suckers rather than tap-roots, and shoots sprang up elsewhere through the departure of some children to seek their fortunes in other districts: there are Minorets who are cutlers at Melun, Levraults at Montargis, Massins at Orleans, and Crémières who have risen to a prosperous position in Paris. Varied are the destinies of these bees from the mother-hive. Inevitably, rich Massins employ working-class Massins, just as there are German princes in the service of Austria or Prussia. In the same administrative district,* a Minoret millionaire is guarded by a soldier with the same surname. With the same blood flowing in their veins, but with their only point of resemblance being their identical surnames, these four shuttles had ceaselessly woven a human cloth each length of which was either a dress or a napkin, superb cambric or coarse lining. The same blood pulsed through the feet, head and heart, through hard-working hands, ailing lungs and foreheads of genius. The heads of each family, faithful to tradition, lived in the township where family links either became closer or more remote according to the circumstances of events within this strange circle of interrelated names. Whatever country you go to, if you change the names, you have still not changed the basic facts, but they are facts devoid of the poetry of Feudalism – the poetry rendered by Sir Walter Scott with so much skill.

*département

39

Looking a little further afield at the history of humanity itself, all the noble families of the eleventh century (which are now almost all extinct – except for the royal line of the Capets) have inevitably contributed to the birth of a Rohan, a Montmorency, a Bauffremont or a Mortemart today; all are inevitably present in the blood of the lowliest gentleman of coat armour, providing he is of truly gentle blood. In other words, every middle-class man is the cousin of other middle-class men, and every nobleman is the cousin of other noblemen. As it is said in that sublime page of biblical genealogy, three families – the lines of Shem, Ham and Japheth – can cover the face of the earth with their descendants within a thousand years. A family can become a nation, and unfortunately a nation can revert to a single, simple family. As proof of this, it is only necessary to apply to the study of one's ancestors, accumulating backwards through time in geometrical progression, the same calculation as was used by the wise man who, as a reward for inventing chess, asked a Persian king for a head of corn in the first square of the chess-board: constantly doubling this head of corn, he demonstrated that the kingdom itself would not be large enough to pay him. The network of the aristocracy, interwoven with the network of the middle classes, that hostile interaction of two centres of privilege, one protected by rigid institutions, the other by the wiles of commerce and the patient activity of hard work, led to the Revolution of 1789. These two classes, now virtually united, today confront disinherited collaterals. What will be the outcome? In the answer to this lies a heavy question-mark over our political future.

The man who in Louis XV's reign had the simple surname of Minoret had so numerous a family that one of his five children – the Minoret whose attendance at church was causing a sensation – left Nemours as a young man to seek his fortune in Paris; his returns home became more and more infrequent but he doubtless came back to his native town on his grandparents' death to draw his share in the inheritance. After enduring many hardships, as do all young men of firm purpose who seek a place within the brilliant world of Paris, young Minoret carved out for himself a finer career than he perhaps dreamed of at his beginnings; he immediately devoted himself to a medical career – one of the professions which demand both talent and good luck, but even more good luck than talent. Backed by Dupont de Nemours, associated by a lucky chance with the Abbé Morellet whom Voltaire used to call *Mords-les,** and protected by the Encyclopaedists, Dr Minoret became an ardent disciple of the great doctor Bordeu, Diderot's friend. D'Alembert, Helvétius, Baron d'Holbach and Grimm, in whose presence he was a mere boy, no doubt took an interest in Minoret eventually, as Bordeu had done; by about 1777 Minoret's practice included a fair number of deists, Encyclopaedists, sensualists, materialists – whichever name you choose to apply to the rich *philosophes* of those days. Although there was very little in him of the charlatan, he invented the famous 'Balm of Lelièvre', so highly praised by the *Mercure de France*, and advertised permanently at the back of that journal, the weekly newspaper of the Encyclopaedists. The chemist Lelièvre, who was an able man, saw a commercial possibility where Minoret had merely seen a new preparation for the Pharmacopoeia, and honestly shared his profits with the doctor, who had gone to Rouelle to study chemistry, just as he was a student of Bordeu in medicine. One would have become a materialist for less. In 1778 the doctor made a love-match; it was the time when *La Nouvelle Héloïse* was on everyone's lips, when people sometimes married for love; his wife, the daughter of the famous harpsichordist Valentin Mirouët, was herself a celebrated musician, but she was weak and delicate, and the Revolution killed her. Minoret was on close terms of friendship with Robespierre, for whom he had once obtained a gold medal for a dissertation on the following subject: *What is the origin of the opinion that attributes to a whole family some part of the shame suffered by a criminal whose sentence involves a loss of civil rights? Is such a state of opinion more harmful than useful? And if so, how can the difficulties resulting from this be obviated?* The Royal Academy of Arts and Sciences at Metz,

*Literally, 'Bite them'.

41

to which Minoret belonged, must have the original text of the dissertation. Although this friendship meant that the doctor's wife need have nothing to fear, she was so afraid of being sentenced to the scaffold that an irresistible terror aggravated the aneurism caused by her excessively sensitive nature. Despite all the doctor's precautions (and he idolized his wife), Ursule happened to meet the very tumbril carrying Madame Roland to her execution, and the sight of this caused her death. Minoret had been full of tender indulgence for his Ursule; he had refused her nothing, and she had led the life of a society belle; he was hard up after her death. Robespierre secured his appointment as senior physician at a hospital.

Although, during the heated debates occasioned by mesmerism, the name of Minoret had acquired a fame that brought him now and again to his parents' notice, the Revolution had such a dissolving influence and broke up family relationships to such an extent that by 1813 Dr Minoret's existence was completely unknown at Nemours. Only a chance encounter gave him the idea of returning, as wild animals do, to die in his old home.

When crossing France, a traveller's eye is so quickly bored by the monotony of its plains; but who has not had the delightful experience of glimpsing a valley from the top of a hill, from its slope or at a bend in the road, when instead a barren landscape seemed to be indicated: a cool, fresh valley with a river running through it, and a small town nestling beneath a rock as a beehive may be seen inside an old, hollow willow-tree? When you hear the 'Gee up!' of the coachman walking alongside his horses, you shake yourself out of your slumber and dreamily admire some beautiful dream-like landscape that seems to the traveller as brilliant an invention of nature as any remarkable passage is to the reader of a book. Such is the feeling caused by the sudden sight of Nemours as you approach it from Burgundy. From that approach you see it encircled by bare rocks, rocks that are white, black, grey, and peculiarly shaped like so many in the forest of Fontainebleau; and, springing up from these rocks, occasional trees stand out clearly against the sky, giving a rural appearance to this sort of tumbledown wall. This point marks the end of the forest-clad hill which crawls alongside the road from Nemours to Bouron. Beneath this half-formed amphitheatre stretches a meadow through which the Loing gently falls from level to level. This delightful landscape, beside which runs the road to Montargis, is like an opera set, so carefully thought out are its effects. One morning the doctor was returning post-haste to Paris from a summons to a rich patient in Burgundy; at the last coaching-inn he had not said which road he wanted to take, and so was driven unawares through Nemours; in his half-waking state he again saw the countryside amid which he had spent his childhood. By that time the doctor had lost several of his old friends. The devoted supporters of the Encyclopaedist movement had witnessed La Harpe's conversion, and attended the funerals of Lebrun-Pindare, Marie-Joseph de Chénier, Morellet and Madame Helvétius. He was an observer of Voltaire's semi-eclipse under the attacks of Geoffroy, who carried on Fréron's work. These things caused him to think of retirement, and so, when his post-chaise halted at the top of the high street in Nemours, he set his heart on inquiring about his relations. Minoret-Levrault came personally to see the doctor, who recognized the postmaster as his eldest brother's own son. His nephew introduced him to his wife, the only daughter of old Levrault-Crémière, who twelve years ago had bequeathed her the finest inn in Nemours together with the coaching business.

'Well, nephew,' said the doctor, 'have I any other family?'

'Aunt Minoret, your sister, married a Massin-Massin.'

'Oh yes, the estate manager at Saint-Lange.'

'She died a widow, leaving an only daughter, who has just married a Crémière-Crémière, a charming young man who is still looking for a job.'

'Very well, so she's my actual niece. My seafaring brother died a bachelor, Captain Minoret was killed at Monte Legino, and then there's me; so we're extinct in the male line; have I any relations on my mother's side? My mother was a Jean-Massin-Levrault.'

'As for Jean-Massin-Levraults,' Minoret-Levrault replied, 'there's only one Jean-Massin left and she's married Monsieur Crémière-Levrault-Dionis, a provender merchant who died on the scaffold. His wife died of despair, a ruined woman, leaving one daughter married to a Levrault-Minoret, a farmer at Montereau, who's in a good way of business; and their daughter has just married a Massin-Levrault, a notary's clerk at Montargis, where his father is a locksmith.'

'So I'm not short of family,' the doctor said gaily, adding that he would like his nephew to show him round Nemours.

The Loing winds through the town, bordered by terraced gardens and tidy little houses that make one think happiness must exist there if it exists anywhere in the world. As the doctor turned from the High Street into the Rue des Bourgeois, Minoret-Levrault pointed out to him the house and garden of Monsieur Levrault, a rich Parisian ironmonger who (he said) had just gone and died.

'There's a fine house for sale, uncle, with a lovely garden overlooking the river.'

'Well, let's have a look,' the doctor answered, seeing a small paved courtyard at the back of which was a house huddled between the outer walls of two adjacent houses: walls hidden by clumps of trees and creepers.

'There are cellars underneath,' Minoret observed as he climbed up a very long flight of steps leading to the front door, between blue and white earthenware vases filled with flowering geraniums.

Like most provincial houses, it was bisected by a passage leading from the courtyard to the garden; to the right, there was only a drawing-room lit by four windows, two of which opened on to the courtyard and two on to the garden; but Levrault-Levrault had used one of these windows as the entrance into a long brick greenhouse stretching from the drawing-room to the river, where it culminated in a horrid Chinese pavilion.

'Hm, if I roofed this greenhouse over and put a floor in, I could use it as my library and convert that strange piece of architecture into a nice study.'

On the other side of the passage a dining-room overlooked the garden; it was painted to resemble black lacquer with green and gold flowers, and was separated from the kitchen by the well of the staircase. A small pantry behind the staircase led into the kitchen whose barred and latticed windows looked out on to the courtyard. There were two rooms on the first floor, and above them attics that were still quite fit to live in. After a rapid inspection of the house, with its green trellis-work completely covering the walls on both the garden and courtyard sides of the house, and with its river-terrace full of earthenware vases, the doctor commented: 'Levrault-Levrault must have spent a mint of money!'

'Oh! an enormous amount – as enormous as he was,' Minoret-Levrault replied. 'He loved flowers, how foolish can you get! "What income does that produce?" says my wife. You see, a painter came from Paris to fresco his passage walls with flowers. He's put full-length mirrors everywhere. The ceilings have been redecorated with cornices costing six francs a foot. The dining-room and wood-block floors are inlaid: such crazy ideas! It hasn't added anything at all to the value of the house.'

'Well, nephew, buy this house for me, and let me know when you've done the deal. Here's my address; the rest I shall leave to my notary. By the way, who lives opposite?' he asked, as he was on the way out.

'Émigrés!' the postmaster replied. 'A Chevalier de Portenduère.'

Once the house had been purchased, the illustrious doctor wrote instructing his nephew to let it, rather than coming to live there himself. The Levrault Folly became the home of the Nemours notary, who then sold his practice to Dionis, his head clerk, and died two years later leaving the doctor with a house to let, just as Napoleon's destiny was being decided in the surrounding districts. The doctor's heirs had been more or less taken in, assuming that his desire to return to his old haunts was the whim of a wealthy man. They were in despair at the thought that sentimental attachments were keeping him in Paris, thus depriving them of his inheritance. Nevertheless, Minoret-Levrault's wife took this opportunity of writing to the doctor. The old man replied that as soon as the armistice was signed, and the roads were free of soldiers and communications restored to normal, he would come and live in Nemours. He made his appearance in the town accompanied by two of

45

his patients, the hospital architect and an upholsterer, who between them took charge of the repairs, interior design and furniture removal. Madame Minoret-Levrault offered the old deceased notary's cook as caretaker; and the offer was accepted. When the heirs discovered that their uncle or great-uncle Minoret was definitely coming to live in Nemours, their families were seized with avid curiosity, despite the political events that were overhanging those very regions of Gâtinais and Brie at the time; yet it was a curiosity which was almost legitimate. Was their uncle rich? Was he thrifty or extravagant? Would he leave a fine fortune, or nothing? Had he any life annuities? With infinite trouble and all manner of devious spying, this is what they discovered.

After the death of his wife Ursule Mirouët the doctor must have earned a sizable income between 1789 and 1813; in 1805 he had been appointed consulting physician to the Emperor; but no one knew the size of his fortune. He lived frugally, his only expenses were a sumptuous apartment and a carriage hired by the year; he never had visitors and almost invariably dined out. His housekeeper, who was furious at not coming with him to Nemours, told Zélie Levrault, the postmaster's wife, that she knew the doctor had 14,000 francs investment income from Government securities. Despite the fact that for twenty years he had occupied the lucrative positions of hospital registrar, physician to the Emperor and member of the Institut, these 14,000 francs investment income – the fruits of his regular savings – denoted a maximum capital of 160,000 francs! If he had only saved 8,000 francs a year, the doctor must have had either many vices or many virtues; but neither the housekeeper nor Zélie, in fact nobody, could make out the reasons for this modest fortune. Minoret, whose departure was deeply regretted in the district in which he lived, was one of the most philanthropic men in Paris and, like Larrey, he kept his benefactions an absolute secret. It was, therefore, with intense satisfaction that the doctor's family saw the arrival of their uncle's fine furniture and well-stocked library; they noted too that he was already an officer of the Legion of Honour, and that the King had just appointed him a knight of the order of Saint-Michel, perhaps because his retirement made way for some royal favourite. But even when the architect, painters and upholsterers had everything arranged in the most comfortable manner, the doctor still did not come. From the indiscreet remark of a young man sent down to set out the library, Madame Minoret-Levrault (who had been supervising the upholsterer and architect as if her own fortune was involved) discovered that the doctor was responsible for an orphan named Ursule. This news caused strange havoc amongst the people of Nemours. Eventually, however, the old man arrived at his new home towards the middle of January 1815, and settled down there on the sly with a baby girl of ten months and her nurse.

'Ursule can't be his daughter. He's seventy-one!' the heirs cried in alarm.

'Whoever she is,' said Madame Massin, 'she'll cause us a lot of *mither*!' (A local expression.)

The doctor did not extend a cordial welcome to his great-niece on the maternal side, whose husband had just bought the clerkship of the Civil Court of Conciliation; they were the first to venture to speak to him of their difficult circumstances. Massin and his wife were not wealthy. Massin's father, a locksmith at Montargis who had had to make a composition with his creditors, was working at the age of sixty-seven as hard as any young man, and would leave no fortune. Madame Massin's father, Levrault-Minoret, had just died at Montereau as a consequence of the battle, seeing his farm burned down, his fields ruined and cattle devoured.

'We shan't get anything from your great-uncle,' Massin remarked to his wife, who was already expecting her second child.

The doctor secretly gave them 10,000 francs, with which the clerk of the Civil Court of Conciliation (a friend of the notary and the tipstaff at Nemours) set himself up as a money-lender, and made such short work of the local peasants that at this time Goupil knew he had about 80,000 francs of unpublicized capital.

As for his other niece, the doctor used his connections in

47

Paris to obtain the Nemours tax-collectorship for Crémière; and supplied them with the caution money. Although Minoret-Levrault was not in any need, Zélie – envious of her uncle's generosity to his two nieces – introduced the doctor to her son, who was then aged ten, and whom she was sending to school in Paris, where (she added) education was very expensive. As he had been Fontanes's doctor, Minoret secured his nephew a half-scholarship at the Collège Louis-le-Grand, where the boy was put into the fourth form.

Crémière, Massin and Minoret-Levrault, who were exceedingly common men, were decisively summed up by the doctor after the first two months in which they tried to corner not so much their uncle as his inheritance. People guided by instinct have this disadvantage as against intellectuals: their characters are quickly read; the promptings of instinct are too natural and too obvious not to be instantly noticed, whereas mental conceptions demand an equal degree of intelligence on either side if they are to be fathomed. After buying off his heirs' gratitude, and in a sense shutting their mouths, the wily doctor excused himself from receiving them, pleading his occupations, habits and the care Ursule required; yet he did not bar them from the house. He was fond of dining alone; he went to bed late and rose late; he had returned to his birthplace to seek rest and solitude. Such old men's whims seemed quite natural, and his heirs were content with paying him a visit once a week, every Sunday, between one o'clock and four – visits which he tried to put an end to by saying: 'Only come and see me when you need something.'

Though he did not refuse to give consultations in serious cases, especially to the poor, the doctor did not wish to become doctor to the little hospital at Nemours, declaring that he would practise no longer.

'I've killed enough people,' he laughed to the Abbé Chaperon, who, aware of his benevolence, would plead to him on behalf of the poor.

'He really is a character!' This comment on Dr Minoret was the innocent revenge of ruffled vanity – for the doctor built up a social circle who deserve to be placed in contrast with the heirs. Those middle-class townsfolk who thought themselves worthy of swelling the court of a man decorated with a black ribbon* nurtured a feeling of jealousy towards the doctor and his favourites. Unfortunately, this jealousy was to produce its effect.

*The ribbon of a knight of the order of Saint-Michel.

3. The Doctor's Friends

By a peculiarity explained in the proverb 'extremes meet', this doctor with his materialistic philosophy very quickly made friends with the parish priest at Nemours. The old man was very fond of backgammon, the favourite game of church people, and Abbé Chaperon was a worthy opponent. Thus, a game was the first link between them. Moreover, Minoret was a charitable man and Chaperon was the Fénelon of the Gâtinais region. Both had had a wide education: thus, the man of God was the only person in the whole of Nemours who could understand the atheist. To have a useful discussion, men must first understand one another. What pleasure is there in making witty remarks to someone who does not appreciate them? The doctor and the priest had too much taste and had moved too much in civilized society not to practise its precepts; they could wage on one another that friendly warfare so necessary to conversation. Although they detested one another's opinions, they admired each other's characters. If such attraction of opposites were not the basis of private life, would not one have to despair of society which, especially in France, demands a kind of antagonism? Antipathies stem from the collision of personalities, not from the clash of ideas. Thus, Abbé Chaperon was the first friend the doctor made in Nemours. Then aged sixty, he had been parish priest at Nemours since the re-establishment of the Catholic Church. Out of devotion to his flock, he had refused to become vicar-general of the diocese. The agnostics were grateful to him for this, and his congregation loved him all the more. Revered by his flock and respected by the whole town, the parish priest practised his philanthropy without inquiring about the religious views of those in need. His presbytery, scarcely furnished with enough furniture to meet the simplest needs of life, was as cold and bare as a miser's house. Miserliness and charity reveal themselves in similar ways: for charity stores up in Heaven the treasure that misers accumulate on earth. Abbé Chaperon's arguments with his maid about household expenses were more meticulous than Gobseck's with his – if indeed that notorious Jew ever did employ a housemaid. The good priest often sold the silver buckles from his shoes and breeches to give the money to poor people who happened to find him short of ready money. Seeing him come out of church with the flaps of his breeches tied in a knot through the buckle-holes, the pious ladies of the town would go for the buckles to the watchmaker's and jeweller's in Nemours, and scold their parish priest when they brought them back to him. He never bought himself any linen or outer clothing and wore his clothes until they were out of fashion. His underwear was so thick with darns that it made marks on his skin like a hairshirt. Madame de Portenduère or other kindly souls would then arrange with the housekeeper to have his old underwear or other garments replaced with new ones whilst he was asleep, and the parish priest did not always notice the substitution immediately. He ate at home on pewter plates with spoons and forks made of forged iron. Whenever he entertained the priests in charge of parishes and chapels of ease on the solemn feast days which are the responsibility of rural deans, he would borrow his atheist friend's silver and table-linen.

'My silver is his salvation,' the doctor would say.

These beautiful actions, which people found out sooner or later and which were always accompanied by witty words of encouragement, had a sublime artlessness about them. Abbé Chaperon's life was the more praiseworthy in that he had a fund of learning as vast as it was varied, and truly remarkable ability. His subtlety and grace, inseparable concomitants of a simple life, enhanced an elocution worthy of a prelate. His manners, character and habits gave his social conduct the exquisite flavour of all that is both sophisticated and guileless in the human mind. Fond of a joke, he was never priestly in a drawing-room. Until Dr Minoret's arrival, the good abbé felt no regret at hiding his light under a bushel; but perhaps he was grateful to the doctor for putting his abilities to use. He had had a private income of two thousand francs a year and quite a good library when he first came to Nemours, but by 1829 all that he had left was his stipend as a priest, almost all of which he gave away each year. His guidance in misfortune or delicate situations was excellent, and many a person who did not go to church seeking consolation went to the presbytery seeking advice. To conclude this portrait of his character, one small anecdote will be enough. Sometimes – though admittedly not very often – peasants who were of bad character claimed they were being sued for debt, or even got themselves fictitiously sued, in order to excite Abbé Chaperon's benevolence. They misled their wives, who, seeing their houses threatened with confiscation and their cows distrained upon, also misled the poor priest with their tears, so that he found them the seven or eight hundred francs they were asking for – which the peasants spent on a patch of land. When pious people, churchwardens, pointed the fraud out to Abbé Chaperon, asking him to consult them so as to avoid becoming a victim to cupidity again, he told them: 'These people might have done something criminal to get their acre of land. Doesn't preventing evil amount to doing good?' Perhaps a sketch of this man may not be out of place here – a man remarkable in that the arts and sciences had left their impact on his heart and powerful mind without in any way corrupting him. Abbé Chaperon was sixty; his hair was as white as snow, so keenly did he feel the misfortunes of others, so strongly had he been influenced by the events of the French Revolution. Twice imprisoned for refusing to swear oaths of allegiance during that Revolution, he had (as he said) twice repeated the Latin words: 'Father, into Thy hands I commend my spirit.' He was of medium height, neither fat nor thin. His face, which was colourless and very wrinkled and hollowed, first attracted attention by the utter tranquillity of its features and by the purity of its outlines, which seemed fringed with light. The face of a chaste man has something inexplicably radiant about it. Brown eyes, with alert pupils, gave life to an irregularly shaped face crowned with an enormous forehead. His look of authority came from a gentleness which did not exclude strength of character. The upper bones of his eyes seemed like two arches shaded by bushy greying eyebrows that held no terror. As he had lost many of his teeth, his mouth was out of shape and his cheeks sunken; but this ravaged appearance was not without a charm of its own, and those gracious wrinkles seemed to be smiling at you. Though he was not gouty, his feet were so sensitive and he found walking so difficult that, whatever the season, he wore shoes made of Orleans calfskin. Believing that trousers were an unseemly dress for a priest, he always wore cloth breeches and stout black woollen stockings knitted by his housekeeper. Out of doors he never wore a soutane, but a brown frock coat, and still kept to the tricorn hat that he had bravely worn even in France's darkest days. This handsome, noble old man, whose face always shone with the sincerity of a faultless soul, was destined to have so deep an influence on the people and things in this story that it was first necessary to trace the source of his moral authority.

Minoret took three newspapers: a Liberal one, a Government one and an extreme right-wing one; also a few periodicals and scientific journals, whose series swelled the size of his library. These newspapers, books and the follower of the Encyclopaedists himself were an attraction for an ex-captain in the Royal Swedish regiment named Monsieur de Jordy, a nobleman of Voltairean principles who was an old bachelor living on a pension and annuity income of 1,600 francs a year. After reading the *gazettes* for a few days (they had been passed on to him by the parish priest), Monsieur de Jordy thought it appropriate to thank the doctor with a personal visit. From the very first time they met, the old captain – who had been an instructor at the École Militaire – won the old doctor's favour, and Minoret was eager to return the visit. Monsieur de Jordy, a thin, lean little man, who suffered from apoplexy although his face was very pale, was particularly noticeable for his handsome forehead, so like Charles XII's, above which his hair was always close-cropped – like that of the Swedish soldier-king. His blue eyes gave the impression that love had not been absent from his life, but they were immensely sad; they at once attracted attention through the memories that seemed to be glimpsed in them – memories about which he kept so strict a silence that none of his old friends ever could detect any reference to his past life, nor any of those exclamations prompted by catastrophes similar to one's own. He concealed the painful mystery of his earlier days beneath a philosophical gaiety; but whenever he thought he was alone, his sluggish movements – sluggish less because he was senile than for a deliberate purpose – revealed one constant and distressing thought: hence the nickname, given him by Abbé Chaperon, of 'the Christian who did not know he was one'.* Always wearing clothes made of blue cloth, he betrayed the former habits of a life of military discipline both in his dress and in his slightly stiff bearing. His sweet, harmonious voice could touch a listener's soul. In his fine hands and the shape of his face he resembled the Comte d'Artois; so clearly did they show how charming he must have been in his youth that the mystery of his life became still more unfathomable. It was impossible not to wonder what the misfortune could have been that had befallen the manly beauty, courage, grace, education – indeed, all the heart's most precious qualities that had formerly been combined in him. At the name of Robespierre, Monsieur de Jordy would always shudder. He was a great snuff-taker, but curiously enough cured himself of the habit to please little Ursule, who showed some dislike for him on account of this addiction. At his first sight of the little girl, the captain gazed at her repeatedly with a long, almost passionate look. So deep was his interest in her, so keen was his joy at seeing her play, that this affection strengthened his friendship with the doctor, who never dared ask the old bachelor: 'I dare say you too have lost children?' There are such people, as kind and patient as he was, who pass through life with a bitter thought locked in their hearts and a sweet but painful smile on their lips, carrying with them to the grave the key to their hidden secret, refusing to divulge it either through pride or disdain or perhaps from some desire for revenge: having only God to confide in and to console them. Like the doctor, Monsieur de Jordy had come to Nemours to spend the twilight of his life in peace; almost the only people he knew there were Abbé Chaperon, constantly at his parishioners' disposal, and Madame de Portenduère, who went to bed at nine. Wearily abandoning the search for company, he too had even-

* 'Le Chrétien sans le savoir': a pun on the title of a comedy by Michel Sedaine, *Le Philosophe sans le savoir* (1765).

tually begun to retire early, despite the thorns that afflicted him in slumber. It was therefore a wonderful stroke of luck for both the doctor and the captain to meet someone who had moved in the same circles, spoke the same language, went to bed late, and with whom it was possible to exchange ideas. The first time Monsieur de Jordy, Abbé Chaperon and Minoret spent an evening together, it gave them so much pleasure that the priest and the soldier turned up every evening at nine o'clock, just when little Ursule had gone to bed and the old man was alone. All three would stay up till midnight or one o'clock.

Soon this trio became a quartet. Another man, the conciliative magistrate, got an idea of the pleasures of these evening sessions, and sought out the doctor's company: a man who had had considerable experience of life and whose exercise of his public duties had given him the tolerance, knowledge, subtlety, conversational talent and wealth of observation that the soldier, doctor and priest owed to their cure of souls, their healing of disease and their teaching. Before becoming conciliative magistrate at Nemours, Monsieur Bongrand had spent ten years as a solicitor at Melun, where he himself also appeared in court – as is the custom in towns where there is no bar. A widower at forty-five, he felt that he was still too active for a life of idleness; he had therefore applied for the post of conciliative magistrate at Nemours, which had fallen vacant a few months before the doctor settled in. The Lord Chancellor is always happy to find practising lawyers, especially people in comfortable circumstances, to carry out the functions of this important judicial post. Monsieur Bongrand lived simply at Nemours on his 1,500 francs salary, and was thus able to devote the rest of his income to his son, a law student at the Sorbonne, who was also studying the practice of the law under Derville, the famous solicitor. Bongrand was rather like an old retired head of some Civil Service department: he had the same kind of face, not pale by nature but worn pale by the public business, the disappointments and the disgust that have left their mark on it, a face wrinkled with thought and with the constant muscular control habitual in people whose job demands discretion; but it was often lit by smiles peculiar to those men who alternately believe everything and believe nothing, and who are used to seeing and hearing everything without showing surprise, and to fathoming the depths of self-interest in the hearts of men. His hair was not so much white as discoloured, wavy but firmly brushed down; the yellow skin on his sagacious forehead matched his few wisps of hair. His thickset face gave him some resemblance to a fox, especially with its short pointed nose. From his mouth, which had the split common to all great talkers, flew dazzling sparks which made his conversation so torrential that Goupil used to say nastily: 'You need an umbrella to listen to him,' or else: 'Judgments are raining down on the Court of Conciliation.' His eyes seemed shrewd when he was wearing spectacles; but taking off his glasses dulled his look to such an extent that he appeared a simpleton. Although he was gay, even almost jovial, his bearing was a little too self-important. He almost always kept his hands in his trouser pockets, and only drew them out to adjust his spectacles with an almost malicious gesture of the hands, denoting some subtle remark or unanswerable argument. His gestures, talkativeness, and innocent pretensions betrayed the fact that he had once been a provincial solicitor; but these slight faults were only superficial: he redeemed them by an acquired good-naturedness which the precise student of human behaviour would describe as the leniency natural to anyone of superior ability. He looked a little like a fox, and was thought of as being immensely cunning – yet he was not dishonest. His cunning was shrewdness in action. But people are called cunning when they foresee a result, and avoid the traps laid down for them! The conciliative magistrate liked whist, a game with which the captain and doctor were familiar, and which the parish priest quickly learned.

To this small group of men Minoret's drawing-room became like an oasis. The Nemours doctor, who was not lacking in either education or good manners, and who respected Minoret as one of the most distinguished medical figures, was another welcome guest; but his tiring duties, which forced him to go to bed early in order to be up at an early hour, made it impossible for him to be as regular in attendance as were the doctor's three friends. The friendship of these five men of ability, the only ones in Nemours with sufficiently wide learning to understand one another, accounts for the aversion Minoret felt for his family: though he had to leave them his fortune, he could scarcely invite them to share his company. Whether it was because the postmaster, tax-collector and clerk of the court took this point, or because they felt reassured by their uncle's loyalty and gifts, they ceased to visit him – much to his satisfaction. Thus, seven or eight months after the doctor's arrival in Nemours, the four old men playing whist and backgammon formed a compact, exclusive group: a group which each felt to be a sort of autumnal brotherhood, and whose delights were all the more to be appreciated because they were unexpected. This kinship of choice minds looked on Ursule as a child to be adopted in different ways: the priest thought of her soul, the conciliative magistrate became her guardian, the soldier was intending to become her tutor; as for Minoret, he was her father, mother and doctor.

After becoming acclimatized, the old man fell into a routine and organized his life in the way lives are organized in every country district. On Ursule's account he never received visitors in the morning, and never gave dinner parties; but his friends could arrive at his house about six in the evening, and remain until midnight. The first arrivals would find newspapers on the drawing-room table and read them whilst awaiting the others, or sometimes they would go to meet the doctor as he was returning from a walk. Such tranquil habits were not only imposed on him by old age, they were also the wise, thoughtful calculation of a man of the world who did not wish his happiness to be disturbed by the anxious curiosity of his family or the tittle-tattle of small towns. He would concede nothing to that fickle goddess, public opinion, whose tyranny – one of the misfortunes that have befallen France – was about to assert itself, transforming our country into a single province. And this was why, as soon as Ursule was weaned and able to walk, he dismissed the cook obtained for him by his niece, Madame Minoret-Levrault, on finding out that she was keeping the postmaster's wife informed of everything that went on under his roof.

Little Ursule's nurse, the widow of a poor workman whose only name was the one given him at baptism and who came from Bougival, had lost her last child when it was six months old; the doctor knew she was a good, honest creature and so took her in as a nurse, feeling pity for her distress. Antoinette Patris, the widow of Pierre 'de Bougival' (as he was called), had no money of her own and came from Bresse, where her family lived in penury; she naturally became devoted to Ursule, just as wet-nurses become attached to their foster-children when they are looking after them. This blind maternal affection was accompanied by keen concern for domestic duties. Forewarned of the doctor's intentions, La Bougival secretly taught herself to cook, became clean and handy and moulded herself to the doctor's habits. She took meticulous care of the rooms and furniture, and never tired. Not only did the doctor want his private life kept utterly private, he also had good reason to conceal his financial affairs from his heirs. By the second year of his residence at Nemours, the only remaining servant in the house was La Bougival, on whose discretion he could absolutely rely, whilst his true motives were concealed beneath the supreme pretext of domestic thrift. To his family's great satisfaction he became a miser. La Bougival was forty-three at the time this story begins; without any humbug or cajolery, and exerting no influence beyond her solicitude and devotion, she acted as housekeeper to the doctor and his favourite: she was the pivot around which the whole house revolved, in a word, a woman whom they could trust. She had been given the name of La Bougival because it was so clearly impossible to call her by her Christian name, Antoinette; names and faces obey the laws of harmony.

The doctor's miserliness was not an inaccurate term, but it was practised with a purpose. From 1817 onwards he cut out two newspapers, and cancelled his subscriptions to periodicals. His expenditure, which the whole of Nemours was able to work out, did not exceed 1,800 francs a year. Like all old men, he had virtually no need for new clothes, linen or shoes.

Twice a year he made a journey to Paris, no doubt to draw his dividends and see to his investments personally. In fifteen years he never said a single word relating to his affairs. His confidence in Bongrand was slow to develop; he only disclosed his plans to him after the 1830 Revolution. Such were the only facts about the doctor's life of which his heirs and the middle-class townsfolk were aware at this time. Political opinions were no concern of his, since his house was only rated at one hundred francs a year; he was as unwilling to subscribe to the Royalist party as to the Liberals. In his deism and his well-known abhorrence of the priestly fraternity, he disliked demonstrativeness so much that he showed the door to a commercial traveller who had been sent by his great-nephew Désiré Minoret-Levrault to persuade him to buy a *Curé Meslier* and the Speeches of General Foy. To the liberals of Nemours, this sort of tolerance seemed inexplicable.

The doctor's three collateral heirs were Minoret-Levrault and his wife, Monsieur and Madame Massin-Levrault junior and Monsieur and Madame Crémière-Crémière, who shall just be called Crémière, Massin and Minoret (such distinctions between namesakes only being necessary in the Gâtinais district); their three families were too busy to build up other social connections, and met as regularly as people do meet in small towns. The postmaster gave a big dinner on his son's birthday, a ball on Shrove Tuesday and another on his wedding anniversary, to which he invited all the middle-class citizens of Nemours. The tax-collector also threw two parties a year for his friends and relatives. The clerk of the Court of Conciliation claimed he was too poor to indulge in such extravagances, and lived modestly in a house halfway down the high street: part of this house, the ground-floor rooms, was let to his sister, who was in charge of the letter post – another of the doctor's good turns. Nevertheless, these three men or their wives met regularly throughout the year, in town, or riding or walking outside the town, at the market in the mornings, on their doorsteps or (as was the case now) in the square on Sundays after mass; in other words, they met every day. Especially in the last three years the doctor's age, miserliness and wealth permitted both vague references and direct comments to be made concerning the inheritance; these remarks spread by degrees and eventually made both the doctor and his collateral family equally famous. For the last six months there had never been a week when the Minoret family's friends or neighbours had not spoken to them with concealed envy of 'the day when the old fellow's eyes would close and his coffers open'.

'Dr Minoret may be a doctor and understand all about death, but only God is eternal,' someone said.

'Oh, I don't know, he'll see us all to our graves; he's in better health than we are,' one of the heirs would reply hypocritically.

'Well, if you don't live to enjoy it, your children will, unless that little Ursule . . .'

'He won't leave her everything.'

As Madame Massin had foreseen, Ursule was the pet aversion of the collateral family, their sword of Damocles. The words, 'Anyway, time will tell!', were Madame Crémière's favourite way of summing the matter up, and made it quite clear that the expectant heirs wished her more harm than good.

The clerk and the tax-collector, who were poor in comparison with the postmaster, had often chosen the size of the doctor's fortune as a topic of conversation. They would look at one another with a woeful air if, when walking along the road or the canal bank, they saw their uncle coming towards them.

'He must have kept an elixir of life for his own use,' one of them would say.

'He's made a pact with the Devil,' would come the reply.

'He ought to do more for us. That big fellow Minoret isn't short of anything.'

'Yes, but Minoret's son will be costing him a mint of money.'

'How much do you reckon the doctor is worth?' the clerk of the court would ask the tax-collector, whose business was in handling money.

'12,000 francs put by every year for twelve years would make 144,000 francs, plus compound interest amounting to at least 100,000 francs; but with a notary in Paris to advise him, he must have made some good investments; besides, until 1822 the yield on his Government bonds must have been $7\frac{1}{2}$ or 8 per cent; so the old fellow must be worth about 400,000 francs today, not counting his 14,000 francs a year investment income in the 5 per cents, which are now standing at 116. So if he died tomorrow and didn't leave Ursule anything, we should get between 700,000 and 800,000 francs plus his house and furniture.'

'Well then, 100,000 ought to go to Minoret, 100,000 to the girl, which would leave us 300,000 apiece: that would be the fair way.'

'Yes, that would really set us up.'

'If he did that,' Massin cried, 'I'd sell my clerkship of the court and buy a nice estate. I'd try to become a judge at Fontainebleau, and then I'd be elected to Parliament.'

'I'd buy a bill-broker's business,' was the tax-gatherer's comment.

'Unfortunately, that girl of his and Abbé Chaperon between them have got him so much under their thumb that we can't do a thing.'

'Anyway, one thing we can be sure of: he won't leave the Church anything.'

The family's consternation on seeing their uncle going to mass can now be easily imagined. People always have enough wit to sense that their self-interest is being endangered. Self-interest is as basic to the peasant mentality as to the diplomat's, and in this respect the man who is most stupid in outward appearance may in reality be the most astute. Even in the mind of the most unintelligent relation one truth was written up in dazzling letters of fire: 'If Ursule is strong enough to get her guardian to go to church, she will be strong enough to get the inheritance.' As for the postmaster, the mysterious words in his son's letter were forgotten. He came running up into the square. If the doctor was in church, following the mass in his prayer-book, it meant a loss to him of 250,000 francs. Let it be admitted that the relatives' fear sprang from the strongest and most lawful of social feelings, concern for the welfare of the Family.

4. Zélie

'WELL, Monsieur Minoret,' said the mayor (a Levrault-Crémière who had once been a miller, and was now a Royalist), 'when the Devil grew old, he became a hermit. I believe your uncle has become one of us.'

'Better late than never, cousin,' replied the postmaster, trying to hide his vexation.

'Wouldn't that fellow laugh if we were done down! He'd be quite capable of marrying his son to that blasted girl, who I wish would go to the Devil,' cried Crémière, clenching his fists and pointing towards the mayor, who was standing in the church porch.

'What's upsetting old Crémière?' asked the butcher at Nemours, the Levrault-Levraults' eldest son. 'Isn't he happy that his uncle has found the way to Heaven?'

'Whoever would have believed it?' asked the clerk of the court.

'Well, you never know what the future holds in store,' observed the notary who, seeing this group of men from a distance, fell out of step with his wife, letting her go on alone into church.

'Look, Monsieur Dionis,' said Crémière, taking the notary's arm, 'what do you advise us to do in these circumstances?'

'I advise you to go to bed and get up at your usual times. Eat your soup before it goes cold. Wear shoes on your feet, and hats on your heads, and just carry on *as if nothing was the matter*.'

'That's not much help,' said Massin, looking at him as if they were confederates.

Despite his small stature, stoutness and thick, heavily built face, Crémière-Dionis was as sharp as a needle. He had made his fortune in a secret partnership with Massin, whom he no doubt informed about peasants who were hard up, and strips of land that were ready to be devoured. This was how these two men did business, never letting a single bargain escape them, and sharing the profits of their money-lending on mortgage, which handicaps – though it does not prevent – the peasants' activity on the land. Thus, Dionis took a keen interest in the doctor's inheritance, less because of Minoret the postmaster, or Crémière the tax-collector, than for the sake of his friend the clerk of the court. Sooner or later Massin's share in the inheritance was due to swell the working capital with which these two men carried out their joint operations in the surrounding district.

'We'll try to find out from Monsieur Bongrand what is at the bottom of this,' whispered the notary, cautioning Massin to keep quiet.

'Well, what are you doing here, Minoret?' a small woman suddenly exclaimed, dashing towards the group at the centre of which the postmaster was standing four-square like a tower. 'You don't know where Désiré is, and yet you stand there gossiping when I was thinking you were out on horseback! Good morning, everybody.'

This thin little woman, pale and fair-haired, was wearing a white chintz dress with large chocolate-coloured flowers; on her head was an embroidered lace cap; across her flat shoulders she wore a small green shawl. She was the postmaster's wife, the woman who put the fear of God into the roughest postilions, servants and carters, who kept the books, sat at the till, and ran her household 'like clockwork' – in the homely phrase used by her neighbours. Like all true housewives, she wore no jewellery whatsoever. She did not 'go in for trashy knick-knacks', to use her phrase. She was concerned with solid realities, and, even though it was a day of celebration, she kept her black apron on, jingling a bunch of keys in her pockets. Her yapping voice almost shattered one's eardrums. Though her eyes were light blue in colour, her set expression clearly befitted her thin lips, tightly closed mouth, and high, bulging, very domineering forehead. Her glance was sharp enough but her gestures and words were sharper still. Needing to have enough will-power to suffice for two, Zélie's will-power had always been enough for three: this was how Goupil put it, as he pointed to the successive reigns of three smartly dressed young postilions, each of whom Zélie set up in life after seven years in her employment. Hence the nicknames of Postilion I, Postilion II and Postilion III bestowed on them by the malicious clerk. But the fact that these young men were perfectly obedient, and exerted practically no influence around the house, proved that Zélie had purely and simply taken an interest in them because of their good characters.

'Well, Zélie likes zeal,' the clerk would reply to those who pointed out such facts to him.

This slanderous talk was lacking in credibility. Since the birth of her son, whom she had fed herself though no one could see how, the postmaster's wife had only been concerned with increasing her fortune, and she unceasingly devoted all her energies to the management of her immense business. It was quite impossible to steal a truss of straw or a few bushels of oats, or to catch Zélie unawares when she was in the middle of the most complex calculations – although her handwriting looked like a cat's scrawl and all she knew of arithmetic was addition and subtraction. She only went for a walk if her hay, oats and second crops needed to be estimated; then she would send her labourer to harvest the crop and her postilions to tie it up, telling them to the nearest hundredweight what quantity of herbage was standing on any given meadow. Although she was the soul in the body of that great hulking fellow Minoret-Levrault, and led him by the end of his silly turned-up nose, she sometimes experienced the alarm which sooner or later always overcomes animal-tamers. For this reason she always worked herself up into a temper before he did, and whenever Minoret gave the postilions a dressing-down they knew that he had just been given a dressing-down by his wife, and that her anger was rebounding on to them. Moreover, Madame Minoret was as clever as she was self-interested. Throughout the town many a household would say: 'Where would Minoret be without his wife?'

'When you know what's happened to us, you'll be as mad as we are,' replied the Nemours postmaster.

'Why, what is it?'

'Ursule has taken Dr Minoret with her to mass.'

The pupils of Zélie Levrault's eyes dilated, she stood for a moment livid with anger, then said: 'That has to be seen to be believed!' and rushed inside the church. It was the Elevation of the Host. The deep devotion of every worshipper enabled Zélie to look along each row of chairs and pews, moving along the side-chapels until she reached Ursule's place – and beside Ursule she espied the bare-headed old man.

If you recall the faces of Barbé-Marbois, Boissy-d'Anglas, Morellet, Helvétius and Frederick the Great, you will immediately have a precise picture of Dr Minoret's head: in his green old age he resembled those famous men. Such heads seem to have been struck on the same die, indeed they are suitable for medals. Their profile is severe and almost puritanical, their colouring pale, they have a mathematical logic about them, and a kind of narrowness in their almost pinched faces; their eyes are shrewd, their mouths serious, and their whole appearance has something of an aristocratic air, less in their feelings than in their habits, more in their ideas than in their character. All have high foreheads, but foreheads that recede towards the crown of the head – indicating a tendency towards materialism. You will find these principal features and expressions on the heads and faces of all the Encyclopaedists, the orators of the Girondist party, and the men of that time whose religious beliefs were more or less non-existent, who claimed they were deists but who were really atheists. The deist is an atheist with reservations. Old Minoret had a forehead of this kind, but it was furrowed with wrinkles, and he had recovered an artlessness all its own through the way in which his silvery hair, brushed back like a woman's when she is still dressing, fell in light fleecy ringlets on his black coat: for he obstinately clung to the dress of his youth, with black silk stockings, gold-buckled shoes, paduasoy breeches, a white waistcoat with a diagonal black ribbon, and a black coat sporting a red rosette. Through a window daylight streamed across his distinctive features, whose chilly whiteness was softened by the yellow tints of age. Just as the postmaster's wife made her entry, the doctor's blue eyes – with their rosy lids and tender outlines – were raised towards the altar, his new-found belief giving them an expression hitherto unknown. In his prayer-book his spectacles marked the place where he had ceased his devotions. With his arms crossed against his chest, this tall gaunt old man – whose stance showed him to be fully in possession of his faculties and quite unshakeable in his faith – never took his eyes for an instant from the altar, looking towards it in humility, and with a youthfulness in his features that was the gift of hope. He felt no impulse to look in the direction of his nephew's wife, who stood there almost facing him as if to blame him for his return to God's fold.

When all the congregation turned to look at her, Zélie hurried out into the market-place – but less hastily than she had gone into the church. She was expecting a share in the doctor's inheritance, and now the inheritance was becoming problematical. On rejoining the clerk of the court, the tax-gatherer and their wives, she found them even more dismayed than they had been before. Goupil had been teasing them for fun.

'We can't talk business in the square, in front of everybody,' said the postmaster's wife. 'Come along to my house. You too, Monsieur Dionis.'

Thus, the probable disinheritance of the Massins, Crémières and the postmaster was to become the talk of the whole district.

Just as the family and the notary were about to cross the square to get to the postmaster's house, an enormous din was heard. It was the stagecoach arriving at top speed at the coaching office, at the upper end of the high street, a few yards from the church.

'Heavens! I'm as bad as you are, Minoret. I'm forgetting Désiré,' Zélie cried. 'Let's go and meet him as he arrives. He's almost a barrister now, and this problem of ours is some concern of his.'

A stagecoach's arrival is always a diversion. But when it arrives late, people assume that something extraordinary is afoot. There was a crowd waiting as *La Ducler* drew up.

'Here's Désiré!' was the general cry.

Désiré was both the tyrant and the life and soul of Nemours. His appearances always set the town agog. Popular with the young men, to whom he was often generous, he stimulated them by his presence; but people were so afraid of the tricks he got up to that many a family was overjoyed when he became a law student in Paris. He was a slim young man, as fair-haired and slender as his mother whose blue eyes and pale complexion he had inherited. He smiled through the coach door at the crowd, and jumped down nimbly to greet his mother. A brief sketch of this young man will show how flattered Zélie felt at seeing him.

The student was wearing fine boots, white trousers made of English material with patent-leather understraps, a well-tied cravat in a costly material, fastened with an even costlier pin, a smart fancy waistcoat with a flat watch in his waistcoat pocket and the chain showing, a grey hat and a short blue frock coat; but the fact that he was a social upstart was clear from his gold waistcoat buttons and the ring he wore over his purplish kid gloves. He carried a walking-stick with a carved gold knob.

'You're going to lose your watch,' his mother warned as she embraced him.

'Oh no! that's done on purpose,' he replied, allowing himself to be embraced by his father.

'Well, cousin, so you'll soon be a barrister now,' said Massin.

'I'll be taking my oath when I go back,' he answered, returning the crowd's friendly greetings.

'We'll be up to some fun,' said Goupil, shaking Désiré's hand.

'Hello, you old scallywag.'

'A licence to practise at the bar isn't a licence to speak at random,' replied the notary's clerk, humiliated at being addressed so disrespectfully before so many people.

'What's that? Is he trying to bar Désiré from speaking at ransom?' Madame Crémière asked her husband.

'You know what luggage I have, Cabirolle!' Désiré shouted to the old stagecoach driver with his purple-blue pimply face. 'Get it all carried up to the house.'

'The horses are sweating all over,' Zélie shouted harshly at Cabirolle. 'Haven't you sense enough to drive them properly? You're dafter than them!'

'But Monsieur Désiré was determined to get here as soon as he could, in case you were becoming anxious . . .'

'But there hadn't been any accident, so why risk ruining the horses?'

The friendly exchange of greetings, the recognition of old friends, the young men's enthusiasm at seeing Désiré again, all the various incidents of the student's return home, and the accounts of the accident which had caused the delay – this took so long that the collateral family and their friends came flocking into the market place when mass was over. By one of those strokes of fate which makes anything possible, Désiré noticed Ursule standing under the church porch just as he was passing by, and stood transfixed by her beauty. The young barrister's impulse inevitably caused his parents to halt too.

Ursule was holding her prayer-book in her right hand and her parasol in the other, as she walked along on her godfather's arm. She had that innate grace which gracious women display as they fulfil the difficult though attractive tasks of a woman's life. If it is true that a person's character is revealed even in the slightest actions, it can safely be said that her demeanour revealed a divine artlessness. She was wearing a white muslin dress loose-fitting like a dressing-gown, and dotted with blue bows. Her cape, edged with a similar ribbon inserted through a large hem, was fastened by bows just like those on the dress itself; it stressed the beauty of her figure. Her neck, which was a lustreless white, was charming when set off by all the blue – blue is the true complement for blondes. Her blue sash with its long floating ends shaped a flat waist, which seemed supple: one of the most graceful of female attractions. She wore a rice-straw hat, modestly trimmed with ribbons similar to those on her dress, but their ends tied beneath her chin – which, whilst setting off the extreme whiteness of the hat, did not detract from the whiteness of her complexion: the beautiful complexion of a fair-haired woman. Ursule arranged her delicate fair hair herself, naturally looping it up in thick plaits; on either side of her face it was entwined in heavy locks, whose little tresses caught the eye with their hundreds of shining twists. Her grey eyes were both gentle and proud, and in keeping with a well-formed forehead. A pink tint, flushing her cheeks like a cloud, enlivened a face that was regular in proportion without being insipid; by a rare privilege of nature, she had both a fine face and purity of facial outline. The nobility of her life was revealed in an admirable harmony between her features, her movements and the general expression of her body, which could have served as a model for either Faith or Modesty. Her health, though excellent, was not too ostentatiously robust, with the result that she was distinguished in appearance. Beneath her light-coloured gloves one imagined she had lovely hands. Her thin, arched feet were daintily shod in bronze-coloured leather half-boots with brown silk fringes. Her blue sash, with a small flat watch tucked into it together with a blue purse with gold tassels, attracted every woman's attention.

'He's given her a new watch!' Madame Crémière said, squeezing her husband's arm.

'What, is that Ursule?' cried Désiré. 'I didn't recognize her.'

'Well, uncle, you really have caused a sensation,' said the postmaster, pointing to the whole town lined up on either side of his way from church. 'Everybody wants to see you.'

'Was it Abbé Chaperon or Ursule who converted you, uncle?' asked Massin, as obsequious as a Jesuit in his greetings to the doctor and the young woman.

'Ursule,' snapped the old man, walking ahead with the air of one weary of being pestered.

The evening before, as he was finishing his game of whist with Ursule, Bongrand and the Nemours doctor, the old man had said, 'I shall go to church tomorrow!' – to which the magistrate had replied: 'Your cousins will never get over it!' But even without this warning, the shrewd, lucid doctor would have fathomed his relatives' minds at a glance, just by the looks on their faces. Zélie's sudden appearance in church, the look on her face that the doctor had caught a glimpse of, this meeting of every interested party in the market place and the expression in their eyes on noticing Ursule, everything denoted a newly revived hatred and sordid mercenary fears.

'So this is your *thing* (i.e. doing),' said Madame Crémière, joining in the proceedings with a deep curtsy. 'Miracles come easily to you.'

'They come from God,' Ursule protested.

'God!' exclaimed Minoret-Levrault. 'My father-in-law used to say that God was the only saddle-cloth many a horse had.'

'He had the mind of a horse-dealer,' the doctor answered sternly.

'Come on then, you're surely going to greet uncle?' Minoret cried to his wife and son.

'I couldn't answer for my actions in front of that little hypocrite,' Zélie replied, walking away with her son.

'Uncle,' said Madame Massin, 'you really oughtn't to go to church without a little black velvet cap. It's such a damp place.'

'Niece,' said the doctor, looking at all the people who were walking along with him, 'the sooner I'm dead and buried, the sooner you'll be celebrating.'

He still kept up his pace, with Ursule walking beside him, and appeared to be in such a hurry that they were soon alone.

'Why do you say such harsh things to them? It isn't nice,' Ursule objected, saucily nudging the doctor's arm.

'I shall hate hypocrites just as much after my conversion as I did before. I have helped all of them, and never asked for any gratitude; but not one of them sent you any flowers on your name-day, the only day I hold special.'

At quite a distance behind the doctor and Ursule, Madame de Portenduère was walking painfully along, seemingly overwhelmed with grief. She belonged to that category of old ladies in whose dress lingers the fragrance of the eighteenth century, who wear pansy-coloured gowns with flat sleeves cut in the style of the gowns in Madame Vigée-Lebrun's portraits; they have black lace capes, and hats whose old-fashioned shapes are in keeping with their slow, solemn step; they still seem to be walking with panniers, whose weight they still appear to be feeling around their waists, just as those who have had an arm amputated sometimes try to move a non-existent hand; with their long pale faces, large haggard eyes and withered foreheads, they are not lacking in a kind of sad, graceful charm, despite their lofty hairstyles and flattened curls; their faces are covered with old lace that no longer flutters against their cheeks; but over all this ruined beauty towers an unbelievable dignity, both in manners and in expression. The old lady's red, wrinkled eyes were proof enough that she had been weeping during the service. She was walking as if agitated and, turning round to look behind her, seemed to be expecting someone. This turning-round by Madame de Portenduère was no less serious a fact than the religious conversion of Dr Minoret.

'Who is Madame de Portenduère angry with?' asked Madame Massin, rejoining the heirs as they stood horror-stricken by the old man's remarks.

'She's looking for the parish priest,' said Dionis, the notary, suddenly striking his forehead like a man gripped by some memory or forgotten idea. 'I know what we need! Your inheritance is intact! Come on, let's have an enjoyable breakfast at Madame Minoret's.'

It is easy to imagine how eagerly Dr Minoret's heirs trooped after the notary to the postmaster's house. Goupil and his boon companion walked along arm in arm, the clerk whispering to his friend with a hideous smile: 'I've got some birds laid on.'

'What does that matter?' replied the rich young man, shrugging his shoulders. 'I'm madly in love with Florine, the loveliest creature on earth.'

'Who is this Florine? Hasn't she a surname? I'm too fond of you to let you be fooled by *creatures*.'

'The famous Nathan is passionately in love with Florine. I'm infatuated too, but it's hopeless. She's positively refused to marry me.'

'Girls who go wild with their bodies are sometimes wise in their heads.'

'If only you could just see her, you wouldn't say things like that,' Désiré sighed languorously.

'If I thought you were going to ruin your career for what should be just a passing whim,' Goupil retorted with a warmth of emotion that would perhaps have taken Bongrand in, 'I'd go and crush that little puppet like Varney crushes Amy Robsart in *Kenilworth*! You must marry a d'Aiglemont or a Mademoiselle du Rouvre, someone who could help you to become a deputy. I have mortgaged my future to yours, so I shan't allow you to do anything stupid.'

'I'm rich enough only to have to consider my happiness.'

'Well now, what are you plotting?' Zélie shouted to Goupil, hailing the two friends, who were still standing in the middle of the vast stable yard.

The doctor vanished into the Rue des Bourgeois, and was as nimble as a young man in reaching the house where a strange event had occurred in the last week: the event that was now the talk of everybody in Nemours, and which calls for further explanation if the notary's advice to Minoret's heirs and, indeed, the whole of this story are to become perfectly clear.

5. Ursule

THE doctor's father-in-law, Valentin Mirouët, was a famous harpsichordist and instrument-maker, as well as one of our best-known organists; he died in 1785, leaving an illegitimate son, the child of his old age, a boy whom he acknowledged and who bore his surname but who was a terrible good-for-nothing. On his deathbed he did not have the consolation of seeing this spoiled child. Joseph Mirouët became a singer and composer who, after making his début at the Théâtre des Italiens under an assumed name, eloped with a young girl to Germany. The old instrument-maker recommended this boy, who was really gifted, to his son-in-law, pointing out that he had refused to marry the boy's mother so as not to damage Madame Minoret's inheritance. The doctor promised to give half of the instrument-maker's estate to this unfortunate young man; Érard purchased the old man's business; Minoret tried to locate his illegitimate brother-in-law Joseph Mirouët through diplomatic channels, but Grimm told him one evening that after enlisting in a Prussian regiment the artist had deserted under a false name, and was baffling every attempt to find him. Nature had endowed Joseph Mirouët with an attractive voice, a flattering figure, and a handsome face; besides which he was a spirited and tasteful composer; for fifteen years he led a Bohemian existence, of the kind so well described by Hoffmann. As a result of this, however, he was in such dire financial straits by the time he was nearing forty that in 1806 he seized the opportunity to become French again. He then settled in Hamburg, where he married the daughter of a good middle-class family, a girl who was mad about music and who fell in love with the artist: a man who had such a fine career ahead of him and was now going to devote himself to it. But after fifteen years of misfortune, Joseph Mirouët could not resist the temptations of affluence; his tendency towards extravagance recurred; and, though making his wife a happy woman, he spent her fortune within a few years. He again fell into abject poverty. His family must have dragged out the most horrible existence for Joseph Mirouët to have reached the point of enlisting as a musician in a French regiment. In 1813, by an incredible coincidence, the regiment's surgeon-in-chief was struck by the name of Mirouët, and wrote to Dr Minoret, towards whom he felt an obligation. A reply followed immediately. In 1814, before Paris surrendered, Joseph Mirouët found a refuge in Paris where his wife died giving birth to a little girl whom the doctor insisted on calling Ursule, after his own wife. Worn out, as she had been, by hardship and destitution, the music captain did not long survive his bereavement. At his death the unfortunate musician entrusted his daughter to the doctor's care and Minoret became her godfather, despite his dislike of what he called Church mumbo-jumbo.

After seeing all his children die through miscarriages, difficult labour or in their first year, the doctor had awaited the result of a final experiment. When a sickly, neurotic, delicate woman starts her married life with a miscarriage, it is not unusual for her to behave in her pregnancies and confinements as Ursule Minoret had behaved, despite her husband's attentions, advice and knowledge. The poor man often blamed himself for their joint persistence in wanting children. The last child, conceived after an interval of two years, died during 1792, a victim of its mother's neurotic condition – if those physiologists are to be believed who claim that, in the inexplicable phenomenon of procreation, a child resembles its father's bodily vigour and its mother in her nervous system. Forced to renounce the pleasures of the strongest feeling in his life, the doctor no doubt practised benevolence as a revenge for his disappointed dreams of fatherhood. During his married life, with all its cruel agitations, the doctor's supreme desire had been for a little fair-haired daughter, one of those flowers that bring joy into a home; so he was glad to take on Joseph Mirouët's legacy, and transferred to the orphan girl all the hopes of his vanished dreams. For two years, like Cato with Pompey, he concerned himself with the smallest details in Ursule's life; he did not wish the nurse to suckle the baby, get her up or put her to bed unless he was present. His experience, knowledge – indeed, everything he had – was at this child's disposal. After undergoing the pains, alternations of fear and hope, and work and joys of a mother, he was happy to find that this daughter of a fair-haired German woman and a French artist had both a sturdy body and a sensitive soul. It made the old doctor happy to watch, like a mother, over the growth of Ursule's blond hair: first like down, then silken, then light and fine, and so soft to his fingers as they ran through it that it seemed to caress them. He often kissed her small, bare feet, whose toes, covered with delicate skin beneath which the blood was visible, were like rosebuds. He was madly fond of this little girl. Whenever she tried to speak or fixed her fine, gentle, blue eyes on the things around her, looking at them with that dreamy expression which is the dawn of thought, and then interrupting herself with a laugh, he would spend long hours in her company discussing with Jordy the reasons (or, as so many others would have it, the whims) underlying the slightest features of that delightful phase in life when a child is both a flower and a fruit, confused in its intellect, ceaseless in its movements, and violent in its desires. Ursule's beauty and gentleness made her so precious to the doctor that he would have liked to change the laws of nature for her benefit: as he sometimes told old Monsieur de Jordy, he himself felt toothache when Ursule was cutting her teeth. When elderly people love children, there are no limits to their passion; their love is a form of worship. For them they silence their own whims and addictions, and recall all the happenings in their own lives. Their experience, indulgence, patience – their acquisitions of a lifetime, all their treasures so painfully accumulated – they sacrifice to a young life through which they themselves become young again, and compensate in intelligence for what they lack in maternal feelings. Their wisdom, constantly alert, is equivalent to a mother's intuition; they recall the gentle ways which a mother has by divination, and practise them in the compassion they show: a compassion all the stronger, no doubt, for their one immense weakness. Their slowness of movement takes the place of a mother's tenderness. With them, as with children, life is reduced to the barest simplicities; maternal feeling turns a mother into a slave, but their indifference to passion and freedom from self-interest make it possible for the elderly to give themselves completely. Consequently, it is not unusual for children to get on well with old people. Delighted by Ursule's caresses and flirtatiousness, the old soldier, priest and doctor never tired of answering her remarks or playing with her. Far from making them impatient, her petulance charmed them, and they satisfied her every desire, turning everything into a useful lesson. So little Ursule grew up, surrounded by old people's smiles, and looking on these elderly men as so many mothers, each of them equally attentive and far-sighted. Thanks to her wise education, Ursule's soul ripened in a favourable climate. This rare plant had found the soil it specially needed, and blossomed into its true life, drinking in the sunlight of life's happiness.

'What religion will you bring the little girl up in?' Abbé Chaperon asked Minoret when Ursule was six.

'In yours,' the doctor replied.

An atheist in the manner of Monsieur de Wolmar in *La Nouvelle Héloïse*, he did not think he had the right to deprive Ursule of the benefits of the Catholic religion. Sitting on a bench beneath the window of the Chinese pavilion, the doctor felt the Catholic priest pressing his hand.

'Yes, abbé, every time she talks to me of God, I shall send her to her friend *Sapron*,' he said, imitating Ursule's childish talk. 'I want to find out whether religious beliefs are inborn. This is why I have done nothing either to assist or resist the tendencies of her young soul; but in my heart of hearts I have already named you as her spiritual father.'

'God will thank you for this, I hope,' Abbé Chaperon answered, gently clapping his hands and raising them towards Heaven as if offering a short mental prayer.

Thus, from the age of six, the little orphan came under the abbé's religious influence, as she had already come under the influence of his old friend Jordy.

The captain, who had once been an instructor at one of the former military colleges, enjoyed studying grammar and the differences between the European languages; he had examined the problem of a universal language. This learned man, as patient as all experienced masters, was therefore delighted to teach Ursule to read and write, instructing her both in the French language and in as much arithmetic as she needed. The doctor's large library enabled her tutors to choose books which could be read by a child, and which would amuse her as well as containing a lesson. The soldier and the priest allowed her mind to develop with the same ease and freedom that the doctor allowed for her body. Ursule learned as she played. Religion gave her food for thought. The divine accent on an education in which Ursule's natural goodness was led by three careful teachers into pure regions of the spirit meant that she was more concerned with feeling than with duty, so that her rule of conduct became the voice of conscience rather than social law. To her, beauty – whether in feeling or in action – had to be spontaneous; mental reflection would afterwards confirm the heart's impulse. She was destined to take pleasure in doing good, before considering good actions as an obligation. This nuance is the peculiar characteristic of a Christian education. Such principles, quite different from the ones men need to be taught, were appropriate to a woman – the genius and conscience of the Family, the secret elegance of domestic life, whose position within the household is almost that of a queen. All three men adopted the same methods with the girl. Far from recoiling from the bold ways of innocence, they explained to Ursule the purposes of things and the known methods of attaining them, never stating anything that was imprecise. Whenever they were discussing a plant, a flower or a star and she at once introduced the notion of God, the doctor and the military instructor would tell her that only the priest could deal with that. None ever trespassed upon the others' territory. Her godfather took complete charge of her material welfare and the practical things of life; the basic teaching was Jordy's domain; the abbé dealt with ethics, metaphysics and other exalted subjects. This fine method of education was not thwarted by careless servants, as often happens in the wealthiest homes. La Bougival had been cautioned in this respect, besides which she was too simple both in mind and heart to interfere; she did not upset the work of these great minds. Ursule was a privileged creature in that she had around her three guardian angels to whom her beautiful character made every task gentle and easy. Such was their manly tenderness, seriousness tempered by smiles, freedom without danger, and constant care of both soul and body that by the age of nine she was an accomplished child, quite delightful to behold. Unfortunately, this paternal trio broke up. In the following year the old captain died, leaving the continuation of his work to the doctor and the parish priest, after accomplishing the most difficult part of it himself. In a soil that had been so well prepared, flowers would grow by themselves. For nine years this man of noble family had put by a thousand francs a year, so that he could bequeath ten thousand francs to his little Ursule as something to remember him by throughout her life. In a will inspired by such touching motives, he invited his legatee to replenish her wardrobe with the whole of the four or five hundred francs a year income from this small capital. When the conciliative magistrate affixed the seals at his old friend's home, a great many toys were found in a small room where no one had ever been permitted to enter; many were broken, and all had been used; these toys piously preserved from the past were to be burned by Monsieur Bongrand himself, at the poor captain's request. About this time, Ursule had to make her first communion. Abbé Chaperon spent a whole year instructing the young girl, whose heart and mind – so well developed, yet each so carefully sustaining the other – demanded special spiritual nourishment. Such was her initiation into a knowledge of the divine that from that moment when the soul takes on a religious form Ursule became the pious, mystical girl whose character was always superior to events, and whose heart overcame every adversity. Now began that secret struggle between an elderly agnostic and a young Christian girl: a struggle which was long unsuspected by the person who had set it afoot, but whose outcome interested the whole town, and which was to have so deep an influence on Ursule's future by unleashing the doctor's collateral relatives against her.

During the first six months of 1824, Ursule spent almost every morning at the presbytery. The old doctor guessed the priest's intentions. Chaperon wished Ursule to become an unanswerable argument for the faith. It was hoped that the agnostic, whom his goddaughter loved as if she was his own child, would believe in her artless simplicity, and be charmed into submission on seeing the touching influence of religion upon the soul of a girl in whom love resembled the trees in tropical climates whose branches are ever laden with flowers and fruits, and always green and fragrant. A beautiful life is more convincing than the strongest intellectual argument. The charms exerted by some images cannot be resisted. The doctor's eyes brimmed with tears – he did not know why – as he saw his heart's delight setting out for church wearing a white crepe dress with white satin shoes, arrayed with white ribbons, with a broad hair-band around her head, tied in place on one side in a large bow, her bodice surmounted by a ruff gathered with baby ribbon, starry-eyed with youthful hope, hurrying tall and happy to take the sacrament of divine union for the first time, loving her godfather all the more now that she had lifted up her heart to God. He saw that thoughts of eternity were feeding a soul that until then had remained in the limbo of childhood, just as when night is over the sun gives sustenance to the earth; and, still not suspecting why, he was annoyed that he had been left at home alone. Sitting on the flight of steps outside his front door, he stared for a long time at the bars of the gate through which his ward had vanished with the words: 'Godfather, why don't you come? Do I have to enjoy my happiness without you?' Although shaken to its foundations, the Encyclopaedist's pride was not yet broken. But he went for a walk so as to see the procession of communicants, and picked out his little Ursule radiant beneath her veil with religious fervour. In the stony corner of his heart the inspired look she gave him touched the recess that remained closed to God. Yet the deist stood firm, saying to himself: 'What mumbo-jumbo! Why imagine that if a Supreme Artificer exists, this God of the Infinite should be concerned with our silly goings-on?' He laughed; and continued his walk along the hilly ground overlooking the Gâtinais road, where pealing bells rang far afield with the joys of family life.

The noise of backgammon is unbearable to people who do not understand the game – one of the hardest in existence. Not to upset his ward, whose exceedingly delicate nerves and organs would not allow her to listen to its meaningless talk and movements without having to suffer for it, the doctor, priest and old Monsieur de Jordy, when he was alive, always waited until their child was in bed or out for a walk. Quite often the game was still in progress on Ursule's return: with infinite grace she would then resign herself to it, and sit down by the window to work. She felt an aversion for the game, whose opening moves are indeed harsh and unfathomable to many minds, and which are so difficult to master that unless one gets into the habit of playing it in one's youth it is almost impossible to learn it in later life. But on the evening of her first communion, when Ursule returned home to find her guardian spending the evening alone, she put the backgammon board in front of the old man.

'Let's see, whose turn is it to throw?' she asked.

'Ursule, isn't it a sin to make fun of your godfather on the day of your first communion?'

'I'm serious,' she replied, sitting down; 'I must think of your pleasures when you're always looking after mine. Whenever Monsieur Chaperon was feeling pleased with me, he would give me a backgammon lesson, and he gave me so many lessons that I'm good enough now to beat you. You won't have to put yourself out any more on my account. Not to spoil your enjoyment, I've overcome every difficulty, and now I like the noise of backgammon.'

Ursule won. The parish priest called on the players unawares, to enjoy his triumph. The next day Minoret, who until then had refused to allow his ward any music lessons, went to Paris, bought a piano, made arrangements with a music-mistress at Fontainebleau, and accepted the tedium of his god-daughter's endless practising. Jordy, who had been a student of phrenology, had predicted that the girl would become an excellent musician; and the prediction came true. Minoret was so proud of his goddaughter that he now had an able music teacher coming down once a week from Paris, an old German named Schmucke; and he was footing the expenses involved in acquiring this skill, which at first he had considered a quite useless attainment from a domestic point of view. Unbelievers dislike music, that heavenly language developed by Catholicism, which has adopted the names of its seven notes for one of its hymns: each note is the first syllable of one of the first seven lines of the Hymn to St John. Although vivid, the impression made on the old man by Ursule's first communion was only transitory. To him the calm and contentment diffused in her young soul by works of religion and prayer were equally ineffectual in their influences. Having no cause either for remorse or repentance, Minoret's state of mind was perfectly serene. Performing his good works without hope of a heavenly reward, he felt himself superior to Catholics, whom he always accused of treating God with a usurer's hope of gain.

'But if everybody wanted to join in such a bargain, you must admit that the world would be a perfect place,' said Abbé Chaperon. 'No one would be unhappy then. To do good in your way, you have to be truly philosophical; you attain your doctrine through reasoning, you are an exception to the general run of men; whereas in our way of doing things you only have to be a Christian in order to lead a good life. With you, virtue requires an effort; to us, it comes naturally.'

'In other words, abbé, I think and you feel. That's what it amounts to.'

However, by the time she was twelve Ursule's feminine subtlety and tact had been developed by a superior education and her blossoming intellect guided by a religious sense (the most delicate of all the senses); and she eventually realized that her godfather did not believe in a Hereafter, or in the soul's immortality, or in Providence, or God. Besieged with questions by the innocent child, the doctor could no longer conceal his fatal secret. At first Ursule's artless consternation made him smile; but on seeing her sometimes sad, he understood how much affection was revealed in that sadness. Utter devotion abhors any kind of discord, even in ideas that are alien to it. Sometimes the doctor yielded to his adoptive daughter's reasonings as if to a caress; they were said so sweetly and gently, voicing the purest and most ardent feeling. Believers and unbelievers speak two different languages, and cannot understand each other. Arguing God's cause, the girl ill-treated her godfather, just as a spoiled child sometimes ill-treats its mother. The parish priest would gently remonstrate with Ursule, telling her that God alone could humble the proud of heart. The girl retorted to Abbé Chaperon that

David had slain Goliath. This religious disagreement, and the regrets of a child wishing to lead her guardian towards God, were the only griefs in her spiritual life, a life which was so sweet and full, and hidden from the prying eyes of the inhabitants of that small town. Ursule grew up, developed, and became the young modest girl of Christian upbringing whom Désiré had admired on her way out of church. The hours, days and months of her calm existence were filled with the growing of flowers in the garden, with music, her guardian's amusements, and all her little attentions to him – for she had relieved La Bougival of the burden of taking care of him. Nevertheless, for the last year the doctor had been concerned that Ursule was showing some symptoms of illness; but their cause was so obvious that he was only anxious about them from the standpoint of her physical health. Later, however, this deeply experienced medical man, who was a shrewd observer, thought he could discern that the physical ailments had had some repercussion upon her personality. He kept a motherly eye on his ward, but could see no one in her circle of acquaintance who was worthy of inspiring her love; and so his anxiety passed.

6. A Brief Digression on Magnetism

AT this juncture, a month before the day when our drama begins, one of those events occurred in the doctor's intellectual life which strike a man's mental outlook to its foundations and turn it upside down; but this event calls for a brief account of a few incidents in the doctor's medical career, which will also add further interest to the story.

Towards the end of the eighteenth century science was as deeply divided at Mesmer's appearance as art was at Gluck's. After rediscovering magnetism Mesmer came to France, to which from time immemorial inventors have come to win approval for their discoveries. Thanks to its clear language France acts as a kind of trumpet to the world.

'If homeopathy gets as far as Paris, it is saved,' Hahnemann said not long ago.

'Go to France,' Metternich advised Gall. 'If people there poke fun at your theory of bumps on the skull, you'll be a famous man.'

So it was that Mesmer's disciples and opponents were both as keen as the followers of Piccini in their opposition to Gluck's disciples. The French scientific world was shaken, and a solemn controversy began. Before a definitive judgement was reached, the Faculty of Medicine imposed a total ban on Mesmer's so-called charlatanism, tub, conducting wires and theories. But it must be admitted that the German scientist unfortunately compromised his splendid discovery through his immense desire to turn it into money. Mesmer failed through the uncertainty of the facts, through ignorance of the part played in nature by imponderable fluids, which at that time had still not been observed, and through his own inability to make a thorough investigation of a science with three distinct aspects. Magnetism has more than one application; in Mesmer's hands its relationship to what it afterwards became was that of cause to effect. But though it is true that the discoverer was lacking in genius, it is a sad fact, both for France and for human reason itself, to have to note that a science dating back to the origins of civilized society, and practised alike in Egypt and Chaldea, Greece and India, should have met with the fate that truth suffered with Galileo in the sixteenth century: in mid-eighteenth-century Paris magnetism was rejected by the two-pronged attack of religious people and philosophical materialists, whom it equally alarmed. Magnetism, the chosen science of Jesus and one of the divine powers entrusted by Him to the Apostles, did not appear to have been foreseen by the Church any more than by the followers of Rousseau, Voltaire, Locke and Condillac. The clergy and the Encyclopaedist movement did not come to terms with an ancient human power that seemed so new. The miracles performed by the Convulsionaries of Saint-Médard were hushed up by the Church and by the indifference of scientific men, despite the valuable writings of Judge Carré de Montgeron; yet they were the first inducement to make experiments on human fluids enabling a man to dispel pains due to external factors by resisting them with sufficient internal strength. But it would have been necessary to admit the existence of intangible, invisible, imponderable fluids, three negations which the science of those days claimed would postulate the existence of a void. To modern philosophy, the void does not exist. If there were ten feet of void, the world would cave in! Especially to materialists, the world is full, everything hangs together, is causally connected and functions like a machine. 'Considered as the result of chance,' wrote Diderot, 'the world is easier to explain than God. Creation can be explained by the multiplicity of causes and countless number of impulses which chance presupposes. Given the *Aeneid* and all the type needed for it to be set up in print, and providing you allow me enough time and space, I shall arrive at the permutation known as the *Aeneid*, simply by putting different combinations of letters together.' These unfortunate men, who made everything into a god rather than admit the existence of God Himself, also recoiled from the concept of the infinite divisibility of matter involved in the nature of imponderable forces. Locke and Condillac delayed by fifty years the immense progress which the natural sciences are making at present thanks to the notion of Unity of Composition advanced by the great Geoffroy

Saint-Hilaire. A few upright men, unfettered by any system but convinced by facts they had conscientiously observed, persisted in Mesmer's doctrine, which recognized the existence of a penetrating influence in man, an influence which enables one human being to dominate another, which is brought into operation by the will, is able to produce cures through an abundance of fluid, and whose action consists in a duel between two opposing wills, an evil to be cured and the wish to cure it. The clinical features of hypnotism, hardly suspected by Mesmer, were established by Monsieur de Puységur and Monsieur Deleuze; but the Revolution put a stop to these discoveries, and thus the scientists and scoffers won the day. Amongst the small number of people who believed in mesmerism there were some doctors. Until their deaths these dissentients were persecuted by their colleagues. The worthy fellowship of doctors in Paris attacked Mesmer's supporters with a ferocity only equalled in the religious wars, and in its hatred of them was as cruel as it was possible to be in an age of Voltairean tolerance. Orthodox doctors refused to confer with doctors who favoured the Mesmerist heresy. The so-called heretics were still victims of underhand condemnation in 1820. The storms and misfortunes of the Revolution did not put an end to this scientific hatred. Only priests, judges and doctors can hate in such a manner. An official robe always makes a man terrifying. But by the same token, are not ideas more terrifying than things? Dr Bouvard, a friend of Minoret, was converted to the new faith, and persisted till death in the science to which he had sacrificed his heart's ease, for he became one of the abominations of the Parisian Medical Faculty. Minoret was amongst the most valiant supporters of the Encyclopaedists, and the doughtiest opponent of Deslon, Mesmer's principal lieutenant, whose writings had an enormous influence in the dispute; he quarrelled bitterly with his colleague; indeed, he did more than that, he persecuted him. His behaviour towards Bouvard was to be the one cause of regret that troubled the serenity of his declining years. Since Dr Minoret's retirement to Nemours, the science of imponderable fluids – the only suitable name for magnetism, whose phenomena are so closely linked to light and electricity – had been making immense progress despite the constant mockery of Parisian scientists. Phrenology and physiognomy, the twin sciences of Gall and Lavater, the first of which stands in relation to the second as cause to effect, convinced a number of physiologists of the existence of traces of imperceptible fluid, which is the basis of the functioning of the human will and gives rise to a man's passions, habits, and the shapes of his face and skull. Magnetic experiences were accumulating, as were the miracles of hypnotism, divination and ecstasy, which give a man access to the spiritual world. The strange story of the visions experienced by the peasant Martin de Gallardon, for which there is so much evidence, and his interview with Louis XVIII; the knowledge of Swedenborg's communications with the dead, which has been so seriously authenticated in Germany; Scott's tales concerning the effects of second sight; the prodigious powers exercised by a few fortune-tellers who merge palmistry, cartomancy and horoscopy into a single science; the established facts regarding catalepsy and the activation of the properties of the diaphragm through certain morbid diseases: all these things, which were curious to say the least and which all stemmed from the same source, allayed many doubts and induced even the most indifferent people to make experiments. Minoret was unaware of this intellectual movement, so strong in northern Europe but as yet so weak in France; yet it was in France that a number of facts were occurring which are called 'marvellous' by superficial observers, and which fall into the vortex of Parisian events like stones into the sea.

At the beginning of that year the rationalist doctor's peace of mind was disturbed by the following letter:

My dear Fellow,

Even when a friendship is over, it still has claims – though they are hard to fulfil. I know you are still alive, and I have a clearer memory of the happy days we spent in that attic by Saint-Julien-le-Pauvre than of our quarrel. As I am about to depart this life, I am anxious to prove to you that magnetism will turn out to be one of the major sciences – though of course science is basically indivisible. I can shatter your doubts with undeniable proofs. Perhaps your scientific inquisitiveness will give me the joy of greeting you again, just as we used to greet one another before Mesmer came along.

Ever yours,
BOUVARD

Like a lion stung by a gadfly, the opponent of Mesmer rushed up to Paris and left his card with old Bouvard, who lived in the Rue Férou near Saint-Sulpice. Bouvard called at his hotel, leaving a card with the words: 'Meet me at nine tomorrow in the Rue Saint-Honoré, opposite the Church of the Assumption.' Minoret felt young again, and did not sleep. He visited the old doctors whom he knew, asking them if the world was topsy-turvy, if there was still a School of Medicine, and if the four Faculties were still in existence. The doctors reassured him that the old spirit of resistance was still alive; only instead of persecuting mesmerism, the Academies of Medicine and Science mockingly classified magnetic phenomena amongst the surprising performances of Comus, Comte and Bosco, and alongside conjuring tricks, sleight of hand and what is known as 'comedy physics'. These remarks did not deter old Dr Minoret from turning up to his appointment with Bouvard. After forty-four years of hostility, the two opponents met again beneath a carriage gateway in the Rue Saint-Honoré. The French are too continually distracted to hate each other for long. Especially in Paris, facts and events seem to extend space and make the life of politics, literature and science too vast for men not to find new lands to conquer in which their pretensions can hold undisputed sway. Hatred calls for so much strength to be constantly on the alert that people counting on a protracted enmity band into groups. Thus, only corporate institutions can have a memory. Robespierre and Danton would embrace one another after an interval of forty-four years. Yet neither doctor extended his hand to greet the other. Bouvard was the first to speak.

'You look extraordinarily well.'

'Oh, I'm not so bad. And how are you?' Minoret answered, once the ice was broken.

'As well as I look.'

'Does magnetism stop a man from dying?' Minoret asked jokingly, but with no bitterness in his voice.

'No, but it nearly stopped me from earning a living.'

'So you're not well off then?'

'What would you think?'

'Anyway, I am,' cried Minoret.

'It's not your money I want, but your intellectual assent. Come with me.'

'How stubborn can you get!'

The champion of mesmerism led the unbeliever into a fairly dark staircase, where the two men groped their way up to the fourth floor.

Just at that time an extraordinary man was active in Paris, a man whose faith gave him incalculable power, and who commanded a whole range of magnetic skills. This great but unknown man, who is still alive, was not only capable of personally curing the cruellest, most deep-rooted diseases from a distance, as suddenly and radically as the Saviour of Mankind once used to do; he could instantly induce the strangest symptoms of hypnotism by quelling even the most rebellious temperaments. He claims to derive his power directly from God and to communicate, like Swedenborg, with the angels; his face is like a lion's, full of concentrated, irresistible energy. His features are peculiarly contorted, with a terrible, overpowering look about them; his voice rises up from the very depths of his being, and seems charged with magnetic fluid; it penetrates its hearers through every pore of their bodies. Disgusted at the public's ingratitude after performing thousands of cures, he has withdrawn into impenetrable loneliness, a self-inflicted limbo. His omnipotent hand, which has restored dying girls to their mothers, fathers to their weeping children, and idolized mistresses to doting lovers; which has cured patients of whom doctors had despaired, which has had hymns sung in its praise in synagogues, chapels and churches by priests of different religious denominations all brought back to the one God by means of the same miracle; which soothed the agony of dying men in whom life was no longer possible; that sovereign hand, a living sun dazzling the closed eyes of mediums, would not even be raised to restore an heir presumptive to a queen. Wrapped in the memory of his good deeds as in a luminous shroud, he holds aloof from the world and lives in the heavens. But in the dawn of his reign, when he was almost surprised at his own power, he allowed a few interested people to witness his miracles: he was as unselfish as he was strong. The news of his immense fame, which could be revived tomorrow, kindled new life in Dr Bouvard as he approached the grave. This persecuted disciple of Mesmer was finally able to see the most radiant display of his science, a science which he had locked up in his heart like a treasure. The old man's misfortunes had moved the great unknown man to pity, so that he was allowed a few privileges. This was why Bouvard savoured his old opponent's jokes with malicious delight as they climbed the stairs. All he replied was 'Wait and see! Wait and see!' giving little nods such as people indulge in when they are sure of their facts.

The two doctors entered a more than modest apartment. Bouvard went for a moment's talk in a bedroom adjacent to the sitting-room where Minoret waited with distrust mounting within his heart; but Bouvard came back for him immediately and ushered him into the bedroom where they found Swedenborg's mysterious disciple, and a woman sitting in an armchair. The woman did not rise from her seat. In fact, she did not appear to have noticed the two men's entry.

'What! aren't there any tubs now?' said Minoret, smiling.

'Nothing but the power of God,' the Swedenborgian answered gravely. Minoret thought he looked fifty years old.

The three men sat down, and the Swedenborgian started to converse. They talked about nothing in particular, much to the amazement of Minoret, who thought a trick was being played on him. The Swedenborgian questioned his visitor on his scientific views, and clearly seemed to be probing what kind of man he was.

'You have come out of simple curiosity,' he eventually said. 'I am not in the habit of degrading a power which, to my mind, emanates from God Himself; if I were to use it frivolously or wrongly, it might be taken away from me. Still, the problem as outlined to me by Monsieur Bouvard is to change an outlook contrary to ours, and to enlighten a well-intentioned scientist; so I shall satisfy you. This woman here' (he pointed towards her) 'is in a hypnotic trance. As is clear both from the admissions and the behaviour of every hypnotic patient, the trance-like state is a delightful existence in which the inner self – freed from all the fetters imposed upon its operations by external nature – moves in the world that we wrongly call invisible. In this condition sight and hearing are more perfect than in the so-called *waking state*, and perhaps they function without the aid of the physical organs that are like sheaths to the dazzling sword-like brightness of sight and hearing! To anyone who has been put into this condition, distances and material objects do not exist or else they are permeated by that inner life for which our bodies serve as a reservoir, a necessary fulcrum, an outer envelope. Words are lacking to describe biological functions that have only recently been rediscovered. Nowadays the words "imponderable", "intangible" and "invisible" have no meaning with regard to the fluid whose workings are demonstrated in magnetism. Light is ponderable in terms of its heat, which increases the volume of bodies it penetrates; and clearly, electricity is only too tangible. We have denied the existence of intangible things rather than condemn the imperfection of our scientific instruments.'

'She's asleep!' said Minoret as he scrutinized the woman, who seemed to him to come from the lower orders.

'Her body is as it were blotted out,' the Swedenborgian replied. 'Ignorant people would think she is asleep. But she will prove to you that a spiritual world exists in which mind does not conform to the laws of the physical universe. I shall send her wherever you want her to go. Whether it's fifty miles away or in China, she'll tell you what's going on.'

'Just send her to my house in Nemours.'

'I don't want to be involved in this. Give me your hand. You'll be both the actor and the spectator, both cause and effect.'

He took Minoret's hand, which Minoret allowed him to do, and held it for a moment apparently in meditation, whilst with his other hand he seized the old woman's as she sat waiting in the armchair; he then clasped the doctor's hand within the woman's, motioning to the old agnostic to sit down beside this prophetess without a tripod. Minoret noticed a slight quivering in her exceedingly calm features after the Sweden-borgian had joined their hands; but, though wonderful in the effects it produced, it was a very simple movement.

'Do what the gentleman says,' the Swedenborgian ordered her, laying his hand on her head and seeming to impart both light and life. 'Remember that anything you do for him will please me. Now you can speak to her,' he added to Minoret.

'Go to the Rue des Bourgeois, in Nemours, to my house.'

'Give her time. Let your hand remain in hers until she can prove by her words that she has arrived there,' Bouvard cautioned his former friend.

'I can see a river,' the woman replied weakly. Though her eyes were closed, she seemed to be looking within herself with deep concentration. 'I can see a pretty garden . . .'

'Why are you entering by the river and the garden?'

'Because they are there.'

'Who?'

'The girl and nurse you are thinking of.'

'What is the garden like?' Minoret inquired.

'As you enter it by the little flight of steps going down to the river, there's a long brick gallery to the right where I can see books, and at the end of the gallery a summer-house with little wooden bells and ornamental red knobs. To the left the wall is densely covered with creepers – virginia creeper and yellow jasmine. In the middle stands a little sundial. There are lots of vases containing flowers. Your ward is looking carefully at her flowers, and pointing them out to her nurse. She's making holes with a dibble, and planting seeds . . . The nurse is raking the paths . . . Though the girl is as pure as an angel, love is stirring within her heart, as delicate as the light of early morning.'

'Whom is she in love with?' asked the doctor, who until now had heard nothing that could not have been told him by someone who was not a medium. He still thought he was being tricked.

'You don't know anything about this, although you have been rather worried recently, now that she has become a woman,' and the old woman smiled. 'Her heart has obeyed the instincts of nature . . .'

'Is it possible for a working-class woman to talk in this way?' the old doctor exclaimed.

'When they are in this state they all speak with peculiar clarity,' Bouvard answered.

'But whom does Ursule love?'

'Ursule does not know she's in love,' the medium replied with a slight nod of the head; 'she is far too angelic to have experienced desire or any of the emotions of love; but she is concerned about him, and thinking about him, and even trying to prevent herself from doing so. But the thoughts return to her though she doesn't want them to . . . She is sitting at the piano . . .'

'But who is he?'

'The son of a lady who lives opposite . . .'

'Madame de Portenduère?'

'Portenduère, is that it?' the medium replied. 'That may well be. But there's no danger. He's out of the district.'

'Have they spoken?'

'Never. They have looked at each other. She thinks he's charming. He is indeed a handsome man, and a kind-hearted one too. She has seen him from her window, and they have also seen one another at church. But the young man has forgotten about her.'

'What is his name?'

'Before I could tell you that, I should either have to read it or hear it pronounced. She has just said it; he's called Savinien. She likes pronouncing that name; she has already looked up St Sabinian's day in the almanac, and put a little red mark against it . . . such childlike behaviour! She will certainly love him with all her heart, but her love will be as pure as it is ardent; she isn't the sort of girl to fall in love twice, and love will colour her soul and penetrate it so thoroughly that she would reject any other feeling.'

'Where can you see that?'

'In her heart. She will be able to bear suffering too; it's in her blood, her father and mother both suffered deeply!'

This last remark astounded the doctor, who was not so much shaken as surprised. It is not irrelevant to point out that between each of the woman's sentences there was a pause of ten to fifteen minutes during which she plunged into deeper and deeper concentration. One could see her seeing into the secrets of men! Her forehead took on the strangest appearances: it reflected her inner tension, growing relaxed or taut under the influence of a power whose workings Minoret had only ever observed in the dying, in those moments when they are endowed with the gift of prophecy. Several times she made gestures resembling Ursule's.

'Go on! ask her more questions!' the mysterious man urged Dr Minoret. 'She will tell you secrets that you alone can know.'

'Does Ursule love me?'

'Almost as much as she loves God,' she answered with a smile. 'So she is very unhappy about your agnosticism. You do not believe in God, as if you could prevent Him from existing! His Word fills the worlds! This is the poor child's only anxiety, and you are its cause. Wait! She is practising scales; she would like to be an even better musician than she is, and she is getting angry with herself. This is what she's thinking. If I was a good singer and had a beautiful voice, when he is at his mother's, my voice would carry across to him.'

Dr Minoret took out his pocket-book and noted the precise time.

'Can you tell me what kinds of seeds she has sown?'

'Mignonette, sweet peas, balsam . . .'

'And what else?'

'Larkspur.'

'Where do I keep my money?'

'At your notary's; but you invest it as you go along without losing a single day's interest.'

'Yes. But where do I keep my money at Nemours for the half-year's expenses?'

'You put it in a big book with a red binding called *The Pandects of Justinian*, volume II, between the next to the last page and the one before that; the book is on top of the sideboard with glass doors, on the shelf with the large folios. You have a whole row of them. Your money is in the last volume, on the drawing-room side. Yes, and volume III comes before volume II. But you haven't got any coins, it's . . .'

'Thousand-franc notes?' asked the doctor.

'I can't see clearly, they are folded together. No, there are two five-hundred-franc notes.'

'Can you see them?'

'Yes.'

'What are they like?'

'One of them is very yellow and old. The other is white and almost new.'

The last part of this interrogation flabbergasted Dr Minoret. He looked at Bouvard with a dazed expression, but Bouvard and the Swedenborgian, who were used to seeing unbelievers' astonishment, were chatting in low voices without seeming either surprised or astonished; Minoret asked them if he might come back after dinner. This opponent of Mesmer wanted to compose himself, to get over his deep terror, and then to experience this immense power afresh, subjecting it to conclusive experiments, and asking questions, the correct answers to which would dispel any further doubt.

'Come back at nine this evening,' replied the mysterious man. 'I shall be back to meet you.'

Dr Minoret was in such a disturbed state that he left the room without saying good-bye. Bouvard, following at a distance, kept crying out: 'Well? Well?'

'I think I must have gone mad, Bouvard,' Minoret answered when they reached the carriage gateway. 'If what that woman says about Ursule is right – and only Ursule knows the truth of what that witch has been saying – then *you'll be right too*. I only wish I had wings to fly back to Nemours and check what she has said. But I'm going to hire a carriage, and I'll be leaving tonight at ten. Oh! I'm going out of my mind.'

'And what would be your reaction if, after knowing someone with an incurable illness for many years, you were to see him cured in five seconds! Supposing you saw that great hypnotist making a man suffering from ichthyosis sweat profusely, or enabling a crippled society belle to walk again?'

94

'Come and have dinner with me, Bouvard, and stay with me till nine. I want to think up some decisive, unexceptionable experiment.'

'Thank you. I'd love to, my dear fellow,' answered Mesmer's disciple.

7. The Double Conversion

THE two enemies, now reconciled, went off to dine at the Palais-Royal. After a lively conversation, which helped Minoret to still the ferment of ideas within his brain, Bouvard remarked: 'If you admit that that woman has the power to abolish or to cross space, if you become convinced that from the Church of the Assumption she is able to hear and see what is being said and done at Nemours, then you will have to admit all the other consequences of hypnosis and magnetism; to an unbeliever, they are equally as impossible as the ones we have just seen. So why don't you ask her for one proof that will really satisfy you – you may think that we've obtained all the information so far; but, for instance, we can't know what's going to happen at nine o'clock tonight in your house, in your ward's bedroom: listen to what the medium sees or hears, memorize it or write it down, and hurry home. Little Ursule, whom I have never met, is not our accomplice; and if it turns out that she really did say or do what you write down, then admit you were wrong about hypnotism, you rebellious infidel!'

The two friends returned to the room, where they again met the medium, who did not recognize Dr Minoret. Her eyes closed gently as the Swedenborgian raised his hand above her, and she resumed the attitude in which Minoret had seen her before dinner. As soon as her hands were linked with the doctor's, he asked her to tell him everything that was going on in his house at Nemours at that very moment.

'What is Ursule doing?'

'She is undressed. She has finished putting in her curl papers. She is kneeling at her prie-dieu, in front of an ivory crucifix set into a frame with red velvet.'

'What is she saying?'

'She is saying her evening prayers, and commending herself to God. She is beseeching Him to drive all wicked thoughts from her heart. She is examining her conscience and thinking over what she has been doing today, in case she has failed to observe any of her self-imposed duties or any commandments

of the Church. The poor little girl is stripping her soul bare!'
There were tears in the medium's eyes. 'She has committed no
sin, yet she blames herself for thinking too much of Monsieur
Savinien. She is interrupting her prayers to wonder what he is
doing in Paris, and asking God to make him happy. Finally,
she thinks of you and prays for you aloud.'

'Can you tell me what the prayer says?'

'Yes.'

Minoret took out his pencil and, at the medium's dictation,
wrote down the following prayer which had evidently been
composed by Abbé Chaperon:

O Heavenly Father, if Thou art content with this Thy servant
who worships Thee and prays to Thee in fervent devotion, who
tries not to stray from Thy holy commandments, who like Thine
only-begotten Son would die with joy to the greater glory of Thy
Name, and who would fain live in Thy shadow, for Thou
readest all human hearts: Of Thy bounty enlighten my godfather,
lead him into the paths of righteousness, and so endue him with
Thy grace that he may live the evening of his life in Thy peace;
deliver him from all evil, and permit me to bear his burden of
suffering. O blessed Saint Ursula, my patroness, and Thou Divine
Mother of God and Queen of Heaven, together with saints and
archangels, hear my prayer, join Your intercessions to mine, and
have mercy upon us.

So perfect was the medium's imitation of Ursule's artless
gestures and holy inspirations that Dr Minoret's eyes brimmed
with tears.

'Is she saying anything else?'

'Yes.'

'Can you repeat it?'

'"Poor godfather! who will play backgammon with him in
Paris?" Now she's blowing out her candle, putting her head
on the pillow and going to sleep. She's asleep already! She
looks so pretty in her little nightcap.'

Minoret said good-bye to the great stranger, shook
Bouvard's hand, hurried downstairs, and rushed to a cab-rank
which at that time still existed outside a house that has since
been demolished to make room for the Rue d'Alger; he found a
cabman, and asked him if he was willing to drive immediately

to Fontainebleau. As soon as the price had been stated and agreed, the old doctor – already looking a much younger man – set off at once. As had been arranged, he allowed his horse a rest at Essonne and caught up with the Nemours coach; finding that it had a spare seat, he dismissed his cab driver. He arrived back home about five in the morning and went to bed, with all his former ideas ruined concerning physiology, physics and metaphysics. He slept till nine, he was so exhausted after his journey.

Convinced, on waking, that no one had crossed his threshold since his return home, the doctor proceeded to verify the facts – but not without feeling an ungovernable terror. He himself was unaware of the difference between the two banknotes and the inversion of the two volumes of *The Pandects*. What the medium had seen was correct. He rang for La Bougival.

'Tell Ursule I wish to speak to her,' he said, sitting down in his library.

The girl came running up to him and gave him a kiss. The doctor seated her on his knees, and her fine blond locks mingled with the white hair of her dear old friend.

'Is anything the matter, godfather?'

'Yes, but promise me, for your salvation's sake, that you will give me straight, honest answers to my questions.'

Ursule blushed to the roots of her hair.

'Oh! I shan't ask anything that you can't tell me,' he went on, noticing the modesty of first love troubling the still childish purity of her fine eyes.

'Go on, godfather.'

'What was your last thought in your prayers yesterday evening, and when did you say them?'

'It was about quarter past nine, or half past nine.'

'And could you repeat your final prayer?'

The girl hoped that her voice would communicate her faith to the unbeliever. She got down from where she was sitting, knelt, joined her hands fervently, her face was illuminated with radiant light, she looked at the old man, and said: 'What I asked God for yesterday I asked for again this morning, and I shall go on asking for it until He has granted my wish.'

She then repeated her prayer with new and more powerful expression; but, to her great astonishment, her godfather cut her short and finished the prayer himself.

'Very good, Ursule!' and the doctor took her back again on to his knees. 'When you went to sleep with your head on the pillow, didn't you say to yourself: "Poor godfather! who will play backgammon with him in Paris?"'

Ursule jumped up as if the doomsday trumpet had sounded in her ears: she uttered a cry of terror; her wide eyes fixed the old man with a horrifying stare.

'Who are you, godfather? Where have you got such power?' she asked, imagining that as he did not believe in God he must have entered into a pact with the Fallen Archangel.

'What did you sow in your garden yesterday?'

'Mignonette, sweet peas, balsam . . .'

'And finally larkspur?'

She fell to her knees.

'Don't frighten me, godfather. You must have been here, mustn't you?'

'An't I always with you?' he joked, wishing to spare the innocent girl's reason. 'Let's go to your room.'

He gave her his arm and they climbed the stairs.

'Your legs are trembling,' she said.

'Yes, I feel quite dumbfounded.'

'So perhaps you do believe in God now?' she cried with artless joy, as tears welled to her eyes.

The old man looked at the bedroom he had fitted up for Ursule. It was so simple and dainty. On the floor lay an inexpensive carpet, plain green in colour, which she kept exquisitely clean. The walls had a linen-coloured paper dotted with roses and green leaves. At the windows, which overlooked the yard, hung cotton curtains, each trimmed with a strip of pink material. Between the two windows, beneath a long high mirror, was a gilt wood console-table with a marble top, on which stood a blue Sèvres vase where she used to arrange flowers, and, opposite the fireplace, a charming little marquetry chest of drawers with a top made of breccia marble from Aleppo. The bed was in old chintz and had chintz curtains with a pink lining. It was one of those stately beds so common in the eighteenth century, with tufts of feathers carved over the four fluted posts at the corners. An old clock, encased in an imposing tortoiseshell structure overlaid with ivory arabesques, adorned the fireplace, whose mantelpiece and marble candlesticks, and mirror and grisaille-painted panel above it, offered a remarkable harmony of tone, colour and style. A large wardrobe had doors depicting landscapes in different kinds of wood, a few of which had green tints not available today; no doubt it contained her underwear and dresses. The room was fragrant with a scent of Heaven itself. The way everything was so precisely arranged showed she had an orderly mind, and a feeling for harmony which would certainly have impressed anyone, even a man like Minoret-Levrault. Above all, one could see how dear to Ursule were the things that surrounded her, and how much she delighted in a room which as it were reflected all her childhood and adolescent life. Looking everything over so as to keep himself in countenance, her guardian established that from Ursule's bedroom one could see into Madame de Portenduère's home. During the night he had carefully considered what attitude he should adopt in the matter of Ursule's blossoming love affair, whose secret he had surprised. An interrogation would compromise him with his ward. He would have either to approve or to disapprove her love: in either case, he would find himself in a false position. He had therefore decided to study the respective circumstances of young Portenduère and Ursule, to see whether he should combat her inclination before it proved to be irresistible. Only an old man could have shown such wisdom. Still gasping from the onslaughts of the established truth of magnetism, he kept walking round and round, looking at the slightest details in Ursule's bedroom. He wanted to have a look at the almanac hanging by the fireplace.

'Those ugly things are too heavy for your pretty little hands,' he said, picking up the copper-encrusted marble candlesticks. He felt their weight, looked at the almanac, picked that up and said: 'This also looks very ugly. Why do you have this postman's almanac in such a pretty room?'

'Oh! let me keep it, godfather.'

'No, I shall get you another tomorrow.'

He went downstairs taking with him this piece of evidence, locked himself in his study, looked up St Sabinian, and found (as the medium had said) that there was a red dot against 19 October; he also found a similar one opposite St Denis's day, his own patron saint, and also against St John's day – the patron saint of the abbé. This dot, which was only as large as a pinhead, had been noticed by the sleeping medium despite the distance and obstacles. The old man pondered till evening on these events, which were even more important to him than to any other person. The facts had to be admitted. A great wall crumbled as it were within him, for his life until then had been based on two principles: his religious indifference and his rejection of magnetism. By proving that the senses, organs which were a purely physical construct all of whose operations could be explained, were bounded by some of the attributes of infinity, magnetism refuted – or at least seemed to him to refute – Spinoza's powerful argument: whereas the latter had claimed that the infinite and the finite were incompatible, these two elements were to be found intermingled. However much power he assigned to the divisibility and mobility of matter, he could not admit that it had semi-divine qualities. In any case he had grown too old to link these observations to a system and to compare them to the observable facts of sleep, vision and light. Founded on the theories of Locke's and Condillac's followers, the whole of his scientific system was now in ruins. As his hollow idols lay shattered on the ground, his agnosticism inevitably faltered. Thus, in this struggle between a Catholic child and a Voltairean old man, all the advantages were to be with Ursule. Across the ruins of the crumbled fortress a light shone. From its rubble rang the voice of prayer! Yet the obstinate doctor kept his doubts at bay. Though he had been struck to the heart, he would not come to a decision; he still struggled against God. But his mind was wavering, he was no longer the same man. He had become exceedingly meditative, and read Pascal's *Pensées*, Bossuet's sublime *History of the Variations of the Protestant Churches*, Bonald and St Augustine; he also tried to skim through the works of Swedenborg and the late Louis-Claude Saint-Martin, which had been mentioned to him by the mysterious man. The edifice of materialism within the doctor's soul was cracking on every side. Now only a final jolt was needed. And, when his heart was ripe for God, it fell like some luscious fruit into the Heavenly Vineyard. As he sat playing cards with the curé in the evenings, with his goddaughter beside him, several times already he had asked questions which Abbé Chaperon thought odd in view of the doctor's opinions: the parish priest was still ignorant of the inner workings of the soul by which God was reclaiming a fine conscience.

'Do you believe in apparitions?' the agnostic asked his parish priest, interrupting the game.

'Cardano, a great sixteenth-century philosopher, said he had seen them,' the abbé replied.

'I know all the apparitions that have preoccupied scientific men, I have just been rereading Plotinus. I am questioning you at the moment from the Catholic point of view, and my question is: Do you think that a man can return from the dead to visit the living?'

'But Jesus appeared to the Apostles after His death. The Church must believe in the appearances of Our Saviour. As for miracles, we're not short of those!' said Abbé Chaperon with a smile. 'Do you want to hear about the most recent one? It occurred in the eighteenth century.'

'I don't believe it!'

'Oh yes! The Blessed Alphonso Maria de' Liguori was a long way from Rome when he had an intuition of the Pope's death at the very moment when the Holy Father was dying, and many people witnessed this miracle. This holy bishop fell into a kind of ecstasy, heard the dying words of the Sovereign Pontiff, and repeated them in the presence of several people. A courier only arrived with the news of the event thirty hours later . . .'

'What a Jesuit you are!' old Minoret joked. 'I'm not asking you for proofs. I'm asking you whether you believe in all this.'

'I believe that the apparition depends a great deal on the person seeing it,' said the curé, continuing Minoret's joke.

'Look, I'm not setting you a trap. What do you believe about all this?'

'I believe that God's power is infinite.'

'If I am reconciled to God when I die, I shall ask Him to let me put in an appearance to you,' the doctor laughed.

'That was precisely the agreement between Cardano and his friend.'

'Ursule,' said Minoret, 'if ever you are threatened with any danger, call me and I'll come.'

'In that one word you've summed up André Chénier's touching elegy *Néère*,' the abbé interposed. 'But a poet's greatness consists in clothing facts or feelings in imagery that is eternally vivid.'

'Why are you talking of your death, godfather?' Ursule asked, griefstricken. 'We Christians don't die; our graves are the cradles for our souls.'

'Anyway,' the doctor smiled, 'I've got to leave this life some time or other, and when I'm gone you'll be very surprised at your wealth.'

'When you're gone, my one consolation will be to devote my life to you.'

'To me, when I'm dead?'

'Yes. Every good work I am able to do will be done in your name to redeem your transgressions. I shall pray to God every day to obtain His infinite mercy, asking Him not to mete out eternal punishment for the errors of a single day but to place a soul that is as beautiful and pure as yours beside His Throne, amongst the everlasting saints.'

The angelic candour of her reply, which was said in a tone of utter conviction, dispelled Dr Minoret's ignorance, converting him in the manner of St Paul's conversion. A ray of inner light dazzled him, and such tender concern for his future life brought tears to his eyes. The sudden working of grace had an electric quality. The abbé clasped his hands and stood up in agitation. Ursule, surprised at her victory, began to weep. The old doctor sat bolt upright as if someone had called out to him, and stared into space as if seeing the break of dawn; he then knelt by his armchair, joined his hands together and lowered his eyes to the ground in the gesture of a deeply humble man.

'O Lord God!' he cried, deeply moved, and raising his forehead, 'if anyone can bring about my salvation and lead me towards Thee, surely it is this spotless child! Forgive a repentant old man, whom a radiant child has brought close to Thee!' He silently lifted his heart to God, begging Him to complete the conversion by enlightening him with knowledge after electrifying him with grace, and turned towards the parish priest, offering him his hand: 'Dear father!' he said, 'I am a small child again. I am yours, and I offer you my soul.'

Ursule kissed her godfather's hands, covering them with tears of joy. The doctor seated her on his knee and gaily called her his godmother. Quite overcome with emotion, Abbé Chaperon recited the *Veni Creator Spiritus* with spontaneous fervour. This hymn was the vesper prayer of three kneeling Christians.

'What's the matter?' La Bougival asked in astonishment.

'At long last godfather believes in God!' Ursule cried.

'Well, all to the good! It only needed that to make him perfect,' cried the old peasant woman from Bresse, making the sign of the cross in all simplicity and earnestness.

'My dear doctor,' said Chaperon, 'you will soon understand the grandeurs of religion and the need for religious observances. You will discover that the human aspect of its philosophy is far more exalted than that of the boldest minds.'

With almost childlike joy, the parish priest then agreed to give the old man religious instruction twice a week. Thus, the conversion which people attributed to Ursule's sordid calculation was in fact spontaneous. Chaperon, who for fourteen years had refrained from touching the wounds in Minoret's heart, though deeply regretting them, had been approached just as a man seeks out a surgeon if he feels he has been wounded. Every evening after the scene just described, Ursule's prayers were said in the doctor's company. With every moment that went by, the doctor had felt the turmoil in his soul being subdued by peace. Thinking (as he said) of God as the 'person responsible in the last resort' for the inexplicable in life, his mind was at ease. His dear goddaughter would reply that it was quite obvious from this that he was making forward strides in the Kingdom of Heaven. During the mass he had been concentrating his intellect on the prayers he was reading, for in one of his early classes with Chaperon he had attained the divine notion of the Communion of Saints. This old newly converted believer had understood the eternal symbolism of the consecrated Bread, necessary to those whose faith has entered into its deep, intimate, radiant meaning. If he had seemed eager to return to his home, it was to thank his dear little goddaughter for having 'brought him to God', in the beautiful phrase of time past. And so he had her sitting on his lap in his drawing-room and was placing a holy kiss on her forehead just as, besmirching so saintly an influence with their ignoble fears, his collateral family were heaping the coarsest insults upon Ursule. The old man's eagerness to return home, his apparent contempt for his near relations, his sarcastic replies as he left the church – all these things his family naturally attributed to the hatred Ursule fostered against them.

8. A Double Consultation

WHILST the young girl was playing variations on Weber's *Last Waltz* for her godfather, a careful plot was being hatched in Minoret-Levrault's dining-room, which was to lead to the appearance on the scene of one of the principal characters in this drama. The lunch, which lasted more than two hours, was noisy like all provincial lunches, and enlivened by excellent wines that come by canal to Nemours from both Burgundy and Touraine. Zélie had ordered shellfish, saltwater fish and a few gastronomic delicacies to celebrate Désiré's return. The dining-room, at the centre of which the round table had a cheering aspect, looked like a room in an inn. Content with the size of her outbuildings, Zélie had built herself a pavilion between her vast courtyard and garden – the latter planted with vegetables and full of fruit-trees. Everything in her house was above all clean and solid. Levrault-Levrault's example had had a terrifying effect upon the surrounding district. She therefore forbade her master architect to land her in similar follies. The dining-room had varnished wallpaper, walnut chairs, walnut sideboards, a stove with earthenware tiles, a wall-clock and a barometer. Though the dinner service was made of ordinary white china, the table gleamed with linen and plentiful silver. As soon as Zélie had served the coffee – rushing hither and thither like a shuttlecock, for she had no servant except a cook – and after Désiré, the budding barrister, had been informed of the great event that had occurred that morning, and of its consequences, Zélie shut the door and it was time for the notary Dionis to speak. The silence that fell over the room, and the ways in which each member of the family looked at his unique face, clearly showed the influence that such men exert over families.

'Dear friends,' he began. 'Your uncle was born in 1746. He's eighty-three now. Old men are prone to folly, and that little . . .'

'Viper!' cried Madame Massin.

'Wretch!' exclaimed Zélie.

'Just let's call her by her Christian name,' said Dionis.

'She's a thief, anyway,' added Madame Crémière.

'But a pretty thief,' was Désiré's comment.

'Little Ursule,' Dionis went on, 'is the person he's really fond of. Now, you are all my clients, and I represent your interests. I haven't waited till this morning to gather information. What I've been able to find out about this young . . .'

'Plunderer!' cried the tax-collector.

'Fortune-hunter!' exclaimed the clerk of the court.

'Silence, my friends!' said the notary, 'or else I'll get my hat, bid you good-bye, and that'll be the end of it.'

'Come on, old fellow,' Minoret intervened, pouring him a little glass of rum, 'have some of this . . . It actually came from Rome. Come on now, there was a five-franc carriage charge.'

'Well, it's true that Ursule is Joseph Mirouët's legitimate daughter; but he was the illegitimate son of Valentin Mirouët, your uncle's father-in-law. So Ursule is the illegitimate niece of Dr Denis Minoret. As his illegitimate niece, any will the doctor might draw up in her favour might perhaps be open to dispute; and if he did leave her his fortune, you would bring a legal action against Ursule which might not turn out very favourably for you, because although it might be argued that there is no family relationship between Ursule and the doctor, such an action would certainly alarm a young defenceless girl, and produce some form of compromise.'

'The law is so strict concerning the rights of illegitimate children,' said the young graduate, eager to air his knowledge, 'that by the terms of a judgment of the Supreme Court of Appeal on 7 July 1817, the illegitimate child is not entitled to claim anything from his *natural ancestor*, not even food. So you can see that the notion of the illegitimate child's *parenthood* has been widened. The penalties imposed by the law on illegitimate children extend to their legitimate descendants, in that it assumes that bequests to grandchildren are being *vicariously* made to the illegitimate son. This is clear from a comparison of Articles 757, 908 and 911 of the Civil Code. And for this reason the High Court in Paris, in its judgment of 26 December last, reduced the amount of a legacy made by a grandfather to the legitimate child of an illegitimate son. The grandfather was certainly as unrelated in blood to his illegitimate grandson as the doctor is to Ursule.'

'But in my opinion,' Goupil interjected, 'all this only concerns bequests from ancestors to their illegitimate *descendants*. It has nothing at all to do with uncles, who do not seem to me to have any family relationship to the legitimate children of their illegitimate brothers-in-law. Ursule is no relation of Dr Minoret. I remember a judgment of the High Court at Colmar, delivered in 1825 whilst I was finishing my law studies, in which it was stated that, if the illegitimate child was dead, his descendants could not inherit *vicariously*. Well, Ursule's father is dead.'

Goupil's line of argument produced what journalists call 'uproar' when they are writing up their parliamentary reports.

'What does all this amount to then?' cried Dionis. 'That the courts have never yet tried the case of a bequest from the uncle of an illegitimate child. But if it did come before the courts, French law would show its usual strictness towards illegitimate children, particularly as we are living in an age when religion is respected. I can guarantee that this lawsuit would end in a compromise, especially if it became known that you were determined to take it as far as the Supreme Court of Appeal.'

The smiles, sudden starts and jerky gestures of the heirs gathered around the table meant that they did not notice Goupil's gesture of dissent; they looked as if they had discovered heaps of gold. This outburst was followed by deep silence and anxiety when the notary uttered one further word – the terrifying 'But! . . .'

As if he had just pulled the string on one of those little puppet theatres whose characters jerk along driven by mechanical controls, Dionis found all their eyes riveted on him, every face angled in the same direction.

'But no law can prevent your uncle from adopting or marrying Ursule,' he continued. 'As far as an adoption is concerned, it would be disputed and I believe you would win the case: the High Courts do not consider adoption any laughing matter, and you would have a voice in the legal proceedings. Even though the doctor has the order of Saint-Michel, and is an officer of the Legion of Honour and a former physician to the ex-Emperor, he would lose! But though you would be forewarned of any adoption, how would you know about a marriage? The old fellow is wily enough to go and get himself married in Paris after a year's residence there, and then give his bride a dowry of a million francs in the marriage settlement. So the only thing endangering your inheritance is the prospect of a marriage between Ursule and her uncle.'

The notary paused.

'There is another danger,' Goupil added in a knowing way, 'and that is a will drawn up in favour of a third party, such as old Bongrand, who would receive the money on trust for Mademoiselle Ursule Mirouët.'

'If you annoy your uncle,' Dionis continued, interrupting his head clerk, 'if you don't treat Ursule really kindly, you will egg him on either into marrying her, or else to setting up a trust as Goupil has just mentioned; but I don't think he's capable of resorting to a trust, it's a dangerous method. As far as marriage is concerned, that's easy to prevent. Désiré need only pay her the slightest attention, she'll always prefer a charming young man, the smartest fellow in Nemours, to some old crock.'

'Mother,' whispered the postmaster's son, attracted by Ursule's wealth as much as her beauty, 'if I married her, we'd get everything.'

'Have you gone mad? One day you'll have a private income of 50,000 francs a year! You must become a deputy! As long as I live, I shan't let you ruin yourself in a foolish marriage. 700,000 francs, what's that?!!! The Mayor's only daughter will have a private income of 50,000 francs a year; and they've already suggested her to me as a suitable match . . .'

For the first time in her life his mother had spoken to him harshly. Her reply killed any hopes Désiré might have had of marrying the lovely Ursule. He and his father would never prevail against the decision written in Zélie's terrifying blue eyes.

'Here, but wait a minute, Monsieur Dionis,' Crémière exclaimed after a nudge from his wife, 'if the old chap took this seriously and married his ward off to Désiré, giving her absolute control over the whole fortune, bang would go our inheritance! And if he lives another five years, uncle will certainly be worth a million.'

'Never!' Zélie protested. 'As long as I have breath in my body, Désiré will never marry a bastard's daughter, a girl taken in out of charity, picked up out of the gutter! Goodness gracious! my son will become head of the Minoret family at his uncle's death, and the Minorets have been good solid bourgeois for five hundred years. That's equal to being an aristocrat! You can rest assured of this: Désiré will only marry when we know what sort of future is cut out for him in the Chamber of Deputies!'

Goupil approved this haughty statement, adding: 'With 24,000 francs investment income, Désiré will become either a High Court judge or Attorney General; but a stupid marriage would be the end of him.'

At this point the family all started talking to one another simultaneously. But there was silence when Minoret banged his fist on the table, to enable the notary to continue.

'Your uncle is a good, worthy man. He thinks he's immortal; and, like all clever men, he'll suddenly find he's dying without having made a will. So I think for the time being we should get him to invest his money so that it's very hard for you to be done out of it; and we have an opportunity to do this. Young Portenduère is imprisoned at Sainte-Pélagie, in debt to the tune of just over 100,000 francs. His aged mother knows he's in gaol, she's weeping her eyes out, waiting for Abbé Chaperon to come round to dinner, no doubt to discuss the disaster with him. Now I'll go and see your uncle this evening, and persuade him to sell his 5 per cent Consols, which are now at 118, and to lend enough money to Madame de Portenduère, with her house and the farm at Les Bordières as securities, to get the prodigal son out of his fix. I'm only playing my part as a notary if I plead to him on that young idiot Portenduère's behalf, and it's only natural for me to want to get him to change his investments: that way I get business, contract fees, legal instruments to be signed. If I can become his adviser, I'll suggest that he invests the remainder of his capital in other real estate: I've got some marvellous property investments on my books. Once we've got his money invested in local real estate or mortgages on local property, he can't make away with it that easily. If he wants to cash his land investments, we can always raise objections about actually cashing them.'

The family, impressed with the force of this argument (a far cleverer one than the one used by Monsieur Josse), murmured their approval.

'So let's be agreed on one thing,' the notary concluded, 'and that is to keep your uncle at Nemours, which he is used to and where you can keep an eye on him. The marriage can be prevented by getting the girl a lover . . .'

'But supposing the marriage did take place?' asked Goupil, seized with an ambitious idea.

'That actually wouldn't be so bad. At least we'd know the extent of the loss, we'd know how much the old chap intended to give her,' the notary answered. 'But let Désiré loose on her. He can string her along till the old man's death. Marriages are made and unmade.'

'The easiest way,' said Goupil, 'in case the doctor still has a long time to live yet, would be to marry her to some worthy fellow who'd take her off your hands with a dowry of 100,000 francs and settle at Sens, Montargis, or Orleans.'

Dionis, Massin, Zélie and Goupil, the only intelligent people in the gathering, looked at each other thoughtfully.

'He'd be the nigger in the woodpile,' Zélie whispered to Massin.

'Why did we let him come?' asked the clerk of the court.

'That would be just your job!' Désiré exclaimed to Goupil; 'but could you ever keep yourself tidy and clean enough to satisfy the doctor and his ward?'

'You'll be puffing yourself up no end,' said the postmaster, eventually stumbling on Goupil's meaning.

This coarse joke was enormously popular. The head clerk looked round the laughing circle so threateningly that there was immediate silence yet again.

'Nowadays,' Zélie whispered to Massin, 'notaries are only

concerned with number one. Supposing Dionis took Ursule's side when it came to drawing up the documents?'

'I have every confidence in him,' answered the clerk of the court, looking at his cousin with his spiteful little eyes. He was going to add: 'I can ruin him!' But he restrained himself. 'I entirely agree with Dionis,' he said aloud.

'So do I,' cried Zélie, who however was already beginning to suspect some collusion between the notary and the clerk of the court.

'My wife has spoken!' said the postmaster, drinking a small glass of spirits, though his face was already blue with the after-effects of digesting his lunch and imbibing a sizable quantity of liquid.

'That's all right by me,' said the tax-collector.

'So should I go after dinner?' asked Dionis.

'If Monsieur Dionis is right,' Madame Crémière remarked to Madame Massin, 'we shall really have to visit uncle just like we used to, every Sunday evening, and do everything Monsieur Dionis has just said.'

'To be treated like he used to treat us!' cried Zélie. 'After all, we've got a private income of over 40,000 francs a year, and he's turned down all our invitations. We're just as good as him! Even though I can't write prescriptions, I know a thing or two!'

'Well, as I haven't got 40,000 francs a year investment income,' Madame Massin retorted, rather offended, 'I certainly don't feel inclined to lose 10,000!'

'We're his nieces,' said Madame Crémière. 'We'll look after him. We'll get to the bottom of this business, and one day you'll have cause to thank us, cousin.'

'Handle Ursule carefully. Old Jordy left her his savings!' advised the notary, raising his right index finger to his lips.

'I'll mind my p's and q's,' cried Désiré.

'You were as skilful as Desroches, and he's the best solicitor in Paris,' Goupil remarked to his employer as they left the postmaster's premises.

'And they quibble about our fees!' the notary answered with a bitter smile.

The family, with faces rather flushed by their lunch, were all walking away with Dionis and his head clerk just as vespers were ending. As the notary had predicted, Abbé Chaperon came out of church with old Madame de Portenduère on his arm.

'She's dragged him to vespers,' cried Madame Massin, pointing Madame Crémière's attention to Ursule and the doctor as they left the church.

'Let's go up and have a word with him,' said Madame Crémière, walking towards the old man.

Dr Minoret was surprised to note the change which the legal conference had brought about in all their faces. He wondered what was the reason for this trumped-up friendship, and out of inquisitiveness helped Ursule into a meeting with the two women, who eagerly greeted her with exaggerated affection and feigned smiles.

'Uncle, would you permit us to call on you this evening?' asked Madame Crémière. 'We sometimes thought we were intruding upon you; but our children haven't been to pay you their respects for a very long time, and now our daughters are old enough to make friends with dear Ursule.'

'Ursule lives up to her name,' the doctor answered. 'She's very shy.'

'Well then, let us make her feel at ease,' said Madame Massin. 'Besides, uncle,' this good housewife added, trying to conceal her plans beneath an appearance of thrift, 'we're told that your dear goddaughter is wonderfully gifted on the *pianoforte*: we should be really delighted to hear her. Madame Crémière and I are thinking of employing her music-master for our little girls; you see, if he had seven or eight pupils, he'd be able to charge for his lessons at prices we could afford . . .'

'Certainly,' the old man replied, 'that would be a very good arrangement, particularly as I also want Ursule to have a singing-master.'

'Very well, we'll see you this evening, uncle, and bring your great-nephew Désiré with us. He's a barrister now.'

'Good-bye until then,' replied Minoret, eager to fathom their small-minded plans.

His two nieces shook hands with Ursule, wishing her good-bye with artificial grace.

'Godfather, you can read the secrets of my heart!' cried Ursule, giving the old man a grateful look.

'You have a good voice. And I also want you to have drawing and Italian masters. A woman,' he added, looking at Ursule as he opened the iron gate leading to his house, 'must have an education that fits her for whatever situations she has to face in married life.'

Ursule blushed as red as a cherry: her guardian seemed to be thinking of the man whom she herself had in mind. She felt like confessing to the doctor the spontaneous impulse that led her to be so concerned about Savinien and to make him her ideal of perfection, and sat down under the clump of creepers, against which she stood out from a distance like a blue and white flower.

'Godfather, look how kind your nieces were to me; they were so nice,' she said, seeing what he was driving at and trying to conceal the thoughts that were making her wistful.

'Poor child!' the old man exclaimed.

Placing Ursule's hand on his arm and patting it, he walked her along the terrace by the river, where they could not be overheard.

'Why do you say: "Poor child"?'

'Can't you see they're afraid of you?'

'And why should they be?'

'My family are all worried at the moment about my conversion. No doubt they have put it down to your influence over me, imagining I shall deprive them of their inheritance by giving my money to you.'

'But surely you won't do that?' was Ursule's artless reply as she stood looking at her godfather.

'God has sent you to be a comfort to me in my old age!' said the old doctor, lifting the girl off her feet and kissing her on both cheeks. 'It wasn't for my own sake but for yours that I prayed to God just now to let me live long enough to see you married to a good man worthy to be your husband. You just see, my angel, the play-acting that the Minorets, Crémières and Massins will put on when they come. You want to enhance and prolong my life; they can only think of my death.'

'God has forbidden us to hate; but if what you say is true, oh! I really despise them.'

'Dinner's ready!' cried La Bougival from the top of the outside steps, which on the garden side of the house were at the end of the passage.

Ursule and her guardian were eating their dessert in the pretty dining-room decorated with Chinese lacquer-style paintings (they had been Levrault-Levrault's ruination!) when the magistrate arrived. As a great token of friendship, the doctor offered him a cup of his Mocha coffee blended with Bourbon and burned Martinique coffees, ground by himself, and personally made in a silver coffee-pot of the Chaptal variety.

'Well,' said Bongrand, pushing up his spectacles and giving the old doctor a sly look, 'the whole town is in a fever of excitement. Your attendance at church has flabbergasted your relations. People think you're leaving your money to the priests, or the poor. You have stirred them up and now they have got stirring! I saw their first rumpus in the market-place. They were as agitated as ants disturbed in their anthill.'

'What did I tell you, Ursule? Even if it distresses you, mustn't I teach you the way of the world, and how to guard against undeserved hostility!'

'I'd like to have a word with you about that,' said Bongrand, seizing the opportunity to discuss Ursule's future with his old friend.

The doctor put a black velvet cap on his white head, the magistrate kept his hat on so as not to catch a chill, and the two men walked up and down the terrace discussing the ways and means of making sure that Ursule would get whatever fortune her godfather intended for her. The magistrate knew of Dionis's opinion that any will the doctor might make in Ursule's favour would be null and void; Nemours was so absorbed in the question of Minoret's inheritance that the matter had been argued amongst the legal experts in the town. Bongrand had decided that Ursule had no legal relationship to Dr Minoret, but he was well aware that the spirit and intention of the legislation was averse to over-elaborate constructions that were *ultra vires*. The parliamentary draughtsmen of this particular law had only foreseen the tendency of fathers and mothers to provide for their illegitimate children, they had not imagined that uncles or aunts might favour the affection of an illegitimate child for its own descendants. Clearly there was a loophole in the law.

'In any other country,' he remarked after giving the same outline of the legal position which Goupil, Dionis and Désiré had just spelt out to the family, 'Ursule would have nothing to fear; she's a legitimate child, and her father's illegitimacy ought only to concern his claims on the estate of your father-in-law Valentin Mirouët; but in France judges are unfortunately of a very legalistic, logic-chopping turn of mind; they are concerned with finding out what the law really intends. Barristers will bring ethics into their submissions, pointing out that the loophole in the law stems from the good nature of legislators who didn't reckon with that particular contingency, but who have nevertheless laid down a principle. It will be a long, expensive case. With Zélie involved, it would go as far as the Supreme Court of Appeal, and I'm not sure whether I'll still be alive when the lawsuit comes up.'

'Even the best lawsuits have no value,' cried the doctor. 'I can already see dissertations on the question: *Should an illegitimate child's lack of succession rights affect his descendants?*, and a good barrister glories in winning doubtful cases.'

'Well, I couldn't positively declare that judges wouldn't interpret the meaning of the law so as to extend the protection given to marriage as the eternal basis of human society.'

Without voicing his intentions, the doctor ruled out the idea of creating a trust. But as to the possibility of marrying Ursule, which Bongrand suggested to him as a means of making her fortune secure, the doctor replied: 'Poor girl! I might live another fifteen years yet, and what would become of her?'

'Well, in that case what do you intend to do?' asked Bongrand.

'We'll think about it! I'll see!' said the doctor, obviously embarrassed as to what to say.

Just then Ursule came to tell the two friends that Dionis was asking to speak to the doctor.

'Dionis here already?' cried Minoret, looking at the magistrate. 'Very well,' he said to Ursule, 'show him in.'

'I'd bet anything he's the front man for my relatives; they've all been lunching with Dionis at the postmaster's house, and hatching some plan.'

With Ursule leading the way, the notary came down to the bottom of the garden. After the usual greetings and a few commonplace remarks, Dionis was allowed a few minutes' private talk. Ursule and Bongrand retired into the drawing-room.

'We'll think about it! I'll see!' Bongrand kept saying to himself, echoing the last words spoken by the doctor. 'That's how clever people are; death catches them unawares, and they leave their nearest and dearest in difficulties!'

It is remarkable how much distrust is inspired in business people by men of superior intellect, who are not considered to have the *lesser* abilities though they are credited with the greater ones. But perhaps this distrust is a form of praise. Seeing them move on the loftiest of planes, business people do not believe that men of brilliant intellect are capable of stooping down to deal with the infinitely small details of life which, like interest in the realms of finance or animalcules in the natural sciences, accumulate to such an extent that they become equal to capital and create worlds of their own. But this is a mistaken assumption! Both the magnanimous man and the genius see everything. Bongrand, offended at the doctor's silence, but no doubt prompted by the thought of Ursule's welfare, which he considered threatened, decided to take her side against the collateral family. He was in despair at not knowing anything of Minoret's interview with Dionis.

'However pure Ursule may be,' he thought, looking at her carefully, 'there is one matter whose legal and moral aspects girls usually solve for themselves. Let's see!'

'The Minoret-Levraults,' he said, adjusting his glasses more firmly on his nose, 'may consider you a suitable bride for their son.'

The poor child went pale: she was too well brought up, and had too delicate a sense of honour, to eavesdrop on the conversation between Dionis and her uncle; but, after a short period of mental deliberation, she thought it permissible to show herself, thinking that if her presence was not required her godfather would tell her so. The slatted shutters of the French window were open in the Chinese pavilion where Dr Minoret had his study. Ursule's idea was to go and close them herself. She apologized for leaving the magistrate alone in the drawing-room, but Bongrand smilingly said: 'Do, by all means!'

9. The First Confession of a Secret

URSULE reached the steps leading down from the Chinese pavilion to the garden and stood there for a few minutes, slowly manipulating the shutters and watching the sunset. It was at this point that she heard the doctor say the following words as he came walking up to the pavilion.

'My family would be delighted if I had my money invested in real estate and mortgages; they imagine my wealth would be much more tied up: I see what they're getting at, and perhaps you've come as their spokesman? Well, sir, my mind is firmly made up as to how I shall leave my money. My family will have the capital of the fortune I had when I came here. Now they know, so I hope they will leave me alone. If any of them tried to upset any arrangements I feel I must make for that poor child' (he pointed to his goddaughter) 'I would come back and torment them from the grave! Consequently, if anyone is depending on me to get him out, Monsieur Savinien de Portenduère can remain in prison. I shan't sell any of my Government securities.'

Hearing the tail-end of the doctor's remarks, Ursule was stricken with pain – the first and only time she was ever to be so. She leant her forehead against the shutter, clinging on to it to keep herself from falling.

'Good Heavens! what's the matter with her?' cried the doctor, 'she's as white as a sheet. Such a shock after dinner could kill her.' He stretched out his arm towards Ursule, who fell down almost in a faint. 'Please leave us alone, and good-bye,' he said to the notary.

He carried his goddaughter to a huge cushioned armchair dating from the reign of Louis XV, which was in his study, and took a bottle of ether out of his medicine chest, giving it to her to inhale.

'See Dionis out,' he said to Bongrand, who was alarmed. 'I want to be alone with her.'

The magistrate showed the notary to the iron gate, asking

him, without betraying the slightest eagerness: 'What on earth's happened to Ursule?'

'I don't know,' Monsieur Dionis answered. 'She was listening to us from the steps; and when *her uncle* refused to lend a large enough sum of money to young Portenduère, who's been imprisoned for debt (he wasn't lucky enough, like Monsieur du Rouvre, to have a Monsieur Bongrand to defend him), she went pale and tottered over . . . Could she be in love with him? Could there be . . . ?'

'At fifteen?' Bongrand interrupted Dionis.

'She was born in February 1814. She'll be sixteen in four months' time.'

'She's never seen her neighbour,' the magistrate retorted. 'No, it's probably a touch of sickness.'

'Lovesickness,' the notary slipped in.

Dionis was quite delighted with his discovery, which would prevent the terrifying prospect of a marriage *in extremis* whereby the doctor could thwart his family's interests, whilst Bongrand's castles in Spain were razed to the ground: he had long been hoping to marry Ursule to his son.

'If the poor girl does love that fellow, it'll be hard lines for her. Madame de Portenduère comes from Brittany. She's crazy about noble rank,' the magistrate commented after a pause.

'Yes, that is fortunate . . . for the sake of the Portenduères' honour,' replied Dionis, almost giving away his true meaning.

Let it now be said in honour of that honest, worthy magistrate that as he walked back from the iron gate to the drawing-room he renounced his hope that one day he might be able to call Ursule his daughter-in-law; but he still felt distressed for his son. He intended to give the young man 6,000 francs a year investment income the day he became a deputy public prosecutor; and if the doctor had been willing to allow Ursule a dowry of 100,000 francs, the young couple would have made a perfect match; his son Eugène was an honest and charming fellow. Perhaps he had been a little too generous in his praise of Eugène, so arousing old Minoret's distrust.

'I'll plump for the mayor's daughter,' he thought. 'But even without a dowry Ursule would be a better bride than

Mademoiselle Levrault-Crémière with her million francs. Anyway, now let's try and get Ursule married to young Portenduère if in fact she loves him.'

After closing the door leading to the library and garden, the doctor had taken his ward to the window overlooking the water's edge.

'What's the matter with you, you cruel girl?' he asked. 'Your life is my life. What would become of me if I couldn't depend on your smiles?'

'Savinien in prison!'

Having said these words she burst into a flood of tears, and began to sob.

'She's safe,' thought the doctor, who had been feeling her pulse with a father's anxiety. 'Alas! she's just as sensitive as my poor wife,' he said to himself as he went to get a stethoscope, which he placed against Ursule's heart and began to listen in to. 'Anyway, everything's all right!' – 'I didn't know, my dear, that you were so much in love with him already,' he resumed, looking at her. 'But just confide in me as if you were thinking aloud, and tell me everything that has passed between you.'

'I'm not in love with him, godfather. We've never even spoken to one another,' she sobbed. 'But to think that that poor young man is in prison and that you were so cruel as to refuse to get him out, when you're really so good.'

'Ursule, my darling angel, if you're not in love with him, why have you put a little red dot beside St Sabinian's day, just like St Denis's day? Come on, tell me all the little details of this love affair!'

Ursule blushed, held back her tears, and a moment's silence ensued between the niece and her uncle.

'Are you afraid of your godfather, your friend, father, mother and doctor, whose feelings have been even warmer towards you these last few days than ever before?'

'Well, godfather, I'll confess. In May Monsieur Savinien came to see his mother. Until this visit I'd never paid him the slightest attention. When he went away to live in Paris I was a child, and I assure you I couldn't see any difference between a young man and you older men, except perhaps that I loved you without ever imagining that I could love anybody more tenderly. Monsieur Savinien came by the mail-coach on the eve of his mother's name-day, without our being aware of it. At seven in the morning, after saying my prayers, I opened the window to let air into my bedroom – and I saw Monsieur Savinien's bedroom windows open, and Monsieur Savinien in a dressing-gown, getting shaved – oh! ever so gracefully, I really did think he was handsome! He combed his black moustache and the tuft under his chin, and I saw his round, white neck ... Do I have to confess everything? I noticed that his fresh neck, face and fine dark hair were very different from yours, when I've watched you getting shaved. Something came over me, I don't know what it was: it filled my heart, throat and head, with such a rush that I had to sit down. I couldn't stand, I was all of a tremble. But I was so eager to see him again that I stood on tiptoe; then he saw me and, just to tease me, blew me a kiss and ...'

'And? ...'

'And then I hid, ashamed of myself but happy, without being able to understand either my shame or happiness. The impulse that dazzled my heart, exerting such a strange power over it, has recurred every time I have thought of that young man's face. And I was glad to be feeling the same emotion again, even though it was so violent. As I was on my way to mass, I just couldn't help looking at Monsieur Savinien walking along with his mother on his arm: everything about him seemed attractive, his way of walking, his clothes, even the sound of his boots on the pavement. Even the slightest thing about him, such as his finely gloved hand, cast a kind of spell over me. However, I was strong enough not to think of him during mass. When it was over, I lingered behind in church so as to let Madame de Portenduère go out first, and then walk along behind him. I can't tell you how interested I was in all these little contrivances. When I got home, as I turned round to shut the iron gate ...'

'And what about La Bougival? ...' asked the doctor.

'Oh! I'd let her go off to the kitchen,' Ursule replied artlessly. 'It was then quite natural and easy for me to see Monsieur Savinien standing there looking at me. Oh! godfather, I felt so proud when I thought I could detect in his eyes a sort of surprise and admiration, so proud that I don't know what I wouldn't have done to give him a chance to look at me. I felt that all I ought to be concerned with from now on was pleasing him. His look has become the sweetest reward for my good deeds. From that moment I have been constantly thinking about him, even though I've tried not to. Monsieur Savinien left the town that same evening, I haven't seen him since. The Rue des Bourgeois has seemed empty. He's sort of taken my heart away without being aware of it.'

'Is that all?'

'Yes, godfather,' she said, with a sigh in which regret at not having more to say was stifled beneath her present grief.

'Dear girl,' said the doctor, seating Ursule on his knee, 'you're nearly sixteen now and you'll soon be leading a woman's life. You are between a blissfully happy childhood, now almost over, and the turmoils of love which will make your life a stormy one, because you've got the nervous system associated with extreme sensitivity. What is on its way, my dear, is love' – and the doctor had a look of deep sadness as he said this – 'love in its purest candour, love as it must be: spontaneous, swift as a robber to take everything ... yes, everything! And I expected it, I've observed women carefully, and I know that whereas most only fall in love after lots of courtship and proof of miraculous affection, only speaking and yielding when they are already conquered, others fall in love at first sight – as the result of a mutual sympathy explainable nowadays by the properties of magnetic fluids. Today is the day to tell you this: the very first time I set eyes on the charming woman whose name you bear, I felt that I would faithfully love her, and her alone, before knowing whether our characters and personalities were compatible. Is there such a thing as second sight in love? How are we to answer that, when so many marriages celebrated under the heavenly auspices of matrimony are later broken, and give rise to almost eternal hatred and total antipathy? The senses can as it were be in communion, and the mental outlooks at variance: and perhaps some people live more through their ideas than their bodies. On the other hand, often the characters are in harmony yet there is personal dislike. These two facts, although so different, explain many misfortunes, and justify the wisdom of the law in allowing parents authority over their children's marriages; a girl is often the victim of one or other of these hallucinations. So I don't blame you. It's quite natural to experience these feelings, the happiness it gives you to think of Savinien, the sensitive impulse overwhelming your heart and mind from a centre within yourself that you didn't even know existed! But, dear child, as Abbé Chaperon has explained to you, Society demands the sacrifice of many of our natural inclinations. Men's destinies are quite different from women's. I was in a position to choose Ursule Mirouët as my wife, and to go up to her and tell her how much I loved her; whereas a girl is untrue to feminine virtue if she invites the attentions of the man she loves: women haven't got the option, as we have, to pursue their objectives openly. And so with women, and especially with you, modesty is the impregnable barrier guarding the secrets of your heart. The way you hesitated before confiding your earliest feeling has made me quite sure that you would suffer the harshest tortures before confessing to Savinien . . .'

'Yes, oh! yes,' was her reply.

'But you must do more than this: you must curb and even forget your impulses.'

'Why?'

'Because, darling angel, you must only love the man who will become your husband; and even if Monsieur Savinien de Portenduère loved you . . .'

'I haven't even thought about it.'

'Listen, even if he did love you, even if his mother asked my permission for you to be his bride, I would not agree to the marriage till I had given Savinien a long and probing trial. His behaviour has incurred every family's suspicion and placed barriers between heiresses and himself which will be hard to remove.'

An angelic smile dried Ursule's tears as she said: 'It's an ill wind that blows nobody any good!' The doctor was speechless at her simplicity. 'What has he done, godfather?' she went on.

'In two years he has run up about 120,000 francs of debts in Paris! He has been foolish enough to allow himself to be locked up in Sainte-Pélagie, a blunder which nowadays discredits a young man's reputation for ever. A spendthrift who's capable of plunging his poor mother into grief and poverty is also capable of what your poor father did: killing his wife with despair!'

'Do you think he can mend his ways?'

'If his mother settles his debts, he'll have ruined himself, and I know of no better amends or punishment for a nobleman than to be destitute.'

This reply made Ursule thoughtful. She brushed her tears away, saying to her godfather: 'If you can rescue him, please do, godfather; if you do him this favour, you'll be entitled to give him advice: you can remonstrate with him . . .'

'And,' said the doctor, imitating Ursule's way of speaking, 'he'll be able to come here, the old lady will come, we'll see them, and . . .'

'I'm only thinking about him at the moment,' Ursule replied with a blush.

'Don't think about him any more, my dear. It would be foolish!' the doctor said in a serious voice. 'Even if she only had 300 francs a year to live on, Madame de Portenduère – a Kergarouët – would never agree to Vicomte Savinien de Portenduère marrying you: the great-nephew of the late Comte de Portenduère who was deputy commander of the Navy, the son of Vicomte de Portenduère, a naval captain, marrying Ursule Mirouët! – a regimental musician's daughter, a destitute girl whose father (I'm afraid the time has come to tell you this!) was an organist's illegitimate son – and that organist was my father-in-law.'

'Oh how right you are, godfather! We are only equal in God's eyes. I shall only think of him in my prayers now,' she sobbed, moved to tears by Dr Minoret's disclosure. 'Give him everything you were planning to leave me. What can a poor girl like me need? And he's in prison!'

'Offer up all your mortifications to God, and perhaps He will come to our assistance.'

There was silence for a few moments. Ursule did not dare

to look at her godfather, but when she did look up at him she was deeply touched to see tears streaming down his withered cheeks. An old man's tears are as terrifying to behold as a child's are natural.

'Heavens! What's the matter?' she cried, throwing herself at his feet and kissing his hands. 'Don't you trust me?'

'I want to satisfy your every wish, yet I've had to cause you the first great suffering in your life! It grieves me as much as it grieves you. I've only ever wept when Ursule and my children died. Look, I'll do anything you ask,' he cried.

Through her tears Ursule looked at her godfather, and her look was like lightning. She smiled.

'Let's go into the drawing-room,' the doctor said, leaving his ward in the study, 'and remember not to tell anyone else about all this, my dear.'

The fatherly man felt so weakened by her divine smile that he was about to utter a word of hope, and thus mislead his goddaughter.

10. The Portenduères

At this moment Madame de Portenduère was sitting alone with the curé in her chilly little ground-floor sitting-room. She had finished relating her troubles to the good priest, her only friend. She was holding letters that Abbé Chaperon had just handed back to her after reading them – letters which had raised her wretchedness to its highest pitch. Sitting in her armchair by the square table on which stood the remains of dessert, the old lady was looking at the parish priest who, slumped in his armchair opposite, was stroking his chin in a gesture common to stage servants, mathematicians and priests, signifying deep thought about an intractable problem.

This small sitting-room, lit by two windows looking on to the street and panelled with grey-painted wainscoting, was so damp that the lower panels showed those geometrical cracks that you find in rotten wood when only the paint is still holding it together. The floor, red and polished by the old lady's one and only servant, called for little esparto foot-rests to be placed in front of each chair, and the abbé had his feet on one of these. The curtains were made of old damask, light green in colour with green flowers; they had been drawn, and the slatted shutters closed. Two candles cast a light over the table, whilst leaving the rest of the room in semi-darkness. Need it be said that between the two windows there was a fine Latour pastel portrait of the famous Admiral de Portenduère, the rival of the Suffrens, Kergarouëts, Guichens and Simeuses? On the wainscoting opposite the mantelpiece was a portrait of the Vicomte de Portenduère and the old lady's mother, a Kergarouët-Ploëgat. Thus, Savinien's great-uncle was the Vice-Admiral de Kergarouët, and his cousin the Comte de Portenduère, the admiral's grandson; and both these men were extremely rich. The Vice-Admiral de Kergarouët lived in Paris, and the Comte de Portenduère resided at the mansion in Dauphiné that bears his name. His cousin the count was the head of the senior line, and Savinien was the only descendant of the junior. The count, who was over forty years of age, had married a rich wife, by whom he had three children. His income, enriched by several inheritances, amounted (it was said) to 60,000 francs a year. He was deputy for the Isère constituency, and spent his winters in Paris where he had bought back the Hôtel de Portenduère with the compensation due to him under the law passed by Villèle. The Vice-Admiral de Kergarouët had recently married his niece, Mademoiselle de Fontaine, solely to make sure that she would inherit his fortune. Savinien's misconduct would therefore lose him the support of two powerful friends. Being a handsome young man, if he had entered the navy, he might have become a lieutenant-commander by the age of twenty-three – what with his family name and the support of an admiral or a deputy; but his mother was opposed to her only son's taking up a military career. She had had him educated at Nemours by one of Abbé Chaperon's curates, and had fondly imagined she would be able to keep her son beside her until her dying day. She wanted him to make a prudent marriage with a Mademoiselle d'Aiglemont, who had a private income of 12,000 francs a year, and to whom the family name of Portenduère and the ownership of the farm at Les Bordières entitled him to aspire. It was an unassuming plan, but a wise one, in that it could have restored the family fortunes in the second generation; but it would have been frustrated by events. At that time the d'Aiglemonts were ruined, and one of their daughters – the eldest, Hélène – had disappeared in circumstances so mysterious that the family had never been able to elucidate them. The boredom of a closed-in life, a life without either purpose or action, and sustained by nothing other than a son's love for his mother, proved so wearisome to Savinien that he broke loose from his chains – delightful though they were – and vowed that he would never live in the provinces, realizing rather late in the day that his future did not lie in the Rue des Bourgeois. At twenty-one he had therefore left his mother to gain acknowledgement from his cousins and try his fortune in Paris. The contrast between his Nemours life and the way of life he led in Paris was to prove a disastrous one for a young man of twenty-one, free, without anyone to restrain or contradict him, inevitably craving for pleasure, and whose surname of Portenduère and wealthy relations made him an acceptable visitor in every drawing-room. In the certain knowledge that his mother had twenty years' savings hidden away somewhere, Savinien had soon spent the 6,000 francs she gave him to see Paris with. This amount did not cover his first six months' expenses: he owed twice that sum to his hotel, his tailor, bootmaker, jobmaster, a jeweller and all the tradesmen who contribute to a young man's luxuries. Hardly had he managed to get himself known, to know how to converse, make a favourable impression, choose and wear his waistcoats, order his clothes and tie his cravat than he found himself in debt to the tune of 30,000 francs, and had only reached the point of casting around for a delicate way to broach his love for the Marquis de Ronquerolles's sister, Madame de Sérizy, an elegant woman but one whose youth and brilliance belonged to the days of the Empire.

'How did you others manage?' Savinien inquired one day after lunching with a few dandies with whom he had become friendly, as young men do become friendly nowadays when their goals are identical in every way – demanding for themselves an equality of status that is impossible to achieve. 'You weren't any richer than I, and yet you haven't a care in the world. You can support yourselves whereas I am already in debt!'

'We all began that way,' laughed Rastignac, Lucien de Rubempré, Maxime de Trailles and Émile Blondet, the then princes of fashion.

'The fact that de Marsay was born rich was pure chance!' said their host, an upstart named Finot who was trying to hobnob with these young men. 'And if he hadn't been the man he is,' he added, bowing towards him, 'his wealth could have been his ruin.'

'You've hit the right word,' said Maxime de Trailles.

'And the right idea,' interjected Rastignac.

'My dear fellow,' de Marsay said gravely to Savinien, 'debts are the business capital subscribed by experience. A good university education, with tutors for your social graces and academic ratraces, costs 60,000 francs – and it teaches you nothing. A worldly education costs twice that much, but it teaches you about life, business, politics, men – and sometimes women.'

Blondet completed the lesson with the following adaptation of a line from La Fontaine:

Le monde vend très cher ce qu'on pense qu'il donne! *

Instead of giving thought to the sensible words spoken by the ablest navigators of the Parisian archipelago, Savinien merely thought they were joking.

'Take care, my dear fellow,' warned de Marsay. 'You have a distinguished surname, and if you don't acquire the wealth that must go with a name such as yours, you might end up as a sergeant in some cavalry regiment.

Nous avons vu tomber de plus illustres têtes! †

he added, declaiming this line from Corneille and taking Savinien's arm. 'Nearly six years ago now, a young Comte d'Esgrignon joined our circle, but he didn't last more than two years in this paradise known as high society! Alas! he had a meteoric existence. He rose to the dizzy heights of being the Duchesse de Maufrigneuse's lover, then fell back again to his native town, where he is paying for his mistakes with an old father plagued by catarrh and games of whist where the stakes are two sous a rubber. Confess your position openly and unashamedly to Madame de Sérizy. She will be very helpful to you. But if you cast yourself as the smitten lover, she will play the part of a Raphael madonna, flirt with you without ever letting things get out of hand – and your excursion into love-making will cost you very dearly!'

Savinien was still too young. He was entirely dedicated to the idea of a nobleman's purity and honour. He did not dare to confess his financial position to Madame de Sérizy. When her son no longer knew where to turn, Madame de Portenduère

* 'The world sells very dearly what people think it gives.' An adaptation of La Fontaine's line (*Philémon et Baucis*, 1.12): . . . *La Fortune vend ce qu'on croit qu'elle donne* (Fortune sells what people believe she gives).

† 'Greater heads than his have been seen to fall!' This line is not from Corneille.

sent him 20,000 francs, everything she possessed – prompted to do so by a letter in which Savinien, guided by his friends in the art of attacking a parent's strongboxes, spoke about bills of exchange that needed to be paid and the disgrace of having one's signature to bills dishonoured by legal protest. With this help, he got by until the end of his first year. During his second, whilst still attached to Madame de Sérizy, who was genuinely in love with him and giving him a good social education, he resorted to the dangerous expedient of borrowing from money-lenders. One day when he was in straits, des Lupeaulx, a friend of his who was a deputy and a friend of his cousin de Portenduère, advised him to turn to Gobseck, Gigonnet and Palma, who – fully and duly informed of the value of his mother's property – discounted his bills without objection or difficulty. For about eighteen months he led a happy life thanks to money-lending and deceptively helpful renewals. Without daring to break with Madame de Sérizy, the poor fellow fell madly in love with the beautiful Comtesse de Kergarouët – who was as prudish as any young woman expecting the death of her elderly husband, and cleverly carrying her virtue forward into a second marriage. Unable to realize that calculated virtue is unconquerable, Savinien courted Émilie de Kergarouët with all the display of a wealthy man: he never missed a ball or a show at which she was to be present.

'You haven't got enough explosive to topple her, my dear fellow,' de Marsay jokingly said one evening.

Even though this young king of Parisian dandies was pitying enough to explain Émilie de Fontaine's character to the poor boy, it needed the sombre light of misfortune and the darkness of a prison to enlighten Savinien. With the agreement of the money-lenders, who did not want to be involved in the odious business of an arrest, a jeweller on whom Savinien de Portenduère had rashly drawn a bill of exchange had him committed to Sainte-Pélagie for debts amounting to 117,000 francs – without his friends knowing anything about it. As soon as Rastignac, de Marsay and Lucien de Rubempré heard the news, they all visited Savinien and each offered him a thousand-franc note on finding him completely destitute. Savinien's valet, bribed by two of his creditors, had told them where his master had a secret flat, and everything in it had been seized except for his clothing and the small amount of jewellery he was in the habit of wearing. After an excellent dinner, and over the sherry de Marsay had brought along with him, the three young men questioned Savinien about his position, ostensibly to make plans for his future, but really no doubt so as to form a judgement of him.

'When your name's Savinien de Portenduère,' Rastignac cried, 'and when you're a cousin of a future peer of France and the great-nephew of Admiral de Kergarouët, if you commit the enormous blunder of allowing yourself to be slung into Sainte-Pélagie, you mustn't stay there long!'

'Why didn't you let me know?' exclaimed de Marsay. 'You had only to ask for my carriage, 10,000 francs and letters of introduction to people in Germany. We know Gobseck, Gigonnet and other sharks and we'd have forced them to back down. In any case, what idiot led you to them in the first place?'

'Des Lupeaulx.'

The three young men looked at one another with the same meaning, or rather suspicion, on their faces; but they did not express it aloud.

'Outline your financial resources. Tell us the position,' urged de Marsay.

After Savinien had described his mother and her looped bonnets, her little home with its three casement windows in the Rue des Bourgeois, its only garden a backyard with a well and a shed for drying wood; after working out the value of the sandstone house rendered in reddish mortar, and valuing the farm at Les Bordières, the three dandies again looked at each other, and in a phrase used by the priest in *Les Marrons du Feu*, one of Alfred de Musset's recently published *Contes d'Espagne*, they solemnly commented: 'How sad!'

'Send your mother a skilfully composed letter, and she'll pay up,' said Rastignac.

'Yes, but what then?' cried de Marsay.

'If only you'd been got out of the way in time,' said Lucien,

132

'the Government would have you in the diplomatic service; but Sainte-Pélagie isn't exactly a stepping-stone to an embassy.'

'You're not up to living in Paris,' was Rastignac's verdict.

'Listen,' de Marsay continued, looking Savinien up and down as a horse-dealer sizes up a horse. 'You've got beautiful blue eyes, large wide-open ones, a white finely chiselled forehead, magnificent black hair, a little moustache that looks good against your pale cheeks, and a slim figure; it's obvious from the shape of your foot that you're an aristocrat; your shoulders and chest are not too much like a street-porter's yet at the same time they're robust. You're what I call a dark handsome stranger! Your face is rather like Louis XIII's, not much colour, but a well-shaped nose; besides which you've got the knack of appealing to women, something that men themselves aren't aware of – something in your look, manner, voice, gestures, the expression in your eyes, a thousand and one little things that women notice, giving them a meaning that's beyond us. You don't know your advantages! In six months, providing you behave yourself a bit, you could bewitch some Englishwoman with £100,000, especially if you took the title of Vicomte de Portenduère which is yours by right. My charming stepmother Lady Dudley, who hasn't got an equal when it comes to fixing up marriages, could find you one somewhere in the alluvial regions of Great Britain. But you would have to have the knowledge and ability to defer the repayment of your debts for ninety days by skilful manoeuvring in the world of high finance. Why didn't you let me know? The money-lenders would have looked up to you in Baden-Baden, and perhaps helped you; but they despise you now you've got yourself thrown into jail. The money-lender is like Society itself, like the Populace too: they worship the man who's strong enough to trifle with them, and are ruthless towards the innocent lambs. To some people, Sainte-Pélagie is a Scarlet Woman who devilishly corrupts young men. Do you want to know what I think, my dear boy? I'll give you the same advice I gave young d'Esgrignon. Pay your debts off in an orderly manner, leaving yourself enough to live on for three years, and get married back home in the provinces to the first girl you meet with a private income of 30,000 francs. Within three years you'll have found some good-living heiress who'd like to be called Madame de Portenduère. Now that's sound advice! So let's drink on it! Here's a toast: To a girl with some money!'

The young men did not leave their former friend until the end of the official visiting hour, and at the prison gates summed him up in the words: 'He's not up to it! Hasn't he got himself in a mess? Will he ever get out of it?'

The next day Savinien wrote his mother a general confession extending to twenty-two pages. After weeping for a whole day, Madame de Portenduère first wrote to her son promising to get him out of prison, then to the Comtes de Portenduère and de Kergarouët.

The letters which Abbé Chaperon had just read and the poor mother was still holding, moist with her tears, had arrived by that morning's post – and had broken her heart.

TO MADAME DE PORTENDUÈRE

Paris, September 1829.

Madam,

You cannot have any doubt of the sympathy the Admiral and I feel for you in your distress. What you announce to Monsieur de Kergarouët is particularly distressing to me as your son was always a welcome visitor to our home: we were so proud of him. If Savinien had shown more confidence in the Admiral, we would have taken him in hand, he would already have a suitable position; but the poor boy never breathed a word to us! The Admiral is unable to pay 100,000 francs. He owes money himself, and has incurred great debts on my behalf; I knew nothing about his financial affairs! He is so dreadfully sorry about this – particularly when Savinien has tied our hands for the present by letting himself get arrested. If my nephew had not been foolish enough to fall in love with me, thus stifling the voice of a relation beneath the pride of a lover, we would have arranged for him to travel in Germany whilst his affairs were being sorted out here. Monsieur de Kergarouët could have asked for a posting for his great-nephew in the Admiralty; but no doubt the fact that he has been imprisoned for debt will frustrate any steps the Admiral might take. Settle Savinien's debts, let him serve in the Navy and he will make his way like a true Portenduère, whose fire shines in his handsome dark eyes; we shall all help him.

So, Madam do not despair. You still have friends, amongst whom I hope you will consider me one of the truest. With my best wishes and respects,

Your affectionate servant,
ÉMILIE DE KERGAROUËT

TO MADAME DE PORTENDUÈRE
Portenduère, August 1829.

My dear Aunt,

I am both grieved and annoyed by Savinien's escapades. Being a married man with two sons and a daughter, and with a fortune that even now is barely sufficient for my position and aspirations, I cannot afford to reduce it by the 100,000 francs needed to ransom a Portenduère from the money-lenders. Sell your farm, pay his debts and come and stay at Portenduère. You will be welcomed as is your due, even though our hearts are not entirely yours. You will be happy, and we will find Savinien a wife – my wife thinks he's a charming young man. This prank is of no consequence. Don't be upset. People in our district will never hear of it, and we know several very rich girls around here who will be delighted to belong to our family.

My wife joins me in saying how much pleasure you will give us, and begs you to accept her best wishes for the fulfilment of this plan.

With our affectionate regards,
LUC-SAVINIEN, COMTE DE PORTENDUÈRE.

'What letters for a Kergarouët to receive!' cried the old lady, wiping her eyes.

'The Admiral doesn't know his nephew's in prison,' Abbé Chaperon finally remarked; 'only the Countess has read your letter, and she alone has replied to it. But you must make up your mind,' he went on after a pause, 'and this is the advice I am honoured to give you. Do not sell your farm. The lease has nearly expired, after a period of twenty-four years; in a few months you will be able to push the rent up to 6,000 francs, and also wangle yourself another two years' rent on the side. Borrow from some honest man, not from the towns-people who deal in mortgages. Your neighbour is a worthy man who's used to good society; he moved in fashionable society before the Revolution; from being an atheist, he is now a Catholic. Don't feel reluctant to call on him this evening.

He'll be very touched by your action; forget for a moment that you are a Kergarouët.'

'Never!' cried the old lady in a harsh voice.

'Just show the Kergarouët charm. Call on him when he's alone, he'll only ask for $3\frac{1}{2}$ per cent interest, perhaps only 3 per cent; and he'll do you this favour discreetly. You will be satisfied. He himself will go and get Savinien released from prison, as he'll have to go and sell Government securities; and he'll bring him back home to you.'

'Do you mean that little fellow Minoret?'

'That little fellow is eighty-three!' smiled Abbé Chaperon. 'My dear Madame de Portenduère, show a little Christian charity. Do not offend him. He may prove useful to you in more ways than one.'

'How do you mean?'

'An angel lives with him in his house, the sweetest of young girls.'

'Oh yes, little Ursule ... Anyway, go on.'

The poor priest did not dare continue after the words, 'Anyway, go on,' whose harshness and asperity cut short the proposal he was wanting to make.

'I believe Dr Minoret is extremely rich ...

'Good for him!'

'You've been the cause – admittedly, a very indirect one – of your son's present misfortunes in not getting him to follow a career. Beware of the future!' the abbé warned harshly. 'May I tell your neighbour that you'll be coming to visit him?'

'But knowing that I need him, why doesn't he come to see me?'

'Because if you go to see him, you'll only pay 3 per cent interest; but if he comes to see you, you will be paying 5 per cent,' answered Chaperon, thinking up this brilliant reason to persuade the old lady. 'And if you were compelled to sell your farm by either Dionis the notary or Massin the clerk of the court, who would refuse to loan you any money in the hope of making a profit out of your disaster, you would lose half the value of Les Bordières. I haven't got the slightest influence over people like Dionis, Massin and Levrault, the wealthy people about here who have their eyes on your farm and who know your son is in prison.'

'They know about that! They know about that!' she cried, raising her arms. 'Oh! dear curé, you've let your coffee go cold ... Tiennette! Tiennette!'

Tiennette, an old Breton woman aged sixty wearing a blouse and a Breton cap, hurried in and took the priest's coffee away to warm it up.

'Don't worry, Rector,' she urged, seeing that Abbé Chaperon wanted to drink it, 'I'll put it in the saucepan. It won't harm.'

'Well,' added the curé persuasively, 'I'll go and tell the doctor about your visit, and then you will come over.'

The old lady only yielded after an hour's discussion, during which the priest had to repeat his arguments ten times over. And even then the haughty Kergarouët was only finally convinced by his parting words: 'Savinien would go!'

'Then it had better be me,' she said.

11. Savinien is Rescued

IT was striking nine as the wicket closed behind the abbé, who rang sharply at the doctor's iron gate. From Tiennette to La Bougival it was a change without a difference, for the latter greeted him with: 'You're very late, Monsieur le Curé!' whereas the former had asked: 'Why do you leave Madame so early when she's distressed?'

The curé found quite a gathering in the doctor's green and brown drawing-room, for Dionis had called in at Massin's to reassure the collateral family, repeating their uncle's words to them.

'Ursule,' he said, 'has, I think, a love-affair on her mind which will only cause her trouble and distress; she seems romantic [the word notaries apply to extreme sensitivity], she'll be a spinster for a long time yet. So don't show any distrust. Make a fuss of her, and do as your uncle bids you. He's smarter than a hundred Goupils,' added the notary, unaware that 'Goupil' is a corruption of the Latin word *vulpes*, meaning a fox.

Thus, Madame Massin and Madame Crémière, their husbands, the postmaster and Désiré joined with Bongrand and the Nemours doctor to make up an unusual and rowdy gathering of people in the doctor's house. On his arrival at the house Abbé Chaperon could hear the piano. Poor Ursule was coming to the end of Beethoven's symphony in A. With the guile of innocence, the young girl – enlightened by her godfather and unfriendly towards the collateral heirs – chose this grandiose music, which must be studied before it can be understood, so as to dispel the women's envy. The more beautiful music is, the less it is appreciated by ignorant people. Thus, when the door opened to reveal Abbé Chaperon's venerable face the heirs cried out: 'Hello! here's the rector!', happy to get up from their seats and put an end to their torture.

Their cry found an echo at the card-table where Bongrand, the Nemours doctor and Minoret were victims of the tax-collector's impertinence: to please his great-uncle, Crémière had suggested he should make a fourth at whist. Ursule left the *pianoforte*. The doctor stood up as if to greet the parish priest, but really so as to end the game. After flowery compliments to their uncle about his goddaughter's talent, the heirs withdrew.

'Good night, my friends,' cried the doctor as the iron gate clanged to.

'Well! so that's what all the money's going on,' Madame Crémière remarked to Madame Massin after they had gone a few paces.

'Heaven preserve me from spending money for little Alice to kick up a racket like that in my house,' was Madame Massin's reply.

'She says it's by *Bethovan*, but he's supposed to be a great musician,' said the tax-gatherer. 'He has quite a reputation.'

'He'll never have one in Nemours!' Madame Crémière went on. 'People are right to call him *Bête à vent*.'*

'I think Uncle deliberately laid it on so we wouldn't come again,' said Massin. 'He winked as he pointed out the green volume to that little minx.'

'If that's the kind of din they enjoy,' said the postmaster, 'then let them mix amongst themselves.'

'The magistrate must certainly like card games to listen to such *sopratas*,' said Madame Crémière.

'I'll never be able to play to people who don't understand music,' said Ursule, sitting down beside the card-table.

'In people with abundant constitutions, feelings can only develop in congenial circles,' observed Chaperon. 'Just as the priest couldn't give a blessing in the Devil's presence, just as the chestnut tree dies in heavy soil, so a brilliant musician suffers inward defeat when confronted by ignorant Philistines. In the arts, we must receive from circumambient souls just as much strength as we communicate to them ourselves. This axiom governing human affections has led to the proverbs: "When in Rome, do as Rome does", and "Birds of a feather flock together". But the suffering you must have experienced only affects tender, delicate natures.'

'And therefore,' the doctor added, 'a thing that would only

* 'Windbag'

139

cause distress to a woman might kill little Ursule. When I'm no longer alive, fence off this dear little flower from the world with that protective hedge referred to in the lines of Catullus: *ut flos*, etc.'

'Still, those ladies were flattering to you, Ursule,' smiled the magistrate.

'It was gross flattery,' the Nemours doctor commented.

'I've always noticed some grossness in sham flattery,' replied old Minoret. 'I wonder why?'

'A true feeling has its own peculiar subtlety,' Chaperon suggested.

'Did you dine with Madame de Portenduère?' asked Ursule, questioning Abbé Chaperon with a look full of anxious curiosity.

'Yes; the poor lady is very upset, and may well call to see you this evening, Dr Minoret.'

'If she's distressed and needs to see me, I'll go across to her,' exclaimed the doctor. 'Let's finish the last rubber.'

Beneath the table Ursule squeezed the old man's hand.

'Her son,' said the magistrate, 'was a little too simple-minded to live in Paris without anyone to guide him. When I found out that people were approaching the notary for information about the old lady's farm, I realized that he was reckoning in advance on his mother's death.'

'D'you think he's capable of that?' asked Ursule with a terrible glare at Monsieur Bongrand, who said to himself: 'Yes, she does love him, unfortunately!'

'Yes and no,' said the Nemours doctor. 'Savinien has good qualities, and the proof of this is that he's in prison: rogues never get put there.'

'My dear friends,' cried old Minoret, 'that's quite enough for this evening. One mustn't allow a poor mother to weep a moment longer than she need when one can relieve her sorrow.'

The four friends rose and left the house. Ursule walked with them to the iron gate, watched her godfather and the parish priest knocking at the door opposite and, when Tiennette had let them in, sat down on one of the boundary-stones outside the house with La Bougival beside her.

'Madame la Vicomtesse,' said the curé, walk.ng ahead into the little sitting-room, 'Dr Minoret did not wish you to go to the trouble of calling on him . . .'

'I am too old-fashioned in my ways, Madame,' the doctor interrupted, 'not to know the respects a man should pay to someone of your rank and, from what I have heard the curé say, I am only too happy to be of some help to you.'

Madame de Portenduère was so put out by the course they had agreed on that since Abbé Chaperon's departure she had been thinking of approaching the Nemours notary; but such was her surprise at Minoret's tact that she stood up to return his greeting, motioning him to an armchair.

'Pray be seated,' she said with a regal look. 'Our dear Abbé Chaperon will have mentioned to you that the viscount is in prison on account of a few debts, a young man's wild oats, 100,000 francs . . . If you could lend him this sum, I would allow you my farm at Les Bordières as security.'

'We'll talk of that, Viscountess, when I've brought your son back – if you will permit me to act as your man of business on this occasion.'

'Very well, doctor,' the old lady answered with a bow of the head, and giving Abbé Chaperon a look that implied: 'You're right, he is a man who has moved in good society.'

'My friend the doctor,' the curé then remarked, 'is, as you can see, entirely devoted to your family's interests.'

'We shall be grateful to you for it,' she replied with visible effort. 'At your age, chasing round Paris tracking down the misdeeds of a young scatterbrained . . .'

'Madame, in 1765 I had the honour of meeting the illustrious Admiral de Portenduère at the home of that excellent man, Monsieur de Malesherbes, and also at the Comte de Buffon's when the latter was wanting to question him about several curious facts relating to his voyages. It's not impossible that the late Monsieur de Portenduère, your husband, was also present. At that time the French navy was in the ascendant, it was holding out against the British, and the captain threw his courage into the struggle. How impatient we all were in 1783 and 1784 to get news of the camp at Saint-Roch! I nearly enlisted as an army doctor. Admiral de Kergarouët, your great-uncle, who is still alive, fought his famous engagement about then. It was on the *Belle-Poule*.'

'Oh! if he were to find out that his great-nephew is in prison!'

'The viscount won't be in prison two days from now,' replied old Minoret, rising to go.

He held out his hand towards the old lady's, and was allowed to take it in his. Kissing it respectfully, he gave Madame de Portenduère a deep bow and left the room. But he entered it again to ask the curé: 'Would you book me a seat on the coach for tomorrow morning?'

The parish priest stayed on for another half-hour or so singing the praises of Dr Minoret, who had set out to conquer the old lady and had done so.

'He's an astonishing man for his age,' she said. 'He talks of going to Paris and dealing with my son's business as if he was only twenty-five. He has moved in good society.'

'In the very best, Viscountess; and today many an impoverished peer's son would be very happy to marry his ward, with her fortune of a million francs. Ah yes! if Savinien were to take a fancy to her, things are so different now that it wouldn't be you who would object most – not after the way your son has been behaving.'

The deep amazement which the old lady felt as a result of this last sentence allowed the curé to finish his remarks.

'You must be out of your mind, dear Abbé Chaperon.'

'Think it over, Viscountess, and Heaven help your son to behave himself properly from now on, so as to win the old man's respect!'

'If it was anyone but you, curé,' said Madame de Portenduère, 'if anyone else spoke to me like that . . .'

'You would never see them again,' smiled Abbé Chaperon. 'Let's hope your dear son will tell you how marriage alliances are treated in Paris. You must think of Savinien's happiness, and after you've already compromised his future don't stop him from achieving an establishment.'

'And are *you* telling me that?'

'If I didn't tell you, who else would?' exclaimed the priest, standing up and beating a happy retreat.

Abbé Chaperon could see Ursule and her godfather walking round and round the courtyard. In his weakness the doctor had been so pestered by his goddaughter that he had eventually given in: she wanted to go to Paris, and advanced innumerable pretexts for doing so. He called for the curé to come, and asked him to book the whole of the coupé for his use and to make the reservation that very evening if the coach office was still open. The next day, at half past six in the evening, the old man and the girl arrived in Paris, where without more ado the doctor went off to consult his notary. The political situation was threatening. The conciliative magistrate at Nemours had told the doctor several times the previous evening, during their conversation, that it was madness to keep any money invested in Government securities so long as the quarrel between the Court and the press remained unsettled. Minoret's notary agreed with the advice indirectly given by the conciliative magistrate. So the doctor put his visit to good use by selling his equities and Government securities, which at that time were all at a peak; he paid his capital into the bank. The notary urged his old client also to sell the stocks that Monsieur de Jordy had bequeathed to Ursule, which he had been looking after like a good parent. He promised to engage an extremely shrewd business agent to negotiate with Savinien's creditors; but if success was to be achieved in this, the young man had to be brave enough to remain in prison for a few more days.

'Undue haste in these matters costs you at least 15 per cent,' the notary remarked to the doctor. 'And in any case you won't have the cash from your securities for seven or eight days.'

When Ursule was told that Savinien would be at least another week in prison, she begged her guardian to allow her to go there with him just once. Old Dr Minoret refused. The uncle and his niece were staying at a hotel in the Rue Croix-des-Petits-Champs, where the doctor had taken a large and suitable apartment; knowing his ward's piety, he made her promise not to leave it whilst he was out on business errands. The doctor took Ursule for walks around Paris, showing her the arcades, shops and boulevards; but nothing amused or interested her.

'What do you want to do?' the old man would ask.

'I want to see Sainte-Pélagie,' was her stubborn reply.

Minoret then hired a cab and drove her up to the Rue de la Clef, where the carriage halted in front of the shabby exterior of the former convent, now converted into a prison. The sight of its high greyish walls with all their windows barred, the wicket gate where you have to bow your head as you enter (a terrible lesson!), and the gloomy pile surrounded by empty streets, rising up in that wretched area like some supreme symbol of wretchedness: all these melancholy things made a deep impression on Ursule, causing her to shed a few tears.

'How can they imprison young men for money?' she cried; 'how can a debt give money-lenders a power which not even the King has? To think that *he* is there! Oh! whereabouts, godfather?' she added, looking along from window to window.

'Ursule, you're making me do stupid things. *That* isn't forgetting him!'

'But if I do have to give him up, does that mean I can't show any interest in him? I can love him, and not get married.'

'Oh! there is so much sense in all this nonsense that I regret bringing you with me.'

Three days later, the old doctor had the receipts duly signed, and the certificates and all the documents pertaining to Savinien's release. Including the business agent's fees, the liquidation had cost 80,000 francs. The doctor was left with 800,000 francs, which his notary persuaded him to invest in Treasury bonds, so as not to lose too much interest. He kept back 20,000 francs in banknotes for Savinien. On the Saturday at two o'clock the doctor went in person to obtain Savinien's discharge, and the young viscount, already informed of all this in a letter from his mother, thanked his rescuer with heartfelt sincerity.

'You mustn't lose any time in coming to visit your mother,' old Dr Minoret told him.

Savinien replied with some embarrassment that he had incurred a debt of honour during his time in prison; and he related his friends' visit.

'I thought you had some preferential debt,' smiled the

doctor. 'Your mother is borrowing 100,000 francs from me, but I've only paid 80,000. Here's the remainder, take care of it, and think of what is left over as your stake in the game of chance known as Life.'

During the last week Savinien had been giving thought to the times he was living in. Competition in every walk of life demands immense hard work from those wishing to make a fortune. Illegal methods call for greater talent and more underhand dealings than a frank, honest search for wealth. Far from conferring any status on a man, social success eats up his time and requires an enormous outlay of money. Though his mother claimed it was all-powerful, the name of Portenduère counted for nothing in Paris. The Comte de Portenduère, his cousin who was a deputy, was of small account in the elective Chamber alongside the peerage and the Court, and barely enjoyed sufficient prestige for his own purposes. Admiral de Kergarouët was only important because of his wife. He had seen orators and people of lower social standing than the nobility, together with members of the lesser gentry, rise to positions of influence. Above all, money was the fulcrum, the be-all and end-all and sole driving force of a society which Louis XVIII had wished to organize on the model of England. From the Rue de la Clef to the Rue Croix-des-Petits-Champs the nobleman briefly outlined his ponderings to the old doctor, ponderings which were in line with de Marsay's advice.

'I must fade out for three or four years, and look around for a career. Perhaps I might make myself a name with a book on some serious political subject or on moral statistics, or some treatise or other on one of the burning questions of the day. Anyway, while looking around for a young wife whose private fortune can qualify me to stand for Parliament, I'll go on working silently in the shadows.'

Carefully studying the young man's face, the doctor could see that it revealed the earnestness of a man whose pride has been wounded and who is now seeking revenge. He thoroughly approved of the plan.

'Yes,' he concluded, 'providing you break with the ways of the old nobility, which are irrelevant nowadays, after three or four years of sensible behaviour and hard work I'll undertake to find you a young woman of unusual attainments, who's beautiful, agreeable, religious and with a fortune of 700,000 or 800,000 francs. She's someone you'll be proud of and she'll make you a happy man – but her only nobility is her nobility of heart.'

'But doctor,' cried the young man, 'there's no such thing as a nobility today, there's only an aristocracy now.'

'Go and settle your debts of honour, and meet me back here. I'm going to book the private compartment at the front of the stagecoach – my ward is with me,' said the old man.

That evening at six o'clock the three travellers set off in *La Ducler* from the Rue Dauphine. Ursule, wearing a veil, did not utter a word. After the day when, on an impulse of thoughtless gallantry, he had blown her the kiss that wrought as much havoc in Ursule as any love story, Savinien – in his Parisian inferno of debt – had completely forgotten the doctor's ward. Besides, his hopeless infatuation for Émilie de Kergarouët did not give him any occasion to recall a few glances exchanged with a girl in Nemours; so he did not recognize her when the old doctor climbed up after her into the closed carriage and sat down beside her so as to keep her apart from the young viscount.

'I'll have some accounts to render,' the doctor remarked to the young man. 'I'm bringing all your papers along with me.'

'I nearly didn't make it,' said Savinien. 'I had to order some new clothes and linen shirts. The Philistines took everything away from me, and I'll arrive home like the Prodigal Son.'

Interesting as were the topics of conversation between the young man and Dr Minoret, and though Savinien made some witty replies, Ursule sat silent until dawn broke, her green veil lowered over her face and her hands crossed on her shawl.

'Mademoiselle doesn't seem to have enjoyed Paris,' Savinien finally remarked, with wounded pride.

'I shall be glad to be back in Nemours,' she replied with emotion, raising her veil.

In spite of the darkness Savinien then recognized her from the size of her plaits, and her sparkling blue eyes.

'And I too have no regrets at leaving Paris, and coming to

live in the obscurity of Nemours – I shall be close to my beautiful neighbour again,' he said. 'I hope, doctor, you will allow me to visit you; I'm fond of music, and I remember hearing Mademoiselle Ursule playing the piano.'

'I don't know,' the doctor replied gravely, 'whether your mother would like you to visit an old man who has to show this dear girl all the loving attention of a mother.'

His carefully phrased reply gave Savinien much to think about, and the young man then remembered the kiss that he had so thoughtlessly blown. Dusk had fallen, the heat was oppressive, and Savinien and the doctor were the first to doze off. Ursule stayed awake for a long time making plans, but she too fell asleep about midnight. She had taken off her little hat made of ordinary woven straw. Her head, with its embroidered bonnet, was soon lying against her godfather's shoulder. By daybreak they were at Bouron, and Savinien was the first to waken. He noticed that the jogging of the coach had thrown Ursule's head into disarray: her bonnet was crumpled and twisted up; her loose plaits fell down on either side of her face, which was flushed with the heat of the carriage: a horrifying situation for women who have to pay careful attention to their dress and make-up, but one in which youth and beauty are triumphant. Innocent people always sleep beautifully. Her half-open lips revealed pretty teeth; beneath the folds of a printed muslin dress her disarranged shawl disclosed the firmness of Ursule's breasts, without any offence to her modesty. And the purity of her virgin soul shone in her face, all the more visibly in that it was untroubled by any other expression. Old Dr Minoret, waking up, placed his goddaughter's head back in the corner of the carriage, so that she should be more comfortable; she let him do so without even noticing the fact, so deeply was she asleep after all the nights she had spent thinking of Savinien's misfortune.

'Poor girl!' he remarked to his neighbour. 'She's sleeping like a child, which is what she is.'

'You must be proud of her,' replied Savinien, 'she seems as good as she is lovely!'

'Yes, she brings joy to my home. Even if she were my own daughter, I couldn't be fonder of her. She'll be sixteen on 5

147

February. May God grant me strength to live long enough to see her married to a man who'll make her happy! I wanted to take her out to the theatre in Paris, it was her first visit; she didn't want to go, the parish priest at Nemours had forbidden her to do so. "But," I said, "when you're married, supposing your husband wanted to take you?" "I'll do anything my husband wants," was her reply. "If he asks me to do something wicked and I am weak enough to obey him, he will be answerable for those offences before God; and so I shall find the strength to resist him – in his own best interest, naturally."'

On arriving at Nemours at five in the morning, Ursule woke up quite ashamed of her disorderly appearance, and bashful at noticing Savinien's admiring look. During the hour that the coach took to get from Bouron, where it stopped for a few minutes, the young man had fallen in love with Ursule. He had studied the artlessness of her soul, the beauty of her body, the whiteness of her complexion, the delicacy of her features, the charm of her voice uttering the short yet so expressive sentence in which the poor child said everything without wishing to say anything. Besides which he had a feeling that Ursule was the wife the doctor had been describing to him, encircling her image with the golden magic words: '700,000 to 800,000 francs!'

'In three or four years' time she'll be twenty, I'll be twenty-seven; the old fellow has spoken of trials, hard work and good behaviour! Although he seems a shrewd man, he'll eventually reveal his secret.'

The three neighbours parted in front of their homes, and Savinien's good-byes were advances in themselves as he glanced at Ursule with an appealing look. Madame de Portenduère let her son sleep till midday. Though tired after their journey, the doctor and Ursule attended High Mass. Savinien's release and return home with the doctor had explained the purpose of Minoret's absence to the politically minded townsfolk and the collateral heirs gathered together in the market-place in an assembly similar to the one they had held there a fortnight before. To the great astonishment of the various groups, Madame de Portenduère stopped old Dr Minoret as they were coming out of mass, and the doctor offered her his arm and walked home with her. The old lady wanted to ask him into dinner along with his ward, that very day, saying that the curé would be the other guest.

'He will have wanted to show Ursule round Paris,' said Minoret-Levrault.

'Damn it,' cried Crémière, 'the old fellow won't go a step without the little girl being with him.'

'For old mother Portenduère to have offered him her arm,' said Massin, 'there must be some real monkey business going on between them.'

'But don't you realize that your uncle's sold his investment income to get young Portenduère out of clink?' cried Goupil. 'He refused my master, but he hasn't refused his mistress ... Oh yes, you're all done for! The viscount will suggest entering into a marriage settlement rather than a recognizance, and the doctor will convey to his darling goddaughter – through her husband – the amount that will have to be put down for such a marriage to be arranged.'

'It wouldn't be a bad idea to marry Ursule to Monsieur Savinien,' said the butcher. 'The old lady's inviting Dr Minoret to dinner today. Tiennette came round at five o'clock to order a fillet of beef.'

'Well, Dionis, this is a fine how-d'ye-do,' said Massin, running up to the notary as he came walking into the square.

'What do you mean? Everything's all right!' answered the notary. 'Your uncle has sold his investment income, and Madame de Portenduère has asked me to call to witness a recognizance for a mortgage of 100,000 francs on her property advanced by your uncle.'

'Yes, but supposing the young people get married?'

'That's as likely as saying that Goupil is my successor,' answered the notary.

'Both are possibilities!' said Goupil.

On getting back from mass, Madame de Portenduère sent Tiennette to tell her son that she wished to see him.

Her little house had three bedrooms on the first floor. Madame de Portenduère's and the one used by her late husband were on the same side, with a large bathroom between them lit by a window overlooking a neighbour's property, and linked by a little anteroom which opened on to the staircase. The other bedroom, which had always been occupied by Savinien, was like his father's in that it looked out over the street. The staircase at the back was so designed as to allow this bedroom a small dressing-room lit by a small circular window facing the courtyard. Madame de Portenduère's bedroom, the gloomiest in the whole house, overlooked the courtyard; but she spent her life in the sitting-room on the ground floor, which was linked by a passage to the kitchen at the far end of the courtyard; so that this room was both drawing-room and dining-room combined. Monsieur de Portenduère's bedroom had been left just as it was on the day of his death: all that was lacking was the deceased husband! Madame de Portenduère had made the bed herself, placing on the counterpane the captain's uniform worn by her husband and his sword, red ribbon, orders and hat. The gold snuff-box from which the viscount had taken his last pinch of snuff stood on the bedside table beside his prayer book, watch and the cup from which he had drunk. His white hair, arranged in a single lock, had been framed and hung above the crucifix with its holy-water stoup in the alcove. And the knick-knacks he used to use, his newspapers, furniture, Dutch spittoon, the telescope that had served him in his campaigns and now hung by his mantelpiece: nothing was missing. His widow had stopped the old wall-clock at the hour of his death, and so it would remain for ever. The dead man's snuff and wig-powder could still be smelt. The hearth was untouched. To enter his room was to see him again, reminded of his habits by all the things one found there. His large gold-pommelled walking-stick lay where he had left it, with his thick doeskin gloves close by. On the console-table shone a gold vase, which was crudely modelled but worth 3,000 francs; it had been presented to him by Havana, which he had protected from a British attack during the American War of Independence by engaging superior numbers after leading the fleet he had been escorting safely into port. In recompense the King of Spain had made him a knight of the Spanish orders of chivalry. Raised because of this to the rank of commodore at the next naval promotion, he was given the order of St Louis. He was now certain of appointment to the first vacancy, and so able to marry; his wife brought him a fortune of 200,000 francs. But the French Revolution prevented his promotion, and Monsieur de Portenduère sought refuge abroad.

'Where's mother?' Savinien asked Tiennette.

'She's waiting for you in your father's bedroom,' the old Breton replied.

Savinien could not control a shudder. He knew the rigidity of his mother's principles, her cult of honour, loyalty, and faith in nobility; and he foresaw a scene. And so he went to his interview as to an assault, with pallid face and beating heart. In the half-light filtering through the shutters he found his mother dressed in black; she had assumed an air of solemnity in keeping with the funereal bedroom.

'Viscount,' she said as soon as she saw him, taking his hand to lead him over to his father's bed, 'there your father died. He was a man of honour. He died without any cause for self-reproach. His spirit is still present here. He must indeed have groaned in Heaven to see his son tarnish his reputation in a debtors' prison. In the days of the old monarchy, you would have been spared this stigma by being granted an order under the King's personal seal and then being shut up in a state prison for a few days. But here anyway you are in your father's presence, and he is listening to you. You know everything you did before entering that ignoble jail. Can you swear to me, before God who sees everything, and in the presence of your father's memory, that you committed no dishonourable action, that your debts were caused by the waywardness of youth, that your honour is untarnished? If your blameless father were here, alive in that armchair, and asked for an account of your behaviour, would he embrace you after hearing your story?'

'Yes, mother,' answered the young man with respectful gravity.

She stretched out her arms to him and clasped him to her heart, shedding a few tears.

'Well then, let everything be forgotten,' she said. 'We've only lost money. I shall pray to God that He may help us to recover it. And as you are still worthy of your name, embrace me: I have gone through so much!'

'I swear, mother,' he said, stretching his hand over the bed, 'never to give you any anxiety of that kind again, and to do everything possible to make amends for my early mistakes.'

'Come and have lunch, my boy,' she said, leaving the room.

If the laws of the stage are to be applied to the novel, then Savinien's arrival, bringing to the town the one character still missing from its *dramatis personae*, concludes our Exposition.

PART TWO

12. The Lovers Meet with Obstacles

THE action of the story began with an impulse so frequently used in literature, both past and present, that no one could believe it to be possible in 1829, if it were not the work of an old Breton woman, a Kergarouët, an aristocratic refugee from the Revolution! But let the fact be immediately admitted: by 1829 the nobility had recovered in its ways of life a little of the ground that it had lost in politics. Besides, the feeling that sways grandparents wherever the suitability of a marriage partner is concerned is an imperishable feeling, closely linked to the very existence of civilized societies and stemming from a notion of family solidarity. It is to be found in both Geneva and Vienna, as in Nemours where Zélie Levrault had been refusing to allow her son to marry a bastard's daughter. Nevertheless, there is an exception to every social law. Savinien hoped therefore to bend his mother's pride by showing her Ursule's inner nobility of character. The confrontation was immediate. As soon as Savinien had sat down at the table, his mother spoke to him of the horrible letters (as she called them) written to her by the Kergarouëts and Portenduères.

'There's no such thing as the Family nowadays, mother,' Savinien replied, 'there are only individuals! The members of the nobility no longer stand solidly in support of one another. Nowadays people don't ask you whether you're a Portenduère, whether you're brave, whether you're a statesman, they only ever ask you: How much tax do you pay?'

'And what about the King?' asked the old lady.

'The King is torn between the two Chambers like a man between his wife and his mistress. And so I must marry a wealthy girl, whatever family she comes from, even a peasant's daughter if she has a million francs dowry and is sufficiently well brought up – if she's been to a boarding school, that is.'

'That's different!' answered the old lady.

Savinien frowned at these words. He well knew the granite will-power, or Breton stubbornness, that characterized his mother, and was anxious to find out immediately what her opinion was on this delicate question.

'So supposing I loved a girl such as our neighbour's ward, for example, young Ursule. Would you object to my marriage?'

'Yes, as long as I live. After my death, you alone will be answerable for the honour and blood of the Portenduères and Kergarouëts.'

'So you'd let me die of hunger and despair for the sake of a phantom ideal which only becomes a reality nowadays if it's backed up by the prestige of wealth!'

'You would serve France and trust in God!'

'You would prevent me from being happy until after your death?'

'It would be a horrible thing for you to do, that's all.'

'Louis XIV nearly married Mazarin's niece, and Mazarin was a parvenu.'

'Mazarin himself was against the idea.'

'And what about Scarron's widow?'

'She was a d'Aubigné! Besides, it was a secret marriage. But I am very old,' she added, shaking her head. 'When I'm no longer alive, you will marry as you please.'

Savinien both loved and respected his mother; he immediately decided, though only in his heart of hearts, to resist this old Kergarouët stubbornness with an equal stubbornness of his own. He vowed never to have any wife other than Ursule, who (as always happens in such circumstances) derived from his mother's opposition the merit of forbidden delight.

When Ursule, wearing white and pink, and Dr Minoret entered this cold room after vespers, she was seized with a nervous trembling as if she was in the Queen of France's presence, with some favour to ask of Her Majesty. After her frank discussion with the doctor, this little house had taken on the proportions of a palace and the old lady had assumed all the social prestige that a duchess must have had in the Middle Ages in the eyes of a villein's daughter. Never did Ursule realize more despondently than now the distance that separated a Vicomte de Portenduère from the daughter of a military director of music, an organist's illegitimate son and formerly a singer at the Théâtre des Italiens: a girl who depended for her very existence on a doctor's goodwill.

'What is the matter, child?' the old lady asked her, motioning to her to sit down beside her.

'Madam, I am overcome by the honour you have condescended to do me . . .'

'But, my dear girl,' answered Madame de Portenduère in her bitterest tone, 'I know how much your guardian loves you and I wish to please him, since he has brought my Prodigal Son home to me.'

'But dear mother,' protested Savinien, stricken to the heart at the sight of Ursule's vivid blush and the horrible contortion of her face as she held back her tears, 'even if you were under no obligation at all to Chevalier Minoret, I think we could still be happy at the pleasure Mademoiselle is kind enough to give us by accepting your invitation.' And the young nobleman clasped the doctor's hand meaningfully, adding: 'I see, sir, you are wearing the order of Saint-Michel, the most ancient of French orders of chivalry, one that always confers nobility.'

Ursule's extreme beauty, and the fact that her almost hopeless love had given her during the last few days that depth of character which great painters have imprinted upon portraits of theirs that strongly suggest qualities of soul, had suddenly struck Madame de Portenduère, leading her to suspect that beneath the doctor's generosity lay ambitious scheming. Her reply to Savinien was therefore phrased with the object of wounding the old man in what he held most dear; but he could not help smiling at being called 'Chevalier' by Savinien, and he saw in this exaggeration the boldness of a lover who does not shrink from any ridicule.

'People once used to commit many absurdities, Viscount, in order to obtain the order of Saint-Michel,' said Dr Minoret. 'But it has fallen into as much decay as so many other privileges! Nowadays it is only given to doctors and impoverished artists. It was wise of the kings of France to unite it with the order of Saint-Lazare – I believe Lazarus was a poor fellow miraculously called back to life! In this sense the orders of Saint-Michel and Saint-Lazare have a symbolic value for us.'

After this reply, full of both mockery and dignity, there was a silence which no one seemed inclined to break. It had become embarrassing when there was a sudden knock at the door.

'Here is our dear curé,' said Madame de Portenduère, rising to her feet, leaving Ursule on her own and walking to meet Abbé Chaperon, an honour which she had not paid either to Ursule or the doctor.

Dr Minoret smiled as he looked in turn from his ward to Savinien. To complain of Madame de Portenduère's manners, or to take offence at them, was a trap into which a small-minded man would have fallen; but Minoret had too much experience of the world not to avoid it: he began to chat with the viscount about the danger Charles X was then running in appointing the Prince de Polignac as his Prime Minister. When enough time had gone by for the doctor not to seem to be taking revenge in turning the discussion to business matters, he half jokingly presented the old lady with the files relating to creditors' claims and those containing receipted accounts supporting his notary's bill.

'Has my son agreed it?' she asked, looking towards Savinien, who nodded his assent. 'Well then, Dionis must deal with it,' she added, pushing the papers to one side and treating the whole episode with the contempt she considered money to deserve.

In Madame de Portenduère's eyes, to denigrate wealth was to exalt nobility and deprive the bourgeoisie of all its importance. A few moments later Goupil arrived with a message from his employer asking for a settlement of accounts between Savinien and Dr Minoret.

'Why do you want them?' asked the old lady.

'As the basis for the recognizance. There has been no transfer of cash,' replied the head clerk, impudently looking around the room.

Ursule and Savinien, both of whom were now seeing this horrible character for the first time, felt as if they were in contact with a toad, but it was a feeling overlaid with sinister foreboding. Both had a dim and indefinable vision of the future, such as no words can describe but which could be explained by one of those inner impulses of character mentioned by the

Swedenborgian to Dr Minoret. Ursule trembled at the certainty that this venomous lawyer would prove fatal to them both, but overcame her agitation through the unspeakable joy it gave her to see that Savinien was sharing her feeling.

'Monsieur Dionis's clerk isn't what you would call handsome!' said Savinien as the door closed behind Goupil.

'And what does it matter whether such people are handsome or ugly?' asked Madame de Portenduère.

'I don't mind his ugliness,' commented Abbé Chaperon, 'but I do mind his extraordinary capacity for evil. He's a rogue with it, too.'

Despite his wish to please, the doctor grew reserved and chilly. This embarrassed the two lovers. But for Abbé Chaperon's friendly good nature, enlivening the dinner with gentle gaiety, the position of the doctor and Ursule would have been almost unbearable. At dessert, noticing Ursule growing paler, he remarked: 'If you're not feeling well, dear, you've only to cross the road.'

'What's the matter, child?' asked the old lady.

'Alas!' was the doctor's harsh reply, 'she feels chilled to the heart – she is so used to seeing nothing but smiles.'

'Then she has been very badly brought up, doctor. Hasn't she, curé?'

'Yes, Madame,' answered Minoret with a look at the curé, who was at a loss for words. 'I realize I have made life impossible for her angelic nature if she had to move in worldly circles; but before I die I shall have placed her beyond the reach of coldness, indifference and hatred.'

'Godfather! don't say any more, please! I'm quite all right!' she said, facing towards Madame de Portenduère rather than give away her meaning by looking in Savinien's direction.

'I don't know whether Mademoiselle Ursule is unwell,' said Savinien to his mother, 'but I do know that you are putting me through tortures.'

On hearing these words wrung from the warm-hearted young man by the way his mother had been behaving, Ursule went pale and begged Madame de Portenduère to excuse her; she rose, took her guardian's arm, bowed, left the room, returned home, and rushed to her godfather's drawing-room where she sat down beside her piano, buried her head in her hands, and burst into tears.

'Why don't you let me guide you in your feelings, you cruel girl? I have much more experience!' cried the doctor in despair. 'Aristocrats never have any feelings of gratitude towards us middle-class folk. If we help them, we're just doing our duty. Besides, the old lady has noticed Savinien's interest in you; she's afraid he's in love with you.'

'Well anyway, he's saved, isn't he? But to try and humiliate a man like you! . . .'

'Wait here for me, my dear.'

When the doctor returned to Madame de Portenduère's home, he found Dionis had arrived along with Monsieur Bongrand and Monsieur Levrault, the mayor, the witnesses required by the law for the validation of deeds in districts where there is only a notary. Minoret took Monsieur Dionis to one side and whispered something into his ear, after which the notary read the recognizance aloud: in it Madame de Portenduère mortgaged all her property until the repayment of the 100,000 francs lent by the doctor to the viscount, on which the interest rate was stipulated as 5 per cent. When this clause was read out the curé looked at Minoret, who answered Chaperon with a slight nod of the head. The poor priest then whispered a few words into Madame de Portenduère's ear, to which she replied in an undertone: 'I don't want to owe those people anything.'

'My mother is giving me a fine part to play,' said Savinien to the doctor. 'She'll repay you all the money, but she asks me to sign the recognizance.'

'But you'll have to find 11,000 francs the first year, because of the expenses over the contract,' the curé remarked.

'As Monsieur and Madame de Portenduère are in no position to pay for the registration,' Minoret said to Dionis, 'add the contract fees to the loan capital. I'll settle them.'

Dionis made some alterations, and the loan capital was then agreed at 107,000 francs. When everything was signed, Minoret excused himself from the company on the pretext of tiredness, and left along with the notary and witnesses.

The parish priest remained alone with the Viscount and

Madame de Portenduère. 'Why,' he asked her, 'did you upset that excellent man, Dr Minoret, when he has saved you at least 25,000 francs in Paris, and was considerate enough to leave your son 20,000 francs to pay off his debts of honour?'

'Your friend Minoret is a sly fellow,' she replied, taking a pinch of snuff. 'He knows what he's about.'

'Mother thinks he wants to force me to marry his ward by swallowing up our farm, as if a Portenduère, the son of a Kergarouët, could be forced into marrying someone against his will.'

An hour later Savinien called at the doctor's house, where the collateral family had already arrived, attracted there out of curiosity. The young viscount's appearance caused a keen sensation – all the keener as the emotions it aroused were different in each one of the persons present. Mademoiselle Crémière and Mademoiselle Massin whispered together, watching as Ursule blushed. The mothers remarked to Désiré that Goupil could well be right about the marriage. All eyes then turned to the doctor, who did not rise to welcome the nobleman but simply greeted him with a nod of the head without putting down his dice box – he was playing a game of backgammon with Monsieur Bongrand. The doctor's coldness surprised everyone.

'Ursule, dear,' he said, 'play us a little music.'

Seeing the young girl run towards her instrument, happy to have a way of keeping her composure, and handling the green-bound music volumes, the doctor's heirs resigned themselves with a show of delight to the silence and torture that were about to be inflicted upon them – they were so eager to know what was afoot between their uncle and the Portenduères.

It sometimes happens that a piece of music which, though poor in itself, is played by a young girl with deep feeling can make more of an impression than a grand overture pompously performed by a skilful orchestra. Besides the musical ideas of the composer, all music expresses the soul of the performer, who by a privilege solely confined to that art can give meaning and poetic feeling to musical phrases of little value. Chopin's mastery of the awkward piano is again proving the truth of this fact, which Paganini has already demonstrated for the violin. This brilliant genius is not so much a musician as a soul of great sensitivity which could express itself in any kind of music, even in simple chords. Ursule's sublime and delicate constitution placed her amongst that group of rare geniuses; but old Schmucke, the master who came each Saturday and who saw her every day during her stay in Paris, had developed his pupil's talent to its fullest perfection. The Dream of Rousseau, the piece chosen by Ursule and one of Hérold's youthful compositions, is not in any case lacking in a certain depth that can be developed in performance; filling it with the feelings that troubled her, she fully justified the title of Capriccio by which this fragment is known. Through her playing, which was at once pleasant and dreamy, her soul communicated with that of the young man, enfolding him as in a cloud with ideas that were almost visible. Seated at the end of the piano, with his elbow against the lid and his head resting in his left hand, Savinien was admiring Ursule, who stared at the wooden panelling, her eyes seemingly concentrating on another mysterious world. It would have been possible to fall deeply in love for less. Genuine feelings have their own magnetic appeal, and Ursule wanted somehow to reveal her soul, like a flirtatious girl dressing up in order to please. So Savinien gained insight into that delightful realm, led along by his heart, whose self-expression derived strength from the unique art of communicating with the thoughts of another through one's own thoughts, without the aid of words, colours or form. Artlessness has the same captivating effect on a man as childhood, it has the same attraction and irresistible charm; moreover, Ursule was never more artless than in this moment when she was spiritually reborn. The parish priest arrived and tore the nobleman away from his reverie, asking him to make a fourth at whist. Ursule carried on playing and the heirs departed, except for Désiré who wanted to know what the intentions of his great-uncle, the viscount and Ursule were.

'You are as talented as you are soulful,' Savinien said as the young girl closed her piano and came to sit beside her godfather. 'Who is your teacher?'

'A German who lives close by the Rue Dauphine, on the Quai Conti,' the doctor answered. 'If he hadn't given Ursule a lesson every day during our stay in Paris, he'd have come down this morning.'

'He's not only a great musician but an adorably simple man,' Ursule added.

'The lessons must be expensive,' cried Désiré.

The card-players exchanged an ironical smile. When the game was over, the doctor, who had been anxious until then, looked at Savinien with the air of a man grieved at having a painful duty to fulfil.

'Monsieur,' the doctor began, 'I am most grateful to you for the kindly feeling that has caused you to call on me so promptly; but your mother suspects me of very unworthy ulterior motives, and I would give her grounds for believing them true if I did not beg you not to visit me again, even though I should be honoured by your visits and delighted to know you better. My honour and peace of mind demand that we should cease all neighbourly intercourse. Tell your mother that if I do not ask her to do my ward and myself the honour of dining with us next Sunday it is only because I am certain that on that day she would be ill.'

The old man held out his hand to the young viscount, who shook it respectfully, saying: 'You're right, sir!' And he withdrew, with a parting bow to Ursule that revealed more melancholy than disappointment.

Désiré left at the same time as the nobleman, but could not exchange a word with him as Savinien hurried home.

For two days the quarrel between Dr Minoret and the Portenduères was the staple topic of conversation amongst the doctor's family, who paid tribute to Dionis's ability and now considered their inheritance secure. And so it came about that in a century when social distinctions are disappearing, when the craze for equality puts all men on an equal footing and threatens everything, even military subordination, the last stronghold of power in France, a century in which therefore no other obstacles remain to the fulfilment of passion than personal antipathy and disparities of wealth, a stubborn old

163

Breton woman and a proud doctor raised barriers between the two lovers, whose passion (as always happens) they strengthened rather than destroyed. A passionate man prizes a woman for the difficulties experienced in winning her. The struggles, efforts and uncertainties which Savinien saw ahead of him made Ursule seem all the more precious; he was eager to gain her love. Perhaps our feelings obey the laws of nature concerning the longevity of its creatures, those destined to a long life being also destined to a long childhood!

13. A Betrothal of Hearts

THE next morning both Ursule and Savinien had the same thought as they rose. Such an accord would give rise to love, if it were not the most delightful proof of it. When Ursule gently drew her curtains apart so as to have just enough space to peep through at Savinien, she glimpsed her admirer's face above the espagnolette of the window opposite. In view of the immense benefits that windows confer on lovers, it is only natural to impose a window tax! Having thus protested against her godfather's strictness, Ursule let the curtains fall to again and opened her windows to close the slatted shutters through which she could then see without being seen. She must have gone up to her bedroom seven or eight times during the day, always to find Savinien writing away, tearing up his paper and beginning again: no doubt he was writing to her!

Next morning La Bougival handed Ursule the following letter as she awoke.

TO URSULE

Mademoiselle,

I am under no illusion about the distrust a young man must create when he has got into the situation from which I only escaped through your godfather's intervention; from now on I must give more guarantees of good conduct than any other man. And this thought makes me deeply humble in protesting my love to you. It is no mere passion which dictates this declaration, but a certainty that will last for a lifetime. I was thrown into jail because of my foolish infatuation for my young aunt, Madame de Kergarouët; I hope you will accept as proof of my sincere love for you the fact that she has completely vanished from my thoughts, her image having been driven from my heart by yours. From the very first moment I saw you looking so lovely and child-like when you were asleep at Bouron, you have reigned over my heart like a queen over her empire. I only wish you to be my wife. You have all the refinements I could hope for in the woman who is to bear my name. Your education and nobility of heart fit you for the highest of social stations. But I am too uncertain of myself to attempt to describe you to yourself, I can only love you. After hearing you yesterday, I remembered these sentences which seem as if they were written about you:

'Born to appeal to the heart and bewitch the eye, both gentle and indulgent, witty and sensible, as polished in manner as if she had spent her life in courts, as artless as a solitary who has known nothing of the world, her eyes in their divine modesty temper the ardour of her soul.'

I have felt the full worth of the beautiful soul which you reveal even in the smallest things. And this gives me the boldness to ask whether, if you are not already in love, you will allow me to prove by my attentions and behaviour that I am worthy of you. My whole life is involved in this. Do not doubt that all my strength is devoted not only to pleasing you but also to deserving your respect, which is all the world to me. With this hope, Ursule, and if you will allow me to worship you in my heart, Nemours will be like Paradise itself, and the hardest of ventures will present nothing but delights that I shall offer up to you as one offers up everything to God. Pray allow me, therefore, to sign myself

> Your
> SAVINIEN.

Ursule kissed this letter; then, after rereading it and handling it with frantic impulsiveness, she dressed and went to show it to her godfather.

'Heavens! I nearly missed saying my prayers,' she said, coming back into her bedroom to kneel at her prie-dieu.

A few moments later she went down into the garden, where she found her guardian and got him to read Savinien's letter. Both sat on the garden-seat, under the clump of creepers opposite the Chinese pavilion: Ursule waited for the old man to speak, and the old man spent far too long in thought for an impatient girl. Their secret discussion resulted, however, in the following letter, written no doubt partly at the doctor's dictation.

Monsieur,

I am most honoured by the letter in which you offer me your hand; but, at my age and according to the dictates of my up-bringing, I had to show it to my guardian, who is the only family I have and whom I love both as a father and a friend. Here now are the cruel objections he has raised, objections which must serve as my reply.

I am, sir, a poor girl whose future fortune entirely depends not only on my godfather's goodwill but also on the risky steps he will be taking to thwart his family's ill-will towards me. I am the legitimate daughter of Joseph Mirouët, director of music in the 45th Regiment of Foot; but as he was the illegitimate brother of my guardian's wife, a lawsuit could unjustifiably be brought against a defenceless young girl. As you can see, monsieur, my slender means are not the greatest of my misfortunes. I have many reasons to be humble. It is for your sake, not mine, that I am making these remarks, which are often easy to endure for loving devoted hearts. But please also bear in mind that if I did not put these remarks to you I should be suspected of wanting your love to triumph over obstacles which would appear invincible to outsiders and especially to your mother. I shall be sixteen in four months' time. Perhaps you will admit that we are both of us too young and inexperienced to battle with the hardships of a life entered into with no other fortune than the money I have inherited through the kindness of Monsieur de Jordy. Besides, my guardian does not want me to marry before I am twenty. Who knows what fate may have in store for you during those four years, the finest in your life? So do not ruin your life for a poor girl's sake.

Far from opposing my happiness, my dear godfather wishes to promote it to the utmost. His protective care will soon grow weaker, but he hopes it will be replaced by a love equal to his own. I have now explained his reasons to you, and can only add how touched I am both by your offer and by the affectionate compliments that go with it. This letter reflects the prudent outlook of an old man with much experience of life, but also the gratitude of a girl to whom all other feelings are unknown and who can therefore sign herself

Your sincere servant,
URSULE MIROUËT.

Savinien did not reply. Was he trying to win over his mother? Had his love been killed by Ursule's letter? Innumerable questions of this kind – all insoluble – were horrible torments both to Ursule and (through her) to the doctor, who was pained by the slightest signs of anxiety in his dear godchild. Ursule would often go upstairs to her bedroom and look across at Savinien, sitting there so thoughtfully at his table and often turning his eyes towards her windows. Not until the end of that week did she receive the following letter from Savinien, whose delay had been due to an excess of love.

Dear Ursule,

I have a little of the Breton in me; once I have made my mind up, nothing can change it for me. Your guardian, whose life may God preserve for many years, is right; but does that mean I am wrong to love you? I am only anxious to know whether you love me. Tell me yes, or just hint it with a sign, and then these next four years will become the finest in my life!

A friend of mine has handed my great-uncle, Vice-Admiral de Kergarouët, a letter in which I ask him to support me for a ranking in the Navy. Touched by my misfortunes, the worthy old man has replied that if I wished for a commission naval regulations would prevent the exercise of the King's favour. However, after three months' study at Toulon the Admiralty will give me the rank of yeoman of signals; then, after a cruising expedition against the Algerians with whom we are at war I can sit an examination and become a midshipman. And if I distinguish myself in the offensive being mounted against Algiers, I shall certainly become a sub-lieutenant; but how long will that take? . . . It is impossible to say. All I know is that the regulations will be bent as far as they possibly may in order to get the name of Portenduère back on to the Navy list. I realize I can only obtain your hand with your godfather's consent; and in your respect for him you are all the dearer to me. Before replying to you, I shall seek an interview with him: my whole future hangs on *his* reply. But whatever happens, I want you to know that, rich or poor, a king's daughter or the daughter of a director of music, you are the girl marked out for me by the promptings of my heart. Dear Ursule, we live in an age when prejudices that would once have kept us apart no longer have the power to prevent our marriage. To you I give all the affection of my heart, and to your uncle guarantees that will assure him of your happiness! He does not realize I have loved you more in a few moments than he has loved you for the past fifteen years. Till this evening!

'Look, godfather,' said Ursule, proudly handing him the letter.
'Yes, child,' the doctor answered after reading it, 'I am

happier than you are. The young nobleman's decision has made up for all his faults.'

After dinner Savinien called on the doctor, who was strolling with Ursule along the balustraded terrace overlooking the river. The viscount's clothes had been sent down from Paris, and the young suitor had taken care to enhance his natural advantages by dressing as neatly and elegantly as if he had been trying to attract the proud and beautiful Comtesse de Kergarouët. As he came down the steps towards them, the poor girl gripped her uncle's arm just as if she was struggling to avoid falling over a precipice and the doctor shuddered to hear her deep, muffled palpitations.

'Leave us to ourselves, my dear child,' he told his ward, who sat down on the steps of the Chinese pavilion after first giving her hand to Savinien, who kissed it respectfully.

'Sir, will you allow this dear girl to marry a naval captain?' the young viscount whispered to the doctor.

'No,' Minoret smiled; 'we might have to wait too long; but . . . a naval lieutenant is another matter.'

Tears of joy moistened the young man's eyes as he shook the old doctor's hand with deep affection.

'So now I shall go away to study, and try to pick up in ten months what naval cadets take six years to master.'

'Go away?' cried Ursule, rushing down the steps towards them.

'Yes, Mademoiselle, so as to become worthy of you. You see, the greater my eagerness, the greater my affection for you.'

'Today is the 3rd of October,' she said, looking at him with eyes overflowing with tenderness. 'Stay till the 19th.'

'Yes,' interposed the doctor, 'then we can celebrate St Sabinian's day.'

'Good-bye then. I must be in Paris this week, making the necessary contacts and preparations, buying books and mathematical instruments, obtaining the Minister's protection and getting the best possible conditions of entry.'

Ursule and her godfather walked back with Savinien as far as the iron gate. They saw him returning to his mother's house, and then leaving it, with Tiennette carrying a small trunk.

'You are rich. Why are you making him serve in the Navy?' Ursule inquired of her godfather.

'Before long it will be my fault he ran up his debts!' Minoret smiled. 'I'm not making him do anything; but lots of faults can be wiped out by a naval uniform and the cross of the Legion of Honour gained in battle. Within six years he may have command of a ship; that's all I'm asking of him.'

'But he may be killed,' she answered the doctor, growing pale at the thought.

'Lovers are like cats. They have nine lives,' he replied facetiously.

Unknown to her godfather, and with La Bougival's help, the poor girl cut off as much of her beautiful, long, blond hair that night as was needed to make a chain; then two days later, she artfully persuaded her music-master, old Schmucke, to make sure that the hair was not changed and that the chain would be ready by the following Sunday. On his return, Savinien informed the doctor and Ursule that he had signed on. He was due to report for duty at Brest on the 25th. The doctor invited him to dine on the 18th, and he spent almost the whole of those two days at the doctor's house. Despite the most prudent warnings, the two lovers could not help betraying their innermost feelings to the curé, the conciliative magistrate, the Nemours doctor and La Bougival.

'You are putting your happiness at risk if you don't keep your secret to yourselves,' the doctor warned them.

Savinien's name-day finally came round. A few looks were exchanged during mass; afterwards, secretly watched by Ursule, the young man crossed the road and entered the little garden, where the couple were almost alone. The doctor had favoured them by reading his newspapers in the Chinese pavilion.

'Dear Ursule,' Savinien began, 'will you on my name-day give me even greater joy than my mother could, by giving me life for a second time?'

'I know what you want to ask me,' Ursule interrupted. 'Look, here's my reply,' and from her pinafore pocket she took out the chain made of her hair and gave it him with a nervous trembling that betrayed her boundless happiness. 'Wear this if you love me. May this gift shield you from every danger, as it reminds you that my life is bound up with yours!'

'The little scamp is giving him a chain of her hair,' thought the doctor. 'How has she managed that? Cutting at those lovely blond plaits! ... She'd even shed my blood for his sake!'

'Would you think it very awful of me to ask you before I leave for a solemn promise not to marry anyone else?' asked Savinien, kissing the hair-chain and unable to hold back his tears as he looked at Ursule.

'Haven't I made that clear enough to you already, when I came to gaze at the walls of Sainte-Pélagie when you were there?' she answered, blushing; 'I promise you again, Savinien: I shall never love anyone except you, and never marry anyone except you.'

Seeing Ursule half-hidden by the clump of creepers, the young man could not resist the pleasure of hugging her to his heart and kissing her forehead; but she gave a feeble cry, sank on to the garden-seat, and when Savinien sat down beside her asking her forgiveness, he saw the doctor standing in front of them.

'Young man,' said Minoret, 'Ursule is a really sensitive girl who would be killed by a harsh word. For her sake, you must control your passionate love. Ah! if you had loved her for sixteen years, you'd have been satisfied with her word,' he added out of revenge for Savinien's closing remark in his last letter.

Two days later, Savinien left Nemours. Despite his regular letters to Ursule, she developed an illness that seemed without physical cause. Just as a beautiful fruit is devoured by maggots, so one thought gnawed at her heart. She lost her appetite and beautiful complexion. The first time her godfather asked her what was the matter, she replied: 'I would like to see the sea.'

'It's not very easy to take you to a seaport in December,' the old man answered.

'Shall I ever go, then?'

Whenever it blew a gale Ursule went through paroxysms of anxiety, thinking, despite the learned distinctions between gales and storms drawn by her godfather, the parish priest and the magistrate, that Savinien was battling against a hurricane. For a few days she was filled with happiness when the magistrate gave her an engraving of a midshipman in full uniform. She read the newspapers, imagining that they would have news of Savinien's expeditionary voyage. She voraciously read Fenimore Cooper's seafaring novels, and tried to learn nautical terms. Such proofs of constant thought, often feigned by other women, were so natural in Ursule that she dreamed in advance of every letter that ever came to her from Savinien, and regularly predicted them on the very morning of their arrival as she described the premonitory dreams.

'Now I can rest content,' she said to the doctor on the fourth occurrence of this phenomenon, which did not surprise the parish priest and doctor; 'whatever distance I am from Savinien, I shall know immediately if he's wounded.'

The old doctor sat deep in meditation and from the expression on his face the magistrate and the parish priest could see that they were painful thoughts.

'What's the matter with you?' they asked when Ursule had left them.

'Can she survive?' answered the old doctor. 'Can such a tender, delicate flower withstand emotional stress?'

Nevertheless, the 'dreamy child' (as the parish priest nicknamed her) was intensely active; she realized the importance of a thorough education to any woman of fashion, and whenever she was not engaged in singing or studying harmony and composition she was reading the books chosen for her by Abbé Chaperon from her godfather's extensive library. Though leading a busy life, she suffered but did not complain. Sometimes she would sit for hours on end looking across at Savinien's window. On Sundays she would follow Madame de Portenduère out of church after mass, gazing at her affectionately, for however harsh the old lady was she loved her for the fact that she was Savinien's mother. Her religious zeal increased, she attended mass every morning – firmly believing that her dreams came by the grace of God. Alarmed by the havoc wrought by her hankering after love, Dr Minoret promised Ursule on her birthday that he would take her to Toulon to watch the expeditionary fleet set sail for Algiers:

Savinien would be on board, but would not be informed of their visit. The magistrate and the parish priest did not divulge the doctor's secret as to the purpose of his journey, which seemed to have been planned for the benefit of Ursule's health and which greatly intrigued the Minoret heirs. Ursule saw Savinien dressed in his midshipman's uniform, and went aboard the fine flagship of the admiral to whom young Portenduère had been recommended by the Admiralty Minister; then, at her guardian's request, she went with him to take the air at Nice, travelling along the Mediterranean coast as far as Genoa, where she learned of the fleet's safe arrival and debarkation at Algiers. The doctor would have liked to prolong their journey through Italy, not only for Ursule's enjoyment but to help complete her education, widening her outlook through contact with different places and cultures, and through the delights of a country rich in artistic masterpieces and in the brilliant vestiges of so many civilizations; but he came hurrying back to France at the news of the King's opposition to the now notorious Parliament of 1830, and with him came Ursule, radiant in health and the proud owner of a charming little model of Savinien's ship.

14. Ursule Becomes an Orphan Again

THE 1830 elections gave solidity to the doctor's heirs who, through the efforts of Désiré Minoret and Goupil, set up a committee in Nemours which succeeded in getting the Liberal candidate elected at Fontainebleau. Massin had enormous influence over the country voters. Five of the postmaster's farmers had the vote. Over eleven votes were controlled by Dionis. Through their meetings at the notary's house, Crémière, Massin, the postmaster and their supporters eventually developed the habit of gathering there together. On the doctor's return, Dionis's drawing-room had become the headquarters of the Minoret heirs. The magistrate and the mayor combined in opposition to the Nemours Liberals, but despite the support of the neighbouring magnates they were defeated by the Opposition, and out of their defeat grew into close unity. When Bongrand and Abbé Chaperon informed the doctor of the result of this contest, which for the first time set up two rival political parties in Nemours, making the Minoret heirs into important people, Charles X was already on his way from Rambouillet to Cherbourg. Désiré Minoret, who shared the political views of his barrister colleagues in Paris, sent down to Nemours for fifteen of his friends, with Goupil as their leader; the postmaster supplied them with horses for the dash to Paris, where they joined Désiré during the night of 28 July. Goupil and Désiré took part with their followers in the capture of the Town Hall. Désiré Minoret was given the Legion of Honour, and appointed deputy public prosecutor at Fontainebleau. Goupil received the Croix de Juillet. Dionis was elected Mayor of Nemours in place of Monsieur Levrault, and the town coucil now consisted of Minoret-Levrault, as deputy mayor, Massin, Crémière and all the regular attendants at Dionis's drawing-rooms. Bongrand only kept his post thanks to his son's influence; the latter had been appointed public prosecutor at Melun, and his marriage with Mademoiselle Levrault now seemed likely. As the Three Per Cents fell to 45, the doctor set off post-haste for Paris, where he invested 540,000 francs in bearer bonds. The rest of his wealth, roughly amounting to 270,000 francs, was invested in his own name in the same securities, ostensibly yielding a private income of 15,000 francs. The money bequeathed to Ursule by old Monsieur de Jordy was invested in the same way, as were the 8,000 francs that had been accumulated in interest over nine years: so that, with the aid of a small contribution from the doctor to make her slender means up to a round sum, Ursule's investment income amounted to 1,400 francs. On her master's advice, old Bougival invested her five or six thousand francs savings to produce 350 francs interest. These wise moves, planned by the doctor and the magistrate, were carried out in the greatest secrecy thanks to the political disturbances. When things were more or less quiet again, the doctor bought a little house adjacent to his, which he demolished along with his courtyard wall to make room for a coachhouse and stable. All the Minoret heirs thought it the height of folly to spend on outbuildings capital that would have produced a thousand francs a year. With this so-called folly a new era began in the doctor's life; at a time when horses and carriages were almost being given away, he had a barouche and three superb horses sent down from Paris.

It was on a rainy day early in November 1830 that the old man went to mass for the first time in his barouche. As he stepped out, offering his hand to Ursule, all the inhabitants of Nemours came hurrying into the square, not only to see the doctor's carriage and interrogate his coachman but also to title-tattle about Minoret's goddaughter, to whose extreme ambition Massin, Crémière, the postmaster and their wives attributed their uncle's follies.

'Well, Massin! what about the barouche?' cried Goupil. 'It's a fine look-out for your inheritance, isn't it?'

'You must have got yourself a good wage, Cabirolle?' the postmaster asked the son of one of his own drivers, as he stood waiting beside the doctor's horses. 'Let's hope you don't wear out many horseshoes with an employer aged eighty-four. What did the horses cost?'

'Four thousand francs. The barouche was two thousand, even though it was second-hand; she's a wonderful job, the wheels are in patent.'

'What's that, Cabirolle?' asked Madame Crémière.

'He said *impotent*,' Goupil interjected. 'That's an idea the English have thought up; they invented that type of wheel. See, just look here! You can't see anything at all; everything's neat and boxed in, you can't catch yourself in it, they've got rid of that nasty piece of square ironwork that stuck out from the axle.'

'What does that mean, *impotent*?' Madame Crémière asked innocently.

'Don't be *impatient*!' joked Goupil.

'Oh! now I understand,' she replied.

'No,' Goupil continued. 'You're a decent woman. It's not right to mislead you. *Latent* is the proper word, because the axle-pin's hidden.'

'That's right, Madame Crémière,' Cabirolle agreed, completely taken in by Goupil's explanation, which the clerk had given in such earnest.

'Anyway, it's a lovely carriage!' Crémière exclaimed. 'You've got to be rich to travel in style like that.'

'Ursule's doing all right,' said Goupil. 'But quite right too. She's showing you how to enjoy life. Why don't you have barouches and fine horses, papa Minoret? Are you going to be outdone? If I was you, I'd have a carriage fit for a prince.'

'What do you think, Cabirolle?' asked Massin. 'Is it Ursule who's getting Uncle to go in for all these luxuries?'

'I don't know, but she's more or less in charge at home. If it's not one teacher coming down from Paris, it's another. They say she's going to study painting.'

'I'll have my *likeness* painted while I have the opportunity,' said Madame Crémière.

(In the provinces they still use the word 'likeness' instead of portrait.)

'But they haven't sacked the old German,' Madame Massin joined in.

'He's there today,' Cabirolle volunteered.

'Money flowing like milk and honey!' said Madame Crémière, at which everyone laughed.

Goupil summed up: 'You can't expect the inheritance now. Ursule will be seventeen soon, and she's prettier than she ever was. Travel educates youth, and the little hussy has got your uncle where she wants him. Every week there are five or six parcels arriving for her with the carriers. Dressmakers and milliners come down to try on her gowns and accessories. That's why my boss's wife is so furious. Just wait till Ursule comes out of church: the little shawl she's wearing round her neck is a genuine cashmere, worth 600 francs.'

If a thunderbolt had struck the assembled heirs it would not have caused more consternation than the last sentence spoken by Goupil, who stood there rubbing his hands.

Dr Minoret's old green drawing-room was redecorated by a Parisian upholsterer. Judging by the luxury of the redecoration, people accused the old man either of concealing the extent of his wealth (they believed he might have 60,000 francs a year) or else of delving into his capital for Ursule's amusement. By turns he was thought of as a Croesus and a libertine. 'He's a senile fool!' was the general opinion of him in the district. The advantage of this misjudgement of the situation by ordinary townsfolk was that it fooled the heirs, who did not suspect that Savinien loved Ursule, yet this was the real reason for the doctor's expenses: he was delighted to accustom his goddaughter to her future role as a viscountess, and having a private income of more than 50,000 francs, he enjoyed lavishing gifts on his idol.

On her seventeenth birthday in February 1832, just as she was getting up, Ursule noticed Savinien standing at his window dressed in sub-lieutenant's uniform.

'Why wasn't I told about this?' she wondered.

Since the capture of Algiers, at which Savinien distinguished himself and was awarded a cross for bravery, his corvette had been at sea for several months and it had been quite impossible for him to write to the doctor; but he did not want to leave the Navy before asking his advice. Eager to keep a man of his illustrious name in the service, the new government had been able to promote Savinien sub-lieutenant as a result of the upheaval occasioned by the July Revolution. The new sub-lieutenant had obtained a fortnight's leave and had travelled up on the mail-coach from Toulon to share in Ursule's birthday and also to ask the doctor's advice.

'He's here,' cried Ursule, rushing into her godfather's bedroom.

'Very good!' he answered. 'I can guess why he's leaving the Navy, and now he can stay in Nemours.'

'What a happy birthday surprise!' she replied, embracing the doctor.

On a signal from Ursule, the nobleman came over immediately; she wished to admire him, thinking there had been an improvement in his appearance. And indeed, service in the armed forces imparts such decisiveness, gravity and rectitude to a man's gestures, gait and general manner that even the most superficial observer can detect a military man in civilian clothing: there is no better proof that man is born to command. The result was that Ursule fell even more in love with Savinien, and felt as happy as a child walking with him in the little garden with her arm in his, getting him to relate his part, *as a midshipman*, in the capture of Algiers. As far as she was concerned, Savinien had captured Algiers! Whenever she looked at Savinien's decoration, she believed that the whole world was red. The doctor, who had been watching them from his bedroom as he dressed, now came down to join them. Without completely revealing his mind to the viscount, he told him that if Madame de Portenduère consented to his marrying Ursule the private fortune his goddaughter would enjoy made any service pay – whatever rank he might reach – quite unnecessary.

'Alas! my mother's opposition will take a long time to overcome. Before I left, she was faced with the choice between having me close by her if she agreed to my marriage with Ursule or otherwise of only seeing me very occasionally and knowing I'd be exposed to the dangers of a military career; and yet she allowed me to go . . .'

'But Savinien, we'll be together!' said Ursule, seizing his hand and shaking it about half-impatiently.

To her, love entirely consisted in being together and never

parting again. She could think of nothing beyond that; and such was the innocence of her pretty gesture and mischievous accent that Savinien and the doctor were touched by it. The letter of resignation was sent off, and Ursule's birthday was truly enhanced by her fiancé's presence. A few months afterwards, as May approached, life in Dr Minoret's household resumed its former calm, but with one extra participant. The young viscount's persistent attentions were rapidly seen as those of a future husband – especially as, for all their restraint, his manner towards Ursule and her manner towards him revealed their deep sympathy, both when they were at church together and when they were out driving or walking. Dionis pointed out to the heirs that the old doctor had ceased to ask Madame de Portenduère for interest, and that she was already three years behind with her payments.

'She'll be compelled to give in, and agree to her son marrying beneath himself,' said the notary. 'If this misfortune happens, then (as Basile puts it) a large part of your uncle's fortune will serve as an irresistible argument.'

On realizing that their uncle's preference for Ursule was so great that he would not fail to ensure her happiness, even at a loss to themselves, the family's annoyance became as secret as it was intense. Since the July Revolution they had been gathering every evening at Dionis's house, and there they cursed the two lovers: scarcely ever did the evening end without their trying to devise methods of thwarting the old man – always in vain. The most relentless person of all towards Ursule and the Portenduères was Zélie, who, like the doctor, had no doubt taken advantage of the fall in government securities to find a profitable investment for her enormous capital. Goupil took care not to show boredom at these evening gatherings, but one evening when he had looked in to keep himself abreast of all the gossip that went on there about the town Zélie gave vent to a fresh outburst of hatred: that morning she had seen the doctor, Ursule and Savinien returning home in their barouche from a drive in the neighbourhood, and their friendly intimacy had revealed everything.

'I'd willingly give 30,000 francs for Uncle to be gathered

to his forefathers before Portenduère's marriage to that minx,'
she said.

Goupil walked home with Monsieur and Madame Minoret
as far as the middle of their main courtyard, and said to them,
after first looking about him to make sure they were quite
alone: 'If you'll give me the money to buy Dionis's practice,
I'll break up the marriage between Monsieur de Portenduère
and Ursule.'

'How?' asked the colossus.

'Do you think I'm daft enough to tell you my plan?'
replied the head clerk.

'Well, my boy: you break up that marriage, and we'll see,'
said Zélie.

'If you want me to get involved in this business, *we'll see*
isn't enough! That swaggering fellow might kill me, and I'll
have to get in plenty of practice to be as good as him with the
sword and pistol. Promise me the money, and I'll keep my
word.'

'Stop the marriage, and I'll set you up,' answered the postmaster.

'For nine months you've been thinking about lending me
15,000 francs – a mere pittance – to buy Lecoeur's tipstaff's
practice: and you expect me to believe a promise like that!
Look, you're going to lose your uncle's inheritance, and
it'll serve you right too.'

'If it was only 15,000 francs for Lecoeur's practice, that
would be fair enough,' said Zélie; 'but to put down 150,000
francs caution money!'

'But I'll actually be paying,' said Goupil, glancing at Zélie
with a magnetism in his eyes that confronted her dominating
look. It was like poison being poured over steel.

'We'll wait and see,' said Zélie.

'To hell with you, then!' thought Goupil. 'If ever I have
them in my power,' he thought on his way out, 'I'll bleed
them white.'

As he became better acquainted with the doctor, magistrate
and parish priest, Savinien convinced them how excellent his
character was. The three friends became so keenly interested
in the young man's love for Ursule, a love that was so disin-

terested and constant, that they always associated the two young people in their minds. It was not long before the monotony of this patriarchal life and the lovers' certainty as to their future made their affection into a kind of brother–sister relationship. The doctor frequently left Ursule alone with Savinien. He had formed a shrewd judgement of this charming young man who kissed Ursule's hand as he arrived and would not have asked her for it if he had been alone with her, so great was his respect for the innocence and artlessness of a girl whose extreme sensitivity he had often experienced and who he knew could be killed by a harsh word, or a stern glance, or alternating kindness and severity. The two lovers' most daring moments came when they were in their old friends' company, in the evenings. And so two years passed by, full of secret joys but with no external event other than the young man's fruitless attempts to gain his mother's consent to his marriage with Ursule. Sometimes he would speak for a whole morning; and his mother's only reply to his arguments and entreaties would be either a Breton silence or a refusal. At nineteen, Ursule was elegant, well brought up and an excellent musician; she had every accomplishment, and was perfection itself. The fame of her beauty, grace and education spread far and wide. One day, the doctor had to refuse the Marquise d'Aiglemont's request for Ursule's hand for her eldest son. Six months later Savinien accidentally found out about this even though it had been kept a closely guarded secret by Ursule, the doctor and Madame d'Aiglemont. Touched by such delicacy, he used this line of conduct as an argument to overcome his mother's obstinacy, but she replied: 'If the d'Aiglemonts choose to marry beneath themselves, why should we?'

In December 1834 there was a marked decline in the health of the good, pious old man. Seeing him emerge from church with a yellow, drawn face and pale eyes, the whole town spoke of the doctor's imminent death; he was then aged eighty-eight. 'Then you will know how things stand,' people said to the heirs. And indeed, the old man's death had the fascination of an enigma. But the doctor did not know he was ill, he was under an illusion, and poor Ursule, Savinien, the magistrate and the parish priest were all too considerate to wish to enlighten him as to his condition; the Nemours doctor, who visited him every evening, did not dare to prescribe any treatment. Old Minoret felt no pain, his life was just ebbing away. His mind was as calm, lucid and powerful as ever. In old men of his stamp the soul dominates the body, giving them the strength to die on their feet. So as not to hasten his death the parish priest gave him a dispensation from attending mass in church, allowing him to read the service at home; for the doctor was meticulous in accomplishing his religious duties: the closer he drew to the grave, the more he loved God. All kinds of difficulty became increasingly illuminated by the light of heaven. Early in the new year Ursule persuaded him to sell his carriage and horses and dismiss Cabirolle. The magistrate, whose anxieties as to Ursule's future were far from being allayed by hints from the old man, broached the delicate subject of the inheritance one evening, pointing out to his old friend how necessary it was that Ursule should be emancipated. If that were done, Minoret's ward would be able to have her guardianship accounts settled, and to own property in her own right: which would mean she could then be endowed. Despite this approach, and though the doctor had already consulted the magistrate, he did not let him into the secret of his arrangements regarding Ursule; but he adopted the suggestion that she should be given her freedom. The more the magistrate insisted on being told what steps his old friend had taken to endow Ursule, the more distrustful the doctor became. In short, Minoret was positively afraid to entrust the magistrate with his 36,000 francs investment income in bearer bonds.

'Why aren't you getting chance on your side?' asked Bongrand.

'When you have to choose between two chances, you avoid the riskier.'

Bongrand proceeded so briskly with the matter of Mademoiselle Mirouët's emancipation that it was settled by her twentieth birthday. This birthday was to be the last red-letter day in the old doctor's life; no doubt sensing that his end was near, he celebrated it lavishly, giving a little ball to which he invited the young members of the Dionis, Crémière, Minoret and Massin families. Savinien, Bongrand, the parish priest and his two curates, the Nemours doctor and Madame Zélie Minoret, Madame Massin and Madame Crémière, together with Schmucke, were asked to a grand dinner before the ball.

'I feel I haven't much longer to live,' Dr Minoret said to the notary as the evening drew to its close. 'So please come round tomorrow to draw up the guardianship account I have to give Ursule, so as not to complicate my inheritance. Thank Heaven! I haven't done my family out of any of their dues, and I have only spent my income. Monsieur Crémière, Monsieur Massin and my nephew Monsieur Minoret are members of the family council that has been officially set up for Ursule. They'll be present when the accounts are handed over to her.'

These words, overheard by Massin and broadcast round the ballroom, spread joy amongst the three families, who for the last four years had been living between perpetual extremes, sometimes thinking they would be rich, sometimes thinking they had been disinherited.

'His tongue is nearing its end,' said Madame Crémière.

About two o'clock in the morning only Savinien, Bongrand and Abbé Chaperon were left in the drawing-room. Pointing to Ursule, who looked charming in her ball-dress and who had just said good-bye to the young Crémière and Massin girls, the doctor remarked to his friends: 'I entrust her to you! In a few days' time I shall no longer be here to look after her; act as a shield between her and the world, until she marries . . . I am afraid for her.'

His words made a painful impression. A few days later, the guardianship accounts were handed over at a family council: they declared that Dr Minoret had a balance of 10,600 francs on account, partly from the interest on the scrip for 1,400 francs investment income bought with the legacy from Capitaine de Jordy, partly from a small capital sum of 5,000 francs accumulated from the doctor's gifts to his ward over fifteen years, on their respective birthdays or name-days.

This formal rendering of accounts had been strongly advised by the magistrate, who dreaded the consequences of Dr Minoret's death and who unfortunately was right. The day after the acceptance of the guardianship accounts, by virtue of which Ursule had capital amounting to 10,600 francs and a private income of 1,400 francs, the doctor was stricken with an illness that forced him to keep to his bed. Despite the discretion surrounding the doctor's house, the rumour of his death spread across the town, and the heirs ran round the streets like beads in a rosary when the thread is broken. Massin, calling to hear the news, was told by Ursule herself that the old man was in bed. Unfortunately the Nemours doctor had said that as soon as Minoret took to his bed he would be bound to die. From then on, in spite of the cold, the heirs stood in the streets, in the market-place or on their doorsteps, talking about the event that had been expected for so long, and watching for the moment when the parish priest would take the sacraments to the old doctor in the receptacle used in provincial towns. Two days later Abbé Chaperon crossed the high street, accompanied by his curate and choir-boys and with the sexton walking ahead of them carrying the cross; and it was then that the heirs joined in his procession, and occupied the house, to prevent anything from being taken away and to get their greedy hands on the presumed treasures. When the doctor noticed that his heirs were kneeling behind the clergy but, far from praying, were watching him with eyes as bright as the candle flames, he could not restrain an ironic smile. The priest turned round, saw them and recited the prayers quite slowly. The postmaster was the first to get up from his uncomfortable posture, followed by his wife; Massin, afraid that Zélie and her husband would get their hands on some trinket, joined them in the drawing-room, and soon all the heirs were standing there.

'He's too much of a gentleman to steal the Extreme Unction,' said Crémière, 'so we're bound to be all right.'

'Yes, we'll each get about 20,000 francs investment income,' replied Madame Massin.

'I have an idea,' said Zélie, 'that for the last three years he had stopped *investing*, he was *fond* of hoarding . . .'

'Perhaps the treasure's in his cellar?' Massin asked Crémière.

'Let's hope we find something,' said Minoret-Levrault.

'But after what he said at the ball,' cried Madame Massin, 'it's absolutely certain.'

'Anyway,' Crémière continued, 'how shall we arrange it? Shall we divide up? or auction everything jointly? or draw lots? I mean, we're all of full age.'

A discussion followed as to how they should set about it; it soon became acrimonious. Half an hour later the courtyard and even the street rang with the hubbub of voices, Zélie's shrill voice piercing above the rest.

'He must be dead,' remarked a group of inquisitive people in the street.

This uproar reached the doctor, who heard the following words: 'But the house is worth 30,000 francs! I'll have it for 30,000 francs' – yelled, or rather bellowed, by Crémière.

'Well, we'll pay the going price,' Zélie answered tartly.

'Father,' said Dr Minoret to Abbé Chaperon, who remained with his friend after administering the last rites, 'make sure I'm left in peace. My heirs, like Cardinal Jimenes's, are capable of ransacking my house before I'm dead, and I haven't a monkey to make me better again. Go and tell them I don't want anyone in here.'

The priest and doctor went downstairs and repeated the dying man's orders; in an indignant outburst they added some sharp words of criticism.

'Madame Bougival,' said the doctor, 'shut the gate and let no one in; can't a man die in peace? Then mix flour and mustard into a paste, so we can apply poultices to Dr Minoret's feet.'

'Your uncle isn't dead, and may live a long while yet,' Abbé Chaperon said, dismissing the Minoret heirs who had come along with their children. 'He must be kept absolutely quiet, and only wants his ward to be with him. How differently that girl behaves from you!'

'The old humbug!' cried Crémière. 'I'll keep watch. Something may very well be hatched against our interests.'

The postmaster had already vanished into the garden, intending to sit up with his uncle along with Ursule and gain admittance into the house as a helper. He crept back without making the slightest noise with his boots – there were carpets in the passage and on the treads of the staircase. He was then able to reach his uncle's bedroom door without being heard. The parish priest and the doctor had left, and La Bougival was preparing the mustard poultice.

'Are we quite alone?' the old man asked his ward.

Ursule stood on tiptoe and looked out into the courtyard.

'Yes, Father Chaperon pulled the gate to himself as he went out.'

'My darling child,' said the dying man, 'my hours – even my minutes – are numbered. I haven't been a doctor for nothing: the doctor's poultice won't keep me alive till evening. Don't cry, Ursule,' he went on, interrupted by his goddaughter's tears, 'listen to me carefully. You must marry Savinien. As soon as La Bougival has come upstairs with the poultice, you go down to the Chinese pavilion: here's the key. Lift the marble top on the Boulle sideboard, and underneath you'll find a sealed letter addressed to you. Pick it up, and come back and show me it; I shan't die happy till I see it in your hands. When I'm dead, don't let it be known at once; send for Monsieur de Portenduère, read the letter with him, and promise me in his name and yours to carry out my last wishes. As soon as he has obeyed me and done this, you must announce my death – and the farce played by the heirs will begin. I hope to God those monsters don't ill-treat you.'

'Yes, godfather.'

The postmaster did not hear the remainder of the scene; he hurried off on tiptoe, remembering that the lock to the study door faced the library. He had been present in time past at a discussion between the architect and the locksmith, when the latter had argued that if one were to let oneself into the house by the window opening on to the river, then the lock must be placed on the library side as a precaution because the study was intended as a pleasure room during summer. Dazzled by self-interest, his ears throbbing, Minoret was as deft as a thief in unscrewing the lock with a knife. He entered the study, picked up the packet of papers without troubling to break the seal, screwed the lock up again, put everything back in its place, and went and sat down in the dining-room, waiting till La Bougival had gone upstairs with the poultice before leaving the house. He effected his escape very easily, particularly as poor Ursule thought it was more urgent to watch the poultice being put on than to follow her godfather's instructions.

'The letter! the letter!' cried the old man in a dying voice, 'do as I say, here's the key. I want to see you with the letter.'

The doctor's look was so distraught as he spoke these words that La Bougival said to Ursule: 'Do as your godfather bids, or it'll be the death of him.'

She kissed his forehead, took the key and went downstairs; but she was soon recalled by shrieks from La Bougival, and came running back. The old man looked at her tenderly, saw that her hands were empty, sat bolt upright, tried to speak and died with a horrible sigh on his lips and his eyes wild with terror! The poor girl, seeing death for the first time, fell to her knees and burst into tears. La Bougival closed the old man's eyes and laid him out on his bed. When (in her phrase) she had *decked out* the corpse, the old nurse ran to inform Monsieur Savinien; but the heirs, who were standing at the street corner surrounded by inquisitive onlookers and looking for all the world like ravens waiting for a horse to be buried before scratching the earth and digging into it with their feet and beaks, ran up with the rapidity of those birds of prey.

15. *The Doctor's Will*

WHILST these events were taking place, the postmaster had gone home to see what the mysterious packet contained. This is what he found.

TO MY DEAR URSULE MIROUËT, DAUGHTER OF MY
NATURAL BROTHER-IN-LAW JOSEPH MIROUËT AND
DINAH GROLLMAN

Nemours, 15 January 1830.

My darling Angel,

My fatherly affection, of which you have proved to be so worthy, has been founded not only on the vow I swore to your poor father that I would take his place but also on your resemblance to my wife Ursule Mirouët, whose grace, wit, artlessness and charm you have constantly recalled to my mind. Your status as the daughter of my father-in-law's illegitimate son could lead to the challenging of any bequests I might make to you in my will . . .

'The old wretch!' exclaimed the postmaster.

If I had adopted you, that would have led to a lawsuit. And I have always shrunk from the idea of marrying you so as to convey you my fortune – I might have lived a long time and upset your future happiness, which is now only delayed for as long as Madame de Portenduère is alive. Having given these difficulties thought, and wishing to leave you the fortune needed for a fine style of life . . .

'That rascal's thought of everything!'

. . . without in any way harming my heirs . . .

'The hypocrite! As if all his fortune didn't belong to us!'

. . . I mean you to have the savings I have put by over eighteen years, savings which I have constantly increased in value thanks to my notary's help, so as to make you as happy as wealth can make anyone. If you had no money, your education and high ideals would lead you into misfortune. Besides, the charming young man who is in love with you deserves a fine dowry. Look inside the middle pages of volume III of *The Pandects*, the folio volumes bound in red morocco – it is the last book in the bottom row above the shelf, in the last compartment of the bookcase close to the drawing-room – and there you will find three bearer bonds in Three Per Cent Government stock, each worth 12,000 francs a year . . .

'The low cunning!' cried the postmaster. 'No! God won't allow me to be thwarted like this.'

Pick them up at once, together with the small amount of interest I will have saved at my death: this will be in the previous volume. And remember, darling child, you must blindly obey an intention which has filled me with happiness throughout the whole of my life and which would compel me to invoke God's assistance if you disobeyed me. But to forestall any twinge of conscience you may feel – I know how skilful your conscience is at tormenting you – I enclose a properly executed will bequeathing these scrips to Monsieur Savinien de Portenduère. Thus, whether you possess them in your own name, or whether they come to you through the man you love, they will be your lawful property.

Your loving godfather,
DENIS MINORET.

To this letter was appended the following document, written on a square piece of officially stamped paper:

This is the last will and testament of me Denis Minoret, doctor of medicine, resident at Nemours and being sound in both mind and body, as is attested by the date of this my will. I commit my soul to God, beseeching Him to forgive me my long errors in consideration of my sincere repentance. And having seen the true affection that Vicomte Savinien de Portenduère bears towards me, I bequeath to him in fee simple the capital of 36,000 francs investment income in Three Per Cent Government bonds, this sum to be a prior charge on my estate before any bequests made to my family.

Signed and delivered entirely by my hand at Nemours this eleventh day of January one thousand eight hundred and thirty-one,

DENIS MINORET.

Unhesitatingly the postmaster, who had shut himself up in his wife's bedroom so as to be quite alone, looked around for the phosphorous match box, and received two warnings from heaven as successive matches refused to light. The third caught fire. He burned both the letter and the will in the fire-place. As a superfluous precaution, he buried the remains of the wax and paper in the ashes. Then, tempted by the idea of having 36,000 francs investment income unknown to his wife, he came running back to his uncle's house, spurred on by the only thought, so simple and precise, that could enter his unintelligent head. Seeing his uncle's house invaded by the three families who had now taken over control of the place, he trembled at perhaps being unable to fulfil a plan he did not give himself time to consider – thinking only of the obstacles ahead.

'And what are you doing?' he asked Massin and Crémière. 'Do you think we're going to let the house and securities be vandalized? We three are heirs to the estate, we can't just stand around! Crémière, you rush over to Dionis and tell him to come and certify the death. Although I'm the deputy mayor, I'm not able to issue Uncle's death certificate ... Massin, you go and ask old Bongrand to affix the seals. And,' (now addressing his wife, Madame Massin and Madame Crémière) 'you keep Ursule company. That way nothing will get lost. And remember to shut the outside gate, so no one can leave the house!'

The women, realizing the appropriateness of this remark, ran to Ursule's bedroom and found that noble creature, already the object of such cruel suspicion, kneeling in prayer, her face covered in tears. Sensing that the three women would not be with Ursule for long, and fearing his coheirs' mistrust, Minoret went into the library, saw the volume, opened it, took out the three scrips, and in the other volume found about thirty banknotes. For all his coarse, brutish nature, this colossal man thought he could hear bells ringing out in his ears, and felt blood rushing across his temples, as he carried out his theft. Despite the severity of the weather at this time of year, his shirt was bathed in sweat. And his legs were trembling so much that he collapsed into a drawing-room armchair as if he had been struck on the head with a sledge-hammer.

'Ah! how talkative that great hulk Minoret gets when he has an inheritance to deal with!' Massin had said to himself as he rushed across the town. 'Did you hear him?' he asked Crémière. 'Do this! do that! He knows all the moves.'

'Yes, considering he's such a big fool he did seem to ...'

'Here,' cried Massin in alarm, 'his wife's still there, two of them's too many! You attend to the errands, I'm going back.'

Just as the postmaster was sitting down, he noticed the clerk of the court's excited face at the outer gate; Massin had come rushing back to the deceased's house as fast as a ferret.

'Well! what's up?' asked the postmaster, walking across to open the gate for his coheir.

'Nothing. I'm coming back for the seals to be affixed,' answered Massin, glaring at him like a wildcat.

'I wish they'd been affixed already, then we could all go home.'

'Well, we'll engage someone to make sure they aren't tampered with,' the clerk of the court continued. 'La Bougival is capable of doing anything to help that minx. Let's have Goupil.'

'Him! He'd make off with the loot and we'd be completely foxed.'

'Look,' said Massin. 'Tonight there'll be a vigil over the body, and we'll have finished the seals in an hour's time; our wives can keep an eye on them. We'll hold the funeral to-morrow at noon. We can't start on the inventory for a week.'

'Anyway,' replied the colossal postmaster with a smile, 'let's kick that little hussy out, and we'll put the town crier in charge of the seals and house.'

'Fine! You take charge of this business, you're the head of the Minoret family.'

'Ladies, ladies,' cried Minoret, 'will all of you please remain in the drawing-room. There's no time now for dinner, we must set about affixing the seals to protect all our interests.'

He then took his wife to one side to tell her Massin's ideas regarding Ursule. The women, whose hearts were thirsting for revenge and who hoped to get their own back on 'that minx', immediately and enthusiastically welcomed the plan to expel her. Bongrand arrived, and was indignant at the proposal Zélie and Madame Massin put to him (in his capacity as a friend of the late doctor) that he should ask Ursule to vacate the house.

'*You* chase her from the doctor's house! He was her god-father, her father, her uncle, her guardian and her benefactor!

Go on! It's only thanks to her noble character that you've got your inheritance! Grab her by the shoulders, throw her out into the street, with the whole town looking on! Do you think *she* would rob you? Very well then, appoint a caretaker for the seals – you're entitled to. But bear in mind I shan't affix any seals on her bedroom; that's her home, and everything in it is hers. I'll inform her of her rights, and tell her to gather all her belongings together ... Oh! in your presence,' he added, hearing a growl from the heirs.

'Well?' the tax-collector asked the postmaster and the women, the latter stupefied by Bongrand's dressing-down.

'There's a magistrate for you!' exclaimed the postmaster.

Sitting on a small sofa, half-fainting, with her head tilted back and her plaits undone, Ursule could not prevent an occasional sob. Her eyes were filmy, her eyelids swollen, she was suffering from a physical and mental collapse that would have brought pity to the hearts of the fiercest men – excepting heirs to fortunes.

'Ah! Monsieur Bongrand! To think that my birthday should be followed by death and mourning,' she said with that poetic feeling which is second nature to exalted souls. '*You* know what he was like: he never uttered an impatient word to me in twenty years! I thought he would live to be a hundred! He was a mother to me,' she cried, 'and a good mother too.'

The mere expression of these thoughts brought on two fits of weeping broken with sobs; then she slumped back again.

'Dear child,' the conciliative magistrate continued, hearing the heirs on the staircase, 'you have the whole of your life to mourn him, but only a moment to attend to your affairs: put everything that belongs to you in this house into your bedroom. The heirs are compelling me to affix seals ...'

'Ah! his heirs can take everything they like,' exclaimed Ursule, rising in an outburst of fierce indignation. 'Everything that's precious to me is here,' she added, beating her breast.

'How do you mean?' asked the postmaster, who showed his terrifying face along with Massin.

'The memory of his virtues, his life, every word he spoke, an image of his heavenly soul,' she said, and her face and eyes shone dazzlingly as she raised her hand in a superb gesture.

'So you have a key as well!' Massin cried, gliding like a cat and seizing a key which fell from the folds of Ursule's bodice, dislodged by her movement.

'It's the key to his study,' she said blushing. 'He sent me there just as he was dying.'

Having looked at one another with hideous smiles, the two heirs turned to the conciliative magistrate with searing suspicion in their eyes. Ursule noticed and understood this look, which was spontaneous with Massin, but calculated in the postmaster. She stood up, as pale as if her blood were draining away. Her eyes darted those lightning glances that perhaps only shine forth at the expense of life. In a strangled voice she said: 'Monsieur Bongrand, everything in this room came to me through the kindness of my godfather. They can have it all. All I have on me is my clothes. I shall leave and never return.'

She went into her guardian's bedroom from which no entreaty could bring her out; the heirs were in fact a little ashamed of their behaviour. She told La Bougival to book her two rooms at the Old Coaching Inn until she found lodgings in town where they could both live. She went back to her own room for her prayer-book and spent almost the whole night with the parish priest, the curate and Savinien, praying and weeping. The nobleman came after his mother had retired to bed, and knelt down silently beside Ursule, who with the saddest of smiles thanked him for having loyally come to share her grief.

'Dear child,' said Monsieur Bongrand, bringing Ursule a bulky parcel, 'one of your uncle's heirs has got everything you needed out of your chest of drawers – the seals won't be removed for a few days yet, and then you'll get your belongings back. For your sake, I've affixed the seals to your bedroom as well.'

'Thank you,' she replied, walking up to him and shaking his hand. 'Just look at him once again: wouldn't you think he was asleep?'

At that moment the old doctor presented that ephemeral

sheen of beauty which descends upon the faces of those who have died painless deaths. He looked radiant.

'Didn't he secretly give you anything before he died?' the magistrate whispered to Ursule.

'Nothing. He just mentioned about a letter . . .'

'Very well! It'll turn up. If that's so, it's very lucky for you they wanted the seals on.'

At daybreak, Ursule said good-bye to a house in which she had spent her happy childhood, and above all to that simple bedroom where her love had begun, a room which was so dear to her that in the depths of her darkest grief she wept tears of regret at leaving that sweet, gentle home. After gazing for the last time first at her windows and then at Savinien, she left for the inn, accompanied by La Bougival carrying her parcel, the magistrate, who gave her his arm, and by Savinien, who was her gentle protector. Thus, despite the wisest precautions, the cautious lawyer was proved right: he was to see Ursule destitute and at loggerheads with the doctor's heirs.

On the evening of the following day, the whole town turned out for Dr Minoret's funeral. When people learned of the heirs' behaviour towards his adoptive daughter, the vast majority thought that that behaviour was natural and necessary: an inheritance was at stake, the old fellow was *close*, Ursule might imagine she had rights to the money, the heirs were defending their property, and besides she had humiliated them a good deal in the doctor's lifetime when he used to give them such a chilly welcome. Désiré Minoret, who was not doing wonderfully well in his job, or so people said who were envious of the postmaster, arrived for the service. Ursule was in no fit state to attend the funeral. She was bedridden with a nervous fever caused just as much by the heirs' insulting behaviour as by her deep sorrow.

'Look at that hypocrite weeping!' a few of the heirs said pointing to Savinien, who was keenly afflicted by the doctor's death.

'The question is whether he's justified in weeping,' said Goupil. 'Don't be too hasty with your laughter, the seals haven't been removed yet.'

'Phhh!' said Minoret, who knew just what the situation was, 'you've always put the wind up us for no reason.'

Just as the procession left the church on its way to the cemetery, Goupil experienced a bitter rebuff: he tried to take Désiré by the arm; but the deputy public prosecutor would not let him do so, and so snubbed his old friend in the sight of everyone in Nemours.

'Let's not get agitated. I would miss my revenge then,' thought the head clerk whose dry heart swelled up within his chest as if it had been a sponge.

16. Two People at Loggerheads

BEFORE removing the seals and proceeding to draw up the inventory, time had to be allowed for the public prosecutor, the legal guardian of orphans, to appoint Bongrand to act as his substitute. The itemization of the Minoret inheritance, which people talked about for ten days, then began; it was carried out with the rigorous formalities of the law. Dionis made money out of it, Goupil quite enjoyed doing harm; and as it was a large estate, there were plenty of fees. There was almost always a luncheon after the first session. The notary, his clerk, the heirs and the witnesses drank the choicest wines from the cellar.

In the provinces, and especially in small towns, where everyone owns his own house, it is fairly difficult to find accommodation. For this reason, whenever business premises are purchased, a house is almost always thrown in with the sale. The conciliative magistrate, urged by the public prosecutor to protect the orphan girl's interests, could think of no other way of removing her from the inn than to get her to purchase a small house at the corner of the High Street, by the bridge over the Loing. This house had a single-leaved front door which opened on to a corridor; on the ground floor it had only one sitting-room with two casement windows overlooking the street, and behind this room was a kitchen with a glazed folding-door leading into an inner courtyard about thirty feet square. A small staircase lit by ancient lights on the side facing the river led up to the first floor, which consisted of three bedrooms, above which were two attics. The magistrate borrowed 2,000 francs of La Bougival's savings to pay the deposit on this house, which was worth 6,000 francs; he was allowed to repay the remainder of the money in instalments. To make room for the books Ursule wanted to buy back, Bongrand had the dividing wall demolished between two rooms on the first floor, having noticed that the depth of the house was equivalent to the length of the library bookcase. Savinien and the magistrate put so much pressure on the workmen who were cleaning up, painting and completely renovating the small house that towards the end of March Ursule was able to leave the inn, and found in her ugly new home a bedroom resembling the one from which she had been driven by the Minoret heirs – it had been furnished with her own furniture, which the magistrate had recovered when the seals were removed. La Bougival's room was above Ursule's; she could come down whenever the little bell rang by the head of her young mistress's bed. The room which was intended as the library, the ground-floor sitting-room and the kitchen still stood empty. They had merely been colourwashed, decorated with new wallpaper and repainted. They awaited whatever purchases Ursule might make at the sale of her godfather's furniture. Although they knew the sort of person she was, the magistrate and the parish priest were afraid about her rapid transition to a life devoid of the refinements and luxury to which the late doctor had wished to accustom her. As for Savinien, he was in tears. And so he had given the workmen and the upholsterer many a secret bonus so that Ursule should find no difference between her old bedroom and her new one, at any rate from the inside. But the young girl, who derived all her happiness from Savinien's eyes, showed the gentlest resignation. On this occasion she charmed her two old friends, proving to them for the thousandth time that only the troubles of the heart could cause her suffering. The grief caused by her godfather's death was too deep for her to feel any bitterness at this reversal of fortune, which however put still further obstacles in the way of her marriage. Savinien's sadness at seeing her so reduced in circumstances gave him so much distress that on emerging from church after mass, on the morning of her removal to her new home, she had to whisper to him: 'Lovers must have patience. We'll wait!'

As soon as the inventory abstract was drawn up, Massin – on Goupil's advice (the latter turning to Massin out of a secret hatred of Minoret and hoping for better things from the money-lender's calculation than from Zélie's prudence) – had writs served on Monsieur and Madame de Portenduère, their loan repayment having fallen due. The old lady was stunned by a summons to pay the Minoret heirs 129,517 francs 55 centimes within twenty-four hours on pain of attachment of real property; interest on the sum to be calculated from the day of the summons. It was impossible to borrow money to pay this. Savinien went off to consult a solicitor at Fontainebleau.

'You're up against nasty pieces of work who won't come to terms with you. They'll sue you to the bitter end; what they want is the farm at Les Bordières,' the solicitor said. 'The best thing would be to turn a compulsory sale into a voluntary one, to avoid expense.'

This sad news disheartened the old Breton woman, whose son gently pointed out to her that if only she had consented to his marriage whilst Minoret was alive the doctor would have made over his property to him, as Ursule's husband. Now their household would be rolling in affluence instead of facing wretched poverty. Though there was no tone of blame in his words, Savinien's argument was just as devastating to the old lady as the idea of an imminent and forcible eviction. On learning of this disaster, Ursule, who had hardly recovered from the feverishness and shock caused by the Minoret heirs, was stupefied with despondency. To be in love yet unable to help the man one loves is one of the most terrible sufferings that can distress the hearts of tender and noble women.

'I wanted to buy Uncle's house. I'll buy your mother's,' she said.

'But is that possible?' cried Savinien. 'You're under age and can't sell the scrip for your investment income without going through formalities to which the public prosecutor wouldn't agree. Besides, we shan't try to resist. The whole town is delighted to see a noble family discredited. These middle-class folk are like hounds tearing a stag to pieces. Luckily I've still got 10,000 francs which my mother can live on until this deplorable business is over. Anyway, they haven't finished drawing up your godfather's inventory yet, and Monsieur Bongrand still hopes to come across something left for you. He's as astonished as I am that you've been left without any fortune. The doctor spoke so many times both to him and to me about the fine prospects he had in store for you and we simply can't understand the way things have turned out.'

'Phhh!' she said 'Providing I can buy my godfather's library and furniture to avoid them being dispersed or falling into strangers' hands, I'm happy with my lot.'

'But what price will those abominable heirs be ready to pay for the things you want?'

From Montargis to Fontainebleau people could talk of nothing but the Minoret heirs and the million francs they were looking for; but they made no such discovery, even after the most meticulous search of the house after the seals were removed. The 129,000 francs owed by the Portendučres, the 15,000 francs investment income in the Three Per Cents, which stood at that time at 76, implying a capital of 380,000 francs, and the house whose value was estimated at 40,000 francs together with its costly furniture produced a total capital of about 600,000 francs which everyone considered quite a nice consolation prize. Minoret began to feel nagging anxieties. At the end of each inventory session La Bougival and Savinien, who still believed – as did the magistrate – that there must be a will somewhere, would come up and inquire of Bongrand the latest result of the house search. Sometimes the old doctor's friend would exclaim, as the heirs and officials were leaving the house: 'I just can't understand it!' As the 200,000 francs received by each heir seemed to many superficially minded people to be a fine enough fortune by provincial standards, no one thought of investigating how the doctor could have kept up the standard of living he did on only 15,000 francs a year – since he had not drawn any interest on the money lent to the Portendučres. Bongrand, Savinien and the parish priest were the only people to ask themselves this question in Ursule's interests, and more than once the postmaster went pale as they discussed the matter.

'Yet they've made a thorough search everywhere – they've been looking for money, I've been looking for a will drawn up in Monsieur de Portendučre's favour,' said the magistrate on the day when the inventory was finally settled. 'They've raked through the ashes, lifted up slabs of marble, felt inside slippers, bored into bedframes, emptied mattresses, made holes in counterpanes and bedspreads, turned his eiderdown inside out, gone through his papers one by one, examined the drawers, dug up the soil in his cellar, and I urged them on in this ransacking of the house!'

'What do you think?' asked the parish priest.

'One of the heirs has made off with the will.'

'And what about the securities?'

'You have a look for them! Can you make any sense of people's behaviour when they're as sly and cunning and mean as the Massins and Crémières? Can you explain a fortune like Minoret's, when he draws 200,000 francs from the doctor's estate and, according to what people say, is selling his post-master's warrant, house and stagecoach business for 350,000 francs? . . . What huge sums! not to mention the savings from his 30,000 francs a year or more in rents from land. The poor doctor!'

'Perhaps the will has been hidden in the library,' Savinien suggested.

'That's why I'm not putting the girl off from buying it! Except for that, it would be sheer madness to let her spend all her ready money on books she'll never open!'

The whole town believed that the doctor's goddaughter was in possession of hidden sums of capital; but when it was positively established that her 1,400 francs a year investment income together with her savings were the only fortune she had, the doctor's house and furniture began to arouse every-one's curiosity. Some thought that money in the form of banknotes would be found concealed in furniture; others believed that the old man had stuffed money inside books. And because of this the auction sale presented the strangest spectacle of the precautions to which the heirs went. Dionis, acting as official auctioneer and valuer, announced as each object was being put up for sale that the heirs were only intending to sell the object itself and not whatever securities it might happen to contain; then, before handing it over, all the heirs subjected it to their niggardly investigations, tapping it to test it and make it ring; finally parting with it with the same looks on their faces as a father might have if his only son were setting sail for the Indies.

'Oh Mademoiselle!' said La Bougival, coming back in dismay from the first session. 'I shan't go there again. Monsieur Bongrand is right, you couldn't stand the sight. Everything is all over the place. People are rushing about everywhere like in a street. They use the best furniture for anything and everything. *They* climb on to it, and it's such a scramble a hen couldn't find her own little chicks! It's like being at a fire. Cupboards are open, with nothing inside, the things are out in the courtyard! Oh! that poor dear man! It's just as well he died, his auction would have killed him.'

Bongrand, who was buying back for Ursule the furniture that the late doctor had been fond of, in order to use it in furnishing her little house, did not show himself when the library was auctioned. Shrewder than the Minoret heirs, whose greed could have led him to pay too much for the books, he had commissioned a dealer in old books and clothes at Melun to act for him; this man had come specially to Nemours, and had already had several lots knocked down to him. Because of the heirs' distrust, the library was sold off book by book. Three thousand volumes were examined and peered into one by one; they were held up by both back and front covers and shaken so that any hidden papers would fall out; the covers themselves were scrutinized, and the endpapers checked. The total proceeds of the sale amounted for Ursule to about 6,500 francs, half her claims on the estate. The library bookcase was not handed over until it had been carefully examined by a cabinet-maker specializing in secret drawers, who was sent for from Paris. When the conciliative magistrate gave orders for the library bookcase and books to be carried over to Mademoiselle Mirouët's, the heirs were filled with alarm, which later was dispelled when they saw that she was still just as impoverished as before. Minoret bought his uncle's house whose auction price the other heirs pushed up to 50,000 francs, imagining that the postmaster hoped to find a treasure in the walls. And, as a consequence of all this, the articles and conditions of sale contained reservation clauses. A fortnight after the disposal of the personalty, Minoret, who sold his coaching premises to a rich farmer's son, settled down in his uncle's home, where he spent considerable sums of money on furniture, furnishings and improvements. Thus Minoret, of his own free will, was condemned to living within a few yards of Ursule.

'I hope,' he had said at Dionis's house on the day when the writs were served on Savinien and his mother, 'that we shall be rid of those down-and-out aristocrats! We'll chase the others out afterwards.'

'The old girl with the fourteen quarterings won't want to be a witness at her own disaster,' Goupil replied; 'she'll go off and spend the rest of her days in Brittany, where no doubt she'll find her son a wife.'

'I don't think so,' answered the notary, who that morning had drawn up the contract for Bongrand's purchase. 'Ursule has just bought widow Ricard's house.'

'That damned scatterbrain is always thinking up something new to annoy us!' the postmaster exclaimed, very rashly.

'And why do you mind her living in Nemours?' asked Goupil, surprised at the colossal imbecile's exasperated reaction.

'So you don't know my son's been stupid enough to fall in love with her,' answered Minoret, blushing as red as a beet-root. 'I'd give 300 francs for Ursule to leave Nemours.'

From this initial reaction it will easily be understood how much of an embarrassment Ursule, poor and meek as she was, would become to Minoret. The worries of a personal estate that had to be sold off, the disposal of his coaching premises and the errands necessitated by unaccustomed business, his arguments with his wife over the slightest details and also over the purchase of the doctor's house, where Zélie wished to live in true middle-class fashion so as to further her son's career: all this commotion, so different from his ordinary peaceful way of life, prevented Minoret from thinking about his victim. But a few days after he had settled in the Rue des Bourgeois, towards the middle of May as he was on his way back from a walk, he heard the sound of a piano, saw La Bougival sitting by the window like a dragon guarding a treasure, and suddenly within himself he heard a nagging voice.

It would perhaps necessitate a whole treatise on morality to explain why, in a man of Minoret's stamp, the sight of Ursule immediately became unbearable, when she did not even suspect the theft that had been carried out to her detriment; how the sight of such greatness in misfortune filled him with the desire to expel the young girl from the town; and how that desire took on the nature both of a hatred and a passion. Perhaps he did not believe he was the lawful owner of the 36,000 francs investment income so long as the person to whom it belonged lived close by him. Perhaps he had a vague idea that some stroke of fate would reveal his theft, so long as those whom he had robbed were near at hand. Perhaps Ursule's presence aroused remorse in a nature that had something primitive and almost crude about it but which until then had always acted legally. Perhaps this remorse was all the more poignant because he had still greater wealth acquired by lawful means. He no doubt attributed these twinges of conscience to Ursule's mere presence, imagining that if the girl were to disappear his gnawing anxieties would disappear along with her. Above all, perhaps crime has its doctrine of perfection. The beginning of evil ways leads on to its appointed end, the first wound cries out for the death blow. Perhaps the inevitable outcome of theft is murder? Minoret had carried out the theft without giving it the least thought, so rapid had been the train of events: thought came afterwards. If you have gained a true picture of the man's face and build, you will understand the prodigious effect that thought would have upon him. Remorse is greater than thought, it arises from a feeling which can no more be hidden than love can, and which has its own tyrannic force. But just as Minoret had not had the slightest thought in his head when stealing the fortune intended for Ursule, so his wish to expel her from Nemours was mechanical now that he felt wounded by the sight of such innocence deceived. In true imbecile fashion he did not consider the consequences, he went on from danger to danger, urged forward by instinctive greed, just like a wild animal that cannot foresee the huntsman's wiles, relying on its speed and strength. Before long the wealthy middle-class people who used to forgather at the notary Dionis's house noticed a change in the manners and attitude of a man who at one time had been so carefree.

'I don't know what's the matter with Minoret, he's gone so queer!' his wife would remark. Minoret had resolved to conceal his audacious theft from her.

Everybody accounted for Minoret's dejection (for the thoughtful expression on his face resembled dejection) by his complete abandonment of all business and his sudden transition from an active working life to prosperous retirement. Whilst Minoret was thinking of crushing Ursule, La Bougival never allowed a day to pass without some remark to her foster-daughter about the fortune that ought to have been hers, or without comparing her wretched fate to the life that the doctor had intended her to lead, about which he had spoken to her (La Bougival).

'Besides,' she would say, 'and I don't say this because of myself, would the doctor – such a kind man that he was – have forgotten to leave me the slightest little thing? . . .'

'Don't you have me?' Ursule replied, forbidding La Bougival to say a word about this to her.

She did not want self-interested thoughts to sully the sad, gentle, affectionate memories associated with the old doctor's noble face, which her drawing-master had depicted in a black and white pencil sketch that now adorned her little sitting-room. To her fresh, beautiful imagination the sight of this sketch was always sufficient to remind her of her godfather, whom she thought of continually and, above all, by whose favourite objects she was surrounded: his large deep arm-chair, his backgammon board and the furniture from his study, besides the piano which he had given her. The two old friends whom she still had, Abbé Chaperon and Monsieur Bongrand, were the only people she was willing to invite to her house; amidst the things which her regrets almost brought to life, they were like two living memories of her past, connected with her life in the present through the love which had obtained her godfather's blessing. Soon the melancholy of her thoughts was imperceptibly softened, and lightly tinged her waking hours, combining all these things into an indefinable harmony: as was seen in her exquisite cleanliness, in the most precisely symmetrical arrangement of her furniture, a few flowers given to her each day by Savinien, elegant trifles, and in the peacefulness which her way of life imparted to the things around her, making her home agreeable. After breakfast and mass she continued her studies and singing practice; then, sitting at her window overlooking the street, she would do embroidery. At four o'clock Savinien, returning from the ride he always went for whatever the weather, and seeing her half-opened window, would sit on the sill and chat with her for half an hour. In the evenings the parish priest and the magistrate would visit her, but she never wanted Savinien to accompany them. And she certainly did not accept Madame de Portenduère's proposal, which Savinien had talked her into, that Ursule should come to live with her. The young woman and La Bougival lived moreover in the strictest economy: they did not spend more than sixty francs a month, all told. The old nurse was indefatigable: she washed and ironed, only cooked twice a week, and kept the cooked meats, which she and her mistress ate cold; Ursule wanted to save 700 francs a year so as to pay off what she still owed on the house. Such strictness of conduct, her modesty, and her acceptance of a humble, impoverished way of life after enjoying a luxurious existence in which her slightest whims were gratified, obtained a few people's approval. Ursule gained respect, and freedom from slighting criticism. What is more, now that they were satisfied the Minoret heirs did her justice. Savinien admired such strength of character in so young a girl. Occasionally, as they came out of mass, Madame de Portenduère spoke a few kindly words to Ursule, and twice she invited her to dinner and called round for her herself. Though this was not yet happiness, it was at least peace of mind. But a successful negotiation in which the conciliative magistrate displayed his old skills as a solicitor sparked off the persecution of Ursule contemplated by Minoret, which till then had remained no more than a hidden wish. As soon as all the business relating to the inheritance was completed, the magistrate, at Ursule's earnest request, took charge of the Portenduères' case, promising her to get them out of their difficulties; but during his visit to the old lady, whose opposition to Ursule's happiness infuriated him, he made a point of letting her know that he was only supporting her interests in order to please Mademoiselle Mirouët. He chose one of his former clerks to act as the Portenduères' solicitor at Fontainebleau, and personally supervised the plea in abatement of the proceedings. He wanted to take advantage of the interval of time between the annulment of the creditors' action and Massin's revival of proceedings to renew the lease on the farm at a rental of 6,000 francs, and also obtain some consideration from the farmers and the advance payment of the final year's rent. From that time the whist parties were resumed at Madame de Portenduère's, between himself, the parish priest, Savinien and Ursule, whom Bongrand and Abbé Chaperon used to call for and accompany home every evening. In June Bongrand succeeded in getting Massin's lawsuit against the Portenduères quashed. He immediately signed the new lease, obtaining a cash sum of 32,000 francs from the farmer and a rent of 6,000 francs for a term of eighteen years; then the same evening, before news got out of these operations, he went to see Zélie, knowing she was having some difficulty in investing her capital, and suggested she should buy Les Bordières for 220,000 francs.

'I'd agree to the deal immediately,' said Minoret, 'if I knew the Portenduères were going to move out of Nemours.'

'But why?' asked the magistrate.

'We don't want any aristocrats in Nemours.'

'I seem to remember hearing the old lady say that if she could get her affairs sorted out Brittany would be almost the only place where she could live on what money she had left. She's talking of selling her house.'

'Well! sell it to me,' said Minoret.

'Look, you're talking as if you were the master here,' said Zélie. 'What do you want with two houses?'

'If I don't conclude the deal for Les Bordières with you this evening,' the conciliative magistrate continued, 'people will know we've got a lease, we'll be distrained on again in three days' time and I'll have missed the chance of this liquidation, which I've set my heart on. So from here I'm going to Melun, where I know some farmers who'll buy Les Bordières with no questions asked. And you'll lose an opportunity of investing at 3 per cent in agricultural land close to Le Rouvre.'

'Well then, why have you come to us?' asked Zélie.

'Because you've got the money, whereas it'll take my old clients a few days to cough up 129,000 francs. I don't want any difficulties.'

'If *she* leaves Nemours, I'll pay you the money!' Minoret repeated.

'You'll understand I can't make any promise for the Portenduères,' Bongrand answered; 'but I am certain they won't stay in Nemours.'

On the strength of this assurance, Minoret – nudged on by Zélie – promised the money that would pay off the Portenduères' debt to the doctor's estate. The sale contract was then drawn up by Dionis, and the happy conciliative magistrate obtained Minoret's acceptance of the terms of the new lease; only when it was too late did Minoret and Zélie realize they had lost the final year's rent which was payable in advance. Towards the end of June Bongrand brought Madame de Portenduère her final discharge from debts together with what remained of her fortune, 129,000 francs, urging her to invest the money in Government stock which, at 5 per cent interest, would give her a private income of 6,000 francs if Savinien's 10,000 francs capital were also included. Thus, far from losing any money, the old lady was gaining 2,000 francs a year in interest through her liquidation; and so the Portenduère family remained in Nemours. Minoret believed he had been tricked, as if the conciliative magistrate could have known that Ursule's presence was unbearable to him, and this gave rise to a keen feeling of resentment which increased his hatred of his victim. Then began the secret drama, a drama terrible in its consequences, of the struggle between two sentiments, Minoret's which urged him to drive Ursule from Nemours, and Ursule's which gave her the strength to endure persecutions whose cause was for some time unfathomable: a strange, bizarre situation towards which all the previous events had led, which they had originated and to which they are the preface.

17. The Terribly Malicious Tricks that Can be Played in the Country

MADAME MINORET, to whom her husband gave silver plate and a complete dinner service costing about 20,000 francs, held a superb dinner each Sunday, the day when her son the deputy public prosecutor brought along a few friends from Fontainebleau. For these sumptuous dinners Zélie ordered a few delicacies from Paris, thus compelling the notary Dionis to imitate her splendour. Goupil, whom the Minorets strove to banish from their circle as if he was a blemished man tarnishing their splendour, was not invited till towards the end of July, one month after the prosperous middle-class retirement of the former postmaster and his wife had begun. The head clerk, already alive to this premeditated snub, was obliged to use the formal *vous* when speaking to Désiré who, since taking up his post, had adopted a serious and haughty manner even towards his family.

'So you've forgotten about Esther, since you love Mademoiselle Mirouët so much?' Goupil asked the deputy public prosecutor.

'To begin with, sir, Esther is dead. Besides, I've never given Ursule a thought,' he answered.

'Then what did you mean by that, Minoret?' exclaimed Goupil very insolently.

Minoret, caught out in the most flagrant lie by such a formidable man, would not have known what to say or do except for the motive that had prompted Goupil's invitation to dinner: he remembered the proposal the head clerk had once made about preventing a marriage between Ursule and young Portenduère. His only reply was to walk off abruptly with the clerk towards the bottom of the garden.

'You'll soon be twenty-eight, young man,' he said, 'and you're not on the road to a fortune yet. I want to help you. After all, you were my son's best friend as a boy. Listen to me. Young Ursule Mirouët has an income of 40,000 francs a year; if you can persuade her to become your wife, as true as my name's Minoret I'll give you the money to buy a notary's practice in Orleans.'

'No, I wouldn't be sufficiently important there; but at Montargis . . .'

'No,' said Minoret, 'but Sens . . .'

'Sens would be fine!' answered the loathsome head clerk. 'There's an archbishop of Sens, I've got nothing against a religious town. A little hypocrisy helps you along. Besides, Ursule's a churchgoer, she'll be a success.'

'It must be clearly understood,' said Minoret, 'that I shan't hand out the 100,000 francs until my cousin's marriage. I want to provide for her out of respect for my late uncle.'

'And why not a bit of respect for me?' said Goupil mockingly. He suspected there was some secret behind Minoret's behaviour. 'Isn't it thanks to my information you've been able to buy land producing 24,000 francs a year around the Château du Rouvre – lumping it together all in one stretch, with no other landholdings inside yours? With your meadows and mill on the opposite bank of the Loing, you'd add 16,000 francs a year! Look here, old man, do you want to be perfectly frank with me?'

'Yes.'

'Well then, just to let you feel my fangs, I've been dabbling with buying the Rouvre estate for Massin, with its park, gardens, preserves and woodland.'

'What do you think of that?' interrupted Zélie.

'Now then,' said Goupil, glancing at him venomously, 'if I so choose, tomorrow Massin can have it all for 200,000 francs.'

'Leave us to ourselves, wife,' said the colossus, taking Zélie by the arm and leading her away, 'I'm getting on fine with him . . . We've had so many things on our minds,' Minoret continued, coming back to Goupil, 'that we haven't had time to think of you; but I trust your friendship to get us the Rouvre estate.'

'Yes,' said Goupil mischievously, 'a former marquisate, which managed by you would soon be producing 50,000 francs a year: that's capital equal to more than two million francs as things stand at present.'

'And our son the deputy public prosecutor could then marry a field-marshal's daughter, or the heiress of some ancient family who would further his career as a magistrate in Paris,' said the postmaster, opening his large snuff-box and offering Goupil a pinch.

'Well then, are we playing straight?' cried Goupil, shaking his fingers clean.

Minoret seized Goupil's hands and shook them as he replied: 'On my honour!'

Like all wily people, the head clerk believed – luckily for Minoret – that his marriage to Ursule was the pretext for a reconciliation with the postmaster, after his involvement with Massin in opposition to them.

'He didn't dream up that fib,' he thought. 'I see Zélie's fingers in this pie, she's told him what line to take. Phhh! Let's drop Massin. Three years from now,' he thought, 'I'll be the deputy for Sens.' Noticing just then that Bongrand was walking along to the whist party opposite, he hurried out into the street.

'You're very concerned about Ursule Mirouët, dear Monsieur Bongrand,' he said; 'you can't be indifferent as to her future. Here's what I suggest: she could marry a notary with a practice in an important town. This notary, who's bound to become a deputy within three years, would allow her a dowry of 100,000 francs.'

'She's had a better proposal than that,' snapped Bongrand. 'Madame de Portenduère hasn't been too well since her misfortunes; even yesterday she looked terribly different, her grief is killing her. Savinien still has 6,000 francs investment income, and Ursule has 40,000 francs. I'll increase their capital for them, rather like Massin but honestly, and ten years from now they'll have a small fortune.'

'Savinien would be making a mistake. He could marry Mademoiselle du Rouvre whenever he liked. She's an only daughter, and her uncle and aunt want to leave her two superb fortunes.'

'When love holds sway, farewell to prudence, as La Fontaine has written. Anyway, who is this notary? Because after all . . .' Bongrand asked out of curiosity.

'Me,' answered Goupil; and the magistrate trembled.

'You?' Bongrand said, unable to conceal his disgust.

'Ah well, never mind, sir,' Goupil replied, with a look full of bitterness, hatred and defiance.

'Do you want to be the wife of a notary who would allow you a dowry of 100,000 francs?' cried Bongrand, walking into the little sitting-room and speaking to Ursule, who was sitting beside Madame de Portenduère.

Ursule and Savinien, trembling on the same impulse, looked at each other: she smilingly, he without daring to show his anxiety.

'I am not the mistress of my actions,' Ursule replied, holding out her hand to Savinien unseen by the old lady.

'And that's why I turned it down without even consulting you.'

'But why?' asked Madame de Portenduère. 'Surely, child, it's a fine thing to be a notary?'

'I prefer the delights of poverty; compared with what I might have expected from life, this is opulence to me. Besides, my old nurse saves me a lot of trouble, and I shan't go and exchange my present life, which I like, for an unknown future.'

The next day, when the post was delivered, two hearts were filled with the poison of two anonymous letters: one addressed to Madame de Portenduère and the other to Ursule. This is the letter the old lady received:

You love your son, and wish to set him up in a manner which befits his name, yet in inviting Ursule, a regimental musician's daughter, to your home, you are supporting him in his infatuation for an ambitious little minx with no money to her name. Whereas you could be marrying him to Mademoiselle du Rouvre, whose two uncles, Monsieur le Marquis de Ronquerolles and Monsieur le Chevalier du Rouvre, each have a private income of 30,000 francs and are anxious not to bequeath their fortunes to that mad old spendthrift Monsieur du Rouvre; they plan to make arrangements for their niece in the marriage settlement. Madame de Sérizy, Clémentine du Rouvre's aunt, has just lost her only son in the Algerian campaign; no doubt she will adopt her niece. A well-wisher has reason to believe that Savinien would be acceptable.

And this was the letter to Ursule:

Dear Ursule,

There is a young man in Nemours who worships you to distraction. He cannot see you working at your window without feeling emotions which prove to him that his love is lifelong. This young man is endowed with a will of iron and a perseverance that nothing can dishearten. So please look favourably on his love, because his intentions are entirely pure and he humbly requests your hand out of a desire to make you happy. His fortune, though decent enough already, is as nothing compared with what he will make for you when you become his wife. One day you will be received at court as a minister's wife, as one of the leading ladies in the land. As he sees you every day without your seeing him, put one of La Bougival's vases of carnations on your window-sill. This will be your sign that he can declare himself.

Ursule burned the letter without mentioning it to Savinien. Two days later she received another, written in the following terms:

You were wrong, dear Ursule, not to reply to the man who loves you more than his own life. You think you are going to marry Savinien, but you are making a huge mistake. The marriage will not take place. Madame de Portenduère will not invite you to her house any more. Despite her poor state of health, she is walking to the Château du Rouvre this morning to ask for Mademoiselle du Rouvre as Savinien's bride. Savinien will give in eventually. What objection can he have? The young lady's uncles stipulate in the marriage settlement that their fortunes will pass to their niece. Their combined fortunes produce a private income of 60,000 francs a year.

This letter wrought havoc in Ursule's heart, awakening her to the tortures of jealousy, suffering she had never known until then but which – in a constitution so rich with life and so prone to pain – spread grief and mourning over the present, the future and even the past. Immediately she received this fatal piece of paper, she sat motionless in the doctor's armchair, her eyes staring into space, her mind lost in a painful dream. In a moment she felt the cold hand of death supplant the ardent glow of a life of beauty. Alas! it was worse than this: it was really like the dreadful awakening of the dead into a knowledge that God does not exist, the masterpiece of that strange genius Jean Paul Richter. Four times La Bougival tried to get Ursule to eat breakfast: she saw her picking her bread up only to put it down again – unable to bring it to her lips. Whenever she tried to put in a word of protest, Ursule would reply with a motion of the hand and one terrible word: 'Hush!' – pronouncing it as despotically now as her words hitherto had been kind and gentle. Keeping an eye on her mistress through the glass window of the communicating door, La Bougival saw her by turns as red as if she was consumed with fever and as blue as if cold shivering had followed that feverishness. Her condition grew worse towards four o'clock, when every moment or so Ursule would stand up to see if Savinien was coming – and Savinien never came. Jealousy and doubt rob love of all its modesty. Ursule, who until then would never have made any gesture betraying her passion, donned her hat and little shawl and rushed out into the corridor to go and meet Savinien; but a residue of modesty brought her back into her little sitting-room. She wept. When the parish priest arrived that evening, the poor nurse stopped him on the threshold.

'Oh Father! I don't know what's the matter with Mademoiselle; she . . .'

'I know,' the priest answered sadly, interrupting the frightened nurse.

Abbé Chaperon then informed Ursule of what she had not dared to check: Madame de Portenduère had gone to dinner at the Château du Rouvre.

'And what about Savinien?'

'He's gone too.'

Ursule's slight nervous trembling made Abbé Chaperon shudder as if he had received a discharge from a Leyden jar, and the emotional shock he also sustained was slow to pass away.

'So we shan't be going to see her this evening,' said the parish priest; 'and it would be wise, my child, if you didn't go there again. Your pride would be wounded by the reception you'd get from the old lady. We persuaded her to allow discussion of your marriage but we have no idea what has prompted her change of mind.'

'I am ready for anything. Nothing can surprise me now,' said Ursule with heartfelt feeling. 'In these kinds of crisis it is a great consolation to know one hasn't offended God.'

'Be submissive, dear child, and never probe into the ways of Providence,' said the parish priest.

'I wouldn't want to feel any unjust suspicion of Monsieur de Portenduère's character.'

'Why don't you call him Savinien any more?' asked the priest, noticing a slight tone of bitterness in Ursule's voice.

'Yes,' she wept, 'dear Savinien. Oh dearest friend!' she sobbed, 'a voice still cries out to me that his heart is as noble as his breeding. Not only has he confessed to me that he loved me and me alone, he has proved it to me by countless acts of tenderness and by heroically restraining his ardent feelings. Recently, as he took the hand I held out to him, when Monsieur Bongrand was suggesting a notary as my husband, I swear that that was the first time I had ever offered it to him. Though it all began with a joke when he blew me a kiss across the street, since that time his affection has never strayed, as you know, from the strictest bounds of decency; but I can tell you this, since you can read my soul, except that part of it which is reserved for the angels, that with me this feeling is the source of many virtues; it has led me to accept my griefs, it has perhaps softened the bitterness of my irreparable loss, which I mourn more in my outward clothing than in my heart of hearts. Oh yes, I've done wrong! In me love was stronger than my gratitude to my godfather, and God has punished me for it. But, you see, I respected myself as Savinien's wife; I was too proud, and perhaps it's this pride which God is punishing. God alone, as you have told me, must be the mainspring and goal of our actions.'

The parish priest was touched by the sight of tears streaming down a face that was already so pale. The greater the poor girl's security had been, the greater was her fall.

'But,' she went on, 'once I return to my life as an orphan, I'll feel like an orphan again. After all, can I be a millstone round the neck of the man I love? What business has he here? Who am I to aspire to him? Besides, don't I love him with so divine a love that it even extends to the complete sacrifice of my happiness and hopes? . . . And you know I have often reproached myself for basing my love on the grave, and for knowing that it could not be fulfilled until after an old lady's death. If Savinien is made rich and happy by another woman, I have just enough money to pay my dowry for the convent I shall enter immediately. There must no more be two loves in a woman's heart than two masters in heaven. The religious life will have attractions for me.'

'He couldn't allow his mother to go to the Château du Rouvre alone,' the kind priest remarked gently.

'Don't let's mention it again, dear Monsieur Chaperon. I'll write this evening giving him his freedom. How delightful to have to close the windows in this room!'

And she informed the old man of the anonymous letters, telling him she had no wish to allow her unknown lover to continue his courtship.

'Ah! it's an anonymous letter to Madame de Portenduère that's made her go to the Château du Rouvre,' cried the priest. 'It's clear you're being persecuted by evil people.'

'But why? Neither Savinien nor I have done anybody any harm, and we're not in conflict with anyone's financial interests any more.'

'Anyway, my dear, this storm in a teacup will be disrupting our parties but it will also give us an opportunity to set out our poor friend's library. The books are lying about in heaps. Bongrand and I will arrange them all, we're actually thinking of doing some research from them. Put your trust in God; but also remember that you have two devoted friends in the kind magistrate and myself.'

'That's a great deal,' she said, accompanying the priest as far as the beginning of her garden path, and craning her neck like a bird looking out of its nest, still hoping to glimpse Savinien.

Just then Minoret and Goupil, on their way back from a walk in the meadows, stopped as they passed by and the doctor's heir said to Ursule: 'What's the matter, cousin? we're still cousins, aren't we? You look different.'

Goupil was eyeing Ursule with such ardent looks that she was frightened by him; she went indoors without replying.

'She's shy,' said Minoret to the priest.

'Mademoiselle Mirouët is right not to stand at her doorstep chatting to men. She's too young . . .'

'Ha!' said Goupil, 'you must know she isn't short of admirers.'

The parish priest had hastily bowed his farewell and was hurrying off in the direction of the Rue des Bourgeois.

'Well!' the head clerk said to Minoret, 'things are warming up! She's as pale as a corpse already; but she'll have left the town within a fortnight. You'll see.'

'It's better having you as a friend than an enemy,' cried Minoret, frightened by the wicked smile that gave Goupil's face the fiendish expression which Joseph Bridau has conferred on Goethe's Mephistopheles.

'I should think so,' answered Goupil. 'If she doesn't marry me, I'll kill her with grief.'

'If you do that, young fellow, I'll *give* you the money to become a Parisian notary. Then you can marry a wealthy woman . . .'

'Poor girl! What has she done to you?' asked the clerk in surprise.

'She annoys me!' Minoret said roughly.

'Wait till Monday. Then you'll see what tortures I'll put her through,' Goupil replied, studying the former postmaster's face.

The next day old Bougival went to Savinien's house and said, as she handed him a letter: 'I don't know what the dear child has written to you; but she just acts as if she was dead this morning.'

Who, reading this letter to Savinien, cannot imagine the sufferings that had beset Ursule during the night?

My dear Savinien,

I am told your mother wants you to marry Mademoiselle du Rouvre, and perhaps she is right. You stand between an almost poverty-stricken life and a life of affluence, between the fiancée of your heart and a fashionable woman, between obedience to your mother and obedience to your own choice, for I still believe you have chosen me. Savinien, if you have a decision to make, I want you to make it in complete freedom: I release you from the promise you made to yourself, not to me, in a moment that will never fade from my memory – a moment which, like every day that has followed it, was of angelic sweetness and purity. This memory is sufficient for the whole of my lifetime. If you persist in your solemn oath, a dark and terrible idea will now disturb my happiness. Amidst our hardships, accepted so cheerfully today, you might think later on that if you had obeyed the dictates of society things would have been very different for you. If you were a man who voiced such a thought, it would be my sentence to a painful death; and if you did not mention it, I should be suspicious of the very slightest cloud that darkened your forehead. Dear Savinien, I have always preferred you to anything on this earth. I could do so since my godfather, although he was jealous, used to say to me: 'Love him, my girl! You will quite definitely belong to each other one day.' When I went to Paris I loved you with a hopeless love, and that feeling was enough. I do not know whether I can recover that feeling, but I shall try. What are we anyway at this moment? A brother and sister. Let us stay like that. Marry that lucky girl, who will have the joy of giving back to your family name the lustre which it must have, but which your mother thinks I would diminish. You will never hear of me again. The world will give you its approval. I shall never blame you, and always love you. Farewell.

'Wait!' cried the nobleman.

He motioned to La Bougival to sit down, and scribbled these few words:

My dear Ursule,

Your letter breaks my heart in that you have worried yourself a great deal to no purpose, and for the first time our hearts have ceased to be in harmony. You are not my wife because I can't get married without my mother's consent. Anyway, isn't living on 8,000 francs a year in a pretty cottage on the banks of the Loing a fortune in itself? We've worked out that with La Bougival we'd save 5,000 francs a year! One evening in your uncle's garden you allowed me to consider you as my fiancée; you cannot break our common ties just by yourself. So need I tell you that yesterday I told Monsieur du Rouvre flatly that, if I were free, I wouldn't want to obtain my fortune from a young woman I did not know! My mother doesn't wish to see you any more, I shall lose the happiness of our evenings together, but do not rob me of the brief moment when I speak to you at your window ... Till this afternoon. Nothing can come between us.

'There, old girl. She mustn't be anxious a moment longer than necessary . . .'

At four in the afternoon, on his way back from the ride he deliberately went on every day so as to pass by Ursule's house, Savinien found his beloved looking a little pale as a result of such sudden upheavals.

'I think I never realized until now what pleasure it gave me to see you,' she told him.

'You told me,' Savinien replied with a smile, '(you see, I remember every word you say): "Lovers must have patience. I'll wait!" So, dearest, have you lost faith in our love? . . . Ah! This is the last of our quarrels! You were claiming to love me more than I love you. Have I ever doubted you?' he asked, offering her a posy of wild flowers which he had put together as an expression of his thoughts.

'You have no reason to doubt me,' she replied. 'And in any case, you don't know the complete facts,' she added uneasily.

She had given instructions for no letters addressed to herself to be accepted at the post office. But, though she had no idea what magic brought it about, a few moments after Savinien's departure, after watching him turn the corner from the Rue des Bourgeois into the High Street, she found a piece of paper lying on her armchair; it read: '*Beware! The spurned lover will grow fiercer than a tiger.*' Despite Savinien's entreaties, she was unwilling for prudence's sake to confess the terrible secret reason for her fear. Only the unspeakable pleasure of seeing Savinien again after thinking she had lost him could blot out from her mind the deathly chill that had just gripped her. To await an undefined misfortune is a horrifying torture for any-one. Suffering then takes on the proportions of the unknown, which to the soul is certainly an infinite realm; this caused Ursule the greatest pain. She was dreadfully startled at the slightest noise, she was afraid of silence, she suspected that her very walls were accomplices in her misfortune. And even her blissful sleep was disturbed. With his instinct for evil, Goupil – though knowing nothing of a constitution that was as deli-cate as a flower – had discovered the poison that would wither and kill her. However, the following day went by without surprises. Ursule played the piano until very late, and went to bed worn out by tiredness and feeling practically reassured. About midnight she was awakened by a concert consisting of a clarinet, oboe, flute, cornet, trombone, bassoon, flageolet and triangle. All the neighbours were at their windows. The poor child, already shaken at seeing people in the street, received a terrible blow on hearing a hoarse, common man's voice cry out: '*For beautiful Ursule Mirouët, with her lover's compliments.*' The next day, which was a Sunday, the whole town was agog with rumour and, both when she entered and when she came out of church, Ursule saw numerous groups of people standing around the square talking about her and displaying horrible curiosity. The serenade set everybody talking, everyone indulged in wild conjecture. Ursule walked home more dead than alive and did not emerge again; the parish priest had advised her to say vespers at home. As she entered her house she saw that a letter had been pushed under the door into the brick-floored corridor leading from the street to the court-yard. She picked it up and read it from a desire to find some explanation. The least sensitive of beings can imagine what she must have felt on reading these terrible lines:

Resign yourself to becoming my wife, O woman rich and adored! I desire you. If I do not possess you alive, I shall possess you dead. Blame your refusals for the misfortunes which will befall not only you.

Your lover, to whom one day you will belong.

And, strange to relate, just as the gentle, tender victim of this plot was being struck down like a severed flower, Mademoiselle Massin, Mademoiselle Dionis and Mademoiselle Crémière were envying her fate.

'How lucky she is!' they were saying. 'People take notice of her, they pander to her tastes, they're all after her! It seems the serenade was charming! There was a coronet!'

'What's a coronet?'

'A new musical instrument! See, *that* big,' Angéline Crémière explained to Pamela Massin.

Immediately the next morning Savinien had even gone to Fontainebleau to try and find out who had asked for the regimental musicians from the garrison; but as there were two men to every instrument, it was impossible to find out which men had gone to Nemours. The colonel forbade the musicians to play for private individuals without his permission. The nobleman had an interview with the public prosecutor, Ursule's guardian, pointing out to him the serious nature of this kind of scene for a young girl who was so delicate and frail; he begged him to use all the means available to the Crown Attorney's department to find out who had instigated the serenade. Three days later, in the small hours of the morning, three violins, a flute, a guitar and an oboe performed a second serenade. This time the musicians made off in the direction of Montargis, where a troupe of strolling players was then quartered. Between two items a strident, drunken voice had cried out: 'To the daughter of Captain Mirouët, regimental director of music!' In this way the whole of Nemours learned the profession of Ursule's father, a secret so carefully guarded by old Dr Minoret.

This time Savinien did not go to Montargis. During the day he received an anonymous letter from Paris, containing the following horrible prophecy:

You will not marry Ursule. If you want her to remain alive, you must immediately surrender her to a man who loves her more than you do; for he has become a musician and an artist in order to please her, and he prefers to see her dead than to know she is your wife.

The Nemours doctor was coming three times a day to see Ursule, whom these secret persecutions were putting within risk of death. Feeling herself plunged into a quagmire by some infernal hand, this sweet girl maintained a martyr's attitude: she remained in deep silence, raising her eyes to Heaven and ceasing to weep; she awaited the blows in fervent prayer, imploring for the man from whom death would come.

'I'm happy I can't go downstairs into the sitting-room,' she would say to Monsieur Bongrand and Abbé Chaperon, who left her as little as possible; '*he* would come, and I feel I'm unworthy to be looked at in the adoring way *he* looks at me! Do you think he suspects me?'

'But if Savinien can't find the man behind these vile deeds, he intends to go and ask the Parisian police to intervene,' said Bongrand.

'My unknown persecutors must know I have received a fatal blow,' she replied; 'they'll keep quiet now.'

The parish priest, Bongrand and Savinien were beside themselves with conjectures and suppositions. Savinien, Tiennette, La Bougival and two people who were devoted to the priest became spies and kept on the alert for a week; but no indiscretion could betray Goupil, who planned everything by himself. The conciliative magistrate was the first person to think that the instigator of evil had grown frightened of his handiwork. Ursule was taking on the pallor and weakness of young English girls suffering from consumption. Everyone relaxed his efforts. There were no more serenades or letters. Savinien attributed the cessation of these hateful practices to the secret inquiries being carried out by the public prosecutor's department, to whom he had sent the letters which he, his mother and Ursule had received. The armistice did not last long. When the doctor had just halted Ursule's nervous fever, just as she had regained courage, a rope ladder was found one morning towards the middle of July dangling from her bedroom window. The postilion who had been driving the mail coach that night declared that a little man was climbing down just as he passed by; his horses were heading at full speed down the hill to the bridge, at the corner of which stood Ursule's house; despite his attempt to stop, they carried him on well beyond Nemours. According to one view put about at Dionis's drawing-rooms, these schemes were the work of the Marquis du Rouvre, who at that time was exceedingly hard up, with Massin holding bills of exchange against him: through his daughter's prompt marriage to Savinien he would, so it was claimed, deprive his creditors of the Château du Rouvre. Madame de Portenduère was also delighted, it was said, by anything that could attract attention to Ursule and discredit and dishonour her; but faced with the possibility of a youthful death, the old lady found herself almost defeated. Abbé Chaperon was so deeply affected by this last stroke of wickedness that it made him ill, so ill that he stayed indoors for a few days. Poor Ursule, who had suffered a relapse as a result of this odious attack, received a letter from Abbé Chaperon through the post which had not been rejected at the post office as the handwriting was recognized.

Dear Child,
   Leave Nemours, and outwit the malice of your unknown enemies. They may be trying to endanger Savinien's life. I will tell you more when I am able to call on you.

The note was signed: *Your devoted* CHAPERON.

   When Savinien, who nearly went mad, went round to see the parish priest, the poor abbé read and reread the letter – he was so appalled by the perfect way in which his handwriting and signature had been forged: for he had written nothing; and supposing he had written, he would certainly not have sent his letter to Ursule through the post. The fatal condition brought on in Ursule by this last atrocity compelled Savinien to go yet again to the public prosecutor, taking with him the priest's counterfeit letter.

   'A murder is being committed by methods unforeseen by the law, and the victim is an orphan girl whom the law has declared to be your ward,' the nobleman told the magistrate.

   'If you can find ways of stamping this out,' the public prosecutor answered, 'I'll try them; but I don't know of any! This anonymous scoundrel has given the best advice. Mademoiselle Mirouët must be sent here to the nuns of the Adoration of the Holy Sacrament. Meanwhile, the police inspector at Fontainebleau will, at my request, permit you to carry arms in self-defence. I have been over to the Château du Rouvre myself, and Monsieur du Rouvre has been justifiably indignant at the suspicions circulating about him. Minoret, my deputy's father, is negotiating to buy his château. Mademoiselle du Rouvre is marrying a rich Polish count. Anyway, Monsieur du Rouvre was leaving his country estate the day I went over there, to avoid imprisonment for debt.'

   Désiré, questioned by his chief, dared not reveal his thought! He detected Goupil's involvement! Goupil alone was capable of conducting an affair perilously close to breaching the penal code without falling into the precipice of infringing any particular article. Goupil's impunity, secrecy and success increased his boldness. This terrifying clerk got Massin, who had become his cat's-paw, to sue the Marquis du Rouvre, so as to force the nobleman to sell Minoret the remainder of his land. After opening negotiations with a notary at Sens, he decided to have one last try to obtain Ursule. He wanted to imitate a few young Parisian men who have owed their wives and fortunes to a runaway marriage. The services he had rendered Minoret, Massin and Crémière, and the protection given him by Dionis – the master of Nemours – enabled him to hush up the affair. He at once decided to throw off his mask, believing that Ursule would be incapable of resisting him in the weak condition to which he had reduced her. Nevertheless, before making his last move in this dastardly game he thought it as well to have a frank discussion at the Château du Rouvre, where he accompanied Minoret who was making his first visit there since the signing of the contract. Minoret had just received a confidential letter from his son asking for information about what was happening with regard to Ursule, before he himself and the public prosecutor went to collect her from her home and put her into a convent out of reach of any new act of villainy. The deputy public prosecutor urged his father, if it should come to light that the persecution was the work of one of their friends, to give that friend some wise advice. Though justice could not always punish everything, it would eventually find everything out and would bear the facts in mind ... Minoret had attained a great goal. Now the absolute owner of the Château du Rouvre, one of the finest in the Gâtinais district, he had assembled a rich and fine estate around the park yielding him an income of forty odd thousand francs a year. The colossus did not care a damn about Goupil now. Anyway, he was intending to live in the country, where he would no longer be troubled by thoughts of Ursule.

'Young fellow,' he said to Goupil, as he was walking along the terrace, 'leave my cousin alone!'

'What do you mean?' asked the clerk, unable to fathom this strange behaviour; for stupidity has its own depths.

'Oh! I'm not ungrateful. For 280,000 francs you've got me this fine mansion in brick and ashlar which couldn't be built for 600,000 francs nowadays, together with the home farm, the preserves, the park, gardens and woodlands . . . Yes, my word! I'll give you 10 per cent, 20,000 francs, which you can use to buy a tipstaff's practice in Nemours. And I guarantee you can marry one of the Crémière daughters – the eldest.'

'The one who's always talking about coronets?' cried Goupil.

'But my cousin Madame Crémière will give her 30,000 francs,' Minoret continued. 'Look here, young man, you were born to be a tipstaff just as I was cut out to be a postmaster. A man must always follow his vocation.'

'Well then,' said Goupil, his high hopes dashed, 'here are some revenue stamps. Sign me 20,000 francs worth of acceptances and then I can negotiate with ready money.'

Minoret was due to receive 18,000 francs as half-yearly interest on the scrips which his wife did not know he possessed; he thought that by doing this he would get rid of Goupil, and so he signed. The head clerk, seeing this colossal, imbecile Machiavelli of the Rue des Bourgeois in an upsurge of pride in his lordly possessions, took his departure with the words 'I'll be seeing you', and a look that would have struck fear into anyone but a self-made nincompoop, looking from a terrace on to the gardens and magnificent roofs of a château built in the style fashionable under Louis XIII.

'Aren't you waiting for me?' he shouted, seeing Goupil walking away.

'You'll run into me on the way, old man!' answered the future tipstaff, thirsting for revenge and eager to know the key to the riddle presented to his mind by the strange zigzags in Minoret's behaviour.

18. Two Acts of Revenge

SINCE the day when her life had been sullied by the vilest slander, Ursule – suffering from one of those unexplainable illnesses whose cause is in the soul – was rapidly approaching death. She was deathly pale, spoke feebly and slowly at rare intervals, and the looks on her face were gentle but lacking in animation; everything about her, even her forehead, revealed the destructive effects of an overpowering thought. She believed that that ideal garland of chaste flowers had fallen which at all times nations have wished to place upon the heads of virgins. In the emptiness and silence she could hear the discreditable words, the malicious comments, and the laughter of the little town. This burden was too heavy for her to bear, and her innocence had too much delicacy to survive such bruising. She no longer complained, she maintained a sorrowful smile upon her lips, and her eyes often looked up to Heaven to appeal to the Lord of Angels against the injustice of mankind. When Goupil entered Nemours, Ursule had been brought down from her bedroom to the ground floor on the arms of La Bougival and the Nemours doctor. An immense event was to take place. After learning that this pure young girl was dying like a trapped animal, though she was less wounded in her honour than Clarissa Harlowe, Madame de Portenduère was coming to visit and console her. The sight of her son, who during the whole of the previous night had talked of committing suicide, unbent the old Breton woman. Moreover, Madame de Portenduère felt it behoved her dignity to give back courage to such a pure young girl, and considered her visit a counterpoise to all the harm that the townsfolk had done. Her opinion, which was weightier than that of the masses, would no doubt confirm the aristocracy in its power. This step, of which Abbé Chaperon gave news, brought about a transformation in Ursule, and gave hope to the despairing doctor who was talking of bringing in the most famous doctors in Paris for a consultation. Ursule had been placed in her guardian's armchair, and such was the nature of her beauty that, in her grief and suffering, she appeared lovelier than at any time in her happy days. When Savinien appeared, with his mother on his arm, the young patient's cheeks recovered some of their beautiful colouring.

'Don't get up, child,' said the old lady in a commanding voice; 'even though I am ill and weak myself, I wanted to visit you to tell you my thoughts about what is going on: I esteem you as the purest, holiest and most charming girl in the Gâtinais district, and I think you are worthy to make a nobleman happy.'

At first Ursule could not reply. She took hold of the withered hands of Savinien's mother, and dropped tears on them as she kissed them.

'Ah Madame!' she replied in a weak voice, 'I should never have had the boldness to think of raising myself above my social station had I not been encouraged to do so by promises. I was only justified in doing so by a limitless affection; but people have found ways of parting me for ever from the man I love: they have made me unworthy of him ... Never,' she said, with an elation in her voice that was painful in its effect on the onlookers, 'never will I agree to give my hand in marriage to any man if that hand has been defiled and my reputation tarnished. I was too much in love ... I can tell you this in the condition I'm in: I love a human being almost as much as I love God. And so God ...'

'Come, come, my dear, don't speak ill of God! Look, *my daughter*,' the old lady continued, with visible effort, 'don't exaggerate the importance of a sordid joke which nobody believes. I promise you you will live and be happy.'

'You will be happy, darling!' cried Savinien, kneeling at Ursule's feet and kissing her hands. 'Mother has called you *my daughter*.'

'That will be enough,' said the doctor, who came to take his patient's pulse. 'Don't kill her with happiness.'

At that moment Goupil, finding the gate into the side-passage ajar, opened the door into the little drawing-room and showed his terrible face, a face lively with the thoughts of revenge that had blossomed in his heart along the way.

'Monsieur de Portenduère,' he said in a voice resembling the hissing of a viper cornered in its hole.

'What do you want?' replied Savinien, standing up.

'I'd like a word with you.'

Savinien walked outside into the passage, and Goupil led him into the little yard.

'Swear to me on the life of Ursule whom you love, and on your honour as a nobleman which you so much prize, that what I'm going to tell you will make no difference between us; and I'll enlighten you as to the cause of Mademoiselle Mirouët's persecution.'

'Could I get that persecution to stop?'

'Yes.'

'Could I be revenged?'

'Against the instigator, yes; but against his instrument, no.'

'Why?'

'Well, because . . . I am the instrument . . .'

Savinien grew pale.

'I've just glimpsed Ursule . . .' the clerk continued.

'Ursule?' said the nobleman, with a look at Goupil.

'Mademoiselle Mirouët,' Goupil went on, warned by Savinien's tone of voice to become respectful, 'and I should like to shed all my blood to redeem what has been done. I repent . . . Even if you killed me in a duel or in some other way, what use would my blood be to you? Would you drink it? It would poison you at this moment.'

Both curiosity and this man's cold reasoning calmed Savinien's seething blood. He stared at him in a way that made the failed hunchback lower his gaze.

'Who put you up to this?' asked the young man.

'Do you swear?'

'You don't want anything to happen to you, do you?'

'I want both you and Mademoiselle Mirouët to forgive me.'

'She'll forgive you; but I never shall.'

'But you'll forget about it, won't you?'

What terrible power does reasoning have when backed by self-interest? Two men, one of them wanting to tear the other to pieces, stood in a little courtyard within inches of one another, compelled to converse, held together by one and the same feeling!

'I'll forgive you, but I'll never forget.'

'Nothing doing,' was Goupil's chill reply.

Savinien lost patience. He gave that face a slap that rang out in the yard, nearly knocking Goupil down; he himself staggered from the blow.

'I've only got what I deserve,' said Goupil; 'I've been a fool. I thought you were nobler than you are. You took unfair advantage of my offer . . . Now you are in my power!' and he darted a look of hatred at Savinien.

'You're a murderer,' said the nobleman.

'No more than the knife is a murderer,' answered Goupil.

'I beg your pardon!'

'Have you had your fill of revenge?' Goupil asked with ferocious irony. 'Will you stop at that?'

'Let's both forgive and forget,' said Savinien.

'Give me your hand,' said the clerk, holding out his to the nobleman.

'Here,' replied Savinien, swallowing his shame out of love for Ursule. 'But tell me, who was behind this?'

Goupil looked, so to speak, at the two scales on which Savinien's slap counterbalanced his hatred of Minoret. For a couple of seconds he was undecided. Finally a voice cried out inside him, 'You will be a notary!'; and he replied, 'Forgive and forget? Yes, let's both do that,' and shook the nobleman's hand.

'Well then, who's persecuting Ursule?' asked Savinien.

'Minoret! He'd have liked to see her dead and buried . . . Why, I have no idea; but we'll try and find out the reason. Don't get me involved in all this, I wouldn't be able to give you any more help if they distrusted me. Instead of attacking Ursule, I'll defend her; instead of helping Minoret, I'll try to thwart his plans. I only live to bring about his ruin, to destroy him! And I'll trample him under foot, I'll dance on his corpse, I'll make his bones into a set of dominoes! Tomorrow, across all the walls of Nemours, Fontainebleau and Le Rouvre, will be written in red crayon: *Minoret is a thief.* Yes! by . . . Jove!

229

I'll blow him sky high. Now we are allies through our indiscretions; well, if you want me to, I'll kneel at Mademoiselle Mirouët's feet, tell her that I curse the insane passion that urged me to kill her; I'll beg her to forgive me. That will do her good! The conciliative magistrate and the priest are there, those two witnesses are enough; but Monsieur Bongrand must promise on his honour not to harm me in my career. I have a career now!'

'Wait a minute,' replied Savinien, quite dazed by this revelation. 'Ursule, dearest,' he said, entering the drawing-room, 'the cause of all your misfortunes is horrified at what he has done, repents and wants to ask your forgiveness in these gentlemen's presence, on condition that everything is forgotten.'

'What, Goupil?' the priest, magistrate and doctor all said at once.

'Keep his secret,' begged Ursule, raising a finger to her lips.

Goupil heard these words, saw Ursule's gesture, and felt moved.

'Mademoiselle,' he said in heartfelt tones, 'I wish that at this moment the whole of Nemours could hear me confess to you that a fatal passion led my reason astray, suggesting crimes that would incur the censure of decent people. What I am telling you now I shall repeat everywhere, deploring the harm caused by nasty jokes; but these jokes will perhaps have helped you to hasten your happiness,' he said, a little mischievously, as he stood up, 'as I see Madame de Portenduère is here . . .'

'Very well, Goupil,' said the priest; 'Mademoiselle Mirouët has forgiven you; but you must never forget you nearly became a murderer.'

'Monsieur Bongrand,' Goupil continued, turning to the magistrate, 'I'm going to see Lecoeur this evening to negotiate the purchase of his practice, and I hope these amends won't harm me in your eyes, and that you'll support my application to the Public Prosecutor's Office and the Ministry.'

The conciliative magistrate nodded thoughtfully, and Goupil left to go and negotiate for the better of the two tipstaff's practices in Nemours. Everyone remained with Ursule, and tried hard during that evening to restore calm and tranquillity to her soul, where the satisfaction the clerk had given her was already having results.

'The whole of Nemours will find out,' said Bongrand.

'You see, dear child, that God bore you no enmity,' said the priest.

Minoret returned fairly late from the Château du Rouvre, and dined late. Towards nine o'clock, as it was beginning to grow dark, he was sitting digesting his dinner in the Chinese pavilion with his wife beside him, and with her he was making plans for Désiré's future. Désiré had really improved his ways since becoming a magistrate; he was working now, and there was a chance that he might succeed the public prosecutor at Fontainebleau who, it was said, was being transferred to Melun. He had to be found a wife, a poor girl belonging to an ancient and noble family; he might then be appointed a magistrate in Paris. Perhaps they might be able to get him elected deputy for Fontainebleau, where Zélie believed they should spend the winters after living at Le Rouvre during the fine weather. Secretly congratulating himself at having arranged everything for the best, Minoret had ceased to give any thought to Ursule just at the moment when the drama, which he had so foolishly set in motion, was about to come to a terrible head.

'Monsieur de Portenduère is outside and wishes to speak to you,' Cabirolle announced.

'Show him in,' replied Zélie.

The shadows of twilight prevented Madame Minoret from noticing her husband's sudden pallor; he shuddered on hearing the squeak of Savinien's boots on the woodblock floor of the gallery which had formerly been the doctor's library. A vague foreboding of misfortune ran through the thief's veins. Savinien appeared, and stood there with his hat on his head, his cane in his hand, his hands crossed over his chest, motionless before the married couple.

'I am coming to find out, Monsieur and Madame Minoret, the reasons why you have shamefully tormented a young girl who, as everyone in Nemours knows, is to become my wife. Why have you tried to besmirch her honour? Why did you want her to die? And why did you abandon her to the insults of a fellow like Goupil? . . . Give me an answer!'

'Are you trying to be funny, Monsieur Savinien,' said Zélie, 'coming to ask us the reasons for something we can't explain? I don't care two hoots about Ursule! Since Uncle Minoret died, I've never given her another thought! I haven't breathed a word about her to Goupil, another joker I wouldn't employ to look after my dog! Well, what do you say, Minoret? Are you going to let Monsieur de Portenduère insult you? Are you going to let him accuse you of shameful behaviour that's beneath you? As if a man with 48,000 francs a year from land, and a princely château into the bargain, would stoop to such nonsense! Come on, stand up! You're as limp as a rag!'

'I don't know what Monsieur de Portenduère is talking about,' Minoret eventually said, in his thin little voice whose tremulousness was all the more noticeable because it was so clear. 'What reason would I have for persecuting the girl? I may have said to Goupil how vexed I was that she was in Nemours; my son Désiré was falling head over heels in love with her, and I didn't want her to be his wife, that's all.'

'Goupil has confessed everything to me, Monsieur Minoret.'

There was a moment's silence, a terrible moment during which the three characters looked closely at one another. Zélie had noticed a nervous spasm in her colossal husband's coarse face.

'Though you're only insects, I want a signal revenge, and I'll find some way of getting it,' the nobleman continued. 'I shan't ask you, a man of sixty-seven, for satisfaction for the insults to Mademoiselle Mirouët; I'll ask your son. The first time Monsieur Minoret junior sets foot in Nemours, we shall meet. He'll really have to fight me, and he will fight, or he'll be so completely dishonoured that he'll never show his face anywhere! And if he doesn't come to Nemours, then I'll go to Fontainebleau! I'll obtain satisfaction. It shan't be said you were cowardly enough to try and dishonour a poor young defenceless girl.'

'But Goupil's slanderous accusations . . . aren't . . . really . . .' stammered Minoret.

'Do you want me to confront you with him?' Savinien interrupted. 'Take my advice, don't make this affair public! It's a matter between you, Goupil and me. Leave it that way, and God will decide the outcome in the duel to which I shall be honoured to invite your son.'

'Not so fast!' cried Zélie. 'Do you really think I'll let Désiré fight you, when you've been in the Navy and are trained in using a sword and pistol? If you've a complaint against Minoret, here's Minoret! Take Minoret! Have your duel with Minoret! Why should my boy, who you admit is innocent in all this, bear the consequences? . . . Sooner than let that happen, you'd have to reckon with me, my young fellow! Come on, Minoret, why are you sitting there as stupid as a stuffed canary? In your own house you let this young man stand in front of your wife with his hat on his head! You'd better be making tracks, young man. A man's home is his castle. I don't know what you're getting at with your footling nonsense, but beat it quick! And if you lay a finger on Désiré, you and your silly little Ursule will answer for it to me.'

And she rang the bell briskly, summoning her servants.

'Bear in mind what I've told you!' Savinien repeated, ignoring Zélie's tirade, and then walked out, leaving this sword of Damocles hanging over the couple's heads.

'Now just explain, Minoret,' said Zélie to her husband, 'what's all this? A young man must have a reason for coming like that into a middle-class house, kicking up a first-class rumpus and demanding the blood of a respectable young man.'

'It's some trick thought up by that nasty monkey Goupil. I promised to help him become a notary if he got me the Château du Rouvre cheaply. I gave him 10 per cent commission, 20,000 francs in bills of exchange. He obviously isn't satisfied.'

'Yes, but before that what reason would he have had for pestering Ursule with his serenades and shameful tricks?'

'He wanted her to be his wife.'

'Him? A girl without any fortune! Tell me another! See, Minoret, you're spinning me stupid yarns, and you're too stupid yourself, old man, to kid me into believing them.

There's something at the bottom of this, and you're going to tell me.'

'There's nothing.'

'What do you mean, there's nothing? I tell you you're lying. We'll see who's right!'

'Do you mind leaving me alone?'

'I'll go to that poisonous fountain – you know who I mean, Goupil! – and turn the tap on. You'll be the loser then.'

'You can if you like.'

'I know well enough that things will turn out as I want them to! And what I want more than anything is that no one should lay a finger on Désiré. Look, if he came to any harm, I'd do something that would land me on the scaffold! Désiré . . . But . . . and you don't do a thing!'

A quarrel that had begun in this way between Minoret and his wife would not end without prolonged domestic strife. Thus, the foolish thief found that his struggle with himself and Ursule was now magnified by his misdeed and made more complex by a new and terrible adversary. The next day, as he left his house to go and find Goupil, thinking of placating him with money, he read across the walls of the town: *Minoret is a thief!* Everyone he met sympathized with him, asking him personally who was the author of this anonymous statement; all forgave him his confused, tortuous replies, in view of his utter mediocrity. Fools gain greater advantages from their weakness than clever men gain from their strength. No one offers to help a great man struggling against fate, but people will buy shares in a grocer's business when he faces bankruptcy. Do you know why? People derive a feeling of superiority from assisting an imbecile, but they are annoyed at only being the equal of a man of genius. A brilliant man would have been ruined if, like Minoret, he had mumbled absurd replies in a bewildered manner. Zélie and her servants wiped out the avenging sentence wherever it was to be found; but it remained on Minoret's conscience. Although Goupil had exchanged verbal promises with the tipstaff the previous evening, he very rashly refused to finalize his agreement.

'Look, my dear Lecoeur, I've been able to buy Monsieur Dionis's practice, and I'm in a position to arrange for your business to be sold to someone else! Put your agreement away, we've only lost two revenue stamps. Here are the seventy centimes.'

Lecoeur was too afraid of Goupil to complain. The whole of Nemours immediately learned that Minoret had given a guarantee to Dionis, to assist Goupil in buying his practice. The future notary wrote a letter to Savinien contradicting his confessions about Minoret, and informing the young nobleman that his new status, the legislation passed by the Supreme Court and his respect for the law made it impossible for him to fight. Furthermore, he warned the nobleman to be on his best behaviour with him from now on, for he was extremely good at foot boxing; and, at the first attack, he assured him that he would break his leg.

The walls of Nemours spoke no more. But the quarrel went on between Minoret and his wife, and Savinien maintained an unsociable silence. Ten days after these events, the eldest Mademoiselle Massin's marriage to the future notary was widely rumoured. Mademoiselle Massin had 80,000 francs and ugliness to her credit, Goupil had his deformities and his legal practice; the union, therefore, seemed both probable and appropriate.

Two unknown men came out of hiding and seized Goupil in the street at midnight, just as he was leaving Massin's house; they beat him up, and vanished. Goupil kept completely silent about this nocturnal episode, contradicting an old woman who believed she recognized him as she looked out of her window.

These little and yet great events were studied by the magistrate, who realized that Goupil had a mysterious hold over Minoret and vowed to find out the cause.

19. Ghostly Apparitions

THOUGH public opinion in the little town had admitted Ursule's complete innocence, she was making a slow recovery. In that state of bodily prostration which leaves both mind and soul free, she became the focus of phenomena terrible in their results, and of a kind that would have merited scientific investigation – if scientists had been let into such a secret. Ten days after Madame de Portenduère's visit, Ursule had a dream which had every characteristic of a supernatural vision both in its mental impressions and (as it were) in its physical circumstances. The late Dr Minoret, her godfather, appeared to her and motioned that she should come with him; she dressed, followed him through the darkness as far as the house in the Rue des Bourgeois, where she found every single thing as it had been on the day of her godfather's death. The old man wore the clothes he had been wearing the day before he died, his face was pale, he made no sound as he moved; nevertheless Ursule could hear his voice perfectly plainly, even though it was faint and seemingly echoed from a distance. The doctor led his ward into the study in the Chinese pavilion, where he made her lift the marble top of the little Boulle sideboard, just as she had lifted it on the day of his death; but instead of finding nothing there, she saw the letter which her godfather had instructed her to fetch; she unsealed it, and thus read the will drawn in Savinien's favour. 'The handwritten letters,' she told the parish priest, 'shone as if they had been written with the rays of the sun. They dazzled my eyes.' When she looked at her uncle to thank him, she noticed a kindly smile on his colourless lips. Then, speaking in his weak yet clear voice, the spectre showed Minoret eavesdropping in the passage on their confidential talk, going to unscrew the lock and taking the packet of papers. Then with his right hand he took hold of his ward, forcing her to follow Minoret in a dead march as far as the stagecoach offices. Ursule crossed the town, entered the coaching premises, and went upstairs to Zélie's former bedroom where the spectre revealed Minoret unsealing the letters, and reading and burning them. 'He only managed to light the third match to burn the papers,' said Ursule, 'and he buried the remains in the ashes. Afterwards my godfather took me back home and I saw Monsieur Minoret-Levrault slipping into the library where, out of the third volume of *The Pandects*, he took the three scrips each representing 12,000 francs a year investment income, besides the interest which was in bank-notes. Then my godfather said: "He is responsible for the torments which have brought you close to the grave; but it is God's will that you should be happy. You will certainly not die yet, you will marry Savinien! If you love me, and Savinien, you will ask for your fortune back from my nephew. Will you promise me this?"' Radiant as was Our Saviour during his Transfiguration, Minoret's spectre had by then made such a violent impression on her soul that, in her depressed state, she promised everything her uncle wished in order to bring the nightmare to an end. When she awoke, she was standing in the middle of her bedroom, facing the portrait of her godfather which she had put there since she became ill. She lay down again, and after much tossing and turning again went to sleep; on waking, she remembered the strange vision but dared not mention it. Her delicacy and exquisite judgement were offended by the revelations of a dream whose motive and purpose were to defend her financial interests. She naturally attributed it to the chit-chat with which La Bougival had got her to sleep, which had been all about her godfather's generosity towards her and the certainty her nurse still felt on that score. But the dream returned, with so much greater force that she found it an exceedingly formidable experience. The second time, her godfather's icy hand was laid on her shoulder, causing her the cruellest pain; it was an indefinable sensation. 'The dead must be obeyed!' he said in sepulchral tones. And, she added, tears fell from his white, empty eyes. The third time, the dead man took her by her long plaits and showed her Minoret chatting with Goupil and promising him money if he took her off with him to Sens. Then Ursule decided to confess these three dreams to Abbé Chaperon.

'Father,' she said to him one evening, 'do you believe in the reappearance of the dead?'

'Dear child, sacred, secular and modern history offer several testimonies on this subject; but the Church has never made it into an article of faith; and science pokes fun at it in France.'

'What do you believe?'

'God's power, my child, is infinite.'

'Did my godfather speak to you about this kind of thing?'

'Yes, often. He had completely changed his opinion on these matters. He told me dozens of times that his conversion dated from the day when a woman in Paris heard you praying for him in Nemours, and saw the red dot you had put against St Sabinian's day in your almanac.'

Ursule's piercing cry made the priest tremble: she remembered the scene when her godfather, on his return to Nemours, had seen into her soul and seized her almanac.

'If that is so,' she said, 'my visions are possible. Godfather appeared to me like Jesus to His disciples. He was surrounded by a yellow light, he actually spoke! I wanted to ask you to say a mass for the repose of his soul, begging God's help to put an end to these apparitions, which are shattering me.'

She described her three dreams in the greatest detail, stressing the absolute accuracy of the facts, her freedom of movement, and the hypnotism of her inner being which, she said, moved about with extreme ease when guided by the ghostly figure of her uncle. What greatly surprised the priest, who was well aware of Ursule's truthfulness, was the exact description of the bedroom Zélie Minoret had formerly occupied at the premises of the coaching office – a room which Ursule had never entered, and which she had never even heard anyone mention.

'How then can these strange apparitions occur?' asked Ursule. 'What did my godfather think?'

'Your godfather, dear child, worked in hypotheses. He had accepted the possibility of the existence of a spiritual world, a world of ideas. If ideas are a creation peculiar to mankind and if they exist with a life of their own, then they must have forms that are beyond the reach of our external senses but perceptible by our internal senses under certain conditions. Thus your godfather's ideas can surround you, and perhaps you have invested them with his appearance. Furthermore, if Minoret has committed these deeds, they can be resolved into ideas too; for every action is the result of several ideas. Well, if ideas operate in the spiritual world, your mind – by penetrating that world – was able to perceive them. These facts are no stranger than those of memory, and the facts of memory are as surprising and unaccountable as those relating to the scent of plants, which perhaps are the *ideas* of the plant.'

'Dear me, how great you make the world seem! But is it really possible to hear a dead man speak, and see him walking about doing things?'

'In Sweden,' replied Abbé Chaperon, 'Swedenborg has proved beyond all doubt that he was in communication with the dead. But anyway, come into the library and in the life of the famous Duc de Montmorency, who was beheaded at Toulouse and who certainly wasn't a man to talk rubbish, you can read of an incident almost identical to yours, which had also happened to Cardano a hundred years previously.'

Ursule and the parish priest climbed up to the first floor, and the old man found her a small duodecimo edition of the biography of Henri de Montmorency, printed in Paris in 1666; it had been written by an ecclesiastic of the period, a man who had known the prince.

'Read this,' said the abbé, handing her the volume opened at pages 175 and 176. 'Your godfather often reread this passage. Look! there's still some of his snuff here.'

'And *he* is no more!' said Ursule, taking the book and reading the following passage:

The siege of Privas was noteworthy for the death of divers commanders: two brigadier-generals perished there, to wit, the Marquis d'*Uxelles* from a wound sustained in the approach works, and the Marquis de *Portes*, from a musket shot in the head. On the day whereon he was slain, he was to have been named a Marshal of France. Toward the hour when the marquis died, the Duc de *Montmorency*, asleep in his tent, was woken by a voice like unto the marquis's; a voice that bade him farewell. By reason of the love which he felt for a person so near unto him, he ascribed the false-hood of this dream to the strength of his imagination; and the labours of the night, spent, as was his wont, in the trenches, caused him to fall asleep again without fear. But the same voice interrupted him another time, and the spirit which he had seen only in sleep constrained him to wake yet again and to hearken distinctly unto the selfsame words which he had uttered before vanishing. Then the duke remembered how one day, listening unto the discourse of the philosopher *Pitart* concerning the separation of the soul and the body, they had vowed to one another that the one should bid farewell unto the other if the first of them to die were given leave to do so. Whereupon, unable not to fear the truth of this warning, he hastily dispatched one of his manservants unto the marquis's quarters, which were far distant from his. But before that manservant had returned, there came a summons from the King informing him, through persons able to afford him comfort, of the misfortune which he had foreknown.

I leave it for the doctors to dispute the reasons for this happening which I have divers times heard told by the Duc de *Montmorency*, and which I believe so wonderful and true as to be worthy of report.

'Well then,' said Ursule, 'what must I do?'

'Dear child,' answered the priest, 'what is at stake is such a serious matter, and so financially important to you, that you must keep absolutely silent. Now that you have confided in me about these secret apparitions, perhaps they won't take place again. Besides, you're strong enough to go to church; well then! come and thank God tomorrow, and pray that He will grant your godfather peace. You can be certain, by the way, that you have confided your secret into safe hands.'

'If only you knew how terrified I am to go to sleep! The looks on my godfather's face! The last time he clung to my dress to remain with me longer. I woke up with my face bathed in tears.'

'Be at rest, he will not return,' said the priest.

Without a moment's delay Abbé Chaperon went over to see Minoret, asking him for a moment's interview in the Chinese pavilion, and insisting that they should be alone.

'No one can hear us, can they?' Abbé Chaperon asked Minoret.

'No.'

'Monsieur,' said the old man, looking at Minoret with a gentle but attentive expression, 'my character must be known to you. I have to speak to you about serious, extraordinary things, things which only concern you and about which you can be sure I shall remain absolutely silent; but I cannot avoid informing you about them. At the time your uncle was alive, over there' – and the priest pointed to where the cabinet had stood – 'was a small Boulle sideboard with a marble top' (Minoret grew pale) 'and, beneath that marble, your uncle put a letter for his ward . . .'

Without omitting the slightest details, the priest informed Minoret of Minoret's own behaviour. On hearing the point about the two matches that had failed to light, the retired post-master felt his hair quivering in his scalp.

'But who's thought up such rubbish?' he asked the priest, in a strangled voice, when the account was over.

'The dead man himself!'

This reply caused Minoret a slight shudder, as he too saw the doctor in his dreams.

'God, Monsieur Chaperon, is very kind to perform miracles on my behalf,' said Minoret, inspired by his dangerous position to make the only joke he ever made in his life.

'Everything that God does is natural,' replied the priest.

'I'm not frightened by your wild nonsense,' said the colossus, recovering a little of his composure.

'I haven't come to frighten you, dear Monsieur Minoret; I'll never speak to anybody at all about this. You alone know the truth. It's a matter between yourself and God.'

'Look, Monsieur Chaperon, do you think I'm capable of such a horrifying breach of trust?'

'I only believe in the crimes people confess to me and repent,' said the priest in apostolic tones.

'A crime? . . .' exclaimed Minoret.

'A crime that has had terrible consequences.'

'In what way?'

'In that it is immune from human justice. The crimes which are not paid for in this life will be paid for in the next. God Himself avenges innocence.'

'Do you believe God is concerned with these wretched trifles?'

'If He did not see the worlds at a single glance, in all their details, just as you can take in the whole of a landscape at one glance, He would not be God.'

'Monsieur Chaperon, do you give me your word that you only obtained these details from my uncle?'

'Your uncle appeared three times to Ursule, to repeat them to her. Weary of her dreams, she has secretly confided their contents to me; she thinks they are so senseless she won't ever speak about them. So you can set your mind at rest about that.'

'But it's at rest in any case, Monsieur Chaperon.'

'I hope so,' said the old priest. 'Even if I thought these dream-warnings were absurd, I should still think it necessary to tell you about them, because of the unusualness of the details. You are an honest man, and you've gained your fine fortune too legally to want to add to it by theft. Besides, you are almost primitive in your simplicity, you would be too tormented by remorse. We have within ourselves, the most civilized and the most savage man alike, a feeling of what is just which will not allow us the peaceful enjoyment of ill-gotten gains: ill-gotten, I mean, according to the laws of the society in which we live, for well constituted societies are modelled upon the very order which God has laid down for the worlds. In this respect, human societies are of divine origin. Man doesn't discover ideas or invent forms, he imitates the eternal relationships that surround him on all sides. So what are the results? No criminal on his way to the scaffold, and able to take with him to the grave the secret of his crimes, allows himself to be beheaded without making confessions to which he is urged on by a mysterious power. Thus, dear Monsieur Minoret, if your mind is at rest, I leave this house a happy man.'

Minoret had become so stupefied that he did not see the abbé out of the house. As soon as he thought he was alone, he worked himself up into a temper, like the full-blooded man that he was: he came out with the strangest blasphemies, and called Ursule the most abominable names.

'Well, what has she actually done?' asked his wife, who had tiptoed up after seeing the abbé to the door.

For the first and only time in his life Minoret, maddened

with anger and exasperated by his wife's persistent questioning, gave her such a hiding that when she fell bruised to the ground he had to pick her up in his arms and carry her very ashamedly to bed himself. He became slightly ill: the doctor had to bleed him twice. When he was on his feet again, everyone in time noticed that he had changed. Minoret went for lonely walks, and often passed through the streets looking like an anxious man. He seemed absent-minded as he listened to people – he, who had never had two ideas to put together! Finally, one evening, he came across the conciliative magistrate in the High Street; Bongrand no doubt was coming to call for Ursule and walk with her to Madame de Portenduère's house, where the whist parties had begun again.

'Monsieur Bongrand,' he said, taking the magistrate by the arm, 'I have something quite important to tell my cousin, and I'm quite glad that you are here. You'll be able to act as her adviser.'

They found Ursule at her studies. On seeing Minoret, she rose in a cold, dignified manner.

'My child, Monsieur Minoret wants to speak to you about business,' said the conciliative magistrate. 'By the bye, don't forget to give me the scrip for your investment interest; I'm going to Paris, and I'll draw your half-yearly interest, as well as La Bougival's.'

'Cousin,' said Minoret, 'in our uncle's day you were used to more comforts than you have now.'

'One can be very happy on little money,' she said.

'I thought money would assist your happiness,' Minoret continued, 'and I was coming to offer you some, out of respect for Uncle's memory.'

'There was one straightforward way you could have respected it,' Ursule said sharply. 'You could have left this house just as it was, and sold it to me; you only pushed it up to such a high price hoping to find treasures inside it . . .'

'Anyway,' said Minoret, visibly overcome, 'if you had a private income of 12,000 francs a year, you'd be in a position to make a better marriage.'

'I haven't got that amount.'

'But supposing I offered it to you on condition you bought

an estate in Brittany, in the district where Madame de Portenduère comes from? She'd agree to your marrying her son then! . . .'

'Monsieur Minoret, I have no right to such a considerable sum, and could not accept it from you. We are only distantly related, and still less are we friends. I've suffered too much distress from slander already to want to give rise to any scandal-mongering. What have I done to deserve such money? On what grounds would you give me such a present? I am entitled to ask you these questions. People would answer them in their own different ways. They would see your gift as making amends for some harm done to me, and I don't want to have anything to do with it. Your uncle didn't bring me up to have unworthy feelings. One must only accept things from one's friends: I couldn't feel any affection for you, and so I would be bound to be ungrateful. I don't want to put myself into the position of being lacking in gratitude.'

'You refuse?' cried the colossus, to whom the idea of refusing a fortune would never have occurred.

'I refuse.'

'But on what grounds would you offer Mademoiselle such a fortune?' asked the former solicitor, staring at Minoret. 'You must have an idea! What is the idea?'

'Well, the idea of getting her out of Nemours so that my son doesn't give me any more worry. He's in love with her, and wants to marry her.'

'Well, we'll see about that,' answered the conciliative magistrate, putting his spectacles firmly into position. 'Give us time to think it over.'

He walked back with Minoret to his house, approving the concern he felt about Désiré's future, slightly blaming Ursule's hastiness, and promising he would get her to see reason. As soon as Minoret had gone in, Bongrand went over to the postmaster, borrowed his horse and gig, rushed up to Fontainebleau, asked to see the deputy public prosecutor and was told he was expected at a party given by the sub-prefect. Delighted at this, the conciliative magistrate announced himself. Désiré was playing whist with the public prosecutor's wife, the sub-prefect's wife and the colonel of the garrison regiment.

'I've come with some good news,' Monsieur Bongrand told Désiré: 'you love your cousin Ursule Mirouët, and your father is no longer against the marriage.'

'*I* love Ursule Mirouët?' laughed Désiré. 'What's all this about Ursule Mirouët? I remember seeing her occasionally at old Minoret's house, he was my umpteen-greats-grand-uncle. The girl's certainly a great beauty, but she's a terrible religious maniac; and though I've paid tribute to her charms, like everybody else, my head's never been turned by that rather insipid blonde,' he said, smiling at the sub-prefect's wife (she was a dark handsome woman, in the old-fashioned expression of last century). 'What's put this idea into your head, dear Monsieur Bongrand? As everyone knows, my father is lord paramount of the manors around his mansion at Le Rouvre, manors with a rental of 48,000 francs a year; and everyone realizes I have 48,000 freehold landed reasons for not loving a girl who's a ward of court. If I were to marry a mere nobody, these ladies would think me an utter fool.'

'You've never pestered your father about Ursule?'

'Never.'

'Did you hear that?' the conciliative magistrate asked the public prosecutor who had been listening to them; Bongrand then took him into a window recess where they stood talking for about a quarter of an hour.

An hour later the conciliative magistrate was back in Nemours at Ursule's house. He sent La Bougival to fetch Minoret, who came immediately.

'Mademoiselle . . .' Bongrand began, on seeing Minoret enter.

'Will accept?' Minoret interrupted.

'No, not yet,' answered the magistrate, giving his spectacles a touch, 'she has had doubts about your son's attitude; you see, she was treated very badly as a result of a similar passion, and she knows how valuable it is to have peace of mind. Can you swear to her that your son is madly in love, and your only intention is to preserve our dear Ursule from any more of Goupil's tricks?'

'Yes, I swear that is so.'

'Wait a minute, Minoret!' said the conciliative magistrate,

taking a hand from the fob pocket of his trousers and striking Minoret on his shoulder so that the man shuddered. 'Don't be so ready to commit perjury.'

'Perjury?'

'It's either you or your son. At the sub-prefect's house in Fontainebleau, in the presence of four people and the public prosecutor, your son has just sworn he'd never given his cousin Ursule Mirouët a thought. So have you other reasons for offering her such an enormous sum of money? I could see you were making wild statements, and I've been over to Fontainebleau myself.'

Minoret was completely dumbfounded at his own stupidity.

'But there's no harm done, Monsieur Bongrand, in offering to make a marriage possible for a relative, when that marriage seems likely to make her happy. There's no harm in thinking up excuses for overcoming her modesty.'

Minoret, whose dangerous predicament had just suggested an almost plausible excuse, wiped his forehead on which large beads of sweat were glistening.

'You know the reasons for my refusal,' Ursule replied. 'I must ask you not to come here again. Monsieur de Portenduère has not explained his reasons to me, but his feelings of contempt and even hatred towards you make it impossible for me to receive you in my home. My only fortune is my happiness, I'm not ashamed of confessing this to you. I don't want to put it at risk. Monsieur de Portenduère is only waiting for me to come of age before marrying me.'

'The proverb *Money is everything* is very misleading,' said her tall, stout cousin, looking at the conciliative magistrate, whose watchful eyes greatly embarrassed him.

He stood up and walked out, but outside he found that the atmosphere was as oppressive as it had been inside the little sitting-room.

'But there must be an end to this,' he said to himself as he walked home.

'Bring me your scrip, my dear,' said the magistrate, fairly astonished at Ursule's composure after such a curious event.

On coming back with both her scrip and La Bougival's, Ursule found the magistrate pacing up and down.

'Haven't you any idea what that great clod was aiming at with his visit?'

'None that I can say,' she replied.

Monsieur Bongrand looked at her in surprise.

'Then we have the same idea. Here, keep the numbers of these two scrips in case I lose them: you must always take care to do that.'

Bongrand himself then wrote the numbers of Ursule's and La Bougival's scrips on a card.

'Good-bye, my girl; I'll be away two days, but I'll be back on the third to preside at court.'

That same night Ursule had a strange vision. It seemed as if her bed was in the graveyard at Nemours, with her uncle's grave at the foot of her bed. The white stone on which she read the funeral inscription gave her the most violent shock as it opened like the oblong cover of an album. She shrieked, but the spectral figure of the doctor rose slowly up. First she saw his yellow head and white hair shining within a kind of halo. Beneath his bare forehead his eyes were like rays of the sun, and he rose as if drawn upwards by a superior power. Ursule's bodily form trembled terribly, her flesh was like a sheet of flame and, as she said later, there was another person moving within her. 'Have mercy, godfather!' she cried. 'There is no time left for mercy!' he answered in a voice from the dead – in the unfathomable expression the poor girl used when relating her new dream to Abbé Chaperon. '*He* has been warned! *He* has ignored advice! His son's days are numbered. Unless he admits everything, unless he returns everything quite soon, he will lament the death of his son, who will die a horrible, violent death. Let him be told!' The spectre pointed to a row of figures sparkling on the wall as if written in tongues of fire. 'This is his judgment!' he said. When her uncle returned to rest in his tomb, Ursule heard the noise of the stone slab falling to, and then in the distance a strange noise of horses and men's yells.

The next day, Ursule had no energy. She could not rise from her bed, she was so overwhelmed by the dream. She begged her nurse to go immediately to Abbé Chaperon, and bring him over. The old man came after saying mass; but he was in no way surprised by Ursule's tale: he believed the theft was true, and no longer tried to explain away the abnormal happenings in his dear little 'dreamy child's' life. He immediately left Ursule and rushed over to Minoret.

'Oh dear! Monsieur Chaperon,' said Zélie, 'my husband has grown so embittered, I don't know what's the matter with him. Till now he was like a child; but these last two months he's been a different man. To get so angry as to strike me, when I'm such a gentle person, that man must have completely changed. You'll find him up amongst the rocks, he spends his whole life there! What's he doing?'

Despite the heat – it was then September 1836 – the priest crossed the canal and cut along a path, noticing Minoret sitting below one of the rocks.

'You are a very troubled man, Monsieur Minoret,' said the priest, on coming into the culprit's presence. 'You are my concern, because you are suffering. Unfortunately, I shall no doubt increase your dread. Last night Ursule had a terrible dream. Your uncle raised the stone slab from his grave to foretell misfortunes for your family. I am certainly not coming to frighten you, but you must know whether what he said . . .'

'Really, Monsieur Chaperon, I can't have a peaceful moment anywhere, not even amongst these rocks . . . I don't want to know anything of what's going on in the next world.'

'I shall withdraw, Monsieur Minoret. I didn't walk all this way in the heat just for pleasure,' said the priest, mopping his brow.

'Well then, what did the old fellow say?'

'You are threatened with losing your son. If he has related things that only you knew, it's terrifying to think of the things we don't know about. Hand the money back, dear Monsieur Minoret, hand it back! Don't damn your soul for the sake of a little gold.'

'But hand what back?'

'The fortune that the doctor meant Ursule to have. You took those three scrips, I am sure of it now. You began by persecuting the poor girl, and now you're offering her a fortune. You're sinking into a morass of lies, you're getting

248

thoroughly caught up in them and you're taking false steps all the time. You're a blunderer, and you've been ill served by your accomplice Goupil, who is laughing you to scorn. Hurry! for you're being watched by shrewd, intelligent people – Ursule's friends. Hand the money back! And if you don't save your son, whose life perhaps isn't really threatened, you will save your soul; and you will save your honour. Can you conceal an ill-gotten fortune in a society constituted as ours is, and in a little town where everybody is watching everybody else and where people guess what they don't know? Come, my dear son, an innocent man wouldn't allow me to go on talking for so long.'

'Go to hell!' cried Minoret. 'I don't know what you *all* have against me. I prefer these stones, they leave me alone.'

'Farewell, you have been warned by me, dear Monsieur Minoret, and neither that poor girl nor I have said a single word to anyone. But beware! . . . there is a man who has his eyes on you. May God have mercy upon you!'

The priest walked away, and then after a few yards turned round for another look at Minoret. Minoret was sitting with his head between his hands: his head was torturing him. Minoret was a little mad. At first he had kept the three scrips, not knowing what to do with them. He did not dare to go and draw the interest himself, he was afraid he would be noticed. He did not wish to sell them, and was trying to think of a way of transferring them. He of all people was thinking of his business in terms of novelistic plots whose ending was always the transfer of those damnable scrips! Even in this horrible predicament, he considered confessing everything to his wife so as to obtain her advice. Zélie, who had played her cards so well, would be able to get him out of this difficulty. At that time the Three Per Cent stock stood at 80; so, taking the interest into account, nearly a million francs would have to be returned! It was no small matter to hand back a million francs when there was no proof against him that he had taken the money. And so during September and the early part of October Minoret remained in the grip of his hesitation and remorse. To the great astonishment of everyone in the town, he lost weight.

20. The Duel

A TERRIBLE circumstance hastened the confession Minoret wished to make to Zélie: the sword of Damocles moved overhead. Towards the middle of October Monsieur and Madame Minoret received the following letter from their son Désiré:

Dear Mother,

The fact that I haven't been to see you since the vacation is because, first, I have been standing in for the public prosecutor in his absence and, secondly, I knew that Monsieur de Portenduère was waiting for me to come and stay in Nemours in order to pick a quarrel with me. Perhaps because he was tired of the constant delays to the revenge he wishes to take on our family, the viscount has come to Fontainebleau, having asked one of his Parisian friends to meet him here, after making sure of the support of the Vicomte de Soulanges – a major in the regiment of hussars garrisoned in our town. He called on me very politely, accompanied by these two gentlemen, and told me that my father was undoubtedly responsible for the shameful acts of persecution perpetrated against Ursule Mirouët, his future wife; he provided me with proofs, explaining that Goupil had made confessions in the presence of witnesses and referring to my father's behaviour. At first, father had refused to carry out the promises he made Goupil as reward for his treacherous devices; then, after giving him the money to negotiate for a tipstaff's practice in Nemours, he had felt frightened enough to offer Monsieur Dionis a guarantee for the price of his practice; and thus finally he set Goupil up. The viscount, not being able to fight a man of sixty-seven, and absolutely insistent on avenging the insults Ursule has suffered, formally requested me to give him satisfaction. His decision, taken after much silent thought, was unshakable. If I refused to meet him in a duel, he had decided to come up to me in a drawing-room, in the presence of the people whose respect I most valued, and to insult me so grossly that I should then have to fight, or else my career would be finished. In France everyone shuns a coward. Besides, his motives for insisting on satisfaction would mean only one thing to a man of honour. He said he was sorry to have to go to such lengths. According to his seconds, the wisest thing I could do would be to arrange a duel as men of honour were in the habit of doing, so that the quarrel would not have Ursule Mirouët as its motive. Finally, to avoid any scandal in France, we and our seconds could make a journey across the nearest frontier. That would be the best arrangement. His name, he said, was worth ten times my fortune, and his future happiness put more at stake for him than for me in this fight, which would be a fight to the death. He urged me to choose my seconds and get these questions decided. The seconds I chose met his yesterday, and they unanimously decided that I owed him satisfaction. So in a week's time I shall be leaving for Geneva with two of my friends. Monsieur de Portenduère, Monsieur de Soulanges and Monsieur de Trailles make up the other side. We shall fight with pistols; all the conditions of the duel have been worked out: we shall each fire three times; and after that, whatever happens, it will be the end. Not to make such a sordid business public, for I am unable to justify my father's conduct, I write this at the last moment. I do not want to visit you because of the violent emotions to which you might give way; they would be unseemly. To make my way in the world I must obey its laws; and where a viscount's son has ten reasons for fighting, a postmaster's son has a hundred. I shall pass through Nemours at night, and bid you farewell.

After they had read this letter, there was a scene between Zélie and Minoret which ended with confessions about the theft, all the circumstances relating to that and the strange scenes to which it gave rise everywhere, even in the world of dreams. The million francs fascinated Zélie just as much as it had fascinated Minoret.

'Just you stay quietly here,' Zélie said to her husband, without making the least remonstrance about his stupid behaviour, 'I'll take charge of everything. We'll keep the money, and Désiré won't have to fight.'

Madame Minoret donned her hat and shawl, rushed with her son's letter to Ursule, and found her alone: it was about midday. Despite her self-assurance, Zélie Minoret was struck by the coldness of the orphan's look; but she rebuked her cowardice, as it were, and adopted a carefree tone.

'Look, Mademoiselle Mirouët, do me the pleasure of reading this letter here, and tell me what you think about it,' she cried, handing Ursule the deputy public prosecutor's letter.

Ursule felt a thousand contradictory emotions on reading the letter, which informed her how deeply she was loved and what care Savinien took to defend the honour of the woman he was taking to wife; but she had both too much religion and too much loving-kindness to wish to be the cause of either the death or the suffering of her cruellest enemy.

'I promise you, Madame Minoret, I will prevent this duel, and you can set your mind at rest; but I beg you to leave me the letter.'

'Look, my little angel, can't we do better than that? Just listen to me. We've bought up land worth 48,000 francs a year around the Château du Rouvre, a really royal mansion; in addition, we can give Désiré 24,000 francs a year in Government securities – making a total of 72,000 francs a year. You must admit there are not many young men who can match him. You're an ambitious young woman, and quite right too,' said Zélie, noticing Ursule's emphatic gesture of denial. 'I'm coming to ask for your hand for Désiré, then you will bear your godfather's surname, and that will honour him. Désiré, as you've been able to see for yourself, is a handsome young fellow; he's very highly thought of at Fontainebleau, and he'll soon be appointed a public prosecutor. You have captivating ways, and you'll help him to get on in Paris. In Paris we'll give you a fine house, you'll lead a brilliant social life, you'll be somebody there because with a private income of 72,000 francs plus the salary from Désiré's position, you and he will belong to the highest society. Talk it over with your friends, and you'll see what they say.'

'I need only consult my heart, Madame Minoret.'

'Tut! don't talk to me about that little lady-killer Savinien! Good Lord! You'll pay very dearly for his surname, his little curled-up moustache, and his black hair. There's a fine specimen for you! You'll go a long way with a household to keep up on a private income of 7,000 francs a year, and a man who ran up 100,000 francs of debts in Paris in two years. You don't know this yet, but the fact is that all men are the same, my girl! And, without flattering myself, my Désiré is equal to any prince.'

'You are forgetting, Madame Minoret, the danger your

son is in at this moment, a danger that can only be avoided through Monsieur de Portenduère's desire to please me. That danger would be impossible to avert if he were to find that you are making dishonourable proposals to me ... Remember, Madame, that I shall be happier living on the modest fortune to which you refer than in the opulence with which you seek to dazzle me. For reasons as yet unknown, though everything will become clear eventually, Monsieur Minoret's abominable persecution of me has brought to light my affection for Monsieur de Portenduère; I can admit to that affection, because his mother will undoubtedly give it her blessing: and I must tell you that, being approved and lawful, it is all I have to live for. No destiny, however exalted or brilliant, will change my attitude. The love I feel will never change or cease. It would, therefore, be a crime for which I should be punished if I married another man when I cared in my heart only for Savinien. Now, Madame, since you compel me to do so, I shall tell you something more: even if I didn't love Monsieur de Portenduère, I still couldn't bring myself to face the joys and sorrows of life in your son's company. Monsieur Savinien may have incurred debts, but you have often paid off Monsieur Désiré's. In character we have neither those resemblances nor those differences which enable people to live together without any concealed bitterness. Perhaps I shouldn't feel the tolerance towards him that wives should feel towards their husbands; and so I should soon be a burden to him. Stop thinking about a marriage of which I'm unworthy and which I can turn down without causing you the slightest grief. With your advantages, you're bound to find more beautiful girls than me, girls who are wealthier and of higher social status.'

'Will you swear to me, young woman,' asked Zélie, 'that you will stop those two young men from going off on that journey and fighting?'

'I can foresee that it will be the biggest sacrifice Monsieur de Portenduère can make me; but my bridal crown must not be sullied by bloodstained hands.'

'Well, thank you, cousin, and I hope you'll be happy.'

'And I, Madame,' said Ursule, 'hope you will be able to provide your son with a fine future.'

This reply struck the deputy public prosecutor's mother to the quick, for she recalled the predictions in Ursule's last dream. She stood there with her little eyes staring at Ursule's face, which looked so white, so pure and so beautiful in her half-mourning dress. Ursule had risen as a signal for her so-called cousin to go.

'So you believe in dreams?' she asked.

'I suffer from them too much not to believe in them.'

'But then . . .' said Zélie.

'Farewell, Madame,' said Ursule, bowing to Madame Minoret as she heard the priest's footsteps approaching.

Abbé Chaperon was surprised to find Madame Minoret with Ursule. The anxiety on the retired postmistress's thin, made-up face naturally led the priest to look closely at each of the women in turn.

'Do you believe in spiritualism?' Zélie asked Monsieur Chaperon.

'Do you believe in materialism?' the priest answered with a smile.

'They're a tricky lot, that crowd,' thought Zélie, 'they're trying to lead us up the garden path. The old priest, the old magistrate and that little rascal Savinien are in league. There are no more dreams than I have hairs on the palms of my hands.'

She made two short sharp curtsies and left.

'I know why Savinien was going to Fontainebleau,' Ursule said to Abbé Chaperon, informing him of the duel and begging him to use his influence to prevent it.

'And I suppose Madame Minoret offered you her son's hand?' asked the old priest.

'Yes.'

'Minoret has probably confessed his crime to his wife,' the priest added.

The conciliative magistrate, coming up at this moment, learned of the overture and offer Zélie had just made; he well knew her hatred of Ursule, and looked at the priest as if to say: 'Come outside. I want to talk to you about Ursule out of her hearing.'

'Savinien will find out you've turned down 80,000 francs a year and the swellest young blood in Nemours!' he said.

'But is that a sacrifice?' she replied. 'Is there such a thing as sacrifice when one is truly in love? And is there any merit in my refusing the son of a man we despise? Let others glorify their dislikes into virtues. That mustn't be the morality of a girl brought up by Monsieur de Jordy, Abbé Chaperon and our dear doctor!' she said, looking at the portrait.

Bongrand took hold of Ursule's hand, and kissed it.

'Do you know what Madame Minoret came for?' the magistrate asked the priest once they were in the street.

'What?' said the priest, looking at the magistrate with a shrewdness that seemed to be mere curiosity.

'She wanted to put things right.'

'Do you think so? . . .' Abbé Chaperon replied.

'I don't think it, I'm certain. See, look over there.'

The magistrate pointed to Minoret who was coming towards them on his way home: on leaving Ursule's, the two old friends were walking back up the Nemours high street.

'Having had to plead cases at the Assize Court, I have naturally studied many cases of remorse, but I have never seen anything like this! Now who has caused that flabbiness and paleness in cheeks whose skin, as taut as a drumskin, used to be bursting with the genial rude health of people without a care in the world? Who has put black rings round those eyes, and deadened their peasant-like liveliness? Did you ever think there'd be wrinkles on that forehead, and that that colossal fellow could ever be troubled in his brain? At last his emotions are beginning to tell! I'm an expert in remorse, just as you're an expert in repentance, my dear abbé; the cases of remorse that I've observed up to now awaited their punishment or else were ready to undergo it so as to be quits with the world, they were either resigned or else eager for vengeance; but this is remorse without expiation, remorse pure and simple, avid for its prey and tearing it to pieces.'

'Do you not know yet,' asked the conciliative magistrate, stopping Minoret, 'that Mademoiselle Mirouët has just refused your son's hand?'

'Don't worry,' said the priest, 'she'll prevent his duel with Monsieur de Portenduère.'

'Oh! so my wife has been successful,' said Minoret. 'I'm very glad because I felt nearly dead.'

'Indeed, you're so changed you no longer look the same man,' said the magistrate.

Minoret looked at Bongrand and the priest in turn to find out if the latter had committed any indiscretion; but the motionless expression on Abbé Chaperon's face and his calm sadness were a reassurance to the guilty man.

'And it's even more surprising,' the magistrate continued, 'because you ought to be feeling nothing but contentment. I mean, you're the owner of the Château du Rouvre, to which you've added Les Bordières and all your farms, mills and meadows ... You've 100,000 francs a year including your investments in Government stock.'

'I've nothing in Government stock,' said Minoret hastily.

'Phhh!' answered the magistrate. 'Look, it's the same with this as with your son's love for Ursule. At one moment he couldn't care less, the next moment he's asking to marry her. After trying to kill Ursule with grief, you want her as your daughter-in-law! Dear Monsieur Minoret, there's something behind this ...'

Minoret tried to reply, he fumbled for words, but all he could think of was: 'You must be joking, Monsieur Bongrand. Good day, gentlemen.'

And he turned slowly back into the Rue des Bourgeois.

'He's stolen poor Ursule's fortune! But where's the proof?'

'May God ...' the priest began.

'God has placed within us a feeling that is already at work within that man; but we call that *presumptive evidence*, and human justice demands something more.'

Abbé Chaperon maintained a priestly silence.

21. How Difficult it is to Steal What Seems Easiest

As happens in such circumstances, Abbé Chaperon thought much oftener than he wished about the theft which Minoret had almost admitted, and about Savinien's happiness, which was clearly being delayed by Ursule's lack of fortune; for the old lady admitted in secret to her confessor how wrong she had been not to consent to her son's marriage during the doctor's lifetime. The next day, as he was descending the altar steps after mass, he was struck by a thought which grew within him into the urgency of a voice; he beckoned to Ursule to wait for him, and went to her house without breakfasting.

'Dear child,' he said, 'I want to see the two volumes in which your visionary godfather claims he put his scrips and banknotes.'

Ursule and the priest went upstairs to the library and took down volume III of *The Pandects*. As he opened it, the old man noticed – not without surprise – the mark that papers had made on the pages which, giving less resistance than the cover, still had the scrips' imprint. Then in the other volume he recognized the sort of depression caused by the prolonged presence of a packet and the trace of that packet between two folio pages.

'Come upstairs, Monsieur Bongrand!' cried La Bougival to the magistrate who was passing by.

Bongrand arrived just at the moment when the priest was putting on his spectacles to read three numbers written in the late Dr Minoret's handwriting on the coloured wove endpaper glued inside the cover by the bookbinder, which Ursule had just noticed.

'What's the meaning of that? The dear doctor was much too fond of books to spoil an endpaper,' said Abbé Chaperon. 'Here are three numbers written down between a first number preceded by an M and another preceded by a U.'

'What do you say?' exclaimed Bongrand. 'Let me have a

look. Heavens! Wouldn't this open any atheist's eyes by pointing out the truth of your belief in Providence? Human justice, I think, is the extension of divine thought moving over the face of the worlds!' He clasped Ursule and kissed her forehead. 'Oh my dear child! you're going to be happy and rich, and all through me!'

'What's the matter with you?' asked the priest.

'Dear Monsieur Bongrand,' cried La Bougival, taking hold of the magistrate's blue frock coat, 'let me hug you for what you've just said!'

'Explain yourself,' urged Abbé Chaperon, 'so that we know whether our happiness is justified.'

'If becoming rich involves causing anyone any trouble,' said Ursule, half foreseeing the possibility of a criminal prosecution, 'I . . .'

'And just think,' the magistrate interrupted Ursule, 'of the joy you will give dear Savinien.'

'But you're mad!' cried the parish priest.

'No, dear abbé, listen. There are as many series of scrips in the Great Book of the Public Debt as there are letters in the alphabet, and each number bears a series letter; but scrips for bearer bonds cannot have any letters as they are not recorded in anyone's name. So what you see here proves that on the day the old fellow invested his money in Government stock he noted the number of his scrip worth 15,000 francs a year bearing the letter M (for Minoret), but he also noted the numbers without letters which are the numbers of three bearer scrips, and at the same time he took down the number of Ursule Mirouët's scrip, which is 23,534, and which – as you can see – immediately follows the number of the scrip for 15,000 francs. This coincidence proves that these numbers are the numbers of five scrips bought on the same day, and noted down by the old man in case he lost them. I had advised him to invest Ursule's fortune in bearer scrips, and he must have invested his own money, the money he meant to leave Ursule and the money that belonged to his ward all on the same day. I am going off to Dionis's to have a look at the ledger; and if the number of the scrip that he left in his own name is 23,533 preceded by the letter M, we'll be sure that all on the same day he invested through the same stockbroker: first, his own capital in one single scrip; secondly, his savings, in three bearer scrips, numbered but with no series letter; and, thirdly, his ward's capital. The transfer register will give unchallengeable proof. Ah! Minoret! I've got you now, for all your slyness! Not a word, about this, my friends!'

The magistrate left the priest, La Bougival and Ursule in deep admiration of the ways in which God was leading towards the triumph of innocence.

'The hand of God is in this,' exclaimed Abbé Chaperon.

'Will they do him any harm?' wondered Ursule.

'Ah Mademoiselle!' cried La Bougival, 'I'd like to see him strung up by the neck!'

The magistrate had already arrived at Goupil's premises (Goupil being Dionis's appointed successor), and strolled into the lawyer's office looking fairly unconcerned.

'I need a small piece of information about the Minoret estate,' he told Goupil.

'What's that?' asked Goupil.

'Did the old fellow leave one or several scrips in the Three Per Cents?'

'He left 15,000 francs a year in a single scrip in the Three Per Cents. I recorded it myself.'

'Well, have a look at the ledger,' said the magistrate.

Goupil took down a cardboard file, rummaged about in it, got out the record, looked through it, found what he was looking for, and read out: '*Item*, one scrip . . . Here, you read it for yourself! . . . It's number 23,533, letter M.'

'Do me the pleasure of producing an extract of that ledger item within an hour. I'll wait for it.'

'What use can it be to you?' asked Goupil.

'Do you want to be a notary?' replied the conciliative magistrate, glaring at Dionis's appointed successor.

'I should think so!' cried Goupil. 'I've pocketed enough insults on the way to being called Notary Public. I would have you believe, my dear magistrate, that the wretched head clerk called Goupil has nothing in common with Maître Jean-Sébastien-Marie Goupil, notary at Nemours, the husband of

Mademoiselle Massin. Those two beings are not on speaking terms, they don't even resemble one another now! Can't you see that just by looking at me?'

Monsieur Bongrand then paid attention to Goupil's dress. He was wearing a white necktie, a dazzling white shirt with ruby buttons, and a red velvet waistcoat; his trousers and coat were in a fine black material, tailored in Paris. He wore smart boots. His hair, pressed down and carefully combed, had a nice smell about it. Indeed, he seemed to have been transformed.

'The fact is you're a different man,' said Bongrand.

'Both in mind and body, Monsieur Bongrand! Wisdom comes with the right *practice*; and besides, money is the source of *propriety* . . .'

'Both in mind and body,' echoed the magistrate, adjusting his spectacles.

'But, Monsieur Bongrand, is a man with a private income of 300,000 francs a year ever a democrat? So accept me as an honest man who knows all about the finer feelings, and who's very inclined to love his wife,' he added, as Madame Goupil came in. 'I'm so changed that I think my cousin Madame Crémière is very witty, I'm educating her; so her daughter doesn't talk about coronets any more. In fact, do you know, only yesterday she said that Monsieur Savinien's dog was superb *under arrest*. Well, I didn't repeat that expression, however pretty it may be, and I immediately explained to her the difference between *being under arrest*, *having a rest* and *making a set*. So, as you can see, I'm quite a different man, and I'd prevent a client from *fouling* the language.'

'Well, hurry up,' Bongrand urged. 'Let me have that in an hour, and the notary Goupil will have made amends for some of the head clerk's misdeeds!'

After asking the Nemours doctor to lend him his horse and gig, the conciliative magistrate went to fetch Ursule's scrip and the two incriminating volumes; then, armed with the ledger extract, he rushed to Fontainebleau to see the public prosecutor. Bongrand easily proved that the three scrips had been embezzled by one of the heirs, and, leading on from this, that Minoret was the culprit.

'That explains his behaviour,' said the public prosecutor.

As an immediate safety measure, the Crown attorney wrote a minute to the Treasury objecting to the transfer of the three scrips, and instructed the conciliative magistrate to go and collect the amount of investment interest due from the three scrips, and to find out whether they had been sold. Whilst the conciliative magistrate was busy in Paris, the public prosecutor wrote a polite note to Madame Minoret inviting her to call in at his office. Uneasy about her son's duel, Zélie dressed herself up, had the horses harnessed to her carriage, and drove to Fontainebleau *in fiocchi*. The public prosecutor's plan was simple and formidable. By separating the wife from the husband, he would find out the truth – so great is the terror caused by the Law. Zélie found the Crown attorney in his chambers, and was absolutely dumbfounded by these words spoken without any ceremony:

'Madame Minoret, I don't believe you were an accomplice in the embezzlement that occurred from the Minoret estate, which the Law is investigating at this moment; but you can save your husband from going to the assizes by making a complete confession. Besides, the punishment your husband will incur is not the only thing to be afraid of; you must save your son from being dismissed, you mustn't ruin him. In a few moments it would be too late, the police are in the saddle and the committal warrant will be sent off to Nemours.'

Zélie felt unwell. When she came back to her senses, she confessed everything. After easily proving to the woman that she was an accomplice, the magistrate told her that, so as not to ruin either her son or her husband, he was going to proceed prudently.

'You've been dealing with the man, not the magistrate,' he said. 'There's been no complaint from the victim, nor has the theft received any publicity; but, Madame Minoret, your husband has committed horrible crimes, which are the concern of a court that is less lenient than I am. In the present state of affairs, I shall have to hold you a prisoner . . . Oh! but in my house, and on parole,' he added, seeing that Zélie was about to faint. 'Remember that, strictly speaking, my duty would be to demand a committal warrant and get a judicial inquiry under way; but I'm acting at the moment in my capacity as Mademoiselle Ursule Mirouët's guardian; and in her own interests, properly understood, a compromise is necessary.'

'Ah!' cried Zélie.

'Write these words to your husband . . .' And he dictated the following letter to Zélie, after making her sit at his desk.

Mie deeresst,

Iev bean aristid. and Iev kunfesst avvrithinn. Reeternne the skripps thett ower onckul leffed Monsieur de Portenduère inn the wil you bernnt, bikoz the Pubblik Prosykewtur hazz lojd an obbjeykshunn wiv the Trejjeri.

'This way, you'll save him from denials which would be the ruin of him,' said the magistrate with a smile at the spelling. 'We'll find a convenient way of making restitution. My wife will make your stay under my roof as agreeable as possible, and I urge you not to breathe a word, and not to look in any way upset.'

Once he had obtained a confession from his deputy's mother and arranged for her detention, the magistrate sent for Désiré, related to him point by point the theft which his father had secretly committed to Ursule's detriment, and quite clearly to the detriment of his coheirs, and showed him the letter Zélie had written. Désiré did not need to be asked to go to Nemours to ensure that his father made restitution.

'It's all very serious,' said the magistrate. 'If it gets out that the will has been destroyed, your relations the Massin and Crémière heirs may intervene. I now have sufficient proof against your father. I am releasing your mother, who has had lesson enough about her duties from this little episode. As far as she's concerned, it will look as if I have yielded to your urgent requests in releasing her. Go with her to Nemours and sort out all these difficulties. Don't be afraid of anything or anyone. Monsieur Bongrand is too fond of Mademoiselle Mirouët ever to be indiscreet.'

Zélie and Désiré left immediately for Nemours. Three hours after his deputy's departure, the public prosecutor received the following express letter, in which the spelling has been corrected so as not to make a laughing-stock of a man in his misfortune.

Sir,

God has not been as indulgent to us as you are. We have been stricken by an irreparable disaster. On reaching the bridge at Nemours, one of the traces came unhooked. My wife had no servant behind the carriage, the horses could sense that the stable was near, and my son – afraid of their impatience – did not want the coachman to get down and so got out himself to hook the trace up. Just as he was turning round to climb up beside his mother, the horses bolted. Désiré did not have time to lean back far enough against the parapet, the footboard cut into his legs. Down he fell, and the rear wheel ran over his body. This letter will be brought to you by the express messenger who is hurrying to Paris to fetch the leading surgeons; amidst his sufferings, my son told me to write to you letting you know of our complete acceptance of your decisions in the matter about which he was coming home to his family.

Until my dying day I shall be grateful to you for the manner in which you are proceeding, and shall justify your confidence.

FRANÇOIS MINORET.

This cruel event convulsed the town of Nemours. The emotional crowd standing at the gateway to the Minorets' house informed Savinien that his revenge had been taken in hand by one more powerful than himself. The nobleman promptly went over to Ursule's house, where the priest – just like the young girl – felt more terror than surprise. The following day, after the first dressings had been applied, and when the doctors and surgeons from Paris had given their diagnoses, unanimously agreeing on the need to amputate both legs, Minoret – pale, dejected, dishevelled, and accompanied by the priest – appeared at Ursule's house, where Bongrand and Savinien already were.

'Mademoiselle,' he said, 'I am guilty of a great injury towards you; but even though the wrongs I have done you cannot be completely redeemed, there are some for which I can make amends. My wife and I have vowed to give you the freehold of our estate at Le Rouvre in the event of our son's life being preserved, and the same if we had the terrible misfortune to lose him.'

The man burst into tears at the end of this sentence.

'I can assure you, dear Ursule,' said the parish priest, 'that you can and must accept a part of this gift.'

'Will you forgive us?' the colossus asked, humbly kneeling before the astonished young girl. 'In a few hours' time the operation will be performed by the chief surgeon at the hospital, but I have no faith in human science, I believe in the omnipotence of God! If you would forgive us, and go and ask God to preserve our son, he will have the strength to endure his torture, and, I am convinced, we shall be fortunate enough to preserve his life.'

'Let's all go to church!' cried Ursule, jumping up.

No sooner had she risen than she uttered a piercing cry, fell back into her armchair and fainted. When she came round, she noticed her friends – minus Minoret who had hurried outside to fetch a doctor; all were staring at her anxiously, waiting for her to speak. The words she did speak struck terror into every heart.

'I saw godfather at the door,' she said, 'and he motioned to me that there was no hope.'

On the day following the operation Désiré did indeed die, carried off by the fever and counter-irritation that follow such operations. Madame Minoret, whose heart felt no emotion other than motherhood, went mad after her son's funeral, and was taken by her husband to Dr Blanche's asylum, where she died in 1841.

Three months after these events, in January 1837, Ursule married Savinien with Madame de Portenduère's consent. Minoret was a party to the marriage settlement in that he gave Mademoiselle Mirouët his estate at Le Rouvre and 24,000 francs a year in Government stock; all that he kept for himself out of his fortune was his uncle's house and 6,000 francs a year. He has become the kindliest and most pious man in Nemours; he is churchwarden of the parish and has become a providential blessing to the unfortunate.

'The poor have taken my son's place,' he says.

If ever you have noticed by the wayside, in areas where

oaks are pollarded, some old tree grown white and seemingly blasted by lightning, yet still pushing forth shoots, its sides exposed and begging for the axe, you will have an idea of the old postmaster with his white hair, a thin, broken man, in whom the old inhabitants of the district can discern nothing of the happy imbecile you saw awaiting his son at the outset of this story; he no longer takes his snuff in the same way now, and he conveys in his person a sense of something greater than material things. In a word, one senses in every way that the hand of God has lain heavily on that face, making it into a terrible example. After feeling such hatred of his uncle's ward, the old man – like Dr Minoret – has so concentrated his affections on Ursule that he is the self-appointed steward of her property in Nemours.

Monsieur and Madame de Portenduère spend five months of the year in Paris, where they have bought a magnificent house in the Faubourg Saint-Germain. After giving her house in Nemours to the Sisters of Charity for them to turn it into a free school, old Madame de Portenduère has gone to live at the Château du Rouvre, where La Bougival is lodgekeeper at the main gates. The father of Cabirolle (once the driver of the *Ducler* coach), who is a man of sixty years of age, has married La Bougival; and she has 1,200 francs a year in investment income apart from the ample earnings from her job. Young Cabirolle is Monsieur de Portenduère's coachman.

When you notice passing along the Champs-Élysées one of those charming little low-sprung carriages known as *escargots*,* lined with dove-grey silk with blue trimmings, and admire a pretty fair-haired woman, her face surrounded with a foliage of thousands of curls, her eyes as luminous as periwinkles and full of love, and see her gently leaning against a handsome young man, you may perhaps feel a pang of envy; remember then that this handsome couple, beloved of God, have suffered in advance their quota of life's misfortunes. Those two married lovers will probably be Vicomte de Portenduère and his wife. There is no other such household in Paris.

*'snails'

'Theirs is the most wonderful happiness I have ever seen,' the Comtesse de l'Estorade remarked of them recently.

Bless therefore those happy children, and feel no jealousy, and look yourselves for an Ursule Mirouët, a young girl brought up by three old men and by the best of mothers: Adversity!

Goupil, who is helpful to everybody and who is justly regarded as the wittiest man in Nemours, enjoys the respect of his little town; but he is punished in his children, who are horrible, rickety, and have water on the brain. Dionis, his predecessor, flourishes in the Chamber of Deputies and is amongst its finest adornments, to the great satisfaction of the King of the French, who sees Madame Dionis at all his balls. Madame Dionis tells the whole of Nemours about the minutest details of his receptions at the Tuileries, and the grandeurs of the royal court; her throne in Nemours is founded on a throne which in that case is certainly making itself popular.

Bongrand is presiding judge at the court at Melun; his son is on the way to becoming a very honest public prosecutor.

Madame Crémière still says the loveliest things imaginable. She adds *te* to clarine*te*, allegedly because her pen splutters. On the eve of her daughter's marriage, her final instructions were 'that *a wife must be the queen-pin* of her household, and be *sphinx-eyed* in every detail'. Goupil is actually compiling an anthology of his cousin's gibberish, a *Crémièrana*.

'We have been grieved to lose good Abbé Chaperon,' said Vicomtesse de Portenduère this winter; she had tended him during his illness. 'The whole district was at his funeral. Nemours is fortunate because that holy man's successor is the venerable priest from Saint-Lange.'

Paris, June–July 1841.